Publications by Richard Hernaman Allen

1. Customs & Excise stories

(Already published)

The Waterguard

A well-respected man

The Summer of Love

Nothing was delivered

Something in the air

Bankers' Draught

Along the Watchtower

Heard it on the Grapevine

Brussels Sprout

(Completed, awaiting publication)

Our Friends in the South

Fools' Copper

Copper Kettle

Magic Clarinet

On a Carousel

Old Ghosts

Medicine Man

Ghosts in the Machine

Market Forces

2. Other "Nick & Rosemary" stories

Murder at the Baltic Coast Hotel (already published)

Death on the Volga

The Body in the Marine Buildings

Empty Lands

Sunrise, Sunset

3. Saga novels

Through Fire (already published)

By Water (in publication)

Out of Sight

4. Other novels

Barton Stacey/Stacey Barton – Missing

Sid Mouse & the Electric Cats of Death

The Disappearing Crows of Jurmala

More details on www.richardhernamanallen.com

Contents

INTRODUCTION

When I was writing *"Heard it on the Grapevine"*, I included a passage which would give me the opportunity to write a further tale about Nick and Rosemary Storey's activities while seconded to Brussels as "national experts". I gave it around a ten week window in the autumn of 1975, with an outline impression that it would cover skullduggery within the EEC Commission.

I make the usual apologies for inaccuracies. As I never worked in the Commission and have been unable to get hold of any reliable information about its structure in 1975, I've had to make up a fair amount of stuff. I should also make clear that I am not referring to any real individuals in this book, and even if I've got the designations correct (which would be a less than 10% chance), I am not suggesting that either the Commission or any of the organisations mentioned would be involved in the matters related here, nor do I imagine their procedures were as lax as the ones I have described. If any names of people or organisations which I've invented for the purpose of this book coincide with real ones, I make clear that I am not referring to any person or organisation existing or existed. I've made one exception to this, in the person of Commissioner Harold Marks. I'm not going to say who he is based on. I'll leave that to people who know me to work out.

This book has been revised for publication during the aftermath of the UK referendum on our membership of the European Union. From time to time, I have wondered whether I have been somewhat harsh in my depiction of politicians in my books. However, my experience watching the political class contend for the votes of the British people made me feel that in many respects I have been far too kind to them. And I am more than ever filled with fear for the future of this country when our political and media structures and general political understanding

1

and awareness function so poorly. It may be that I can develop that theme in a future book

As usual, I'd like to thank Vanessa for her patience, tolerance, encouragement, support and love; Jo and Kat for their support and encouragement and Josh for allowing me some writing time.

Richard Hernaman Allen
February 2015 (revised September 2016)

1. INVESTIGATING A DISCREPANCY

It was September 1975. Rosemary and I hadn't been back from our holidays long and were still getting used to the idea that Knud Henriksen was leaving SEFF at the end of the year and the effect that might have on our investigation into what seemed like a likely wine fraud perpetrated by Ceresini, a large wine producer based in Bussolengo, near Verona. But as the next stage of that case would involve one of us being a member of a Wasco team examining Ceresini's premises and accounts, no earlier than December, we were getting on with our other work, as Brussels picked up slowly after the long August holidays.

Nevertheless, we weren't unduly surprised to be summoned to a meeting in Gerry Fitzpatrick's room early one morning. Knud arrived in our wake.

"I understand from Knud that your wine investigations are on hold for a couple of months," Gerry began, in his clipped, highly-educated Irish accent.

"Yes," I replied.

"Do you believe it'll achieve some sort of conclusion?"

"I guess so. Either we'll lay our hands on sufficient evidence to do something about them or we won't….and our chances of laying a glove on them will probably have gone…certainly while Rosemary and I are still here….and who knows who our successors will be…."

"I believe we can be categorical that they won't be like you two…..Apart from it being unlikely we'd get another husband-and-wife team, Giulizzi and Paolotti will be doing their damnedest to ensure they get Brits who want to spend their time behind their desks or in committee meetings, not getting up to the sort of things you two do…."

"And there won't be much Gerry will be able to do about it – as you can be fairly confident that our Italian friends have already been lobbying in København for my successor to be cut from a similar cloth as your successors."

"So there's considerable sense in making full use of your talents before you depart," continued Gerry.

"Oh?" remarked Rosemary. "Where exactly is this leading?"

"I've been approached by the head of the Commission Secretariat, Jérôme Vermeulen, about an extremely tricky and confidential matter. Exactly how he has got to know about your particular talents I know not, but when he took me out to lunch in a somewhat expensive and select restaurant not far from here and proceeded to explain his problem and why he wanted the pair of you, it became clear that he'd been keeping his ear to the ground...."

"....or someone has been doing it for him...." inserted Henriksen.

"He expressed himself impressed by the work you did in unmasking Trebzow and Gozzoli, while preventing Paolitti from being wrongly regarded as a Soviet agent...."

"A matter which appears to have conveniently slipped Paolitti's mind ever since....." observed Henriksen.

"He feels that you are rare people within the Commission. You have practical skills and a preparedness to follow the evidence, but with a sceptical eye. Most people here are wordsmiths in one form or another....wordsmiths or spies, as Vermeulen put it....Not spies for the Soviets, you understand, but for their home countries...."

"What does he want us to do for him?" asked Rosemary, who was always suspicious of flattery....even that offered by her husband!

"I believe he wishes to tell you himself. Apparently it's a matter of such delicacy that it must be kept confidential even from Knud and myself," replied Fitzpatrick. "All he would say was that it concerns a disparity in EEC funds, in particular between records of expenditure and actual cash flowing from Commission banking funds."

"That sounds like a matter for the local police or perhaps that Van Empel's lot," remarked Rosemary. "I don't quite see where we come in. We don't have any jurisdiction – and I guess anyone we have to speak to will know it. So we can't even compel someone to speak to us."

"For reasons which weren't vouchsafed to me, Vermeulen believes that you two are exactly the right people for this work…whatever it may be. I've informed him he can make use of your time for up to ten weeks. But after that, you're back to your day jobs….and I don't expect them to be completely neglected during that time either," explained Fitzpatrick.

"You may very well find you don't lose any of our time," observed Rosemary.

"When are we expected to meet this bloke Vermeulen?" I asked.

"Ideally later this morning, if you've got nothing else on," replied Fitzpatrick.

"Nothing that can't wait," I said.

We arranged to meet Vermeulen at noon. His secretary told us he had an office in the Berlaymont building (the main, new, partly curved building which housed most of the EEC Commission) – and reception guided us to the lifts, indicating we should go to the top floor. We were met at the lobby in front of the lifts by the inevitable flunkey – a brisk and efficient looking young woman from one of the north European countries. We were a few minutes early and were parked in an elegant waiting room about four times the size of the office which I shared with Hans-Georg Meyer. Though I reckoned the view from the windows must be quite good, it was a dismal, grey day, with flurries of rain which reminded us that autumn was already upon us.

Almost on the dot of noon, we were ushered into Vermeulen's office. It was about four times as large again, with a huge meeting table, which I reckoned would seat at least twenty people, a coffee table round which were ranged half a dozen leather chairs, a couple of sofas and, at the far end of the room a vast, ornate desk. The style was gilded baroque and the paintings I glanced at on the walls were all dimly lit internal scenes, reminiscent of what I'd seen at an exhibition of Rembrandt's paintings….Perhaps some were Rembrandts, of course!

Jérôme Vermeulen was surprisingly small – not more than five feet tall in his grey-and-black striped socks, I'd've said, and of indeterminate age. He looked well-groomed, even dapper – but his size meant he seemed more like one of those bustling little sparrows that vied to outsmart each other for crumbs and insects in the garden at the back of our flat in Woluwe St Lambert. As Secretary to the Commission, I would've considered him to be a secretary bird, but I was aware they were larger and more ungainly. He indicated that we should sit in one of the comfortable chairs by the coffee table.

"Good morning, Mr and Detective Sergeant Storey," he began in fairly heavily accented English, after a not very well disguised glance at Rosemary's legs. But his English was almost certainly better than our French. "I'm most grateful for agreeing to this meeting. May I take it that Mr Fitzpatrick has informed to about the tenor of our discussion?"

"He gave us an outline of what you wanted us to do. But no more than that," I replied.

"As an accountant, I'm sure that Detective Sergeant Storey will understand the necessity of ensuring that paper invoices and remittances and the resultant balances should tally with the cash in an organisation's bank account," he went on, continuing to glance furtively at Rosemary's legs. She was wearing a short skirt as usual and some fairly new boots because of the rotten weather – but evidently her knees and five inches of thigh was almost enough to put him off this important matter. "Each year the Commission Secretariat carries out such tallies for each and every Directorate-General in the Commission. Naturally, no-one expects a 100% reciprocity. But in the year ending last December, there was un trou…..a discrepancy of just under 1% between these two elements, for the Commission as a whole. We have subsequently examined such information as we can and it would appear that virtually all of the discrepancy can be ascribed to DGVI – Industrial Support…."

"Please excuse my ignorance, but what exactly does industrial support mean?"

"Essentially it relates to payments made to take outmoded industrial manufacturing facilities out of production and providing suitable alternative employment where possible for the employees in such facilities. I suppose the most well-known example would be closing ancient steelworks in north-eastern France and either modernising them or taking them out of production and investing in the manufacture of other materials – industrial alcohol or other chemicals perhaps. Does that answer your question, Mr Storey?"

"For now. It's possible we may need to know more."

"To continue….The discrepancy which appears to be ascribable to DGVI amounts to the equivalent of around £8 million sterling. That is a very substantial amount."

"And I assume it cannot be ascribed to any accounting error or misplaced documents?" asked Rosemary.

"Our examination indicates that some form of malversation of cash is the only feasible explanation. Because this a matter of such immense sensitivity, the figures have been crawled over many times – and the firm conclusion has been reached that this can only be the result of criminal activity."

"Surely then, the suitable course of action would be to involve the police?"

"You will understand, Detective Sergeant Storey, that we are an international organisation. Though the EEC Commission is located in Brussels, our activities do not, strictly speaking, fall within the purview of the Belgian authorities. Hence our pleasantly low rates of tax and our ability to purchase many goods free of duty. Of course, if, say, a murder took place within this building, we would naturally summon the Belgian police, even though technically the crime would have taken place on international, not Belgian, territory. But when it comes to a malversation of EEC funds, we believe that is primarily a matter to be investigated ourselves."

"But don't you have your own security people? Indeed, we had some dealings with one, a M. Van Empel, earlier in the year."

"I am conversant with that – and with the circumstances. It was precisely those circumstances that made Commander de Klerck suggest you two as the most suitable people to carry out this investigation."

"Doesn't he have his own people to do this? You will appreciate that we have no jurisdiction here, even less than the Belgian police. So anyone we wish to interview can refuse to see us and we couldn't compel them to meet us. Similarly, if we wanted access to any documents, that could be denied us with impunity. I imagine that Commander de Klerck has considerably more clout with Commission employees than either of us does."

"You should understand that the people which Commander de Klerck has under his control are more in the nature of security guards. They have limited experience of interviewing suspects or sifting through evidence and accounts, for instance. If we suspected a member of the Commission staff of theft, for instance, we'd hand them over to the Belgian police to deal with. Van Empel was extremely impressed by your professional competence – and your experience evidently is significantly greater than Commander de Klerck's for instance. There are two further reasons why I should wish you to undertake this work. The first is quite straightforward. Apart from my and their own doubts about their competence for this work, de Klerck's men are known and if they were investigating in DGVI, it would become obvious very rapidly and any evidence which might remain would be destroyed. But if the two of you were seconded for a brief period from SEFF ostensibly to examine the nature of their controls to counter any fraud, that would give you what I believe you call a 'cover story'. The second is that I have the authority to authorise you with the same powers which are given to Commander de Klerck's men. You would be able to require people to attend for an interview with you…."

"Having given them due notice?"

"Yes. Though that might be waived in exceptional cases where evidence was at risk….though they could refuse to speak to you, certainly without a lawyer or other representative present. You would also have the powers to require access to documents and other records."

"I expect there are rules under which interviews must be conducted?"

"I believe so. You would need to speak to Commander de Klerck on such matters of detail."

"I believe Gerry Fitzpatrick has told you we're only available for up to ten weeks?" I said.

"Yes. It may be that you can only get a certain distance and your work may have to be handed on to someone else."

"Before we agree to do this, we need to see what documents and other information is available and some information about the people in DGVI. For instance, is everyone in the DG a potential suspect? Or are there certain people we could talk to?" asked Rosemary. "That will be relevant to whether it's worth our while taking this work on. If we're starting from scratch or there are mountains of documents to work through or dozens and dozens of potential suspects, there probably wouldn't be much point in us even starting. By the end of ten weeks, we'd still be pretty well where we started off."

"I believe it would be best if you spoke with Commander de Klerck, who possesses the relevant detailed information. Perhaps after you've spoken to him and taken the opportunity to peruse these documents, you will have a more informed idea about the length of time this investigation might take. Perhaps you might communicate your thoughts to Mr Fitzpatrick?"

"We shall certainly do so."

That seemed to be the moment when we were expected to depart. So we did. On the way out, I asked Vermeulen's assistant if she could possibly arrange a meeting for us with Commander de Klerck later that day. Since we had so little time, it seemed best to get on with it.

As we walked back to the nearby building where SEFF were located, I asked Rosemary why she'd been so unusually unhelpful – to the point of hostility.

"I didn't like that little man. His air of supercilious superiority and complacency. His comments about why we'd been chosen to be given this poisoned chalice sounded as though he learnt them specially for the occasion. And more than that – this looks to me like a wild goose chase over a marathon course which we're supposed to do in the time it takes to run a half marathon. I kept wondering whether this isn't some trick to take us down a peg or two…or perhaps not us, but SEFF. We did a bit too well with those Soviets – and I bet this wine stuff is rubbing a few people up the wrong way. Why not get us into something where we get some really influential people annoyed with us? Or where we've been set up to make complete fools of ourselves?"

"I guess when we see Commander de Klerck and hear what he has to say and get a chance to look at the documents and accounts, we should get a better idea of whether that's really what's going on. I can't imagine we're so important that they're going to immense lengths to set up some bogus exercise…it'd be a lot easier just to wait until we go back to London in six months' time."

"I suppose you may be right. I just couldn't read that man at all. He just struck me as a consummate liar with an indestructible shell of self-confidence."

"I'd worked out you didn't like him! I can't say I could really read him either. I wondered whether some of his mannerisms weren't those of a very small man who's done rather well for himself…….But perhaps you won't be too bothered by Commander de Klerck, whereas I'll hate his guts."

By the time we got back to the SEFF offices, Fitzpatrick's secretary, a young Irish woman called Niamh, told us that Commander de Klerck would meet us in his offices in the Berlaymont at 3pm. A couple of phone calls later, the time had been brought forward by an hour, so Rosemary could attend for at least an hour before she had to dash off and pick Emily and Sarah up from the international school.

Whereas Rosemary and I usually had a quick lunch in the Commission restaurant and were back in our offices in an hour, we were untypical of Commission and Council staff, who rarely took less than three hours. But we were "National Experts", rather the permanent EC officials, of course. At any rate, Commander de Klerck looked less than gruntled at having his lunch curtailed.

"You've spoken to Vermeulen," he almost snapped, in English so heavily accented as to be barely intelligible. I say "almost", because I doubted he had the energy for his emotions to be stirred so much. He was an extensive man of about my height, but big-boned rather than fat. He had a large round head, with a sallow complexion, with a long strand of dark hair flopping almost over one eye, a moustache suitable for a Belgian detective and sad eyes. But Hercule Poirot or Maigret he was not!

"Yes," I replied. "He said you could fill us in about the details and let us see the relevant documents and accounts.......Would you prefer to speak in French?"

"No. There is perhaps little I can say you at this point. Maybe when you have seen the dossier in these files?"

He handed us four grey box-files, each one secured by a red ribbon, with a label stuck over where the ribbon had been tied, with a "confidential" stamp and an unintelligible signature on it.

"You read and perhaps we speak later," he continued.

"Is there somewhere where we can look at these files?"

"A room has been set aside for you. My assistant will guide you."

A pencil-thin woman in a grey suit, with her hair in a bun so tight it must've constantly hurt her head, led us along the corridor. The room was a typical Berlaymont office – suitable for two people with desks and chairs for each, a small table seating four in the corner, a filing cabinet and a small bookcase. It was by no means luxurious and gave the lie to the assertions in some British newspapers about the "EEC bureaucrats idle life of luxury". Admittedly top brass like Vermeulen did themselves pretty well. But Commander de Klerk had a room about twice the size of this one, but the quality of his furniture was little better than what was in the room we were using temporarily….and our rooms in the SEFF offices were certainly no more luxurious.

The box files were labelled in French – banking and accounts, expenditure, DGVI and background. Rosemary opened the box with the banking and accounts, I looked at expenditure. Of course, we realised quickly that they didn't tell us much on their own. The expenditure papers were largely official forms, completed and certified by various unknown names – mostly in French. They related to things like "decommissioning of rolling mill in Lefebvre et cie 8A" with some incomprehensible technical information. There appeared to be a comprehensive numbering system for each form; and the amounts authorised to be spent seemed to be clearly recorded, with the usual signatures and countersignatures. Without reading each one, it was as I would've expected – the expenditure took place in those areas where coal was mined and iron and steel produced. There were a few oddities – like payments to a British motorcycle manufacturer in the Black Country and a couple of what I guessed might well be china clay operations in Cornwall.

I turned to the DGVI file. The first document was a list of staff, with the responsibilities assigned to them. The Commissioner with the "industry" portfolio was a Frenchman – Jean-Philippe Chevrou de Polignac, a name which suggested a chateau and a knowledge of agriculture, viticulture not least, rather than mining and manufacturing. To my surprise, I discovered that his Director-General was an Englishman, Robin Southern. The "cabinet" (equivalent to a Minister's private office, but considerably larger) was mostly stuffed with Frenchmen, apart from a couple of Brits and a Dutchman. I was just looking at the names of the Directors and trying to see how their responsibilities fitted together when Rosemary interrupted me.

"This stuff is pretty straightforward. Basically it shows that funds get transferred into the industrial restructuring budget every month from the central Commission banking account and then sums are taken out at various points each month. From what I can see some places get a monthly payment, though it's rarely the same amount. Others seem to get a single payment…at least during the period I've been looking at. But the main thing is that each one has an alpha-numeric indicator which I expect must relate to something……I guess the authorisation for the payment or a file reference perhaps? I assume someone has been through both these files and found a discrepancy between what's been paid out from this bank account and what's actually authorised. In which case, it's just a matter of someone working their way painstakingly through these accounts and the authorisations you've been looking at and noting where they don't tally. You could then be able to see who authorised the expenditure and ask them some difficult questions. I don't see why they need us to do any of that."

"If that's it, I agree. But I guess if it'd been that straightforward, they wouldn't've felt the need to involve us. I wonder if there's anything in these files showing how they identified that something fishy had been going on?"

"I can't see why they couldn't've put something like that at the top, instead of dropping us into a mass of detail, which may not even be useful."

"Well…Let's see if there's anything there….."

"Hmmm....there's a balance here. A total of almost 120 million EUAs....which, if I remember correctly is around £80 million....What've you got, Nick?"

"It's the last document in the box, of course....A total of almost 108 million EUAs....so that's a gap of 12 million EUAs or about £8 million."

"I'm guessing that every one of these authorisation forms of yours has an equivalent transfer of funds from the DGVI account....."

She looked into the accounting record and wrote down half a dozen numbers. While she checked them against the authorisation forms, I had a look through the background papers. Inevitably, there were several long Commission documents setting out not just how the industrial restructuring programme was supposed to work in considerable detail, with a series of criteria, provisos and so on – but also why....in a lengthy and verbose preamble.

"All my payments out and authorisations tally exactly in terms of their reference numbers. But in a couple of cases the amounts paid out from the bank account are larger than the amount authorised. I can only assume that no-one checks the amounts paid out against what's been authorised. They just rely on end-year balance checks and then an examination of discrepancies. It seems a pretty dopey way of going about things. If someone checked the requests for payment against the authorisation forms at the time, they'd pick up this sort of thing almost immediately."

"There must be something we're missing.....Otherwise, you'd just have to look at these authorisation forms and question the signatories about why they requested more money than was authorised.....I reckon these are essentially office copies of what payments have been authorised. There must be some separate forms for the actual requests for withdrawal of the cash. Do the same people authorise those? Or someone else? "

"If so, why aren't they among these papers?"

"Presumably they aren't available – otherwise they would've already caught whoever did this red-handed. I wonder what happens to them...."

"I think we need to understand the actual process a lot better than we do. It's easy enough to see how it must work in broad terms, but this is a case where we need to know the details – of exactly who does what, when and where and what exactly gets put down on paper and when."

"I suppose there's nothing in any of these files?"

"Well, I've only looked through the banking one and a bit of the one you looked at about the authorisations. Perhaps the other two have got something useful in them?"

Rosemary started to look through the "background" box and I returned to the "DGVI" one. But after about ten minutes it was time for her to go and pick Emily and Sarah up. So I continued on my own. I managed to work my way through the rest of the two box files and was able to confirm that there was nothing there which explained how the process worked. I'd have to ask a suitable person for that, while remembering that whatever procedures got written down in HQ had a tendency not to be wholly followed on the ground. Certainly, if my experience in the Outfield was anything to go by, people did what they thought either was the best way of doing what was required...or the way that involved least work and hassle.....But, of course, the records on paper were as neatly lined up, spick and span, as any regiment of soldiers being inspected by a visiting Field Marshal.

I wrote down a few notes in a new notebook I'd got from our stationery cupboard. I didn't want this work complicating the wine investigation which we were still in the middle of. It included a note of the top people in DGVI. Apart from the Director-General – Robin Southern – there were four Directors – Helmut Schweid, Joop van Nieukerk, Emil de Kock and Pierre-Henri Dumoulin. Their responsibilities were described as covering certain articles in the relevant EEC legislation or treaty and therefore meant absolutely nothing to me. Another document for us to lay our hands on.

I thought I'd try and have a few words with Commander de Klerck as he might be able to fill in the gaps - or at least, point us to someone who could. But he wasn't in his office – and the pencil-thin woman in the grey suit claimed to have no idea where he was. So I asked her to pass on a message that Rosemary and I needed to meet him or a colleague to have a word about the papers which he'd left us to examine. Naturally, they were collected and locked away the moment I left the room.

There was enough time to go back to the SEFF offices, but Hans-Georg Meyer had a good deal more patience than I with the interminable committees which were giving our proposals for an EEC Directive on information sharing between Customs services a thorough, detailed and incredibly tedious going-over. So there was little for me to do.

When I got home and had heard what Emily and Sarah had been up to, eaten and read them their bedtime stories, I was able to tell Rosemary where I'd got to. Not that it was much further forward.

"I suppose the documents they showed us give us some idea of the problem," I remarked. "But you couldn't exactly say they were particularly helpful. It seems to me they could've put together something a lot more useful – not least a full description about how this system works and those parts where the fraud was most likely to have taken place."

"Either there's something they're not telling us….or they don't really understand how to go about this sort of investigation. I reckon de Klerck and his people just deal with the most straightforward things like Commission staff nicking stationary or over-claiming on their expenses…."

"I must say I get an uncomfortable feeling from time to time that they know exactly who's been carrying out this fraud, but either they're too important or protected to be tackled in the normal way – so we're supposed to uncover it for them…with the great advantage that we'll be out of here by next April, so if we put highly important noses out of joint, it doesn't matter…..And if Commander de Klerck asked for us to be involved in this investigation I'll eat my hat!"

"I suppose we have a bit of previous for putting important people's noses out of joint….But I agree that your non-existent hat isn't in any danger. He looked like a man who'd just found a wasp in the middle of a ripe apple."

"Just as long as we're not being set up to look really bad…."

"Hmmm…I'm still not wholly convinced that we – or SEFF at any rate – aren't being set up to look bad with this wine business…."

"So we do what we always do….take small steps and try and make sure we're on solid ground as long as possible…."

"And then one of us – and I think we know who – takes a giant leap off into the unknown…"

"Well…partly known."

2. MOVING FORWARD – AT SNAIL'S PACE

We decided there was no point in raising our concerns with Fitzpatrick or Henriksen at that stage. Instead, we returned to the Berlaymont building the following morning and went to Commander de Klerck's office to try to get answers to our questions. We had to wait for about twenty minutes until he was ready to see us. I was beginning to wonder whether the information that we were only available for about ten weeks had filtered through to him. And the uncomfortable thought winged its way into my mind that perhaps someone wanted us so deeply embroiled in this matter that we wouldn't be able to take the wine fraud case forward. I told myself that whatever else might happen, the wine fraud case was our priority and I would drop this one wherever it'd got to rather than let the other one fall.

"You have read the documents?" enquired de Klerk, eyeing us with a continuing mixture of suspicion and what seemed like distaste.

"Yes," I replied. "We've now seen the details of this discrepancy and confirmed its scale. We've also seen a series of relevant authorisation forms and various background pieces of information, including an organisational chart for DGVI, which told us practically nothing as it refers to EEC legislation – or perhaps treaty provisions – which are meaningless to us."

"But there was nothing which explained how the system for agreeing and authorising payments works or who is actually responsible for signing off whatever form is required which requires payment of money from the DGVI accounts," added Rosemary. "Evidently it isn't the authorisation forms that were in the box files, as it'd be as plain as the nose on your face who you had to interview as potential suspects....and anyone who did it would have to be a complete idiot, as they'd pretty well signed a confession that they'd committed the fraud. So we need to know a lot more about the system and who exactly is responsible for what in DGVI, in terms we can actually understand."

"You must realise that I cannot answer such questions…." he stated coldly.

"Then who can? Until we know that stuff there's no way we can tell Commission Secretary Vermeulen whether we can take this work on or not," I replied. "And as we've only got ten weeks to do this work, at the moment it seems to us that we're wasting time."

"I will check with Jérôme Vermeulen. For reasons which will be evident to you, you can scarcely ask the sort of questions you wish to ask of a member of staff of DGVI. But there will be those who have worked there who should be able to respond to your questions. I shall speak with Vermeulen this morning and we shall try to arrange that someone may talk with you this afternoon….as soon as possible, so that Detective Sergeant Storey can depart at her due time."

We left. But I felt that it'd been worth reminding Commander de Klerck that we were determined not to spend more than ten weeks on this matter. And it seemed to have worked, as I got a phone call almost immediately after we'd returned to the SEFF offices that a M. Gérard Creac'h, a former employee in DGVI would meet us at noon. Naturally, he wished to meet us at the Berlaymont, so we made our way back there at the appointed time.

Gérard Creac'h was short and stringy, with dark red hair and moustache, both prematurely streaked with grey. If I'd met him anywhere else, I'd probably have assumed he was Welsh. But with a name like that, he was plainly a Breton.

We met in a corner of the large staff restaurant for Commission employees, where we had lunch a few times a week. At this time it was relatively quiet and we got coffees – and I explained a bit about SEFF and went on to our cover story about

19

SEFF wishing to understand the financial control systems of the "spending DGs" - and had picked DGVI out of a hat.

"I have worked in DGVI for six years," he explained in heavily-accented English. "I am an accountant by profession, but my job was to ensure that payments made to companies under Community legislation and regulations were appropriate, justified and the correct amount. What is you wish to know?"

"Before we take a more detailed look at DGVI – when we intend to speak to people working there – we wished to have a better idea than we have about how the whole process works – from expenditure being authorised to the eventual payment to the owners of a redundant steel mill, for instance."

"DGVI mostly operates under the provisions of various Articles of the treaty which set up the European Coal and Steel Community, as modified by later European Economic Community legislation and the recent Accession treaties. In essence, companies wishing to claim funds or compensation from the community – in the one case for investment in new production facilities, in the other for closing down a facility – must make application to the Member State in which they are located for corporate tax purposes. It is the responsibility of the competent authorities in the relevant Member State to assess the application and make a recommendation to the Commission. In some cases, they may be required to supply matching funding themselves. DGVI tend to prefer that, as it makes the relevant Member State more careful about what financial assistance it recommends. But in many cases, the funding or compensation emanates solely from the Commission. When the recommendations accompanying the applications are received in DGVI, they are scrutinised with great care – mostly to ensure that the proposed funding or compensation is consistent with the wording of the treaties and other relevant legal provisions….."

"May I interrupt you for a moment, M. Creac'h," I said. "Do DGVI ever inspect the places which are the subject of these applications?"

"That would be exceptionally rare. Of course, if one received an application for closing a steel mill in Morlaix, my home town, it would be noticed and we should look at it askance. In such a case, it would be so evidently an attempted fraud that it would not even be considered necessary to send someone to check. But perhaps in more marginal cases where there were suspicions, DGVI would request the relevant authorities in the Member state to carry out an investigation. But generally DGVI relies on the honesty and competence of the relevant Member State. Does that answer your question?"

"Yes, thank you. Please go on"

"Sometimes - indeed, quite often – DGVI raise questions about the application. They will write to the relevant Member State and there may be some resulting correspondence, even meetings if significant sums of money are concerned. In some cases, the application is refused – perhaps because it is not compliant with the relevant treaties and legislation, either because of the nature of the activity or because the activity itself….."

"Could you possibly explain that, please?" asked Rosemary.

"Perhaps I might best explain by way of examples. The aim of the coal and steel treaties and subsequent legislation is to modernise Community iron and steel production, taking outmoded, inefficient facilities out of production and replacing them with modern ones – or, indeed, new industries or manufactures if that seems more apposite. If an application was regarded as the equivalent of repainting a rickety fence, rather than rebuilding it, it would be rejected. And the treaties would not extend, for instance, to manufactures where the Community already has a sufficiency or surplus capacity. So an application relating to such manufacture would also be rejected."

"Thank you. I think I understand now."

"When an application is granted, letters pass between DGVI and the relevant officials in the Member State as well as the company which has made the application. In cases where the Commission are providing all or most of the funding, DGVI would normally deal directly with the company. As far as internal procedures are concerned, at that stage approval of funding for the whole would be formally recorded in DGVI. In most cases, it is agreed that a certain amount of the funds may be drawn down at certain stages. Often that is not the full amount. Generally a margin is retained and only paid when the work has been completed and suitable evidence of that has been provided. The stages and amounts of funding drawn down will depend on the nature of the work, of course. DGVI tries its best to release funds only after work has been completed, rather than in advance…for reasons which I am sure you will understand. In virtually all cases, each release of funds is subject to authorisation by a suitable official in DGVI, upon written application from the company, along with suitable evidence of work completed."

"But from what you said previously, presumably DGVI officials rarely inspect the work on site?" I asked.

"That is so. If any doubts were entertained, DGVI would normally request the relevant Member State to carry out a suitable inspection…..And on receipt of a copy of the authorisation, the company completes the appropriate form, with the necessary reference numbers and so on, and seeks payment from the DGVI account in the Commission's banking facility."

"Directly? They don't use their national authorities' banks?" asked Rosemary.

"Directly. All funds emanating from the EEC would be paid into the company's nominated bank from the DGVI account."

"Would anyone in DGVI make such a request on behalf of one of these companies?"

"It'd be highly irregular."

"How easy would it be to get hold of one of the forms used to seek payment from the DGVI banking account?"

"In my time, they were subject to no particular restrictions. But unless someone knew the reference numbers, what activity the funds related to and other details, it would not be possible to complete those forms and expect to receive any money."

"Suppose someone tried to claim more money than they were due to get – how would this be detected and prevented?"

"I doubt it would be discovered until the annual reconciliation takes place. You understand that every application has to be examined and confirmed by the relevant authorities in the relevant Member State. This process is expected to assure DGVI that the applicant companies are reliable and trustworthy. It has not been considered necessary to establish a separate set of controls at the payment stage….I imagine it what you English would call a braces and belt approach. But up to now – at least at the time I left DGVI – it was not considered a rational use of our time and people."

"I understand. Do you know of any case where there had been discrepancies? And if so, what was done about them?"

"I fear I know of none during my years in DGVI. It is possible that some might have occurred. But you understand it is unlikely that such an occurrence would be made widely known."

"Do you know whether there were any procedures that would be brought into effect if a discrepancy was discovered?"

"Not really. It was an occurrence that was widely regarded as unlikely, even exceptional. I would imagine that those involved in the authorisation process – both in DGVI and in the relevant Member State – would be consulted. But as claiming more money than was due would amount to theft, I would expect the police services in the relevant Member State to be encouraged to take the necessary actions."

"Thank you. That's extremely helpful of you."

He was evidently eating elsewhere. Rosemary and I queued up for lunch and returned to a nearby table.

"The naïveté of these people never ceases to amaze me," remarked Rosemary. "Why would you be content to rely on someone else's procedures when it's your money that's at risk!"

"I suppose if you've never had any fraud…or never detected any, at any rate….You believe that the authorities in the Member States are doing a proper job….But that bothers me less than what Creac'h said about this system for getting money paid out. If a steel mill in the Ruhr sends in a form for payment of a million Deutschmarks, when they should only be getting half that, there are bound to be signatories to the form. So it should be possible to identify who was responsible for the fraud in next to no time. Assuming that isn't what's happened in the cases Vermeulen want us to look at, how exactly is this fraud being carried out anonymously?"

"I reckon we need to see the actual applications to the DGVI banking facility and also the forms signed on the original application and the authorisation forms signed by people in DGVI and in the Member State concerned. At least we could spot whether any signatures matched or looked fraudulent."

"So I take it we're going to proceed with this investigation?"

"We'll go as far as we can in ten weeks. Either we can clear it up or we'll leave a neat and tidy file for someone else to take over from us."

"So now we need to get at the original documents…I guess that's Commander de Klerck again…"

"I suppose so. I don't know why he gives off such an air of irritation whenever we meet him….It was his boss who asked us in – we certainly didn't invite ourselves…."

"If it should've been him and his people investigating this matter and it's been taken from him and given to two Brits who he probably thinks are barely out of our nappies, you can see why he might be a bit miffed….I guess I would in his shoes."

"In that case, perhaps he should be asking himself why, rather than messing us about."

"You think he's messing us about?"

"Don't you? Surely he must know enough to have got us where it's taken us two days to get to? If he doesn't, it explains why the work was offered to us. If he does, all he's doing is risking us complaining to Vermeulen that when we've only got ten weeks to complete this work, de Klerck is slowing things down."

"Of course, it's possible he's just not very bright…..?"

As it appeared impossible to get in touch with de Klerck for the rest of the day, I decided to have a word with Knud Henriksen about the snail-like speed of those we were working with in the Commission.

"I'll get Gerry to have a word on the phone with Vermeulen," he replied. "He can put a rocket up their arses. If they don't get up to speed, Gerry will just pull you out from this and they can sort it out for themselves. Is there anything much to it anyway?"

"From what we've seen they definitely lost several millions. But we don't quite understand how it could be accomplished successfully in view of the documents that seem to be used. I can't see anyone signing a form for half a million more than they're entitled to and just waiting until DGVI carry out their annual checks, follow up the paper trail and there your name sits big and bold at the end of it. Either you bugger off to Paraguay or someone's forging signatures or something else we haven't yet thought of."

"Do you reckon someone in DGVI could be doing it?"

"We can't tell at this stage. Once we've seen the original documents, we might get a better idea. It could just as easily be someone from the appropriate Member State or even from the companies involved. I guess we'll need to look at all the fraudulent claims and see whether there's some sort of pattern. It'd be a bit odd if claims from West Germany, France, Belgium, the Netherlands and the UK were all using the same methods of fraud….But stranger things have happened, I guess…..and I guess if word has got around about how DGVI do their checks, crooks may have worked out that they can scarper before anyone is on to them…..But…"

"Scarper?"

"Disappear….run away….But it seems a rather short term fraud for a company or even an individual who can see the possibilities of a successful fraud. Unless there's some way of concealing the fact that you're involved, you can only ever do it once…..and would you be making enough from a single fraud to make it worthwhile? I don't know…."

"Oh well….I'll have a word with Gerry. If you don't hear from me, I suggest Rosemary and you turn up at Vermeulen's office first thing tomorrow and tell him how you expect this work has to be managed. Otherwise, we'll just pull you out and let you get on with other things."

I told Rosemary about the conversation.

"I must admit I hope we don't get pulled off this," she remarked. "I'd quite like to find out exactly who's been up to what. But I'd rather leave it now than find we'd got half way down the road when we had to stop."

The rest of the day was taken up with the usual family things. The tennis season was ending and Emily and Sarah had a fair amount of surplus energy which their tennis training and games took out of them. Unfortunately, as the nights grew darker, there was little for them to do out of doors and children's activities ceased at around six o'clock in the local sports hall. The local park wasn't lit up, so we couldn't use the swings and so on there. A couple of nights a week, we walked to a small restaurant, following the Rue Vervloesem down the hill in the direction of the Roodebeek park. The "Porte de Bois" was a family restaurant, serving typically Belgian food – notably sausages (usually frikandel), waterzooi, stoemp, stoverij, croquettes and hutsepot among the food we enjoyed and fish stew, eels and moules-frites, which we happily avoided. We'd been coming sufficiently often to be regarded as regulars, and being the only foreigners who ever ate there, were treated as something approaching family.

This was perhaps a good thing, as Emily and Sarah, despite the long walk from our flat, still had plenty of energy to burn off, which emerged as noisiness when seated at a restaurant table. Both were now quite used to the international school which they'd been attending for the best part of eighteen months – and Rosemary was already beginning to worry about how they'd settle in back at their former school in Beckenham. One of the latest crazes at the school was to speak English as though it was French. In small doses, it was quite amusing – but having to listen to two little girls doing their version of Inspector Clouseau throughout the meal, (and for much of the way there and back), our enjoyment rapidly palled.

"I know you two think the way you're speaking is very funny," said Rosemary quietly. "But as many of the other people in this restaurant speak French, they might feel it was rather rude. Do you like coming here to eat?"

"Yurse, uv curse," replied Sarah, giggling.

"Well, suppose someone complained that you two were a pair of bad-mannered girls and M. van Haacht asked us not to come here again? Do you know somewhere where everyone is as nice to us as they are here? Or where you like the food as much?"

Silence. Two little brains were turning around – on the one hand, the enjoyment of doing something they found fun, which they also knew irritated their parents – on the other, having to eat somewhere they didn't like, or worse still, being stuck in the flat all evening.

"There's no reason why you can't do it at school – or at home, if you have to…..But not when we're out, especially in places like this," Rosemary continued.

"OK," said Emily. "But you've got to let us be silly sometimes!"

"We don't mind you being silly – provided it doesn't involve being rude to other people."

"We didn't realise people thought we were being rude to them," murmured Sarah, close to tears.

"Just think how you'd feel about someone behaving like you."

There was silence. We walked back up the hill and to our flat with two rather more thoughtful girls – and two parents who probably felt just a little guilty about spoiling their fun. But, as Rosemary said, as she lay in bed with her head on my shoulder later that evening, they were old enough to learn - and returning to their school in Beckenham would be easier if they understood a bit more about how their behaviour might be seen by others.

It was also something we'd do well to remind ourselves – as we noted on our way to meet M. Vermeulen the following morning. Though we both felt irritated and frustrated at the slow progress of the investigation which he'd asked us to undertake for him, there was no point in showing it, as it might just mean we had to put up with a dispiriting and unsuccessful couple of months, when we could be doing something more useful.

"I'm led to believe that you have felt that you haven't been furnished with the information you need fast enough and that you've had to ask for documents that must have been obvious you required?" Vermeulen began, glancing hastily at Rosemary's legs and, as she was wearing trousers specifically for that reason, looking away in barely-concealed disappointment. But he appeared to be in a hurry anyway.

"That's correct," I replied. "We don't believe anyone is being deliberately unhelpful, you understand. But we wanted to make sure that everyone realised that we only have just over two months to complete this work and if we have to wait for days to get the information we need, it's going to make our job harder."

"You must understand that in some instances, those providing the information may have a less clear idea of what you require than you believe."

"I guess that's so. But we feel as if we're having to travel down a path for the first time when there are people and documents who could signpost the way. We don't know anything about how DGVI's systems work and it shouldn't too great a leap to work out what sort of stuff we need."

"Very well. I shall inform Commander de Klerck to pull his finger out….that is your English expression, I believe. I shall also get him to find you someone reliable and trustworthy with experience of DGVI who can guide you. They will be briefed by me in the first instance, so that they are under no doubt about this matter being kept confidential."

"We are very grateful."

He rose – evidently off to some other engagement - so we departed.

We went back to the SEFF offices and went on with our normal work. It wasn't until after Rosemary had left to pick up Emily and Sarah from school that I got a phone call, telling me that by lunchtime the following day we'd have all the documents we'd asked for, along with a Mr Piet Korthuizen, who would be our adviser in regard to DGVI.

We met Korthuizen in a cheap Italian restaurant in the Chaussée de Wavre, about twenty-five minutes' walk from the Commission building, in the direction of the Porte Namur. I didn't know the area, but had heard of it often enough, as it was favoured by many of my former C&E colleagues staying in Brussels because of its cheap hotels and local eateries, which enabled them to eat well and – especially – savour several of the local beers, while being able to take home some £20 to £30 from the "Brussels allowance". As you'd expect for hotels charging £10-£15 per night, it was a fairly down-at-heel area, with a Zairean flavour – not least the several restaurants offering various exotic meats, many of which were probably imported illegally.

Fortunately, Korthuizen hadn't chosen a Zairean restaurant, but "Lago di Garda", which in view of our continuing investigation into the wines of that region, seemed curiously – but I hoped unintentionally – apposite. He was fortyish, tall, broad, but with a narrow, serious face enhanced by thick rimmed glasses, blonde hair cut very short. He was wearing a sports jacket in subdued browns and beiges with a cream shirt and nondescript tie.

"You will understand that I don't work in DGVI," he explained immediately after we'd completed our introductions. "I worked there until a couple of years ago, but I moved on to another den of iniquity – agricultural support to the cereals and ground crops industry. If you think that some of these coal and steel businesses are not beyond trying it on, as you English put it

I believe, you should meet some of the folk I have to contend with. I understand that there appears to have been some significant over-claiming amounting to several millions last year?"

"That's so. I assume you were told it was confidential?" I said.

"Yes. But you should assume that once people outside DGVI started seeking access to relevant documents, noses will have started to twitch in DGVI. One of the reasons why I left was the curious atmosphere there. Whereas virtually every Member State benefits considerably from the CAP – apart from England possibly – support for declining industries is very much concentrated in north-eastern France, Belgium and the Ruhr and Saarland in West Germany. There is substantial competition between those countries for access to as much Community funds as possible, as it helps them solve otherwise difficult political problems of closing down mines, factories and industrial plants, with consequent job losses. The Italians and my fellow-countrymen wish to limit Community spending in this area, for obvious reasons. A multi-national office is a strange place at the best of times – not least because many believe that at least some of their colleagues – if not all – are working as hard for their home countries as they are for the interests of the Commission and the EEC as a whole. So there is much suspicion – which is mostly unspoken, as you might expect."

"Do they suspect their colleagues of doing anything illegal? Or just favouring firms in their own countries and trying to prevent money going to those in other countries?" I asked.

"Primarily the latter. But people tend to work on their own, doing as best they can not to let their colleagues know what they are up to. So if someone was arranging for some sort of over-claim, it could be carried out relatively easily without scrutiny from one's colleagues….provided one could disguise what one had been doing, of course."

"That struck us from the papers we've seen so far," observed Rosemary. "Though there evidently isn't a system of scrutiny which operates while funding decisions are being made or when money is being paid out, there seems to be a pretty clear audit trail of documents all the way from the original application through to the actual payments to the relevant company from DGVI's banking facility."

In the middle of the restaurant was a huge pizza oven, from which three calzones duly emerged. They looked rather larger than I'd imagined and I doubted whether I'd be able to get through mine. Rosemary would eat less than half. We should've shared one, I thought to myself.

"I believe the questions you need to be asking yourselves are how could one devise a way of getting round this audit trail? Someone would need to know how the system operates – or so it seems to me. How could you get money out of DGVI's banking facility without incriminating yourself? And that's not just someone in DGVI, but in the appropriate national administration and the companies concerned. Is it possible to get hold of the relevant information to claim Community funds? Is it possible to get one's hands on the appropriate forms and other necessary documents?"

"Are those rhetorical questions? Or do you have some suggestions to make?" asked Rosemary, conscious I suspected that she'd have to leave in about an hour and wanting to make sure we got as much out of Korthuizen before then.

"It seems to me that in order to outwit the system, you have to know how it operates. That suggests to me someone who works or has worked in DGVI since about six years ago. Before that time, the system and forms have changed. As for the rest, I guess it's for you to check out for yourselves. You will understand that during my time in DGVI, I only dealt directly with the appropriate authorities in the Member States concerned – never directly with the companies who were making the claims. Also I had no reason or opportunity to assist any Dutch companies, so exactly how these matters are managed in the field I do not know. I imagine you would do best to visit some of the companies and national authorities which aren't suspected of anything. My guess is that if you can get the appropriate information and lay your hands on the appropriate forms and documents you could forge the required signatures and alter the banking arrangements. I doubt whether anyone would notice that at the time – though it would be detected during the annual reconciliation, of course. But by then it would be too late. Moreover, the company concerned would undoubtedly claim that it was not responsible for the over-claim and might well be able to prove that."

"But someone has to know how the system works to be able to pull something like this off?"

"Undoubtedly. But you could be looking at someone in DGVI, someone who has worked in DGVI, someone in a suitable place in a national administration – past or present – or someone in one of these companies – past or present. You may need to examine exactly where the false claims came from to be able to narrow it down a bit. For instance, it might be unlikely that a company in the Saarland would try to make claims in relation to companies in Belgium or France. I'd guess the risk of getting something wrong – perhaps just in the language used – would be too great. After all, the skill in this is to get away with the money before anyone knows about it."

"Which suggests whoever did this knows about the way DGVI work – that they don't check at the time claims are presented for payment, but only doing this annual reconciliation exercise."

"But don't assume that'd mean only people who work or have worked in DGVI. Anyone who's used the system must've realised after a year or two of claiming that no claims are challenged at the time they are made, unless the DGVI office code is wrong. You could expect someone within the banking structure to spot that – but no-one would really know whether the amounts were correct unless they went back to the company submitting the claim for payment….."

"…Or DGVI, presumably?"

"Yes. But whoever authorised the original claim might well not know what size the individual requests for payment might be. DGVI's interest would be primarily in whether the total amount had been exceeded."

"And evidently no-one in DGVI keeps any sort of running tally?"

"I guess there might be the odd one or two that do. But they'd be unusual and regarded as over-bureaucratic. I imagine many people believe that the appropriate national administration is doing something like that…."

"But how would they know what was being claimed and paid out from DGVI banking facilities?"

"Frequently Member States provide matching funding up to 50% of Community funding. So a claim for say a million Belgian francs paid out by DGVI is normally likely to have a counterpart of, say, half a million Belgian francs paid out by the Belgian commerce and industry ministry. In theory, something that didn't tally with them should be matched in DGVI. Of course, if you were a criminal and reckoned DGVI was an easier target than the national authorities, you'd only claim what you could legitimately from them and carry out your fraud solely on EEC funds."

"With DGVI relying on Member States spotting something that wasn't actually happening to them."

"Exactly."

"So we need to start with the actual documents used to make the false claims, both individually as also as a possible pattern?"

"I'd reckon so – but you're the experts on that sort of thing. Of course, if there's more than one criminal at it – or someone who's extremely cunning – it may be difficult to detect much of a pattern."

"We can only try."

That was the gist of what we got out of him. He claimed to be happy to help us out when we'd got further along with our investigations. But he doubted whether he'd have much to add to what he'd already told us.

Rosemary left to pick up Emily and Sarah and I returned to the SEFF offices, only to discover that Commander de Klerck wanted to speak to me.....in person, rather than on the phone, unfortunately.

"I regret that you felt the need to complain about my cooperation," he began in a rather petulant tone. "You could have spoken to me directly."

"We pointed out to you the shortness of time that we had for this work on a couple of occasions when we met you," I replied. "We didn't complain. We did wish to alert our managers that we weren't going to be held responsible for this work not reaching a conclusion because we weren't getting the stuff we needed fast enough."

"All the relevant documents are on their way to you in the SEFF offices. If here is anything missing, please contact me – and I will get it done as fast as can be managed. M. Vermeulen has decided that the analysis of these documents should take place away from the Berlaymont, as there will be sharp eyes and flapping ears in this building. I am assuming that you have secure places where the documents can be kept?"

"Depending on the quantity, yes."

"I believe the total will be some eight box files."

"We can certainly accommodate that quantity."

As I left, I received a further glare of self-righteous indignation, but I fear it was water off a duck's back. I realised that communications between different parts of the Commission might not be particularly slick and the normal speed of business quite leisurely compared to C&E practice, but as we had only ten weeks, I couldn't afford to adopt the local customs.

When I got home later I wondered whether I shouldn't have asked Korthuizen to give me a pen picture of some of the top people in DGVI. But it'd only be his perspective and might tempt us along false trails. Rosemary and I agreed she'd work from the banking end and I'd work from the start of the administrative process – looking first at a proper claim and then at the false ones, to see what patterns or even individual lines of enquiry that threw up. Then with the children safely in bed, we had a long - but not entirely relaxing - bath together and forgot about the work completely.

3. THE BORING PROCESS OF ANALYSIS

By the time we arrived in the office the following morning, eight box files of documents were piled up on the desk in the SEFF reception area, with one of de Klerck's men awaiting our signature and to satisfy himself that we genuinely had a secure cupboard in which to store the stuff. Each box was tied up with red tape – much to Rosemary's amusement – and sealed with a stick-on label on which an official date stamp had been stamped, along with the inevitably unintelligible signature.

We took over one of the empty offices on our floor and began to work our way through the piles of documents. Someone – presumably in de Klerck's organisation – had gathered the papers relating to each false claim into separate files, with reference numbers, names and the amount of the false claim. This was helpful, as it enabled us to put to one side all claims for less than £100,000. That still left us with fourteen cases to examine. Inconveniently, it also meant that we couldn't divide up the work in the way we'd intended. So we both set about looking at each case in full. I started on the German ones, while Rosemary took the French ones – on the basis that her German was pretty well non-existent, whereas our French was fairly weak, but on a par.

Fourteen cases might not seem many and we realised it was possible we'd have to dig deeper to find any sort of pattern. But we had to start somewhere. And fourteen cases were enough to work our way through. Fortunately, all the applications for West German firms had gone through the Bundeswirtschaftministrie (Business Ministry) rather than the Länder (regional governments). The French ones had gone through the Ministère de l'Industrie and the Belgian through the Ministère de

Commerce et Manufactures. Inevitably the same names didn't appear too often. But after a day's work, I managed to draw up a schedule.

Country	Company, location & amount of false claim	Company names	National authority names	DGVI names	Bank handling transaction + names
West Germany	Wilhelm Krauss Stahlwerken AG, Voelklingen £0.3m	Dietrich Grueber; Erwin Pfessel; Joachim Goetz	Martin Leinert; Karl-Heinz Hartmann	Louis Chastelin (F); Ronald Griffiths (UK)	Saarbank AG, Stefan Kozlowski
West Germany	Schaar AG, Saarbruecken £0.8m	Helmut Schaar; Ernst Schaar; Franz Eckermann	Martin Leinert; Karl-Heinz Hartmann	Philippe Wouters (B); Ronald Griffiths (UK)	Saarbank AG, Stefan Kozlowski
West Germany	Franz Wehlen AG, Wuppertal £0.9m	Horst Wehlen; Johan Mueller; Georg Frick	Martin Leinert; Paul Heidegger	Louis Chastelin (F); Gianpaolo Ricci (It)	Westfalishes Landesbank AG, Oskar Neidermeyer
West Germany	TKG Kokerei AG, Gelsenkirchen £0.9m	Gregor Goltz; Dietrich Jankowski; Erich Sand	Martin Leinert; Gunther Born	Louis Chastelin (F); Cathal O'Riordan (Ir)	Rheinbank AG, Leopold von Eisenau
France	Polytextiles de Flandres, Roubaix £0.5m	Jean Delasalle; Jean-Pierre Marais; Isidore Gambezzi	Jean-Claude d'Henonville ; Patrick Ploucanet	Heinz Groener (WG) ; Gianpaolo Ricci (It)	Banque de Crédit du Nord, Geoffroi Montgras
France	Acier Escaut Cie, Valenciennes £0.6m	Henri Froche ; Herve Villard ; Robert Herthein	Jean-Claude d'Henonville, Patrick Ploucanet	Heinz Groener (WG) ; Cathal O'Riordan (Ir)	Crédit Flandres, David Simonet
France	EVM Cie, Lille £0.5m	Étienne Boucher; Roger Dupont; Gérard Huguenin	Jean-Claude d'Henonville; Francois Bonnard	Heinz Groener (WG) ; Ronald Griffiths (UK)	Banque de Lille, Marcel Dutoit
France	Deûle Industries, Lille £0.7m	Jean-Pierre Fouchet ; Michel Czerniawski ; Pierre Herne	Jean-Claude d'Henonville ; Francois Bonnard	Heinz Groener (WG) ; Gianpaolo Ricci (It)	Crédit Flandres, Maurice Mervey

France	Charbonniers de Lens, Lens £0.6m	Louis Guillemin ; Pierre Sablouis ; Hubert Ricard	Jean-Claude d'Henonville; Patrick Ploucanet	Heinz Groener (WG) ; Cathal O'Riordan (Ir)	Banque du Pas de Calais, Jules Sercotin
Belgium	Durufle et Cie, Charleroi £0.5m	Maxim de Laan ; Charles Foulnes ; Peter Symons	Marcel Delahaye ; Piet Haan	David Cardle (UK) ; Gianpaolo Ricci (It)	Banque de Tournai, Felix Verlaeren
Belgium	Cie CCR, Charleroi £0.4m	Jan de Mettet ; Marie-Elizabeth Clouet ; Philippe Verstruegen	Marcel Delahaye ; Piet Haan	David Cardle (UK) ; Cathal O'Riordan (Ir)	Namse Krediet Bank, Dirk Verstappen
Belgium	Charbonniers de la Louviere, La Louviere £0.4m	Herve Janvier ; Jean-Claude Louvet ; Vincent Barbouillet	Marcel Delahaye ; Frank van Haarden	David Cardle (UK); Jürgen Schwenk (WG)	Banque de Hainault, Charlotte Benjamin
Belgium	Charbonniers de Courcelles, Courcelles £0.3m	Raymond Leblanc ; Louis Dupuits ; André Gratiolet	Marcel Delahaye ; Piet Haan	David Cardle (UK ; Gianpaolo Ricci (It)	Banque de Hainault, Pierre-Louis Seydmann
Belgium	CW et Cie, Roux £0.3m	Thierry Vloet ; Jean Duvergne ; Luc Grasset	Marcel Delahaye ; Frank van Haarden	David Cardle (UK); Jürgen Schwenk (WG)	Banque de Charleroi; François Millet

Poring through it I found I could detect only one thing of interest. There was no significant pattern. Evidently the same officials in the West German, French and Belgian ministries were responsible for these claims and officials not from the country submitting the claim were responsible for work on the claims in DGVI. But that scarcely amounted to a pattern that was going to be of any use to us.

On the other hand, Rosemary spotted something quickly the following morning.

"Did you notice that none of these claimants ever use a large bank. They invariably use a local one. For instance – none of the French ones have used Paribas or the Crédit Lyonnais. I realise that local banks may understand local businesses better, but if we can get our hands on some kosher claims, I bet we'll find that some have used the big, national banks. I think it's too much of a coincidence that none of these claims have gone through a bank big enough to spot something a bit fishy."

"I suppose we should check whether these are the banks which these companies would normally use."

"And get hold of some valid claims too."

I rang de Klerck's office and explained what documents we needed to his secretary, who appeared more helpful than her boss. I reminded her that this was all supposed to be confidential, but she told me that the documents were coming from "the archives" in the old Commission building, so the only people who would know we were looking at this stuff would be us, the archivist, her and Commander de Klerck, of course. I wasn't sure I felt entirely reassured by that, but, as Rosemary pointed out, the documents we'd been looking at had presumably arrived from the same place by the same route, so it was a bit late worrying whether information was seeping through to DGVI. Indeed, if someone in DGVI was involved, this fraud seemed sufficiently well planned for them either to be out of reach of the authorities or keeping a careful look-out for any investigation of what'd been going on. Though the Commission struck me as being less of a gossipy village than C&E – not least because of the different nationalities working there – I still would've been surprised if our investigation wasn't at least rumoured in DGVI.

"We're almost certainly going to have to interview some of these people," Rosemary observed. "I think we can leave the people in the national administrations for now. It doesn't really seem plausible that Martin Leinert, Jean-Claude d'Henonville and/or Marcel Delahaye have run this fraud. I don't see how they'd lay their hands on the information to make the false claims in the other countries."

"I think we should also leave DGVI out for the time being. It seems to me that though these claims are all handled by separate people in DGVI, the place where all the information comes together and where the process is well known is DGVI. Isn't it likely that someone in DGVI - possibly none of the names on our list – has had access to the original claims and passed on the info to someone else?"

"That's plausible....I agree that it seems a bit unlikely that someone from one of these companies has run the whole fraud. I don't quite see how they'd get the info......But the weak link is probably the bank account. Someone has to set it up...and you have to do that in person. Someone has to present the various forms so that a claim can be made....and collect the money from the bank at the end of the process. Indeed, I reckon we need to interview a few of the bankers pronto. Apart from the fact that they may be the only ones who've actually seen the people carrying out this fraud, they'll also be able to tell us – which these files don't – in what form the money was actually removed from the bank accounts."

"Whoever set this up surely wouldn't be stupid enough to be seen in different places, posing as a series of different people?"

"I guess when you're making £8 million or so, you can afford a few accomplices."

"I suppose so.....But equally he wouldn't be foolish enough to get all the money sent to a single bank account....even in Switzerland."

"I expect not. Though it'll probably all end up in some anonymous bank account there....But I can't see he'd take it in cash. It'd be far too conspicuous. I think it has to be a transfer to the company's bank account, which must be a bogus one he's set up earlier. But we should be able to check that when we see the legitimate claims and after we've spoken to people from the companies and the banks."

"So there's going to be some travelling involved. If Wasco decide to carry out their investigation of Ceresini, we may need my mother to look after Emily and Sarah. We can hardly ask her to come in the next week or two as well."

"And there'd be no point even asking my parents. There's no way Simone would allow them to escape to Brussels to look after Emily and Sarah….Mainly because of the risk that they might like it too much and want to come here more often…They're much too convenient as free and reliable babysitters…..But I don't see that it'd need both of us to go to Ceresini….even less to one of these firms….and some of them – the Belgian ones, at least – should be doable in a day. You could do the West German ones on your own. There wouldn't be much point my going if you were going to be speaking German anyway."

"And the French ones?"

"Let's cross that bridge when we come to it…..But I reckon we could do most of them in a day too."

The legitimate claims came over the next day and a half – each in a box file secured as before.

It rapidly became clear that every single company making a legitimate claim used a different bank from the one used for the false claims – and, as Rosemary had surmised, mostly using large nationwide banks like Paribas, Kommerzbank, etc. It was also clear that legitimate and false claims occurred in no particular order…..and that, from what we could tell, the overpaid claims were invariably a single payment made into a small local bank, which wasn't the same one where previous payments had been made.

"I find it amazing that no-one anywhere seems to have spotted that large sums of money were being paid into completely different bank accounts for the same firm," remarked Rosemary. "They don't seem to have any controls at all. Once the claim has been authorised, it's assumed these companies are legit and honest, so no checks are made until the end-year reconciliation."

"Perhaps it's because we work in law and order areas, but I couldn't see anyone in C&E allowing such lax arrangements…."

"But you lot think everyone is a crook anyway…."

"It didn't stop us setting up VAT with some pretty large holes in it for crooks to exploit…..But I guess this is the same sort of thing, the people in DGVI are interested in softening the decline of some industries while helping others to be competitive. I doubt they ever really think about crooks trying to rip them off."

"Well given that it's other people's money they're spending, they jolly well should have proper controls."

We continued to work our way through the documents covering the legitimate claims. It was a fair slog and even my normal enthusiasm for digging into the detail was beginning to fade. Then something struck me – a breakthrough, of sorts! Everything was the same in the legitimate documents as the fraudulent ones – apart from the bank used and the name of the person who handled the transaction at the bank. But before I opened my big mouth and told Rosemary, my brain clicked into gear with the unwelcome realisation that my breakthrough was nothing of the sort. The fraud was perpetrated in companies whose claims had been recommended by the national authorities and confirmed by DGVI. So someone making a false claim didn't need to know all the details. All they needed to know was which firms were getting money out of DGVI and roughly how much. It'd be taking a foolish risk to try to make a claim for £400,000 when the firm had only been granted £300,000, for instance. You'd need to know enough about the firm to satisfy the bank where you were setting up an account, but I reckoned there'd be safer ways of acquiring that knowledge than purloining it from the DGVI material. Indeed, if someone in DGVI was involved, presumably they'd want it to appear that the fraud could've taken place without anyone in DGVI knowing anything about it.

Indeed, looking more closely at the documents, I realised that most were photocopies of the originals.

"I wonder whether these documents were photocopied just for us, or whether there are a number of photocopies lying around in files which anyone could lay their hands on?" I asked.

"We could check. From what we've seen and heard so far, DGVI doesn't seem a particularly security-conscious place. I'm sure all that red tape and sticky labels stuff was de Klerck and his people trying to show us that they weren't sloppy….in contrast to DGVI."

"The stuff doesn't seem to be handled as confidential anyway. The copies aren't numbered and the originals don't have file page numbers either…."

"You think it's someone in DGVI who's masterminded this fraud, don't you?"

"It's certainly the place where people would know the system inside-out and be able to get hold of the relevant documents. But unless someone has just flown off to Paraguay, it seems to me it'd be the first place anyone would look once the frauds had been discovered. Each payment has to be authorised by the appropriate person in DGVI, but I guess if you've got a copy of documents with all these people's signatures on them you could forge them. DGVI is the obvious starting point to look….but actually I think we should be starting at the other end, with the local banks and firms. If this was masterminded from DGVI, I think whoever it was will've disguised his or her involvement extremely well….or they've shoved off to somewhere that doesn't have an extradition treaty and beyond anyone's reach. However, it seems to me that the only way to get at this is to start with real people doing real things and see where that leads us."

"Just like peeling an onion!"

"Very likely…But do you agree that's the best way to go with this?"

"Yes. It'll take longer, of course. But as you say, because the logical place to find the mastermind is in DGVI, our chances of identifying anyone there without any other evidence seems pretty well impossible., though we should check whether there's anyone who's left DGVI recently and vanished off the face of the earth….But if that'd happened, I doubt whether Vermeulen would've felt the need to involve us…It'd be pretty obvious…. So, leaving that on one side for the moment, you'd have to say that the crime seems well planned – and possibly done only once – so I agree that whoever planned it will have covered his or her tracks well…But if you look at the lists we've been writing out and the officials in these offices, how likely do you think it'll be a 'her'?"

All our further examination of the legitimate claims showed was that though in DGVI, the more senior officer - Martin Leinert, Jean-Claude d'Henonville and Marcel Delahaye – invariably signed the necessary forms, the other signature varied. Indeed it also included Gérard Creac'h and Piet Korthuizen. Both had only signed a couple of the earlier claims. And while that was just about consistent with what Creac'h had told us about when he left DGVI, I recalled Korthuizen telling us he'd left about two years ago. As he was technically our adviser for DGVI, according to Vermeulen, it seemed to me to be worth checking. Indeed, my immediate reaction was that he was less our adviser and more a spy to keep track of where we were getting to.

"Do you think we should raise it with them?" asked Rosemary, when I mentioned it to her – having read through that part of the files after she'd left to pick up Emily and Sarah.

"I think not with Creac'h at this stage. I don't think he was so clear on exactly when he'd left DGVI for it not to look as though we didn't trust him. But Korthuizen is supposed to be our source of advice for things about DGVI. As he plainly signed a couple of claims last November, I don't see how that could be consistent with him telling us he'd left about two years ago."

"You don't think he might be the mastermind, trying to keep an eye on what we're getting up to?"

"I doubt it. Whoever is running this is sufficiently intelligent and cautious not to be caught out in such an obvious lie. I accept he might be a spy working for the mastermind…which suggests that perhaps we don't tackle him directly. When we next see him we'll mention that we've been looking at some kosher claims to see whether and if so how they differ from the bogus ones. Of course, we haven't looked at all the kosher claims by any means, but it'll give him an opportunity to change his story if he wants to...."

"And we can handle him with kid gloves in the meantime."

"Exactly."

Thinking further about it, I realised that Creac'h didn't know what our interest in DGVI was – other than we wanted to know how the processes worked there. There would've been no reason for him to have told us that he'd handled some claims for payment. On the other hand, Korthuizen knew pretty well what we were looking at. So why had he told us such an obvious whopper? There must've been a reasonable chance that we might come across documents that placed him in DGVI within the last two years. Why was he prepared to take such a big risk? After all, if we discovered he'd been lying to us, we might reasonably start to believe he was involved in the fraud in some way. The only answers I could come up with were that he was possibly stupid, a cocky chancer or being used to divert our attention from someone or somewhere else.....for which he was doubtless being rewarded by someone who could be confident he wouldn't lead us to him (or possibly her), because Korthuizen knew nothing about what had really been going on. None of them made me feel particularly comfortable.

But I didn't feel particularly comfortable about this investigation in any case. It seemed to me that there were too many possible suspects but the likelihood of uncovering any evidence that might enable us to narrow the number down a bit, or better still be able to confront a handful of suspects with some hard evidence pointing to them, ranged from small to nil. And as this was presumably a one-off, it could have been carefully planned and the chances of setting a trap for someone trying it on again – as we'd been fortunate to be able to do with Veronica

Anderson and her colleagues in the UDA – were therefore zero. I reckoned we'd spend the next eight weeks visiting various banks and manufacturers and getting plenty of information from them. But it'd get us virtually no nearer to whoever had managed this fraud. Unlike how the UDA had used their part-time hitman, William Hume, to go around setting up various bank accounts in London for their VAT frauds, whoever had organised this would surely minimise the risk – given that this was the weakest link in the chain – by using different people to set up these bank accounts. There'd be no straightforward link between them and the mastermind - wherever, whoever he or she was.

I decided not to mention these doubts to Rosemary, whose days were tiring enough as it was. Not long after we'd returned to work in September, she'd picked up a virus and had been forced to stay in bed for a couple of days, which meant I'd had to shorten my day, collect Emily and Sarah from school and then sort them out – including playing, helping with the small amount of homework they were set, feeding them and getting them to bed. By the time I'd finished reading them their bedtime story and got a light dinner for Rosemary and me, I was completely knackered. So I appreciated just how tiring Rosemary's normal routine was….and I also knew she was spending any few moments of her spare time trying to work through her accountancy textbooks, aiming to be a qualified accountant before she went back to the Met…or as soon after as possible.

Unusually, I couldn't make up my mind whether this digging away at box file after box file of detailed and, frankly, pretty tedious documents was getting to me enough to make me want to unmask whoever was behind the fraud – or whether the chances of getting anywhere were so small that I would carry forward such work as we could do in the time in a completely detached frame of mind. I disliked not bringing things like this to a conclusion. But I knew that if we'd uncovered some possibly fruitful leads by December and had even started to narrow down our list of suspects I'd be extremely frustrated at having to pass the work on to someone else. Apart from a feeling that Commander de Klerck and his men might well not be up to it, I didn't like doing all the hard slog and not being involved in the dénouement. I wondered too why we'd been asked to do this work rather than de Klerck and his people? Was it purely that they didn't have the experience? Or perhaps that Vermeulen couldn't entirely trust them – not to have at least one of their number passing on info to whoever had organised this fraud? And I still had a nagging doubt at the back of my mind that this was an elaborate subterfuge – either intended to get us so embroiled in it we'd prefer to stick with it, rather than go back to the wine fraud investigation or to make us look like callow fools, to damage our credibility in the wine fraud investigation.

Though all the documents which we'd seen had appeared genuine, every one had been a photocopy – and we had absolutely no idea whether the documents that actually passed through DGVI looked like them. We only had Vermeulen and de Klerck's word that the £8m million had actually gone missing as the result of fraud. The claims which we were told were fraudulent could just as easily be legitimate.

But perhaps I was beginning to get a bit paranoid. I suppose it was because somewhere deep down I felt that the Mafia were involved in the wine fraud – and that they had tentacles that could reach virtually anywhere. On the other hand, I reckoned there were less elaborate ways of getting the wine fraud investigation halted, involving fewer senior people in the EEC Commission. And I could certainly test whether the claims which we'd been told were fraudulent really were. Our visits to see the firms and banks involved should tell us that. And it was rather over-sophisticated for the Mafia, it struck me on reflection. They were more likely to make oblique threats to us or Emily and Sarah or plant drugs on us or get us into some sort of compromising situation which would enable them to blackmail us. Of course, there might be a different sort of organisation involved in the wine fraud – or a completely different person might want us to fall flat on our faces, or divert our attention. But again – it seemed rather too elaborate and, for all that I didn't like or trust Vermeulen much, I couldn't see why he'd wish to be associated in something that was aimed at taking Rosemary and me down a peg or three. And by and large, the people we'd annoyed in recent years didn't really have the clout to make something like this happen.

So I resolved to try to take it one step at a time. For once, I'd try to treat this investigation as a sort of exercise, rather than my own personal crusade to unmask a fraudster or gang of fraudsters. If in the highly unlikely event we actually got far enough to have a reasonable chance of bringing it to a conclusion, I could rouse my enthusiasm. But until then, I'd try to take a detached view. But, of course, resolutions like that have a tendency to be overwhelmed by events.

4. A DISAPPEARANCE

I was arranging our first visits to the Belgian firms and companies who were mentioned in the false claim documents. We reckoned that with an early start we should be able to cover both the firms and the banks in a morning. It wasn't as though what we wanted from them was particularly complicated. Indeed, we'd agreed that one of us would phone them in advance to explain the reason for our visit, following up with a letter if they so wished. Vermeulen's office provided suitable credentials – and our cover story essentially was that we were carrying out an audit of a sample of the DGVI transactions undertaken in 1974/5. The first couple of phone calls had caused no problems. None of those we spoke to appeared to have any reservations or could see that what we were doing was anything out of the ordinary. So we agreed we'd head to Cie CCR in Charleroi, as it was only an hour by train from Brussels Central and a little less from Brussels Midi. Fortunately, though the relevant bank was the Namse Krediet Bank, the branch used had been in Charleroi, not Namur. I wondered for an instant whether if the account had been set up in Namur, anyone in DGVI might've questioned it? But, of course, they wouldn't have seen the relevant documents until months after the fraud had been perpetrated.

We arranged the meeting for the Thursday. Though I reckoned it might be possible to knock off both firms based in Charleroi in one morning, we'd no idea how long it'd take to get to them by public transport – having decided to avoid using taxis as far as possible – or how they might wish to deal with us. So we would see just Cie CCR and decide in the light of that whether we could manage two firms in a day, with Rosemary travelling back a little earlier than me, if necessary. The international school which Emily and Sarah attended was able to keep them for much of the afternoon – as many children of British people working in the Commission or UKREP did. But basically it was homework for the older children or sitting around reading for the younger ones…..with the alternative of tennis during the summer. But though both our daughters enjoyed reading, they needed to be more active after the best part of a day cooped up in school. So we'd agreed we'd only make them stay for a long afternoon if it was essential.

A couple of days before our visit to Charleroi, we started to check we'd got all the relevant documents for Cie CCR, as well as re-examining our notes so we didn't come across as complete ignoramuses about the EEC's industrial support processes. While we were in the middle of this, my phone rang with a summons to meet Jérôme Vermeulen. Rosemary was included as well, of course.

"If I'd known this was coming, I'd've worn trousers," she said. "I don't like being leered at."

"Perhaps you should keep a pair of trousers in the office, just in case?"

"Perhaps I should. But I shouldn't really have to. Men like Vermeulen shouldn't behave like that. It's plain bad manners. And I don't see why I should dress to avoid men like him leering at me. All the women of my age wear mini-skirts here – and I like wearing them….And I know well enough I won't be wearing them when I get back to the Met….unless they've lightened up a lot while we've been away."

As it happened, Vermeulen allowed himself but a momentary glance at Rosemary's legs and came straight to the point.

"An employee in DGVI has been reported as having gone missing," he stated, in that curiously accented English. "A Mlle Monique Lefebvre, an accountant. She is French, from Paris, and has been working in the Commission since 1969 and DGVI since 1972. Apparently the last time she appeared in the office was Monday a week ago. When she did not appear in the office for a day or two, her colleagues considered that she must be sick. But when she did not arrive this Monday past, they attempted to contact her by telephone, but received no answer. A colleague who knew her quite well offered to visit her apartment in Uccle, but it was evident that she was not there. Indeed, after the concierge let her colleague into the apartment, it was evident that she had not been there since the previous Monday. Her colleague did not consider it proper to pry, but she could find nothing to suggest where Mlle Lefebvre might have gone. The matter was reported to her superiors, and Mr Southern, the Director-General of DGVI, asked Commander le Klerck to see whether there was anything he could find out. Le Klerck has found no evidence of where she might have gone. She had few friends here in Brussels and in Paris – according to an address book which was left in her flat. But none of those few contacted – nor her mother, who lives in Aubervilliers, a suburb of Paris – had seen her. She does not appear to have been taken to a hospital – or a police station, for that matter. Nor has she left the country – as her passport remains in her flat and there is no record of her on any flight out of Zaventem. She could have left by rail or road – but it would be difficult to leave without a passport. So everyone is at a loss to understand what might have happened to her. But naturally, some people fear the worst."

"Is there some suggestion that this might be linked to the enquiries which we're undertaking about DGVI?" asked Rosemary, looking him in the eye.

"I don't know. Did her name come up in any of the documents you've been examining?"

"I believe she signed a few of the legitimate claim documents. But we haven't looked at the smaller fraudulent claims because of the limited time. Her name is on none of the documents relating to the larger fraudulent claims."

"In that case, I imagine there is a possibility that because she worked in a Directorate-General where such large frauds were being perpetrated, her disappearance is in some way linked to that. I assume you have not been in contact with her?"

51

"No. We'd decided not to contact anyone in DGVI at this stage. If we needed information we'd contact Mr Korthuizen or perhaps M. Creac'h," I explained.

"Is there any reason to suggest that she was involved in any of the fraudulent claims?" asked Rosemary.

"Not that I know of," replied Vermeulen. "I believe the reason for informing you is purely that these frauds have taken place in DGVI's territory, if I might put it like that, and now an apparently competent, hard-working member of DGVI has gone missing."

"It's a bit tenuous," I said. "But we should try to follow it up a bit ourselves. It might be relevant to our work."

"Or not, of course," added Rosemary. "What's being done about her disappearance? Have the local police been informed?"

"I believe that is occurring."

"Would Mr Korthuizen or M. Creac'h know Mlle Lefebvre at all?"

"DGVI is not a large Directorate-General. They will have encountered each other. I will consult Commander de Klerck as to which of them might be most useful for you to meet. This may have nothing to do with your investigations, of course. But if anything emerges from your work, I trust you will keep me in the picture, as I believe you say in England."

"Just before we go, can I confirm that no-one else has left DGVI and disappeared? We'd assumed that if someone had done so, they would be your chief suspect and you would've mentioned their name to us."

"I can confirm that is the case."

We walked back to the SEFF offices.

"What do you think?" we both asked each other at the same time.

"I think someone over there thinks this disappearance may well be connected to the frauds," I got in first.

"I think we're going to have to be careful not to get in the way of the Brussels police," added Rosemary.

There plainly was some enthusiasm for us finding out more about the disappeared Mlle Lefebvre, as we'd not been back in our offices long when Korthuizen rang, suggesting we met for lunch. Though this didn't surprise me, it seemed on the surface less likely for him, rather than Creac'h, to have known Mlle Lefebvre well, as according to what he told us before, he could only have overlapped with her in DGVI for a year or so – and would have no recent information about her.

We met in the Commission restaurant, where subsidies meant you could get a steak, chips and salad, a bottle of Jupiler and a coffee for less than £1.

"You wished to know about Monique Lefebvre, who has apparently gone missing?" Korthuizen began.

"Yes," I replied. "We have no idea whether this might be relevant to the work we're doing or not. But M. Vermeulen appears to think there might be a connection. So we said we'd find out a bit more about it. It may be a path that leads nowhere, of course."

"As many do......You realise that I didn't...don't know Monique well. But DGVI isn't a large office – less than sixty people – so you get to learn a certain amount about most people while you're working there."

"Please tell us what you know about her....especially if it might be relevant to her disappearance," said Rosemary.

"What her name doesn't tell you is that she was half Vietnamese. Her mother was Vietnamese – called Nguyen, of something like that. Her father was a French doctor who met her mother when he was over there before the war. They were separated during the war, but met up in Australia – apparently he'd been working in Brisbane while, once the Australians accepted she wasn't Japanese, Mlle Nguyen was working as a nurse in a hospital in Rockhampton. They married, returned to France and had Monique all in the same twelve months – Monique was born in summer 1946. Her father died when she was still young and she was brought up by her mother in a

Parisian suburb. She – Monique – was bright and did well at school. Not well enough for one of the Grandes Écoles, but enough to qualify as a bookkeeper and accountant. I believe she applied directly for jobs in the Commission rather than any part of the French administration. That is generally quite unusual – expect for Belgians, of course. But I never found out why. Perhaps she never said. She was a competent official, but probably unlikely to rise more than one more grade…and that probably not for ten years or more."

"What sort of work did she do?" I asked.

"Much like the rest of us. Scrutinising claims, checking them against the relevant Community legislation and regulations, dealing with any matters relating to the cases which were assigned to her. For instance, if a company fails to qualify for a Community subsidy or doesn't receive as much as it requested, there may well be complaints and continuing correspondence. She would handle all that sort of thing."

"So she didn't really work as an accountant or bookkeeper?" observed Rosemary.

"That is so. It is perhaps an English peculiarity that public officials are not professionally qualified. You would find it unusual to find someone operating in an administrative position in the Commission who was not a qualified lawyer, accountant or the like."

"How would cases be assigned to people like Mlle Lefebvre?" I asked.

"No member of DGVI would be assigned to a claim from their home country. Otherwise it would be on the basis of current workload. So if a colleague was dealing with ten cases, while she had only six or seven. She would probably be assigned the next case or even two. I understand you English work on letters of the alphabet or postal districts, but we have found that to lead to imbalances in workloads – and changing work parameters like alphabetical case numbers or postal districts requires the agreement of the trade unions. That takes time and may involve some unpleasantness, so it is generally best avoided."

"What was Mlle Lefebvre like as a person?" asked Rosemary.

"She was quiet. My impression of oriental women is that they tend to be self-effacing. As she was largely brought up by her mother, I would imagine her behaviour would rub off on her."

"Any close friends? Or a boyfriend?"

"No close friends in the office. She used to lunch with a few people from DGVI and sometimes from DGIV, where she worked previously. Mostly they were French like her. But most of us tend to lunch with colleagues from our own countries…. unless someone is trying to chat up some sultry Italian woman…and then it's all rather obvious and public. So by and large people who are trying to strike up friendships do it well outside the office."

"Did you ever have lunch with her…along with other colleagues?"

"A couple of times when she joined DGVI and she was being introduced to her colleagues. As you might imagine, conversations on such occasions are somewhat stilted. But in any case, if someone doesn't wish to let their colleagues know much about themselves, no-one would ever pry….and lunchtime conversations tend to be about work, the latest news or television programmes or sport."

"Did you know whether she had a boyfriend?"

"No. I didn't. She never mentioned one – but she wasn't that sort of person. It's quite rare that colleagues meet outside work. This city is big enough fortunately to avoid encountering one's colleagues more than occasionally. Besides, she had an apartment in Uccle, so I believe. I've got a nice flat in Tervuren and I can get away on my bicycle at weekends with fellow cycling enthusiasts. I doubt whether I've ever even been to Uccle. Once I've finished here, I head out for the country."

"Is there anything you can think of that might explain her disappearance? Might she have annoyed someone by refusing their claim for a subsidy? Or had she even been in an argument with anyone in the office?"

"Not really. You'll understand my acquaintance with her was a while back. I've never heard of any company taking a rejection of their claim so hard that they'd kill or kidnap a Commission official. Besides, the rejection would not involve just her – but her manager and possibly even her director. If the company concerned knew her name, it would be just one among several. She might sign certain types of correspondence, but if anything became too antagonistic, letters would be signed at a higher level than her."

"Within the office?"

"I recall there being a couple of the men – not sure which nationality – who used to make rather unpleasant jokes about her Vietnamese nationality. Suggesting she was a Viet-Cong mole in the Commission - that sort of thing. If I remember correctly another man – a rugby player, I believe – punched one of them on the nose in the office. There was quite a lot of blood and a bit of a fuss. But that seemed to stop it. I'm not sure why anything like that would want to make anyone kill her or kidnap her. Other than that – I don't know. As I said, she was quiet and unassuming. But sometimes a few quiet words can be just as wounding than loud verbal bullying. But I've never heard she ever did anything like that or that anyone was doing that to her."

"You don't think she could've killed herself?"

"I guess you can't really tell with people you know so little about. From what little I know, it's supposed to be the quiet ones who do that sort of thing. But as far as I'm aware, she was brought up as a good Catholic. So it'd take a lot to make her kill herself, I guess. I can't think of any obvious reason – nor any reason of ill health…..She took no sick leave, as far as I'm aware. Someone mentioned once that she used to save up her leave days so she could go to Australia, where she had relatives, so I gather. Otherwise, I believe she used to visit her mother for the weekend about once a month. I remember her coming in late one Monday morning because the train from Paris had been delayed for some reason…"

"Anything else you can think of?"

"No….If anything comes to mind I'll get in touch with you."

He didn't ask how our investigation was getting on, so I didn't get the chance to offer him the opportunity to change what he'd said to us previously about when he left DGVI.

"If he left DGVI about two years ago he's got a remarkably good memory," remarked Rosemary after he'd left to join some colleagues for coffee in the coffee lounge outside the restaurant. "He also seems to know a lot more about a colleague he claims he barely knew than I'd expect."

"And we've no idea how much of what he told us was true. I'd like to get a few words with Creac'h if I can, just to see how reliable Korthuizen is."

"I realise this is jumping the gun about whether she's involved in this fraud at all, but I'd like to know more about her. I don't see how we could go to the Belgian police. They've no reason to tell us anything unless someone like Vermeulen tells them to….and the only reason why we're interested is because of the fraud case, which he plainly doesn't want to tell the Belgian police anything about."

"And – other than trying to see Creac'h again – we've no good reason to go chatting to people in DGVI without risking our interest in DGVI becoming known."

Rather than just head back to the SEFF office, we decided to see whether we couldn't organise a meeting with Gérard Creac'h. But it would evidently need to be done through Vermeulen. As it was just after 2pm, he was not in his office, of course. But we managed to leave a message with one of his "assistantes", a buxom Flemish lady of indeterminate age. I also managed to get from her a telephone number for Creac'h, as his name didn't appear in the official Commission telephone book….a matter which struck me as odd, as Korthuizen's and Mlle Lefebvre's were there.

When I got back to the office, I rang Creac'h, to discover that the number was the main line for an organisation called Comité de Liaison des Industries Françaises (CLIF). Fortunately he was still out at lunch, so I had some time to think about what this information meant.

Why had de Klerck or possibly Vermeulen offered Creac'h to us as the best person to tell us about how DGVI worked? Why not an official in the Commission? There must surely be more than just Korthuizen who had worked in DGVI, but no longer did so? A possible reason might be that they wanted to avoid any rumours going around the Commission, inevitably reaching the ears of people in DGVI. But subsequently we'd been put in touch with Korthuizen, a Commission official, and not a wholly reliable one, I felt. Or did they suspect Creac'h – and putting us in touch with him was intended to bring him to our attention? Plainly he seemed to have moved from being a gamekeeper to a poacher, but I couldn't see why that made him suspect. Evidently he'd know his way around the procedures in DGVI and working for CLIF probably gave him opportunities to travel to places where he could put together plans for the fraud. But it seemed to me that the fraud needed copies of various documents – not least authorisation forms – with the correct signatures, dates, etc. Though I knew nothing about how DGVI worked, it seemed to me it was unlikely he could wander into their offices and gather what he needed without it exciting some comment. If something like that had happened, I couldn't see why we shouldn't have been told about it.

Creac'h didn't phone back that afternoon. When I told Rosemary what I'd found out, she was inevitably intrigued – and suspicious.

"It's possible that this is just to avoid rumours going round the Commission, as you say," she observed. "But why did no-one tell us?"

"For an investigation which we were asked to do, it seems odd that we're given so little information. I keep wondering whether

Vermeulen and others have an idea who carried out the fraud or, at least, have a number of suspects and they're trying to send us down a particular route to smoke them out. As we go about this sort of thing in a particular way – seeking documentary evidence, following it up, and so on – they may've been able to predict fairly accurately what direction we'd take."

"I certainly wouldn't trust Vermeulen further than I could throw an elephant….and I can't make out whether de Klerck is untrustworthy or lazy and not very competent. In any case, these are just the people who have been put in front of us. Who knows who's actually running this particular show?"

"Let's see what we get out of Creac'h – assuming we can see him tomorrow. Otherwise we'll have to hope we can pin him down for Friday."

In the event, we were able to meet Creac'h later the following morning. He phoned almost the moment I'd sat down at my desk and suggested a meeting in a nearby coffee bar.

"The CLIF office is just round the corner," he explained, as we sat down with cups of cappuccino, rather than the skull-splitting local version of an espresso. "It's important to be located close to the Commission so that one can get in quickly if they appear to be contemplating something we'd regard as unwelcome."

"You mean you can actually get into the offices of Commission officials?" I asked.

"Not without an appointment. But if I'm nearby and they suggest a meeting in fifteen minutes or they couldn't meet for another fortnight, if I can get there in fifteen minutes, I've outwitted their subterfuge."

"But presumably you can get to see Commission officials more easily as you were one yourself?" suggested Rosemary.

"Not at all! I'm regarded as someone who has gone over to the enemy. Whenever I put my head round the door – as you English put it – in DGVI, I'm treated more as a spy than as a former colleague."

"So why did you leave?"

"Better money and a bit of fun! Promotion in the Commission is based on dead men's shoes, modified only by national quotas. I couldn't see the possibility of a promotion for at least ten years…and that would be it, for me. The money isn't a lot better – and I have to pay proper taxes. But I get a decent expense account and the opportunity to do different things, rather than the same old grind year after year….But I doubt you wanted to hear my life history, Mr and Mrs Storey….?"

"No. It was about a former colleague of yours, Mlle Monique Lefebvre. We've been told that she has gone missing. Apparently she disappeared about ten days ago, leaving no clue as to her whereabouts. So no-one knows whether she's alive or dead," I explained.

"But you work for SEFF. I realise you were doing some work in relation to DGVI. But what interest is Monique Lefebvre's disappearance to you?"

"It appears there have been some irregularities in DGVI and we were asked to have an independent look. We have absolutely no idea whether Mlle Lefebvre's disappearance has anything to do with our work, or with any irregularities. But those who asked us to carry out this work drew her disappearance to our attention and we thought we'd better check whether there might be a connection. But really all we wanted from you was what she was like and whether you could shed any light on why she might disappear like this?"

"I understand you are being cautious. I may be so also, of course……But I'm not sure I need to be in the case of Monique Lefebvre. She was a bit of a mouse – small and quiet. You'd barely notice Monique in a room of two people, so it was said – perhaps a little unkindly. She did her job well enough, but I doubt whether she would ever get herself promoted. Some push themselves forward into the limelight. Others seem almost to draw backwards away from it. Monique was one of those. A woman like that is difficult to get to know. I believe one or two had attempted friendship or a bit more over the years, but so I'm told – as she was never of any interest to me – she rebuffed them with silent indifference. If she had friends – even close ones – outside the office, who knows? She'd certainly never mention them. Too small and discreet. You realise she can't have been taller than a metre and a half…tiny, like a little Vietnamese mouse."

"Her disappearance might have several explanations. Could you imagine any reason why she might be killed or kidnapped? Or whether she might have taken her own life in a way that her body couldn't be found?" asked Rosemary.

"When someone is so quiet and self-contained, it can be difficult to know what is going on inside their heads. Personally I'd say suicide would be more likely than being killed or kidnapped. Certainly, from what I was told, her family had little money – just a mother living in what they call 'reduced circumstances' in a little flat in a Paris suburb. The relatives she used to visit in Australia were refugees, so I gather – and I got the impression that she may have brought some of her savings with her when she visited them to help them out. And why would anyone want to kill someone so insignificant? I'm not saying suicide is likely – merely that it seems more likely than the alternatives…."

"She could be running away from something or someone, I suppose?" I suggested.

"Your irregularities in DGVI, for instance? I suppose anything is possible. But if little Monique Lefebvre was involved in anything even slightly untoward, I'd eat my hat – as you English say, I believe. She was a bit of a fanatic about accuracy and doing things properly. Though she'd never say anything, you could see from her expression – or more accurately, I suppose, her aura – when someone cut a few corners, that she disapproved…to the bottom of her soul. And she was painstakingly accurate and careful with her own work. I suppose if she discovered that someone had been up to something untoward…your irregularities…she was the sort of person who couldn't be persuaded to let it go by. She'd want to inform her managers…So I guess she might have been frightened off sufficiently to wish to disappear without trace. Your irregularities would have to be extremely large stuff for anyone to have her killed in what would appear to be a highly professional manner if she has disappeared so tidily."

"Not something your former colleagues would have any experience of, I imagine?" observed Rosemary.

"No. Like me, they are a bunch of bureaucrats. We can write, calculate, assess, hold meetings – but removing someone without trace isn't one of our talents."

"Someone mentioned us that Mlle Lefebvre had been bullied…or at least, taunted because of her Vietnamese origins. Do you recall anything about that?"

"I think so…I certainly recall a couple of people joking about her being a spy for the Viet-Cong. I'm not sure it was seriously intended."

"But didn't one of the men punch one of those saying such things on the nose?"

"I'm not sure I was actually in the office at the time…." He looked the slightest bit uncomfortable.

"You don't know who punched who do you?"

"The man who did the punching was Piet Korthuizen. A bit of a bully himself, our Piet Korthuizen."

"And the man who was punched?"

"I fear I cannot remember….As I said, I wasn't actually there at the time…and if you've been punched, it's not something you'd go boasting about….and I guess it was the sort of incident which made people feel uncomfortable." He seemed a little more at ease.

Neither Rosemary nor I could think of anything else, so we thanked him and he left.

"What do you make of that?" Rosemary asked me, getting in first this time.

"My guess is that he already knew about Mlle Lefebvre's disappearance and had a pretty good idea what the 'irregularities' I referred to are. For someone so small, silent and insignificant, Mlle Lefebvre seems to have enabled people to find out a fair amount about herself one way or another. And, assuming someone hasn't briefed Creac'h on what to say, he seemed remarkably well-informed about her."

"And though what he said tallied with what Korthuizen told us, we've no reason to assume that it's accurate - merely what people want us to believe. Indeed, they even used some of the same phrases to describe her, almost as if they were working from a script."

"But we've no other way of finding out anything about her."

"But I wouldn't mind betting it was Creac'h who Korthuizen punched. He looked decidedly uncomfortable when we got on to that subject," remarked Rosemary.

"Interesting that Korthuizen was so modest not to mention his part in stopping this bullying….assuming it was bullying rather than a childish bit of joking."

"It does make me wonder why we were favoured with these two!"

"It also makes me keener to get some independent information about her."

"And how do you plan to do that?"

"I thought we might pay a visit to her flat on Friday morning."

"You think anyone will let us in? The Brussels police will probably be watching the place – and they'll then want to know why we've turned up."

"Why couldn't we just turn up as colleagues, perhaps looking for some documents she'd taken home with her which were needed at work? I doubt whether even the Brussels police have so many officers that they can afford to post someone full-time in her flat…or even watching it, for that matter. All we need to do – or so it seems to me – is to persuade the concierge that we need to have a quick look round her flat for the missing documents. I'd even be prepared to let her accompany us."

"The concierge is bound to be a woman, of course?"

"Have you ever seen anywhere where it wasn't?"

"I suppose it's worth a shot. But I'll bet you her apartment will be neat, tidy and sparkling clean – without even a speck of dust out of place. From what we've been told she strikes me as a very 'just so' person."

"She reminds me of my sister Ellen. Do you recall the one and only time we took Emily and Sarah over to see them in Sutton? When the triangular sandwiches appeared on their nice doyleys on her second-best china plates and we all took bites out of them, whereas she, Barry and her two cut each one up into smaller triangles? Of course, she never said a word, but her silent disapproval was as loud as the crowd at Charlton on the rare occasions we score a goal."

"I did feel as though we were a bunch of uncouth savages. I suppose extreme conformity was her reaction to your father's communism."

"I guess so…..I never really knew her. She was already at school when I was born and preferred to play with her friends rather than her snotty little brother. Despite giving her a middle name of Nadezhda, after Lenin's wife, my father didn't consider girls to be proper revolutionary material, so he spent his indoctrination efforts mainly on me. Though she was notionally at home when she was at teacher training college in Eltham, she spent as much time away from home as possible…and took the first job she could get in a school in Croydon so she could escape permanently. She met Barry and they settled down to a life of domestic tranquillity….and no little dullness, in my opinion….But I'm sure it was a conscious choice…..and, to avoid you needing to say it, my sister is a pretty dull person….."

"But the proud owner of a very neat and tidy, spick and span house."

"Indeed. And if that makes her content with her life, who am I to argue with that?"

"At least she's never invited us back….Just Christmas and birthday cards….including Emily and Sarah, to be fair to her."

"That sort of thing is important to her…But I don't think the Romans ever invited the Goths back after the first visit…."

5. MEETINGS –EXPECTED AND UNEXPECTED

The following day we were all up early, leaving Emily and Sarah at school and getting a tram to Brussels Midi station. The countryside between Brussels and Charleroi was scarcely inspired – and under a heavy grey sky that threatened rain, looked dull and depressing. And when we arrived in Charleroi, the view was no better. It was essentially an industrial city that had seen better days. I recall it'd been badly damaged during the First World War, so it was possible that the few older or distinguished looking buildings in the heart of the city were reconstructed. Though I wouldn't have said they looked out of place, they seemed to represent a small monument to the time when it was a market town, rather than an industrial behemoth.

Cie CCR were in the Hainault-Sambre part of the city, right by the River Sambre, presumably because coal to fire the furnaces and finished iron and steel products could be moved as quickly by river as overland, though as the bus taking us from the station made its way towards our destination, we could see several train lines and bridges, doubtless also used for moving coal, coke, iron and steel. Smoke and steam hung in the sky over the area. This was a place of heavy industry of the sort I'd almost never encountered. I recognised some of the port structures by the river, familiar from my childhood in Woolwich and some of my early postings in C&E, but the towering, complex metal structures and other buildings meant nothing to me. It was a huge, complicated mountain of structures, buildings, machinery accompanied by chimneys of varying heights from where black, grey and yellowish smoke and white steam emerged. As we passed, I thought I detected the orange glow of fire in one of the structures. But elsewhere, there were places which seemed dark and silent. I couldn't really fathom it out. Rosemary claimed to have visited a steelworks at Asfordby near Melton Mowbray on a school trip, as well as coal mines near the appropriately named Coalville. But, as she remarked to me, nothing she had seen was remotely on a scale as huge as this.

All I knew was that Cie CCR were in the steel-making business, but that they were being subsidised by the Commission to shut down most of their steelmaking capacity in Charleroi. As we got out of the bus in a dismal road, not improved by the gently falling rain, the huge structures seemed like ancient giants, monuments to a different age – with the only concession to modern times the liberal sprinkling of rather uninspired, mostly political graffiti on many of the walls. Some of the structures could even have been built in the 19th century, though I reckoned probably most would've been destroyed during the First World War, so what I was looking at had probably been constructed in the aftermath, quite possibly funded by German reparations. Ironically, in view of the large contribution West Germany made to EEC finances, it was likely that German money was now funding these buildings being pulled down.

As far as we could tell from the documents about Cie CCR, they were moving out of basic steelmaking into what were termed "special steels" – which meant nothing to either of us, of course. Evidently it required much smaller premises and a vastly reduced workforce, as most of the processes would be automated.

When I'd arranged the visit, I'd been told to head for the main gate, where a gateman would direct me to the company offices. In fact by the time we reached the front entrance, with a brick shelter next to a metal barrier, it seemed pretty plain where the office block was. It was on two floors, built of brick in a style that could've been any time from the 1880s to the 1930s – nondescript, with small windows and a pompous front entrance. It seemed to be the only part of the whole works that had any pretension about it.

We gave our names to the gateman, who already had them on a list. He directed us to the front entrance, without the need for passes or an escort. A couple of men in collars and ties were heading in the opposite direction and about a dozen men in overalls and hard hats were hanging around in front of what looked like a giant barn with a series of huge Heath-Robinson contraptions inside them. Inside the entrance, there was a large lobby, with a receptionist in a familiar cubicle, along with several chairs and tables and pictures of various parts of the works along the walls. At the far end of the room was evidently a war memorial, presumably to employees of the factory who'd been killed in two world wars. The upper memorial was about three times the size of the lower, with, I would've reckoned, more than a hundred names on it. Beneath the two plaques was a large, fresh wreath.

The receptionist, an ordinary looking young woman in glasses, smartly dressed, announced our arrival by way of a tannoy, for M.de Mettet. A couple of minutes later, a dapper young man appeared. He was in his early thirties, with smooth black hair and a sharp face, which seemed to bear the marks of a man who concentrated hard. He wore a dark suit with white shirt and nondescript tie.

"Jan de Mettet," he began, shaking hands. "M. et Mme Storey?"

"Pleased to meet you," I replied. "Do you wish us to speak in French or English?"

"English will be satisfactory. Often in my country a neutral language has advantages. As you may guess from my name, I am Flemish. Many of my colleagues, like Marie-Elizabeth Clouet, who you will meet in a moment, are Walloons. My other colleague you will meet, Philippe Verstruegen, is from Brussels and claims to be both or neither. Not that there is generally much ill-feeling. But as you may imagine, the company's decision to cut back much capacity here and concentrate on smaller scale, higher value-added work has generated a fair amount of ill-feeling, not least on the part of the workforce, of whom virtually all are locals, Walloons. Whereas I, the man the company put in charge of making this change, am a Fleming." His English was virtually free of accent and idiomatic.

"I guess if a manager came from London to carry out such changes at a steel works in Yorkshire or Scotland, he'd be similarly regarded," I said.

"Let us go up to my office. I understand you are carrying out some auditing work for the EEC Commission?"

"That is so."

We went up a functional staircase and into what seemed more like a small conference room, rather than an office. But waiting for us was coffee and almost immediately Marie-Elizabeth Clouet and Philippe Verstruegen. Mme Clouet was short, stocky, with short, mousey hair and glasses, but an intelligent face that struck me as one that enjoyed a fair amount of humour. I guessed she was in her early forties. Verstruegen was perhaps six or seven years younger, balding, pink-faced and rather bland looking. Mme Clouet was the works manager and Verstruegen the company secretary. I wondered whether there were any women works managers in the UK in charge of anything as big as this?

"You have applied for EEC funding to restructure your manufacturing here?" began Rosemary.

"Yes. We have applied in all for grants of just under six hundred million Belgian Francs from the EEC with a further three hundred million coming from the Government of Belgium," confirmed Verstruegen, in a high voice, in only lightly-accented English. (I calculated that quickly to £10 million and £5 million respectively).

"You applications were approved in 1972?"

"That is correct."

"On your application and subsequent drawing down of the grants, you have used the local branch of Paribas?"

"Yes. They've been our bankers for as long as anyone knows. Certainly as long as any of us have been here."

"Is there some problem with our grants or our banking arrangements?" asked Mme Clouet, in a heavily French-accented English.

"Last financial year a payment was ostensibly made to Cie CCR in the sum of 24 million Belgian Francs, paid through the Namse Krediet Bank in its local branch here in Charleroi. You can see on this payment authorisation document that payment and the signatory at the bank - Dirk Verstappen....Please understand, we're not accusing Cie CCR of anything, but we believe someone has used information about your successful application for EEC subsidies to commit a fraud."

"I can assure you that we have no dealings with the Namse Krediet Bank," stated Verstruegen firmly, with a faint note of irritation.

"I bank there in my private capacity," added de Mettet. "Indeed, I know Dirk Verstappen quite well. We play squash together on occasions and share a beer or two. But I know for a fact that the Charleroi branch couldn't handle our accounts, so exactly how someone got Dirk Verstappen to agree to set up an account for Cie CCR and then sign up to it just doesn't make sense. If anyone came into his bank trying to do anything like that, he'd ring me up immediately and ask what the hell was going on."

"It's possible someone has set up your account with another manager there, but has managed to get hold of a document with his signature on it....We have arranged to meet him after our meeting, so he should be able to explain to us how something like that might happen," I explained.

"We are willing to show you our accounts," said Verstruegen. "They will contain details of all sums accruing of a value of a million Belgian Francs or more. But judging by the date on this document, I'd say it was not a time when we sought any money from the EEC....If you will give me a minute of two, I will get the relevant ledgers."

"I'm sure that isn't necessary," I said. "From the checks which we've been undertaking it seems evident that payments of this nature have been taken from several companies like yours, so we've had no reason to suspect that any of these companies have been involved."

"I would prefer to do so, nevertheless."

"That's your privilege."

We sat in silence, sipping coffee so powerful it could make your hair stand on end.

"If it was several companies, evidently someone has worked out the system you use in the Commission," observed Mme Clouet. "You will have to consider new processes, just as we have been doing." There was a faint smile hovering around her eyes.

"Indeed," I replied. "We shall certainly be making a number of recommendations. Whether they are acted on will be a matter for others."

At that point Verstruegen returned and was able to show Rosemary – to his and her satisfaction – that no payment resembling the fraudulent payment had gone through their accounts in any shape or form.

That was all we needed to know, so we thanked them for their time….only to discover that M. de Mettet had arranged for us to be transported to the Namse Krediet Bank in one of the company cars. We thanked him profusely – not least because it was now raining cats and dogs. We drove through the teeming rain, splashing through puddles on the rather battered roads in the industrial area, before getting into a residential area, which was only marginally less depressing. We arrived at the centre of the town, stopping right in front of the Namse Krediet Bank on a double yellow line, which appeared not to bother the monosyllabic driver one bit. In any case, he was speedily away and Rosemary and I made our way into the bank.

I'd already arranged to meet Dirk Verstappen, though we were about forty minutes early – partly because our meeting with Cie CCR had been so quick, partly because we'd expected to travel from the steelworks to the centre of the city by public transport. At any rate, having told one of the clerks who we were and about our meeting, we were about to get out our umbrellas and try to find somewhere we could dilute the taste of the Cie CCR coffee, when Dirk Verstappen emerged from a back office.

He was in his mid-to-late thirties, with straight blond hair cut short, a matching moustache and a friendlier manner than I connected with bank managers. He was fairly tall, plump and very conservatively dressed – in a dark suit and white shirt and faded orange tie. In that he suited his surroundings – a very old-fashioned looking bank, furnished almost entirely in a dark, reddish-brown wood, apart from the metal grilles behind which the clerks sat. He lifted a counter and led us through into a dark corridor and his office – furnished in the same dark wood and looking as though it might well not have altered significantly since the 19th century.

"From what you told my secretary on the telephone, this is a matter concerning the audit of certain payments made by the EEC Commission?" he began, speaking English with only a slight accent. "You are auditing certain suspect payments, at least one of which was paid into this branch into an account nominally for Cie CCR which was set up some time ago, but actually pertaining to someone else, presumably unknown?" As Rosemary sat down, he attempted to disguise a careful look at her legs.

Evidently, while we were driving into the city centre, his friend de Mettet had been on the phone to him. I'd certainly told his secretary less than half of that."

"I believe I told your secretary rather less than that," I replied, "but your recent phone call avoids the need for detailed introductions."

Verstappen gave a slightly shame-faced smirk.

"In a city full of Walloons, we Flemings tend to keep in touch," he observed. "But I understand it is a Cie CCR account which we are supposed to have which interests you?"

"That's so. This is the account, as you can see in this document. In both that one – the confirmation of banking details form - and this other one – the payment details form – you'll see that Cie CCR are named as the company, with these particular account references, and you are both named and appear to have signed the forms," explained Rosemary.

"I have been looking through our records and I can see that we do indeed have an account with Cie CCR. It appears to have been set up in January 1973. The signature on these forms – and indeed in our records – purport to show that I signed off the establishment of the account and these forms. But I have no recollection of any of them. I could see no reason why I would not remember the setting-up of the account. Jan de Mettet is a friend. We play squash and drink a few beers together at least twice a month. I know the business of Cie CCR. It is not such that we could handle here. Their business is too large and too complicated. They undertake various transactions – not least various arrangements relating to foreign currencies – which we are neither competent to handle, nor would we be allowed to handle by our head office. We are essentially a bank who lends to small companies and householders and takes their deposits and manages their money with as little risk as possible. In times of inflation as we have been passing through, this is difficult enough for us, without trying to understand the complexities of trading in foreign currencies, often six months or even a year in advance. But sometimes a transaction for Cie CCR's steel may involve payment in a foreign currency in a year's time and they may, quite rightly, wish to cover themselves to some extent against currency fluctuations which could easily wipe out any profit they might make."

"Has the account been used on any other occasions?"

"No. The only items in the account are the transfer of 24 million Belgian Francs from an EEC Commission account at the Banque de Bruxelles on 15 October 1974 and a payment out to the Banque Luxembourgeois, two days later. The inward payment was sent from Brussels by courier post in a security pouch, so I'm informed. The outward payment was a personal request made in this bank, a cheque payable on an account whose details I shall give you in the Banque Luxembourgeois. If you want my guess, I should say it didn't remain there any longer than it stayed here."

"As the account was set up here and these forms were completed – presumably here – can you account for how your name and signature are on both the account documents and these Commission forms?"

"No. I can't. But let's leave aside the establishment of the account for the moment and just look at these payment forms for now. 24 million Belgian Francs is a large sum – both to be paid in and paid out. That was in October 1974. Apart from there being records in our ledgers, there must also be someone who remembers these transactions. Let me see what I can find out."

Thereupon he leapt to his feet and bolted out of the office. Within a couple of minutes, a secretary arrived with the inevitable tiny cups of overpoweringly strong coffee. Rosemary and I sat in silence, conscious that anything we said might be overheard.

He returned after a quarter of an hour or so.

"These sums definitely went through our accounts….You can see from our ledger…..here ….and here….So your records are certainly accurate. I believe I've also found out how this part of this transaction was managed. As I mentioned before, we received by courier a banker's draft for 24 million Belgian Francs on 15 October 1974 and Mlle Bourdon carried out the necessary paperwork and accounting. On 17 October a man calling himself Philippe Verstruegen from Cie CCR came to the bank and met Eric Kuilwaerts, one of my junior clerks, to arrange the transfer of 24 million Belgian Francs to an account in the name of Industries Utiles et Cie at the Banque Luxembourgeois. The necessary authorisation had been signed by Jan de Mettet, who according to our records had set up the original account. The signatures tallied. So there was no reason why young Kuilwaerts shouldn't have approved the transfer. As for what the so-called

Philippe Verstruegen looked like, I'll ask Kuilwaerts to tell you himself."

He strode to the door and led in a young man who'd evidently been waiting outside in the corridor. He was tall, extremely thin, with straw-coloured unruly straight hair, a narrow face and an extremely callow look about him: indeed, the regulation dark suit, white shirt and nondescript tie emphasised his youthfulness. He looked about seventeen. He spoke in good English, however.

"The man who called himself Philippe Verstruegen was not older than forty. He was slight and not tall, with dark hair and thick glasses. He also had a thick beard. What I saw of his skin was pallid. He spoke French well, but with a slight accent. He was dressed in a dark suit, with a light blue shirt and blue tie. He carried a brown leather briefcase which seemed quite new."

"Definitely not the Philippe Verstruegen we met an hour or so ago at Cie CCR," I commented. "Did the man you met explain why he was making this transfer, rather than Jan de Mettet?"

"He explained that he was the Company Secretary, which I could check if I wished. Indeed, as it was such a large sum of money, I checked the companies register of the region and it showed Philippe Verstruegen to be the Company Secretary of Cie CCR. He said that Jan de Mettet was the Managing Director and it was he who had set the account up, but that it was Verstruegen's job to handle the actual management of the account. It seemed perfectly understandable to me. If M. Verstappen had been in the office, I would probably have consulted him, but he was at Head Office that morning, so I authorised the payment on my own authority."

"As you can see, there was really no reason why he should not have done so," added Verstappen.

"Did you get any feeling for the nationality of the man who claimed to be Philippe Verstruegen?" I asked Kuilwaerts.

"There was nothing particularly unusual about him, other than he was not very tall. So I would have taken him for a Belgian or Luxembourgeois. But perhaps there was something about his eyes that suggested he might have been one of those people from the Dutch East Indies…but his skin was far from brown and his spectacles had extremely thick lenses….I remember saying to myself I doubted whether he could see his hand in front of his face if he took them off."

"Anything else you can think of?" asked Rosemary.

"I don't think so."

Verstappen flicked out his right hand in a gesture of dismissal and Kuilwaerts departed.

"I suspect that the man calling himself Philippe Verstruegen picked Kuilwaerts out as the greenest apple in the bag," he observed.

"Whoever it was plainly managed to learn quite a lot about the bank, presumably to make sure that they called in at a time when you were away," remarked Rosemary. "But we're still at a loss to understand how the account could've been set up in the first place. Do you have any thoughts about that?"

"I'm not really certain I can account for it," replied Verstappen. "That's certainly my signature on those documents and on our record of when the account was set up. I am as sure as anyone can be that I didn't set up that account. I know the business of Cie CCR far too well not to have queried it with Jan de Mettet. I have asked my secretary to see if she can find my diary covering that period, so I can check where I was on that day. I guess it is possible someone in the bank here colluded with the people who appear to have set up this account to move money in and out of our bank with the aim of disguising its true destination."

"Have any employees left the bank since that time? Or would it have to be one of your current employees?"

"Henri-Paul Lemaitre retired in April 1974. You've met his replacement, Kuilwaerts, who had recently completed his training in our head office. Other than that, no-one has left. But I cannot see why any of our staff would've done this."

"If they were offered a sufficient financial inducement, perhaps?"

"In which case, they have either spent it discreetly or have placed the money somewhere it could not be discovered. You understand that whether or not I was here on the day the account was set up, there will be a full internal enquiry by the bank, who will examine all our financial records. It is more than likely that anyone who cannot prove his or her innocence may lose their positions with the bank….and that includes me."

"Could anyone else know how to set up such an account and get hold of the necessary forms and documents – including some document with your signature on it – other than an employee of the bank?"

"We are audited by head office auditors every year. They have access to virtually every document in the bank. But they invariably audit our accounts in June, so the presence of one in the bank in January would undoubtedly be remarked on."

"But presumably someone - whether an auditor or a member of staff, whether retired or not – could pass information on to someone else, along with the appropriate forms and a document with your signature on it?"

"I guess so….But that means almost certainly that who did it is likely to be untraceable…and that none of us will be able to prove that we weren't responsible…So the most likely outcome is the person responsible may well get away with it, while we shall pay for it with our jobs."

"Perhaps that may provide an incentive for you to discover more than we'd be able to do. It's rare that documents go missing without some sort of trace or someone wasn't seen photocopying something? Perhaps a thorough investigation of people's finances may uncover sufficient money to require an explanation?"

"I imagine that may be possible."

At that moment, a middle-aged woman, presumably Verstappen's secretary knocked on the door and entered the room, carrying an A4 size leather-bound book, evidently the diary covering

January 1973. She departed immediately, before I could get any impression of her.

"Now the date the account was set up was 26 January 1973. It seems I was not in the bank that day. I had forgotten that I went for a week's skiing in Austria – a place called Sölden – with several friends…one of whom, if I recall correctly, was Jan de Mettet….That may make my position here a little more secure….But, of course, it makes no clearer who set up the account here…But I doubt there is more I can do to help you today…"

We thanked him and left. It was plain we weren't going to get any more out of him. We walked to the station under our umbrellas in silence, each thinking about what we'd seen and heard that morning. We had to wait about half an hour for a train to Brussels, so we had a soup and a bread roll at a café close to the station, along with a large tumbler of plain water, to try to dilute the effects of the coffee we'd suffered during the morning.

The train had separate compartments and ours was empty apart from us until we reached Nivelles. The weather outside was gloomy, entirely apt for our conversation.

"That skiing holiday and the meeting in head office were certainly convenient for Verstappen," I commented. "I assume they're correct, as they can easily be checked."

"Yes – such good alibis on both occasions does strike me as a bit suspicious. And it's interesting that the person who drew the money out picked on Kuilwaerts, who looked about as green as they come."

"And he could easily have got all the necessary information and documents to someone else. You could even leave the documents setting up the account, including his signature, in someone's tray for them to deal with, assuming all the while that he's agreed to set the new account up….And Cie CCR might've been chosen because he was de Mettet's friend…or he became de Mettet's friend once Cie CCR had been chosen."

"On the other hand, we've no evidence of any of that," Rosemary reminded me. "And we're not seriously thinking that Verstappen masterminded the whole fraud are we?"

78

"No. I'm just assuming he got a fair-sized chunk of the £8 million for his part in facilitating the fraud…..But I reckon we'll find similar difficulties in pinning down how bogus accounts got set up and then emptied of the money transferred from DGVI. This has been meticulously planned."

"At least if DGVI adopt a system of checking claims and bank accounts and that sort of thing as things happen during the year, it shouldn't be possible to do it again….and recommending that may be the best we can do."

"And when we go to one of the other banks involved, we may find completely different circumstances, of course."

Once other passengers joined us at Nivelles, we had to talk about other matters. As we got out of the train at Brussels Midi station, we were just congratulating ourselves that Rosemary wouldn't be much later than usual in picking up Emily and Sarah when we noticed a couple of men coming towards us, evidently searching for someone. One looked like a station official, the other was a young man dressed in a suit.

"Are you Mr and Mrs Storey?" asked the young man as they got within a few yards of us.

"Yes," I replied. "Who are you?"

"I'm Freddie Parsons. I'm in Robin Southern's cabinet. He wishes to have an urgent meeting with you, please."

"Can you tell us what about?"

"He said he assumed you'd be able to guess…But it really is urgent…I've got a car waiting just outside the station."

He led us out of the station on the eastern side where a black Citroen was waiting, parked illegally in the Avenue Fonsny. The driver set off virtually the moment we'd sat down in the back.

"How did you know where to find us?" asked Rosemary.

"Your office said you'd gone to meet certain people in Charleroi, so we phoned and discovered what time you'd left your last appointment. As you were travelling by train, it had to be this one or the next one….and as we'd learnt you'd travelled from the Midi station, it seemed likely you'd come back there."

"How did you know we'd travelled from the Midi station? Or who we'd met?"

"I've no idea. That's what I heard my boss discussing with someone on the phone."

"I guess we can ask him."

We headed through Brussels at speeds well above the limit. I began to wonder that something extremely serious had happened. Or that we'd inadvertently stepped on some highly influential corns in Charleroi and were about to be given a dressing down. I couldn't quite see how or why – but I'd be the first to admit that we'd largely only seen in this case what we'd be allowed to see.

At any rate, we arrived at speed at the Commission building and disappeared into the underground car park as if we were racing in the Monaco grand prix. Parsons led us to a lift, which took us to the third floor. From there we were whisked along a corridor to a room at the far end. We waited briefly in an outer office, where a tough-looking lady secretary was bashing away on a typewriter, and a smooth young Frenchman stared idly out of the window the whole time. Parsons appeared from Southern's room and ushered us is.

Robin Southern was in his early fifties. He was about six feet tall, balding, with glasses and a rather prim face. He looked like my idea of a bishop, of the ascetic sort. He motioned to us to sit down on a plush brown leather sofa.

"So – what's going on?" he demanded.

So that was it! The Director-General of DGVI had, I guessed, learnt about our investigation and seemingly wasn't trusted by Vermeulen to be told what we were up to. And since he appeared not to be trusted by Vermeulen, who was the man who'd asked us to carry out this work, I felt it wasn't our place to reveal it.

"I'm sorry," I replied. "I'm not sure exactly what you're referring to?"

"The two of you – sniffing round my DG. Chatting to former employees here. Examining DGVI files. And today – off in Charleroi nosing around payments made by my DG. Is that clear enough?"

"We've been asked to carry out some work by M. Jérôme Vermeulen, head of the Commission Secretariat. I suggest you get in touch with him. We were asked to do this work on the basis that we were to treat it as confidential."

"That's just not good enough! I demand to know what you two are up to! Don't you believe that a Director-General isn't to be trusted with confidential information? I've got an up-to-date PV in the Civil Service and the equivalent here. There can't be anything you're doing that I'm not cleared to know about! So tell me what you're up to!"

"I'm sorry. It's not a matter purely of clearance. As far as I understand it, you can be cleared to a certain level, but that doesn't mean you're cleared to see every confidential document….As I said, we were asked to do this by M. Vermeulen. I really do think you should take it up with him."

"You don't trust me? Here we are, fellow Brits in the heart of the Belgian Empire, and you'd rather side with that poisonous Belgian dwarf, Vermeulen, rather than me?"

"I'm not siding with anyone. It may seem very bureaucratic, but if I'm working for one individual, I believe I should follow what they ask me to do….I would've thought a phone call to M. Vermeulen should clear this up. I'm happy to phone him, if you wish."

"And what if he tells you not to divulge anything to me?"

"I would do as he requested."

"I'm led to believe that you haven't always been so scrupulous. One of my colleagues when I was in the Cabinet Office was Simon Osbaldistone, who told me you two were both happy to bend the rules when it suited you."

"As was he."

"Then it's evidently a habit of British Civil Servants that we should maintain over here."

"I regret there are certain rules I try my hardest not to bend. The first is not to break my word to whoever is employing me. The second is not to breach security….."

"Osbaldistone also said you were difficult, without respect for your superiors."

"He's entitled to his view. But I don't see why I shouldn't just phone M. Vermeulen. It seems to me we're getting into a difficult position which a phone call could resolve."

I was also thinking that if it hadn't been for Rosemary and me, Osbaldistone might well still be lingering in a prison cell somewhere.

"If anyone speaks to Vermeulen, it'll be me."

I decided to say nothing. There was plainly some reason why he didn't want me to phone Vermeulen and I suspected he didn't wish to either.

He was silent, looking at some papers and then glancing up to give me an occasional glare of hostility. After about ten minutes of this, he appeared to make up his mind.

"You may go!" he almost shouted.

We agreed that Rosemary would go off at once to pick up Emily and Sarah, while I tried to have a few words with Vermeulen. Unfortunately, he was not available that afternoon, so his assistant informed me. So I wrote down a reasonably full account of the meeting with Robin Southern, mentioning also that it seemed to me that someone in Cie CCR or the Namse Krediet Bank had been in touch with him or one of his staff, sufficiently soon after our meeting for officials from DGVI to be waiting for us as Brussels Midi – and, I would've been prepared to bet – Brussels Central too. Moreover, our meetings with Creac'h and Korthuizen had evidently been noticed too.

Unfortunately, neither Henriksen nor Fitzpatrick were around that afternoon either. So I didn't get the chance to get any helpful advice and went home wondering what the hell was going on.

6. GETTING INFORMATION IN ORTHODOX AND UNORTHODOX WAYS

Of course, the following morning was when Rosemary and I had planned to go to the apartment belonging to Monique Lefebvre, née Nguyen.

"Do you think it's wise to go over there when someone might be following us?" queried Rosemary.

"I don't believe they were following us. I reckon Verstappen or someone from Cie CCR phoned a contact in DGVI and they worked out what trains we should be on and had someone waiting at each of the two main stations."

"But Vermeulen or Knud or Gerry might want to have a word?"

"This won't take all day. Besides – they weren't around yesterday afternoon. Why do we have to change our plans just for them! It's all internal politics anyway…otherwise Southern would've just rung Vermeulen up."

"As I guess you'll be the one having to do any explaining later on – let's get going."

"It took a couple of trams from where we'd left Emily and Sarah to get to Uccle. We'd managed to find out that Mlle Lefebvre's flat was on the corner of the rue de la Fourragère and rue de Nieuwenhove. That meant little to us as our street plans didn't extend as far as Uccle. So we got off in the centre and asked. Unsurprisingly, Mlle Lefebvre didn't reside in one of the leafy tree-lined avenues, where many well-heeled eurocrats and diplomats lived, as we headed away along streets of more humdrum character. We discovered the building where her flat was – in a building with a rounded front on what I reckoned was quite a busy street corner, not far from some main roads. For someone who appeared to be as quiet as Mlle Lefebvre, this seemed a bit odd – but I supposed she got what she could afford….in a relatively nice and safe area.

"It doesn't look like the sort of place where you could just pop inside and remove someone without anyone noticing," I observed.

"I wouldn't bet on that. If you got hold of a removal van or perhaps an electrical repairs van, who'd notice anything?"

"I suppose you're right. Perhaps the concierge?"

We opened the front door. Immediately inside was a glorified cupboard full of brooms, mops, various plastic bottles and, inevitably, the concierge. Naturally, she was middle-aged and with a fiercely defensive manner – but unusually she was Asiatic – not Chinese, Japanese or Vietnamese I would've said – more like Indonesian or Malayan.

"What do you want?" she demanded in French, with a distinctly odd accent.

"We are colleagues of Mlle Lefebvre in the EEC Commission," Rosemary explained. "We have been told she has disappeared. But we believe she had some papers with her that we need in the office. We would be extremely grateful if we could have a quick look for them in her apartment, please."

"What sort of papers?"

"You will understand that our work is confidential. All I can tell you is that they are concerned with EEC grants to companies who operate in the coal and steel industries."

"Who are you, please?"

"Rosemary and Nicholas Storey. You can see our Commission identification if you wish."

"I do so wish."

Rosemary and I showed them our Commission passes. She removed a pair of glasses from an ancient leather handbag and examined them minutely. I reckoned this was largely for effect.

"It must be unusual a husband and wife working together in the Commission?"

"We're on secondment from the UK as national experts," I replied. "They either got both of us or neither."

The concierge gave the faintest of smiles.

"Very well. I'll take you to Mlle Lefebvre's apartment. But I'll need to accompany you, you understand."

"Of course."

We followed her up two flights of stairs to a door which had been painted yellow over dark brown some years previously, presumably as a contrast from the fading dark green walls. Between them, it felt as though we were in a narrow tunnel. She opened the door into a small room – evidently the living room. It had a tiny dining table under which two chairs fitted neatly, a rattan sofa and chair, with plain unbleached linen cushions on them, a white wood bureau, the top, glass-fronted, part of which contained a few books and several pieces of oriental china and other artefacts, the lower part of which had drawers and a pull-out board which apparently could serve as a desk. In front of it was a stool, also made of white wood. The only picture on the wall was an oriental landscape, but where was anyone's guess. The furniture was completed by a little red Rigonda 4" screen TV on a white wood coffee table and a Rigonda radio, which might well seem stylish in the Soviet Union, but looked old-fashioned in sophisticated Brussels. The apartment of someone who either had little money or was extremely careful with it.

"I expect you will wish to look in the bureau," said the concierge.

We peered in the drawers. Inside them were three tin boxes which had probably contained biscuits or the like at some stage, containing Mlle Lefebvre's old diaries, an address book and her passport. It would've been interesting to look at the most recent diaries and the address book, but impossible under the concierge's eagle eye. The most recent diary wasn't there anyway. Otherwise, the drawers were filled with unused stationery – cheap stuff, the sort you'd buy in "Woollies" back home…..and two portable typewriters.

That struck me as weird – until we pulled out the board that served as the desk top. Immediately above it, two eight inch high doors pulled sideways, revealing a drawer and shelf on each side. In the drawers on the left were documents typed in what I took to be Vietnamese script. In those on the right, ones in Roman script – all written in French. Mostly they were the sort of documents you'd expect – bills going back six months or so, tax documents, the rental agreement and payment book, etc. There were letters from a hospital and a lawyer or possibly accountant in Paris. I couldn't read the Vietnamese stuff, of course, but I noticed that there were letters with stamps from Vietnam, Indonesia and Malaya.

"There's definitely nothing from the office among these papers," I announced. "Do you mind if we just check elsewhere, just in case Mlle Lefebvre put them somewhere else."

"Do you think that's necessary?" demanded the concierge.

"If we tell our colleagues we've looked everywhere, there's no chance that they'll just ask us or someone else to come back."

"Very well….Go on…"

The bathroom was tiny, with a shower so constricted it would have been a squeeze for me. The cabinet contained exactly what we'd come to expect. It was half full and contained toothpaste, face cream, a tube of antiseptic cream, stomach and headache pills. There were no interesting medicines, nor exotic make-up or perfumes. Everything was in its proper place – including a toothbrush, cake of cheap soap and a small face flannel. The compact airing cupboard which contained the hot water tank had a couple of shelves, on which were half a dozen carefully folded white towels. The bedroom was tidy – evidently her bed had been made before Mlle Lefebvre disappeared. Her clothes hung in a white wood wardrobe, with separate rattan boxes in the bottom containing shoes and underwear. The bedside cabinet contained what looked like a copy of the bible written in Vietnamese, a hot water bottle and two long nightdresses. A plain navy silk dressing down, adorned only by an embroidered yellow marigold, hung on a peg behind the door.

Between the bathroom and the bedroom was a built-in cupboard which contained, among other things the electricity meter. The main things there were several blankets on a shelf, a couple of battered, cheap suitcases, with various airline labels on them, a bicycle and, hanging on the back wall, a handgun in a leather holster along with a bag containing approximately fifty rounds of 25mm ammunition. The gun looked like a cheap, mass-produced thing and a quick examination – while the concierge couldn't see past me – revealed it to be Chinese. I made no comment.

"Well…It'd seem it wasn't Mlle Lefebvre who had the papers that we can't find," I remarked. "I'm sorry to have taken up your time, Mme…."

"..Mme Vliets….You have to carry out your work…I understand."

She ushered us out with slightly less suspicion that when she'd first greeted us. We set off for the nearest café – both to get some coffee, reflect and on the off chance that Mlle Lefebvre ever called in there. The nearest - "La vieille porte verte" - was about fifty yards away on the corner of the Avenue Brugman – more of a snack bar, doing "croques monsieur" at lunchtime and croissants and coffee in the mornings. There was a bar on the other side of the road, but I couldn't see Mlle Lefebvre dropping in there….not unless her private life was utterly at odds with what she showed at work and in the décor of her flat…..apart from that gun.

We sat down and ordered coffees and croissants, conscious that the coffee would be strong enough to blow the top of your head off – and acrid as well.

"It would've been good if we'd been able to have a proper snoop around," Rosemary said. "But there was no point arousing Mme Vliets's suspicions. She'd just've got in touch with DGVI and then any problems we've got with Southern would've multiplied many times over."

"I wonder whether the Belgian police have actually visited the flat? I wanted to ask Mme Vliets, but I couldn't find a way of doing it without making her suspicious. But if they'd been, I wonder why they didn't take that gun away with them? It seems odd just leaving a weapon like that lying around in an unoccupied flat."

"This is Belgium. Perhaps that sort of thing is less unusual than it'd be at home."

"In view of her disappearance, you'd think they'd want to know more about it. Not least because it looks like the type of weapon used by the Chinese military. I imagine guns like that got into the hands of the Viet Cong…and I guess you could get them on the streets of Hanoi.…But though that might explain how Mlle Lefebvre might've got hold of a gun like that, it doesn't explain why she needed to keep it, along with all that ammunition, in her flat."

"It also looked very odd indeed. Everything else was neat and tidy, small and perfectly-formed. Then you get this gun lurking in the back of a cupboard. It didn't fit with anything else in that flat, or anything anyone has told us about her."

"Well, assuming she wasn't some sort of hitwoman, I guess she either had it for her own protection or she was keeping it there for someone."

"I can't imagine we're ever likely to find out," observed Rosemary, sensibly.

"I don't know about that! Why couldn't she be a hitwoman - for the Viet Cong, for instance? She remains in deep cover working in the Commission, looking like a mouse as far as everyone else is concerned, when actually she's a crackshot with nerves of ice. And those holidays supposedly to Australia to meet relatives have actually been operations to bump people off – enemies of the Viet Cong all around the world.…"

"Why on earth would she choose the Commission.........!
OK. You got me there! Try to take this seriously!"

"OK. Why is Mlle Lefebvre so obsessively neat and tidy? Is it
her nature? Or because she's obsessive about security? I'll bet if
she walked in now, she'd be able to tell that someone had been
looking at her things – even without the concierge telling her.
Does it mean she can come and go, staying in different places
perhaps, with only Mme Vliets knowing whether she's been there
or not? Or is she just obsessive about neatness, tidiness,
cleanliness? And if so, why the gun?"

"Yes. I suppose you really can't tell when a flat is as carefully
kept as that whether she'd left in a hurry or not."

"Or even whether she was still living there.....I suspect Mme
Vliets has more in common with Mlle Lefebvre than with the
local police – and certainly than with us."

"That's a lot of speculation, of course. One thing we can say is
that if there was any violence involved in her disappearance, it's
been meticulously cleared up........Oh and by the way, I'm not
standing around doing surveillance on that flat just in case she
might be living there!"

"And as we've no idea whether her disappearance is connected
to our work, it'd be a rather senseless long shot anyway."

A waiter arrived with our coffee and croissants.

"We were hoping to meet a friend here," I said. "A very small,
quiet lady who's half Vietnamese, who lives just around the
corner."

"One such comes in here most days for a coffee and a
croissant on her way to work. Gets the tram further down the
road. Not been in for a couple of weeks. But she seems to have a
fair number of holidays...or perhaps she just doesn't fancy
coming in."

"Oh dear! We're only here for a couple of days. Pity we seem
to have missed her."

"You could try the evening before eight o'clock. The chef is
Indonesian. Does a rijstafel and a crispy duck which brings in

quite a few locals. Your little woman comes in sometimes – usually with a Chinese man…..or from somewhere like that. All I know is, they gabble on in whatever language it is. The only time there seems to be a spark of life in her….Not that she smiles, you understand…But at least she shows she might be human like the rest of us…."

"If we have time, perhaps we'll look in. But if she's away, it might not be worthwhile coming out as far as Uccle again…."

We ate our croissants, drank a rather less powerful coffee than we'd expected, thanked the waiter and left. Two trams and we were back close to the SEFF offices – and it was still before midday.

We arrived to a minor kerfuffle. Robin Southern had evidently phoned Gerry Fitzpatrick to complain about my behaviour the previous evening and SEFF staff being used to spy on his DG. Whether or not he'd also phoned Vermeulen, the latter had evidently now got my message and wished to see us, as of several hours earlier. For obvious reasons, we hadn't wanted to advertise where we were going, so we'd been suitably vague about where we were that morning. So no-one in SEFF knew where we were, of course. Which had complicated matters and raised the temperature, which was already fairly warm.

Being on the spot, Gerry nabbed me first.

"What in heaven's name did you say to Robin Southern yesterday, Nick? I've had him bending my ear for nearly half an hour about your insubordination, rudeness and underhand behaviour."

"I can see why he might consider me insubordinate. But I certainly wasn't rude to him. And the only reason I can think of for my underhand behaviour is that I'm carrying out this work for Vermeulen and wasn't prepared to tell Southern what it was – certainly not off the cuff. I even offered to ring Vermeulen and get his permission to tell Southern what we're doing. But he plainly wanted me to fill him in without clearing it with

Vermeulen. But as we're working for Vermeulen and not him, I refused. Plainly, he didn't like it."

"I see…You might've forewarned me…….Oh, but I was out….and presumably you were out working on this stuff for Vermeulen earlier?"

"I did try to speak to Knud or you yesterday after I'd been grilled by Southern….and I'm afraid I didn't want to delay this morning's visit. I'm sorry I left you holding the baby."

"Not to worry. Robin Southern is a pompous pillock and a man who doesn't trouble himself much about scruples. Not an inappropriate antagonist for Jérôme Vermeulen. I guess there's some sort of power struggle going on between them. No doubt why he didn't want you to phone him……But if this is a daggers' drawn affair, we need to be sure that the two of you aren't Vermeulen's forlorn hope…I take it you know what that is, as a former military man?"

"Only two years' of it….and the British Army didn't go in for that sort of thing in those days…..As I understand it, a forlorn hope leads the advance against the enemy, but then gets left behind to cover the retreat if the attack doesn't succeed."

"That's my understanding as well. I need to put my ear to the ground and make sure Rosemary and you aren't being used……But I'll get back to that poisonous pillock and put him straight. Did you mention your conversation with Southern to Vermeulen?"

"No. He was unavailable. But I left a fairly full message….I gather he's chasing us up."

"Be wary. If you can glean anything about why he and Southern are at each other's throats, it'll probably serve you well."

I left his office thanking my lucky stars again that he was my boss in these circumstances, rather than several who would've assumed Southern, as the senior official, was reporting our conversation accurately. I explained to Rosemary what he'd said and asked her whether she wished to join me when I went over to the Berlaymont to meet Vermeulen in the next few minutes.

"Perhaps if I keep crossing and uncrossing my legs, I'll distract the nasty little man and he'll tell us more than he means to," she remarked with a trademark smirk.

Naturally, Vermeulen was almost instantly available to see us.

"Perhaps you will explain what is going on with Southern?" he demanded, for once forgetting his customary peer at Rosemary's legs.

"You probably have as good an idea as I do," I replied. "We went to Charleroi yesterday to follow up some of the documents used in the fraud. It seems that someone we met contacted someone in DGVI, as we were met by a bloke from Southern's cabinet at the Midi station when we got back to Brussels. I'd also guess they had someone waiting for us at the central station too. We spoke to Southern who demanded to know what we were up to. I told him that we were working to you on this and it was a confidential matter, but I'd happily phone you and see whether you were prepared to authorise me to tell him. He seemed reluctant to agree to this and kept pressing me to tell him. I refused. As you weren't around yesterday afternoon, I left you the note, which I assume you've read."

"It is a pity word of what you're doing has got to the ears of DGVI, but I suppose it was inevitable. I take it there was no other way?"

"Not that we could see. The documents show that in order for the fraud to work, false bank accounts had to be set up for the companies who'd succeeded in their applications for DGVI funds. Since there appear to be legitimate signatures used when the false bank accounts are set up and when the money is taken out, we needed to see the companies to find out how this could happen. In the case of the company we met yesterday, the managing director was a personal friend of the bank manager where the false account was set up, so we needed to check with the bank, as it seemed a bit fishy to us," explained Rosemary.

"And one of these contacted Southern, you suspect?"

"Or someone else in DGVI who told Southern."

"Is this the first visit you have made to one of these companies?"

"Yes. Whether we'll find the same sort of thing with the others we can't tell yet, of course……and I am speaking through my mouth, not my knees!"

Not a whit abashed, Vermeulen shifted his gaze.

"Has Southern contacted you?" I asked.

"No. And I realise he is likely to get some idea of what your work is, but I should be grateful if you continue not to tell him."

"May I ask why?"

"From what I have seen of the documents in this matter and what I have been told, a detailed knowledge of the DGVI processes would be needed to carry out this fraud. While I doubt whether Southern has sufficient detailed knowledge or that he is likely to be involved, I rule nothing out at this stage. Besides, he has a short temper and a flapping mouth, so if he is informed, it is more than likely that anyone and everyone in DGVI will learn what your work is."

"I imagine if someone in DGVI was involved, they'll already have worked that out. That's definitely water under the bridge."

"So, what now?"

"We continue with our enquiries – mostly visiting these companies to see whether there's any sort of pattern or any common factors that lead us in a particular direction, possibly even one or more individuals…..But so far this seems to have been planned quite meticulously, so we may be able to show how the fraud was managed, but there won't be sufficient evidence to prove who did it," Rosemary explained.

For once, Vermeulen kept his eyes on her face.

"We shall have to see."

That seemed to be all he wished to discuss. So we left….heading for the Berlaymont restaurant and lunch. We were standing in the queue for steak, chips and salad when a voice spoke behind us.

"Let's hope there are no bugs in your salad!" remarked Knud Henriksen. "Who knows what they might hear or might want to hear what you say!"

"I think generally we're pretty careful about what we say in public places," replied Rosemary.

"May I join you?"

"Of course."

As the "bien cuit" steaks were being fried – to the evident distaste of the chef – I wondered what Henriksen wanted to say to us. I doubted whether his presence in the queue was pure chance. We sat down at one of the more private tables in the corner of the restaurant.

"Are you any clearer what's going on?" he began.

"Generally…or between Vermeulen and Southern?" I replied.

"I was thinking of the latter primarily…..Gerry believes there's some private war going on between them and you two are a couple of pawns in their game of chess. I guess he told you that?"

"Yes. I'm not sure I fully agree with him."

"Why not?"

"This stuff is too big, too complicated, with far too many people involved for it to have been set up as part of a struggle between Vermeulen and Southern. It's plain that this fraud has been committed and that false bank accounts have been set up, with money put into them by DGVI, and then emptied by a person or persons unknown. Assuming that it's only the larger sums, there are at least fourteen companies and banks involved. That's too many for Vermeulen to set up, just to make Southern look incompetent."

"It's well known that the poison dwarf doesn't like Southern. But Southern is a pompous buffoon who drinks too much and can't control his temper. I'm sure Vermeulen is taking immense pleasure in discomfiting Southern about these frauds in DGVI. I doubt whether anyone believes Southern could have set anything like this up – but incompetence bordering on negligence is a nice hold to have over a senior colleague….and Vermeulen would know enough about you two to know you'd get stuck in and find something – even if you couldn't find out who was responsible in the time available – certainly enough to embarrass Southern."

"So when Southern got the phone call from Cie CCR or the Namse Krediet Bank about the fraud, he panicked."

"I reckon so. He wouldn't want Vermeulen involved in any shape of form until he had a much better idea of what was going on. If you'd phoned Vermeulen as you suggested – so Gerry tells me – he'd be facing Vermeulen not knowing whether he was playing football or rugby."

"Which suggests that Southern will be trying to keep tabs on us, to find out in more detail what we know and what we're up to."

"Exactly."

"Unfortunately, he'll probably get a number of phone calls from people we're visiting. So he should be able to work out pretty quickly what we're doing. I'm surprised he doesn't know about these frauds already," said Rosemary.

"I guess these end-year audits must be undertaken by some of Vermeulen's people….so it's quite possible he didn't know until he got his phone call yesterday…..Of course, that means that if there is someone in DGVI who organised this fraud, they'll know soon enough about your investigation."

"If they don't know already, I'll eat my hat," I observed.

We'd decided not to tell anyone about Mlle Lefebvre's flat – including Vermeulen, unless he asked directly. Not least because we were still trying to work out how the gun fitted in – and also, assuming the woman in the café round the corner was her, who the oriental man was she ate rijstafel or crispy duck with.

"So where do you go from here?" asked Henriksen.

"After a weekend forgetting all about it, we've got three visits next week…one of which will be Nick on his own enjoying a long day travelling to Gelsenkirchen and back next Friday. We've got a company in Lille, otherwise they're all Belgian. We hope to do a couple more of the French ones and another West German in the following week. Hopefully, that'll give us enough to be able to see whether there's some sort of pattern or not," Rosemary explained.

"Well, don't forget to watch your backs. If someone has been making a very large amount of money, he won't want you breathing down his neck."

It was a point worth remembering. Up to now, I'd reckoned that this was a well-planned fraud and whoever had planned it had got away with it, probably leaving virtually no trace. But seeing that gun hanging up in Mlle Lefebvre's cupboard reminded me that the crooks probably had a better idea of where any loose ends were – and if we, perhaps unknowingly, were getting close to them, they might decide that drastic action was needed. And though there was no direct link between Mlle Lefebvre's disappearance and our investigation, the suddenness and apparent completeness of that action could be a warning about the ruthlessness of these people.

But I didn't think much about it during the weekend. The weather had let up a bit, so we took the train to Ostend, mostly deserted by holidaymakers at this time of year. Emily and Sarah were able to go on the rides and other entertainments without queuing; while Rosemary and I enjoyed strolling on the beach. And the chips with mayonnaise were pretty good too! We travelled by train and stayed in a cheap hotel, meaning to do a bit of sightseeing in Bruges or Ghent on the way back. But our daughters were enjoying themselves so much, it seemed a pity to spoil their fun....but we reminded ourselves that we only had about another six months in Brussels and should make at least one more trip to see those two handsome cities before we were back on the other side of the Channel. However, our daughters were going to have to hang around doing not a lot for most afternoons the following week, so we felt we owed them to have a weekend they'd enjoy, rather than "walking for hours and hours round churches and old buildings", as Sarah put it. And, naturally, their parents had taken the opportunity of a separate room with a shower to have a rather late Saturday night.

On Monday, we travelled to CW et Cie, in Roux, a small town, almost a suburb of Charleroi. We'd agreed that when we'd finished there, if there was time, Rosemary would stay for the second visit to Charbonniers de Courcelles in Courcelles, the next stop on the line back to Brussels. Apart from finding out how to get there, we had no idea what CW & Cie did. Roux was a small, nondescript town which seemed quite poor. It was one of those places where the industrial revolution seemed to have caught a small town by surprise, had dominated it, but as the industry slowly died, the town had lost its former identity and was yet to find a new one.

As there appeared to be no public transport that we could see, we took a taxi to the works which were on the southern side of the town. As we got out of the taxi, we realised we were close to the cooling towers of a power station. I guessed that CW & Cie were connected in some way. Indeed, the moment we turned to their entrance, it became plain that they provided coke for the power station. The works were black with coal and coke dust, with small mountains of coal away to our right, with a coking plant almost directly in front of us, pushing noxious yellow-grey-black smoke out of a couple of tall brick chimneys. There was a small brick office block on our left. The whole place was quite old. The brick buildings, though grimy and ageing, had been built by someone with late nineteenth century ideas about industrial style. They weren't elegant – but they were a good deal more than purely functional.

We were met at the front door of the office block by a small woman with short, tidy grey hair – with the unmistakeable air of a concierge.

"You are M. et Mme. Storey?" she demanded in French, of course.

We nodded.

"Follow me."

She led us inside and up a flight of stairs to what I guessed was probably the boardroom. As we entered it, two men entered from another door. The room was furnished in heavy, dark wood, with a couple of paintings of what I reckoned we the founding fathers of CW & Cie, as well as several framed photographs of other men, standing in front of the works – which looked a lot more impressive then. The two men introduced themselves: Thierry Vloet, managing director, who looked like my idea of a French accountant, and Luc Grasset, company secretary, who looked like the sort of man who could carry sacks of coke around all day, down half a dozen pints of beer and then play a game of rugby. We continued to speak in French.

"From your telephone call, I understand this concerns our payments from the EEC for decommissioning these works," began Vloet.

"Yes," I replied. "The end-year audit of the accounts in the EEC Commission has uncovered some discrepancies which we hope we can clear up. This mainly concerns a bank account which you have with the Banque de Charleroi and a payment made to you by the EEC Commission in September 1974 of a little under twenty million Belgian Francs."

"My colleague has brought various ledgers with him and will check this. I am, however, surprised that we should have received such a payment at that time. This factory is closing down. The power station which we've supplied with coke for two generations is being converted to burn oil. There is no other market of comparable size for our coke. So there is nothing for it. This is a small town, M. Storey, and employment prospects for my men are extremely limited. Fortunately, under the EEC's restructuring schemes, we were able to qualify for considerable financial assistance when the plant finally closes. We received a small amount – some three or four million - to assist with the initial redundancies. But I do not expect the rest until the plant closes in about eighteen months' time. So a payment on that scale at that time seems odd. Are you sure there hasn't been some clerical mistake at your end?"

"I don't believe so. You will understand that your name may have been used to perpetrate a fraud on the EEC Commission....Please understand that I'm absolutely not accusing you or any of your staff...Someone had gained access to your information and used it in a fraudulent manner...."

"I can confirm that we have definitely not received any payment at that time," said Grasset in an educated accent, which didn't seem to fit with what he looked like.

"But you do bank with the Banque de Charleroi?"

"No. Our bank is the Banque Bruxelles Lambert and has been since the company was founded. Though we aren't a large company, the Banque de Charleroi couldn't handle our business. It's a bank for people like you and me, to make deposits, take out loans, and so on. They may lend to shopkeepers or very small businesses, but we're too large for them to handle. I don't know how such an account might have been set up, but it certainly was not set up by us."

"Would it be possible to get hold of your signatures, which presumably would be needed to set up such an account?"

"I wouldn't imagine it would be difficult. We've been writing lots of letters – not least to our workers, explaining the firm's position, and to the mayor and other townsfolk, setting out what we are trying to do to ameliorate the circumstances we find ourselves in," replied Vloet.

"Would anyone at the Banque de Charleroi recognise you?"

"I don't bank with them and as far as I'm aware, I don't know anyone who works there. Do you, Luc?"

"Nor I," added Grasset.

"Apparently the man who signed off the payment was a M. Francois Millet. I assume that name means nothing to you?"

Both shook their heads.

Coffee arrived and we happily drank it, as it'd been an early start. But we'd finished what we came for and thanked them for their time and left. Very kindly, Grasset came out with us and suggested we got into his car so he could drive us to the station.

"I see you believe you can tell whether someone is lying when speaking to them face to face, rather than on the telephone," he observed, in impeccable English as he drove along.

"A better chance than on the phone, certainly," I replied. "But that's not our main reason for wanting to meet the firms who've been caught up in this fraud. Someone has to set up a false account at a bank which the firms concerned don't use. It may be helpful to know whether the person who does this resembles the real member of the firm or not. If he does, that suggests it's someone who may be known to you. Besides, it's useful to get a direct feel for what the firms are like, and what the banks are like too. I don't believe you could reliably see any pattern purely from documents or phone calls."

"Well, I wish you luck….I assume the EEC won't consider that we've spent this money and deduct it from what we're due?"

"I can't see why they should. But we'll check that out….."

"If they operated normal commercial accounting procedures this thing would have got stopped in its tracks after the first couple of frauds were detected," added Rosemary, happier speaking English rather than French, which, as she admitted, she found hard work just keeping up with what people were saying.

We didn't have long to wait for a train to Courcelles, where we again had to get a taxi to the works of Charbonniers de Courcelles. We met the three men who'd supposedly signed the false documents – as well as the legitimate ones - Raymond Leblanc (managing director), Louis Dupuits (company secretary) and André Gratiolet (works manager). Like CW & Cie, they produced coke from coal for neighbouring steelworks and power stations. A bigger operation that CW & Cie, they were, nevertheless, also running down their operations and there were already plans afoot to build a large glassmaking plant on the site. What they had to tell us differed little from what we'd learnt at CW & Cie. Like CW & Cie, there seemed to be plenty of opportunities for someone to get hold of their signatures without it being in any way apparent. They were a rather friendlier bunch of people – possibly because they weren't facing the immediate prospect of having to get rid of all their workers with limited prospects of alternative employment. Indeed, if it wasn't for Rosemary having to get back to Brussels, I reckoned we would've enjoyed a convivial lunch there.

As we were so near Charleroi, we decided that it was sensible if I went to see M. Millet at the Banque de Charleroi. Fortunately I was able to phone from the Charbonniers de Courcelles and get a twenty minute slot at 3pm. So, after a farewell kiss, Rosemary and I stood on opposite sides of the platform until our trains arrived, setting off in opposite directions.

The Banque de Charleroi was in the centre of the town, on the corner of the Rue de France and the quaintly-named Rue du Mouton Blanc. It was in a moderately interesting brick building – rather like many in the centre of the city – not exactly elegant or particularly historic, but quite attractive and sometimes quite unusual. It wasn't the sort of place you'd go to specially as a tourist, but, on a less dreary day than when we'd been there before, I realised it was more interesting than I would've expected.

François Millet was middle aged, avuncular and gave all the appearance of being fairly idle. He had carefully cut steel-grey hair, a squareish face with a pug nose and half-moon spectacles. He wore a pinstripe suit with a white carnation in the buttonhole. I explained the purpose of my visit. He explained that this was the central Charleroi branch of the bank, whose main offices were in a more anonymous building a few streets away.

"Why, indeed, I met M. Luc Grasset myself," he stated, speaking French - naturally. "It must've been in early 1973. He told me that the company – CW & Cie – had just been granted some EEC funds which they wished to keep in a completely separate account from their normal banking arrangements, which were with another bank. Essentially, he told me, a few fairly large sums would be paid in by the EEC, which would then be transferred to another bank account. Though we wouldn't make a lot of money out of it – just a few francs for setting up and managing the account and then the cost of managing these inflows and outflows, along with the interest we could get on the money while it was sitting in our coffers, so to speak – it was better than nothing…and we'd hardly have to do any work to make this money. So I was quite happy with the transaction."

"What did M. Grasset look like? Did he have to sign any documents?"

"He was small, with short, straight dark hair – almost black. He was very conservatively dressed. Clean-shaven, but with very thick spectacles. I doubt he could see the end of his nose when he took them off! Pallid skin…..I almost wondered whether he wasn't one of those French half-breeds from Indo-Chine….But he seemed to know his stuff well. He had a couple of documents authorising the setting up of the account - with his signature and that of Thierry Vloet, the managing director…He was the company secretary, if I remember correctly……He had to sign a couple of forms for our purposes, but he signed them without hesitation and I had no doubts that they weren't genuine….Of course, I checked our indices to make sure that these were, indeed, the names of the managing director and company secretary of CW & Cie….."

"So it all seemed entirely genuine. What happened when the eighteen million Belgian Francs were paid into the account? And then when they were paid out?"

"The money arrived by secure messenger of the Belgian Post. In it were copies of a form signed by M. Grasset. M Vloet and a M. Duvergne claiming the subsidy from the EEC and giving the details of the account in the Banque de Charleroi. Because it came in that form, I opened the letter but it was one of my cashiers who would've paid it in….."

"When was this?"

"Early autumn last year……"

"Sorry…Do go on…."

"A couple of days later M Grasset arrived and asked for the necessary forms to transfer the money to a bank in Luxembourg….The exact name escapes me…"

"Could it have been the Banque Luxembourgeois?"

"That sounds about right. There was an account there….something industrial, I think…."

"Industries Utiles et Cie?"

"That sounds about right."

"So you transferred the money to this account?"

"Of course. There was no reason why not to….And M. Grasset told me that there would be other payments, but not for several months….Unfortunately nothing has appeared so far…."

"If it does, I recommend you contact the EEC Commission. It seems likely that your bank has been used by someone committing a very clever fraud to get money from the EEC. Plainly nothing happened with this first transaction which could reasonably have made you suspicious, but if it happens again, questions might well be asked of you…..Though I suspect whoever did this is far too cunning to try and use the same banks twice."

M. Millet looked slightly stunned – and at least it halted his verbal diarrhoea. But it seemed evident that he'd been an innocent party in this, albeit a pretty obvious target because of his laziness. For instance, if he'd actually checked the names of the directors in CW & Cie in his bank's "indices", I was a Dutchman!

There seemed no real point in checking the records, but while I was there I felt happier that I was able to confirm in writing what he'd told me. But, for all his idleness, he had a pretty good memory and I was able to make my way back to Charleroi station and back to Brussels feeling that a pattern was beginning to be established. Indeed, it seemed more likely that our first visit had been unusual because de Mettet had actually known Verstappen. Indeed, what I thought about on the train was how someone had managed to learn this and avoid getting caught out by pretending to be de Mettet when he met Verstappen. And the man who had gone to both banks seemed to me to quite possibly the same one – disguising himself differently, but unable to conceal that he was possibly of oriental origin. Did that perhaps suggest that Mlle Lefebvre's disappearance was more likely to be related to these frauds?

7.   A SMALL MAN WITH SPECTACLES WITH VERY THICK LENSES

At least there was no-one waiting to whisk me off to the Commission for another interrogation when I got off the train at Brussels Midi station. To avoid any possible questions, I decided to head straight home to our flat in Woluwe St Lambert, where I spent an enjoyable couple of hours helping Rosemary play with Emily and Sarah, helping them with the bits of homework they had to do and encouraging Emily with her drawing and Sarah with her recorder. It was only after I'd read them their bedtime stories and they were settling down to sleep, I told Rosemary what had happened at the Banque de Charleroi. Though these were only short day visits, I knew that our daughters remained worried that our investigations might mean that we were faced with men with guns, as had happened when we were in Riga the previous year and which still bothered Sarah, in particular.

"You don't think this Millet might have been got at, possibly bribed?" asked Rosemary.

"I don't see why anyone would've needed to do so. Provided they could get their hands on the right documents, I reckon they'd be able to convince bank managers of relatively small banks like that one that they were kosher….No, the odd thing as far as I'm concerned is how they knew de Mettet was a friend of Verstappen and worked their way round it. Apart from giving us a description of the bloke who actually set up the account and got the money transferred – which may become clearer when we've seen a few more banks – most of these banks or companies won't give us too many leads. But someone had to get some quite detailed knowledge of Cie CCR…How?"

"I wonder whether we might not get more from the other banks. After all, why would you know in advance that de Mettet knew Verstappen? It must've been through some sort of contact with the company or the bank or both. Wouldn't you have to do pretty well the same thing with every company and bank you were going to use? Otherwise you might find the same somewhere else and get yourself caught?"

"That's a very good point……So actually we need to be asking rather wider questions of the companies and the banks to see whether there are any common threads about people getting information out of them, even if it might not have seemed relevant or important."

"Another thing we need to check. For Cie CCR, they used a local branch of a small bank. But for CW & Cie, it was a branch in a different town. We need to keep asking ourselves whether there is any pattern to this or any reason why it was done differently."

"You're right…This does seem to have been too carefully planned…and over several years… for it to be random."

The following day we went to Durufle et Cie, following the familiar train journey to Charleroi. The only thing that could be said about it was that it was a sunny, if cool, autumn day and the countryside looked prettier than I'd noticed before, though that was perhaps not saying a lot. Durufle et Cie were in the middle of a large industrial zone, comprising mostly buildings that looked prefabricated or functional brick, in the west of the city, close to the River Sambre. We were able to get a rather down-at-heel bus to quite close to the works. Judging by the familiarity of the structures, I reckoned they too were in the steel-making business. Although the buildings were probably newer than Cie CCR, they seemed shabbier, possibly because so much was made of some pre-fabricated material – conceivably asbestos.

We met the three men mentioned in the documents relating to the fraudulent claim - Maxim de Laan (managing director), Charles Foulnes (company secretary), and Peter Symons (legal adviser). As they were a Fleming, a Walloon and a British citizen, we spoke in English. They explained the nature of their application to the EEC: a massive transformation of an old-fashioned bulk steel making plant into one specialising in certain sorts of steel, notably that for motor vehicles and the military. Symons explained that he had formerly been employed by NATO in Brussels and had been using his contacts to ensure that Durufle et Cie obtained a decent share of the market for specially hardened steels for use in 'armoured support vehicles and the like', as he put it.

Naturally, they knew nothing of the false claim and could not explain how the company had an account with the local branch of the Banque de Tournai. They banked with Paribas, as we already knew from their original application documents.

"Somehow, someone has managed to set up an account in the name of your company in the Banque de Tournai, here in Charleroi," I explained. "You can see from these documents that they've forged your signatures quite accurately. Would it be fairly easy to get hold of copies of your signatures?"

"We've been writing to the workers and to local politicians and community groups and newspapers about what we're planning to do with the steelworks here," replied de Laan, a squat, pugnacious, spiky-haired middle-aged man. "Close to half the workforce will be losing their jobs over the next two years and the EEC and Belgian government funds won't go very far to creating alternative employment. This is a coal and steel area and we are all facing the same pressures. So when one etablishment cuts jobs, so are all the rest. We've been doing our best to explain that it's either this restructuring or the whole company will go under. But as you may imagine, there are plenty who believe in fairies and that orders come fluttering down from heaven to keep everything the way it was for another fifty years."

"So it'd be relatively easy to get hold of copies of your signatures?"

"No difficulty at all, I'd say."

"In order for this fraud to work, we believe it was necessary to set up a separate bank account in a small local bank – so that's why they used the Banque de Tournai," continued Rosemary. "But they'd have to know that you didn't bank there. Would someone outside the company – other than in the branch of Paribas that you use – know you banked with Paribas?"

"Our audited annual accounts would certainly mention it," replied Foulnes, tall and balding, with rather a beak…not far from my idea of a secretary bird, indeed. "Though we don't publish them widely, they are available as necessary. They would also have been included in our submissions to the Ministère de Commerce et Manufactures for the EEC subsidies, of course."

"It also seems almost certain that someone will've gone to the Banque de Tournai locally to set up the account and to withdraw money from it. We've already come across a case where one of the signatories to the company documents knew the manager of the local bank which was being used for this fraudulent account. Measures were taken by the fraudsters to avoid the manager knowing anything about the account and precautions were taken so he was absent on each occasion the bank was visited. We believe that someone had to get to know a fair amount about the company and the bank they'd selected for the fraudulent account. We were wondering whether anything had been happening that would have allowed someone to get that sort of knowledge about your company?"

"Hmm…We're constantly being inspected by someone or other. If it isn't some expert from NATO or a Belgian Government auditor or tax official…" remarked Symons, a very sleek man, with expensive clothes, haircut, spectacles and a face, round, red-cheeked and shiny, rather like an apple.

"But the man from the EEC was the nosiest. Wanted to know all sorts of things, personal things….and come to mention it, he did ask about whether we knew any of the local bank staff....Claimed it was to ensure there was no possibility of any collusion...though I couldn't quite see what he was getting at," remarked Foulnes.

"What did he look like? Can you remember?"

"Short. Black hair. Moustache. Pale skin...he looked positively unhealthy! But the main thing were his spectacles. Lenses so thick you'd reckon he'd trip over his own feet if he ever took them off," observed de Laan.

"You can't think of anyone else as nosey as him?" I asked.

"Not that I can recall. Most of our visitors tend to stick to their business. This chap – called himself Louis Chastelle, or something like that – claimed that if the EEC were going to grant us millions of Francs they needed to be wholly confident in the company.....I never really caught on at the time – but we were given the go-ahead about a month later. And as it came by way of the Ministère de Commerce et Manufactures here in Belgium, I can't see how his report can have seriously contributed to the decision....Not least because I suspect it was taken before he visited us...from what I know of the bureaucratic procedures of the EEC and the Belgian administration."

"How long was he with you for?"

"The best part of a day...He had all the correct documentation and a male secretary from the EEC telephoned in advance to arrange the visit. There was no reason to suspect anything about him...."

"When was that?"

"November 1972. I'm quite sure about that."

That seemed to empty the well of their knowledge...or, at any rate, of their knowledge that was likely to be useful to us. So we thanked them and went on our way.

We had to wait about twenty minutes for a bus to take us back into the centre of town to the Banque de Tournai. It was a dreary wait, as the scenery consisted of steelworks and other industrial buildings. At least it wasn't raining as it had been when we'd visited the steelworks on the other side of town.

The bank was situated on the corner of the Rue de la Science and the Rue du Governement, in a brick building in a muted "brick Gothic" style. The bank manager, Felix Verlaeren, was tall, blond, with a crewcut, a thin-faced, lean man who gave a strong impression of energy and ambition. He explained that he'd taken the Durufle et Cie business, even though it related to only one aspect of their business, in the hope that if he did it well, they'd give his bank more of their business…and he could also show head office that even in "darkest Charleroi", they could attract some "big players". In other words, the fraudster played to his inexperience and vanity. Evidently the same man had set up the account, with the usual plausible documentation, and arranged in person for the transfer of the money to the Banque Luxembourgeois to the account of Industries Utiles et Cie. These were the only occasions Verlaeren, the "little man" visited the bank and he was fairly sure that no-one else had been snooping around in any obvious way. He was, as he pointed out to us, always on the lookout to prevent any robbers entering his bank. The "little man" fitted the usual description, being clean-shaven on this occasion, but for all his "eagle-eyed" approach, Verlaeren gave us the least detailed description of the man we'd yet had.

But as we said on our way back to Brussels in an empty train compartment, a pattern was beginning to be established. Now it needed testing in West Germany and France. However, we realised that we couldn't sensibly do more than three visits a week. We needed a day between visits to settle our heads, or there was a risk we'd become punch-drunk and see the patterns we expected, possibly missing out on something different, which could make our previous ideas inaccurate. Indeed, we felt we'd already wasted our first few visits because we hadn't asked some of the questions about how the fraudsters got their information about the firms and the banks. It was inevitable, because we hadn't picked up the need for them at that stage, but it meant that there would be gaps….and I doubted whether we or the firms concerned had the time to go back there.

So we spent the next day in our office, partly catching up on our other work, partly preparing ourselves for our visit to Deûle Industries, EVM Cie, Crédit Flandres and the Banque de Lille the following day. As the journey to Lille would take an hour and three quarters, with a fairly hasty change of platforms at Tournai, we'd had to plan quite a strict timetable, which still meant that Rosemary would miss the final meeting – with Marcel Dutoit at the Banque de Lille.

As the connection was so tight, we saw virtually nothing of Tournai, but approaching Lille we realised that this was a real city, much larger than Charleroi, with a historic centre, albeit that the outskirts – both industrial and residential – appeared rather dilapidated. We were only able to get glimpses of the centre of the city as we headed by tram for Deûle Industries to the west, over the river Deûle, and into a district called Lomme, from what we could tell. Deûle Industries were steelmakers, who, like the other firms we'd met, were planning to restructure and produce a range of more specialised steels. The steelworks were as elderly as those we'd seen in and around Charleroi, with perhaps rather more graffiti on the brick walls and less evident activity about the place.

We met only Michel Czerniawski (accountant) and Pierre Herne (company secretary), who explained that the managing director, Jean-Pierre Fouchet, was in Paris meeting officials from the Ministère de l'Industrie. Herne told us about their restructuring plans, which seemed mainly to phase out traditional steelmaking and replacing them with rolling mills to provide steel for the bodies of Renault cars. Naturally, jobs would be lost and with the decline of many heavy industries in the Lille area, there were few prospects for re-employment. Despite our determination not to allow ourselves to fall into a pattern, it seemed that the fraudsters had operated as we would've expected. There seemed to be no problem about getting hold of the signatures used on the fraudulent documents and, naturally, they didn't bank with Crédit Flandres, but with the Société Générale. Neither Herne nor Czerniawski resembled the "little man" with the spectacles with thick lenses – nor, from their description of him, did Jean-Pierre Fouchet. None of them banked with Crédit Flandres. They had received a visit from the EEC Commission a couple of months before they were granted their subsidy. The description of "Philippe Wouters" fitted the "little man with thick spectacles".

They weren't a particularly friendly pair and our conversation was in French naturally. This contrasted strongly with our reception at EVM Cie. We got there using a couple of buses, as it was the other side of the city, not far from railway sidings in the Rue de l'Église Saint-Louis. It was never plain to us exactly what they did, but though the buildings seemed old verging on dilapidated, it was evidently neither a steelworks nor a coking plant. As we only saw the office area and neither Etienne Boucher (managing director), Roger Dupont (company secretary) nor Gérard Huguenin (chef de communications) ever enlightened us as to what they actually made. My guess was this it was textiles. It also struck me as possible that their almost overwhelming bonhomie covered a certain degree of furtiveness. Was it possible that they had connived with the French authorities to apply for subsidies supposedly for coal and steel industries when in fact they were in the textile business, I wondered? But that wasn't the purpose of our visit – though it did underline the unwisdom of DGVI relying on EEC Member States and not undertaking any visits to the places they were subsidizing so lavishly.

With EVM Cie, we stuck very much to the documents and their unwitting involvement in the fraudulent bank account with the Banque de Lille. The story was largely similar to what we'd heard before, including the visit of "Philippe Wouters from the EEC" a couple of months before their application for EEC funds had been granted. His description tallied with what we'd heard before too. The only real difference was that Dupont and

Huguenin had accounts with the Banque de Lille, but in branches in the suburbs where they lived. The fake bank account had been set up in a branch in the centre in the Place aux Oignons and, from the documents we'd seen, had been set up by Etienne Boucher.

"From what we can tell, this fraudulent bank account was set up by a man who signed his name as Etienne Boucher," explained Rosemary, in her careful French, "in the branch of the Banque de Lille in the Place aux Oignons."

"That couldn't have been me," replied Boucher. "As far as I'm aware, I've never been in that branch. Indeed, I can't remember a time when I've even been in the Banque de Lille. As a company we use Paribas and that's what I use as well."

"But both of your colleagues, whose names are on these documents, do have accounts with the Banque de Lille, admittedly in different branches, as they have explained. In other cases we have been looking at, the fraudulent bank account has usually been set up by the company secretary. In your case it was the managing director. A possible reason for this was because the man setting up the fraudulent account knew that the company secretary – M. Dupont – had an account with the Banque de Lille. We were wondering how he night have discovered that?"

"That's easily explained," replied Huguenin, a man of average build, with the face of a fox and matching reddish hair. "The man who called himself Philippe Wouters was insistent that he needed to know where we banked, so that, as the banks would gain from holding large sums of money, albeit perhaps for only a few days, there should seem to be no personal connection."

"So he found out where you banked that way. Didn't he comment on the fact that M. Boucher banked with the same bank – Paribas – where the company has its account?"

"When I explained that my account was in the branch in Hem, close to where I live, he appeared to consider that represented no significant problem," replied Boucher, who bore the close likeness to my idea of a jolly butcher as his name suggested.

Despite their apparent openness and welcoming manner, they were plainly not unhappy to see us on our way – even providing a car to drive us into the centre of the city. I wondered whether "Philippe Wouters" had suspected anything about their application?

From what we saw of it, I would've said that Lille reminded me more of a Belgian city than a French one, but then I knew north-east France barely at all. The Place des Oignons was in the middle of some fairly narrow streets in the old part of the centre. While I wouldn't have gone so far as to say it was an area which looked dilapidated, it certainly felt as though it could do with some freshening up. But then, the city and the region were going through a period of decline in their traditional industries without much replacing it.

The Banque de Lille was in a pleasant building, not particularly elegant or ostentatious, but perhaps eminently suitable for a bank. The branch manager, Marcel Dutoit, looked like an avuncular family solicitor in his early fifties – knowledgeable, dependable, unambitious and a bit dull. A middle-aged secretary who could easily have been his wife brought in the relevant documents.

"I admit that I was somewhat puzzled as to why a company like EVM Cie would wish to set up an account in my branch," he observed, speaking in French, of course. "But M Boucher explained that it was convenient for meetings with EEC officials in the centre of the city. He told me that only a few very high value transactions would be made on the account, but that we would normally have the use of the money for a few days, so it would be financially advantageous for us. It involved very little complication for us and all the necessary documents had been prepared and M. Boucher provided a satisfactory signature and identity card with his photograph on it."

"What did he look like?" I asked.

"Small, with short very dark hair, a small moustache, an extremely pale complexion and spectacles with very thick lenses. I noticed he wore the same tie – and expensive silk one – on both occasions he visited the bank….I confess I was slightly surprised that the photograph on his identity card had him wearing those spectacles, but he explained that his eyesight was so poor that no-one would ever see him without them on….But he had all the necessary documentation - as he did when he came to transfer the money to the Banque Luxembourgeois."

The rest was what we expected, but we went through every detail. Then Rosemary and I headed towards the station so we could have a bite to eat at a small café nearby before she set off back to Brussels. It was as we returned to the station we realised what a fine building it was – a series of large arches at ground level, complemented by three arches and two smaller windows in a classical style on the storey above. I made my way back into the city centre to the Rue des Celestines to meet M. Maurice Mervey, the branch manager of Crédit Flandres. (It was just after I'd kissed Rosemary goodbye outside the station that I realised that because we'd been to EVM Cie second, I'd automatically suggested to their driver that we should head for their fake bank, the Banque de Lille, rather than the one we'd originally intended to visit next, Crédit Flandres).

Crédit Flandres was in the Rue des Celestines. A rather less distinguished building that the Banque de Lille, it was made of brick in a slightly ponderous, but fairly nondescript style. Maurice Mervey struck me as a big fish in a small pond – and a shark-like fish at that. He was about thirty, well-groomed, even slightly dapper. Tall and good-looking, with an air both of self-satisfaction and razor-sharpness about him. I reckoned he probably spoke English well, but we conversed in French. The details were familiar – even the reason why M. Pierre Herne, "a small, moustachioed, black-haired man with spectacles with extremely thick lenses", gave for setting up the account for Deûle Industries.

"I know of Deûle Industries, of course," explained Mervey. "But I could see why they might wish not to complicate their accounts with this money from the EEC, especially as it seemed to be destined to be transferred elsewhere within a few days of its arrival. Evidently it wouldn't be going into their main bank account. Otherwise, why the need for this separate account. Though he didn't say as much, I suspected that M. Herne was putting these millions through us and on their way to the Banque Luxembourgeois, from where it would travel onwards to some tax-free country…or possibly into accounts which would risk more but gain more in returns on the capital invested than sitting in a company account in Paribas or the Société Générale, for instance. Had I the opportunity, I should do the same."

"But you didn't suspect it could be a fraud where EEC money was paid into this account and extracted by someone completely unconnected to Deûle Industries?"

"No. The paperwork looked entirely satisfactory, as did M. Herne's identity papers."

It struck me, as I sat in a largely empty train on my way back to Brussels via Tournai that "the small black-haired man with spectacles with extremely thick lenses" must be a pretty good judge of character. Apart from being able to pick the right sort of bank for these fake accounts, he or perhaps an accomplice – as no-one ever suggested they'd seen him in the bank before the first visit – were able to spot who was lazy, who was busy, who needed to be got out of the way and who was too clever by half. I guess a couple of subtle suggestions would've been enough to get M. Maurice Mervey thinking that the account was to enable some clever financial wheezes, rather than trying to work out whether there were other explanations as to why his branch of a small regional bank should be used for such a large and important transaction.

I half expected to be nabbed by someone working for Robin Southern when I arrived at Brussels Central station, but it appeared either he was biding his time or Vermeulen and he had spoken together and either resolved matters or left them hanging in the air, with further skirmishes to be anticipated.

Rosemary had also been thinking about things on the journey back to Brussels. Once Emily and Sarah were in bed and we'd eaten an un-Belgian dish of cauliflower cheese mopped up with the remains of the morning's baguette, she sat next to me on our settee.

"So the pattern was as we've seen before?" she confirmed.

"Yes. The same little bloke seems to have done everything….though either he or someone else has somehow been able to fathom the characters of the bank managers in particular. They seem to have picked out mostly rather lazy or uninterested bank managers and where that wasn't possible, they seem to have sussed out how to play those that are keener or brighter."

"I wonder whether that was the little man with the glasses or someone else? My guess would be someone else – otherwise the little man would run the risk of being seen somewhere he wasn't supposed to be."

"I guess you're right."

"But something else struck me while I was on the way back here. Though the little man with the glasses changes his appearance to some extent, he never changes those very thick glasses. Is that because he really has got very poor eyesight? Or could it be that he's trying to disguise his eyes? I think we need to ask some of the people who've met him. I reckon if he's got very short sight, his eyes should look larger than normal through such thick lenses. But no-one has mentioned that to us. So I was wondering whether they aren't purely for effect – to disguise his eyes. And why would you do that? Because your eyes would be memorable in some way. And one of the things people might remember about your eyes would be if you were oriental. A couple of those we've spoken to have suggested that he might be like that – but that could be just from his shape and size – but it could've been a suggestion from seeing his eyes, even though disguised. I know it's speculation at this stage - but I wonder whether we aren't perhaps finding a connection with Monique

Lefebvre and the man she used to have dinner with near her flat?"

"That's very clever of you…Miss…."

"Just don't say Miss Marple! Otherwise I'll start dressing like her!"

"OK. Just remember that when you call me Sherlock Holmes. I might invest in a deerstalker cap and a tweed cape….But I can certainly see what the Germans can recall when I meet them on Friday.….I wonder whether there's any other way of checking up on him? ….But I assume he's a foot-soldier, rather than the person who masterminded this fraud."

"That might be preferable to a smoking jacket and playing the violin."

"Well…I'll do my Sherlock Holmes thing and question whether the little man with the glasses is linked to Mlle Lefebvre. Unless they've got their money and done a bunk for good, it seems an unnecessary way of drawing attention to her as the person who supplied the necessary information from the documents which DGVI had. Of course, if they're now in some country that hasn't got extradition arrangements with Belgium, I guess it doesn't matter. But this appears to have been carried out with such care, it seems to me to be a bit clumsy to put her so obviously in the frame. I ask myself whether she mightn't be a decoy."

"But presumably you haven't arrived at an answer?"

"Not at this stage. But I do feel we need to look out for things that are deliberately placed to put anyone investigating this fraud off the scent – or certainly down the wrong track."

"Maybe we need to see if we can get at Monique Lefebvre's personnel file? Perhaps it might tell us a bit more about her?"

"Or not, of course….But it's certainly worth looking….I'll try and get Vermeulen to get us a copy."

I phoned his office the following morning and left our request with them. Shortly before lunch I got a return call telling me that the file would be available to read in an office near his at any time from 11 am the following morning. So Rosemary agreed to have a look at it while I did my long day in Gelsenkirchen.

And it was a long day, indeed! I got a train just before 7.30 am from Brussels Midi, arriving in Gelsenkirchen Hauptbahnhof not long after 11 am. I dozed for a lot of of the journey and spent much of the rest of the time looking out of the train windows without really taking anything in. I got a coffee and a croissant on the station at Cologne, where I had to change trains. I didn't see much of Gelsenkirchen as shortage of time meant that I took a taxi from the station to TKG Kokerei AG, which was on the outskirts. All I could really tell was that this was coal mining country, with the recognisable pit-head buildings and machinery and a heavy grey smoke hanging over one of those gloomy grey days when you think it's going to rain, but never does.

The name suggested a coking plant and that was what I found. It was a mixture of some elderly brick buildings and more modern concrete ones – presumably built after the Allied air raids in the Second World War. As Gregor Goltz, the managing director, explained to me, West German power stations were being converted to either gas, oil or nuclear power, so demand for coke was about to fall off a cliff. He was very much in the mould of a modern West German businessman, with a crewcut, brisk, efficient manner and even spoke English well, with a strong American accent. Nevertheless, in view of his age and Aryan appearance, I reckoned he would've been in the Hitler Youth in his formative years.

But, like his colleagues, Dietrich Jankowski (finance director) and Erich Sand (legal and corporate director), he seemed welcoming and straightforward. They had nothing to hide. The firm was running down its operations. Most of the EEC money was to pay off the workforce, but a small amount was contributing to research into alternative forms of energy – notably obtaining gas from coal and the development of fuel cells that could be powered by the sun. Unless either of these proved fruitful, Goltz observed, there would be no TKG Kokerei AG within five years.

Inevitably, they had been visited by a small man with dark hair and a beard, wearing spectacles with very thick lenses, calling himself "Philippe Wouters" from the EEC Commission, who was undertaking a brief assurance check of applicants for significant amounts of EEC funds. As he had all the requisite documentation, including an EEC Commission pass and identity card, there was no reason to query that he was genuine. (After the first salvo, we conversed in German).

"You say he wore spectacles with very thick lenses," I asked. "Did any of you happen to see his eyes through the lenses?"

"I'm not sure what you mean?" replied Sand, a middling sort of man, with a tidy beard his only distinguishing feature.

"If he was very short-sighted, you'd expect his eyes to seem bigger than they really were through the lenses of his spectacles. I wondered if you'd noticed that?"

"Come to think of it, they didn't," remarked Jankowski, a man who looked like my idea of a Prussian cavalry officer, solely lacking the exuberant Kaiser Wilhelm II moustache. "If anything, his eyes seemed to be affected by light, as they seemed to be half closed."

"Or might he have been oriental?"

"I imagine that would be possible. He didn't strike me as such. He certainly spoke French and English without a discernible accent in either case."

None of them had an account with the Rheinbank and the firm banked with Commerzbank, neither of which came as a surprise. Indeed, the similarities with the other firms we'd visited were much greater than the differences. It was useful to confirm that it seemed likely that "the little man with the spectacles" appeared to do all visiting to these firms. I suppose using only a small number of people to carry out the fraud improved security while cutting down the number who had to share the proceeds.

And I reckoned there was only an infinitesimal risk that any of these companies would compare notes.

However, a thought struck me forcibly as I sat in the TKG Kokerei AG car on my way to the centre of the town to meet Leopold von Eisenau, the manager of the Gelsenkirchen branch of the Rheinbank AG. Why had these particular firms been chosen among the many receiving similarly sized funds from DGVI? Had they been chosen at random? Or was there something about them – perhaps their banking arrangements – that made them more suitable than others? It seemed to me this was not just an interesting question, but one which might help us understand who had chosen them.

Gelsenkirchen struck me as a fairly grimy town. But then somewhere that had been relying so heavily on coalmining for the last hundred years or so – and had then suffered the effects of heavy Allied bombing during the war – was scarcely going to rival Heidelberg or Lübeck, for that matter. What I saw of it was less featureless than I'd expected, but there was little evidence of the growing prosperity which I'd seen when I was in Lübeck earlier in the year.

I wondered what a man called Leopold von Eisenau was doing in a town like Gelsenkirchen. However, he confounded my expectations by being a small, colourless bean-counter. He combined that with a grinding suspicion which meant that getting anything out of him was like drawing blood from a stone – and took twice as long as I'd hoped, having decided to postpone my lunch until after my two meetings. But eventually it became plain that his experience with the TKG Kokerei AG account resembled all the others we'd encountered. The small man with very dark hair and a thick moustache was someone I recognised even before von Eisenau mentioned his very thick spectacles. He, too, indicated that the man's eyes appeared not to look any larger than normal through the lenses, but his interest was in paperwork and figures, not people, so he had no recollection of the what the little man's eyes actually looked like. Naturally, as all the documents were in order, if not actually standing to attention, von Eisenau recalled no doubts about the authenticity of the TKG Kokerei AG account and could readily understand the need for it to be kept separate from their normal account with the Commerzbank to meet EEC requirements. The transfer of the money almost immediately to the Banque Luxembourgeois to the account of Industrie Erfordelich AG appeared to have made his antennae twitch a little, but the "small man" had explained that as the EEC money was essentially to assist with the development of a different sort of manufacturing industry which would, in time, replace TKG Kokerei AG, it had been deemed appropriate to set up what the "small man" called "an interim bridging company"….and Luxembourg was known as a place where the best rates of interest were paid on large sums of money awaiting further use. In any case, it struck me that provided he had an explanation that fitted into his version of the world, he'd be readily satisfied…….though, on reflection, I reckoned that applied to pretty well everyone, including me. It was just that I knew more about what had been going on than he did…and had I been in his position at the time, I might well not have smelled a rat any more than he had.

At any rate, at around 1.30 pm I finally escaped and headed for the station. The bank was close to the city centre – which was more distinguished than I'd expected (not that was saying a lot) in a post-war building – and I decided to walk through some fairly ordinary streets to the station. There I got some bratwurst with sauerkraut and potato salad, along with a bottle of local beer, finishing it in something of a hurry as the train to Cologne arrived a few minutes early.

Unfortunately, that was the only part of the journey which exceeded my expectations. Otherwise it was slow, with more than half an hour to wait on Cologne station. Long enough to drag, but not long enough to pop out of the station and visit the famous cathedral. I tried to make time move a little faster with a "kaffee und kuchen", without much success, other than helping me doze as the train from Cologne to Brussels wended its way through the pleasant, but unexciting countryside, at a distinctly unambitious pace, reaching Brussels Midi station just after 6 pm. I'd like to say that I spent the journey thinking about what I'd been told and how it all related to the fraud case, but in practice I felt too knackered, and just slumped in my seat watching the scenery go past without taking anything in.

We'd got a similar schedule of visits planned for the following week. As I sat on the tram from Brussels Midi towards St Lamberts Woluwe my tired brain kept asking me whether it was sensible. Was there anything new we were likely to learn? Or would the travelling and the essential similarity between the different firms and banks mean that we'd just got ourselves on to a treadmill which we couldn't get off? I realised that we'd both be refreshed after the weekend, but by Wednesday evening, if not before, I reckoned we'd both have got so used to what we were seeing and hearing, we'd be learning nothing – just like filling in the gaps in an easy crossword when the harder clues had already been written in.....But without the satisfaction of having reached any conclusion, other than we now knew how this fraud had been carried out and we had a fair description of one person involved.

We needed a fresh approach. Perhaps Rosemary's examination of Mlle Monique Lefebvre's personnel record might help us get some new information to help us on our way. Otherwise it seemed to me we were risking just going around in circles.

8. AN ENGLISHMAN'S PERSPECTIVE

It was 8 pm before I got home. Someone, either deliberately or accidentally, fell in front of the tram and we had to wait while the local police took all our names and details in case anyone had witnessed what had happened. As the poor driver was evidently in a state of shock, I imagined they hoped one of the passengers might've seen something. Since those of us at the back couldn't possibly have seen anything other than the heads of the people standing next to us – or the road immediately at our side, I was baffled why we were required to hang around, when some thirty of us must have told them we'd seen nothing. Eventually the body was taken away and the tram allowed to continue on its way…after a relief driver had arrived…..on his bicycle, which he then proceeded to squeeze past passengers at the front of the tram. It was probably a good thing that a dozen or more passengers had already given up and made their way on foot. I would've done the same, but we were in a part of Brussels I didn't recognise…and I was well aware I was several miles from home…and had a tendency in Brussels (unlike almost anywhere else) to go in the wrong direction when I wasn't absolutely certain where I was heading.

"You'd better go in to see Emily and Sarah…particularly Sarah," whispered Rosemary as I walked through the door. "Because you said you expected to be back before they went to bed, they're both worried that something might've happened to you….and Sarah still has the occasional nightmare about Riga. When you didn't arrive when you said you would, I'm sure she believed you'd been shot."

124

So I went to the girls' bedrooms and read each of them a late bedtime story and waited until Sarah, at least, was soundly asleep.

"They both look so angelic when they're asleep," I remarked.

"It's pretty well the only time they are…."

"And Sarah looks just what I imagine you looked like at her age…apart from the long hair, of course…."

"Mine was quite a bit longer then - though not as long as hers. I didn't cut it short until I was twelve."

I explained about what I'd learnt about my day in West Germany. In practice, not much more than we knew already.

"So was there anything interesting in Monique Lefebvre's personnel file?"

"You'll be surprised to know that it contained no suggestion that she was a part-time hit-woman, carrying out assassinations at those times she was supposed to be seeing relatives in Australia…"

"So who's not taking this seriously now?"

"OK……There wasn't much. The only interesting things as far as I was concerned were that there were hints that she was….is…a bit anti-French. That's supposedly why she applied directly to work in the EEC rather than in the French equivalent of the Civil Service or local government. Being who she is – or what she wants to appear to be – she didn't give a direct answer when questioned in the EEC Commission interviews, just gave an indication that she might have been bullied or perhaps excluded by other children at school because she was half-Vietnamese…..As we could've guessed from what we saw in her desk, she is reasonably fluent in Vietnamese and claims to have a modest knowledge of Chinese as well. One of the people who wrote a report on her suggested that she might be able to use her talents more fully in the trade or overseas relations DGs. But when it was put to her, it was one of those rare occasions when she was adamant that she did not want to get involved in any work that might require her to go to that part of the world. She didn't explain why and the file contained no suggestions on that score either."

"I guess it's all quite messy in that part of the world and, unless she really is an underground agent for the Vietcong, I doubt - as the daughter of a defector and a colonialist exploiter - she'd receive much of a welcome in Vietnam or China."

"I guess you're right. No doubt there may be other explanations that fit too…..However, a couple of years ago someone did raise a doubt about her supposed relatives in Australia. Although she wasn't….isn't…prone to giving much information away about herself. A former manager – a man called Georges Botsorhel, who is now in a different DG – asked her about a forthcoming trip to Australia. He and his wife had spent a month or so there the previous summer and was interested to know which places she was visiting. Though she could parrot the names, Botsorhel got a feeling that her knowledge of these places was limited to their names and that she'd never been there. He suggested that either she was saving her money to buy property or she was having to subsidize her elderly mother in her Parisian suburb."

"Or she was a fun-loving naturist and went to a nudist island somewhere in the sun, but didn't want to mention it, for obvious reasons."

"Who's not taking things seriously now?"

"She'd certainly have to be a good actress to be a mouse most of the time, while all the time she was an uninhibited thrill-seeker."

"And she probably has no connection to this fraud. The only slight links are that she's disappeared and the little man who goes round organising the fraudulent payments and so on may be oriental."

"Anything else?"

"Not really. There were plenty of the sort of comments you'd expect….quiet, extremely conscientious, careful – even pernickety, and someone mentioned "an occasional air of silent censoriousness when others failed to meet her standards". I wrote it down in my notebook – not least because I hope to be able to use it sometime. Her present manager is Heinz Groener who appears to take very little interest in what she does."

"Any mention of the bullying?"

"No. But there's a definite hint that she kept herself apart from most of her colleagues…whether that was on her side, their side or both, who can tell?"

"So she's someone who gives very little away about themselves. Does their job conscientiously, but seems to make no real effort to befriend anyone….Indeed, the only person we've learnt about she did meet socially was the oriental man she sometimes had a meal with in that café near her flat. It's possible that her upbringing and being bullied or just ostracised at school turned her into someone who kept a thick hedge of silence around themselves and that the person inside was rather different – possibly seething with resentment, if nothing else. But equally, she may have been brought up by a quiet, submissive mother to be that sort of person – and her contact with the rest of the world has merely reinforced those aspects of her character."

"And vanishing without leaving any information about what she was up to would be consistent with that sort of person….On the other hand, it doesn't strike me as the sort of personality who'd decide to kill themselves without leaving any clue as to what they'd decided to do…."

"I'm not very happy with the idea of suicide. For a start, she's supposed to be a good Catholic. Unless something totally unexpected and traumatic had happened, I can't see her risking the fires of hell in that way….And she's also got that mother in the Parisian suburbs who she's been supporting, supposedly…..Could you see someone like that leaving her dear old mother in the lurch?"

"I guess not……And though I'm still not sure she's connected to the fraud stuff, I'd like to get a view of her from someone we've chosen to talk to, rather than someone proposed for us by Vermeulen….Indeed, I'd like to speak to someone in DGVI who could give us some independently verifiable evidence about much of what we've been looking at….and speculating about…and not someone fed to us by Vermeulen or de Klerck…"

"But not Southern……Perhaps we need to look at the DGVI pages in the Commission phone book and see if there's anyone we feel we might be able to trust…at least to some extent."

"Wasn't one of the Directors in DGVI British?"

"No. Southern is the DG. None of the next level were British, from what I remember. I can look through the Directory on Monday….As I was saying earlier, I really don't see we're going to get any more value at this stage from just keeping on with these visits. Unless we can come up with some new angles, we'll be going over the same ground again and again."

"And now let's forget about it for a couple of days….I'm sure you could do with a relaxing hot bath after such a long and tiring day…."

"Perhaps not too hot and not too relaxing….?"

After a relaxed weekend, during which I was able to reassure Emily and Sarah that I had never been in any danger of being shot while on my journey to or from Gelsenkirchen, I returned to work feeling refreshed – and rather more optimistic than I'd been on Friday evening. There were five men and one woman with British names working in DGVI, excluding Robin Southern. One – Philip Deeley – I ruled out because he was plainly in a very junior grade. But I had no reason to choose one of the remaining five rather than another. However the thought came to me that Martin Finlay, now working in the Council Secretariat – a different part of the EEC furniture from Vermeulen's Commission Secretariat – seemed to know pretty well everyone in Brussels, certainly the British, as well as everything that went on.

However, Martin was notoriously difficult to pin down – especially for any sort of meeting. Even though he was no longer part of the diplomatic circuit, he seemed to attend at least as many meetings and social functions, both at lunchtime and in the evening, as he had previously. Eventually I got hold of him, along with a promise to meet for coffee after his lunch appointment. Fortunately, as he appeared to have a meeting in the EEC Council building, next door to the Commission building, I was able to meet him in the "coffee lounge" there, rather than in a nearby restaurant or coffee bar.

I'd been to the modern, but undistinguished Council building on several occasions, generally for Council Working Parties examining SEFF's proposals for information sharing between Customs authorities. Generally they were exercises in tedious nit-picking, which could make ten minutes seem like an hour. I'd used the "coffee lounge" on several occasions, not least because it provided coffee that was marginally less acrid and powerful than the witches' brew that got served at meetings. I confess I'd also popped out of meetings there just to get some relief from the grind.

I had to wait about ten minutes until Martin Finlay appeared.

"I imagine Rosemary and you are up to your necks in yet another piece of investigation," he began. "Not at all what the Italians imagined when they proposed SEFF should be set up. But I guess you're not far off your two years now?"

"A bit less than six months now.....And you're right, we have been asked to look at what were termed discrepancies..."

"In DGVI, I believe.....You have to remember that this place is a multilingual village. Though no-one knows exactly what you're looking at, the fact that Vermeulen put you up to twist Robin Southern's tail has been making its way up and down the Rue de la Loi."

"We realised. I got a bit of a grilling from Southern, but...."

"....But it was water off a duck's back......So, do you need to know more about that pompous pillock?"

"I don't think so. I really wanted to have a discreet word with one of the British people working in DGVI, one that I felt I could trust…and someone who wouldn't go blabbing back to Southern. I wondered whether you'd come across any of them. They're just names on a page to me."

"You'll need to make sure you meet them well away from here if you don't want everybody and his wife in DGVI to know……But who have you got? I can't say I can immediately think of anyone I've come across in DGVI, but who knows?"

"There's a woman – Pauline Stone - and four men – Derek Allenby, James Young, Peter Frazer-Walsh and Graham Peacock."

"I've never met the Stone woman or Young. I have come across Allenby, Frazer-Walsh and Peacock. Did you realise Frazer-Walsh is an AT (Administration Trainee) on a year's secondment from DOI?"

"No. As I said, they're just names on a page."

"Allenby came from DTI, when it was still DTI, before Harold Wilson divided it up again to give all the different Labour Party factions Ministerial posts. He left UKREP five or six months after I arrived. A smooth type, whose loyalties are to Derek Allenby. If you told him anything confidential, he'd judge what was in his career interests as whether or not to pass on what you'd told him. Peacock is the DOI stool-pigeon in DGVI. He's primarily there to find out what's going on and how DOI can get their hands on as much EEC money as possible. I strongly doubt whether that went anywhere near Tony Benn when he was their Secretary of State before the referendum, but there are several parts of the UK Civil Service which have woken up to the gravy train here – MAFF not least – and wish to make sure the UK gets at least our fair share. If I know this, you can bet there are plenty of people in DGVI who suspect it – not least because he'll have equivalents from all the other Member States doing exactly the same thing."

"So anything I say to Peacock is likely to find its way back to DOI in London?"

"Undoubtedly – and what use they might make of it is anyone's guess. But you could probably assume that it'd be unlikely to assist you with whatever you're doing."

"On the other hand, Allenby doesn't exactly seem the sort of bloke to trust."

"You'll need to encourage him to see that keeping it confidential is in his interests as well as yours, it seems to me…But that's up to you, of course……Now I must dash…I've got three members of Coreper to jolly along this afternoon….."

With that, he gulped down the remainder of his coffee and sped off.

I returned to the SEFF office to think which, if either, of these two I might best approach. Though by the time I set off for Woluwe St Lambert, I'd pretty well made my mind up, I thought I'd ask Rosemary for her opinion. After we'd put the children to bed and eaten, I explained what Martin Finlay had told me.

"I certainly wouldn't go for any of those Martin doesn't know," she said. "It seems to me it'd be too much of a risk. But neither of the other two seem particularly trustworthy characters either. I think I'd go for Allenby. It seems to me you know where you stand with him. When you know someone is completely looking out for themselves and their career, it reckon it's not as hard to make use of that. But with the other man – Peacock – I don't think you could judge whether you could trust anything he said to you…and if he really is what Martin says he is, he's likely to pass on whatever you tell him to his colleagues in the Department of Industry…was that it…..? And who knows what someone there might decide to do with the information! It might even get phoned straight back to Southern."

"That was my feeling too. I think if I made it clear to Allenby that if there was any sort of leak, I'd make sure Vermeulen - and any other of the top brass in the Commission I could think of – knew that he was the source of it. If you're fixed on your glittering career, I guess you want as few as possible influential enemies or, at least, people who don't think you're trustworthy…."

"Of course, when you mention influential enemies, it's a good thing you aren't fixed on a glittering career…."

"I'm sure there's still time…."

"What for a glittering career?"

"No. I'm confident that's beyond me…No – I was thinking more about influential enemies I'm probably making at this moment…and no doubt a few more when we get back to London….I seem to have a fair knack of stepping on people's corns…."

"But generally for good reasons…..You may be a bit bolshie, but even you don't tread on people's corns for no reason."

"Thank you for that vote of confidence!"

"Let's see how you get on with this man Allenby…But first, you can help me with the washing up and then we both need to relax…or were you intending to go jogging?"

"Only indoors."

Of course, as Derek Allenby worked in DGVI and I didn't want to arouse any suspicions, I had to work out how to get in touch with him without giving the game away. But I suddenly realised I could kill two birds with one stone. So I rang Vermeulen's office and asked for a quick word on the phone. After a few minutes, he was put through to me. I decided to speak in French as I could scarcely understand a word of Vermeulen's English over the phone.

"We've got to the point in our investigations where we need to speak to someone who is currently working in DGVI," I explained. "In view of the timing of when this fraud was planned, certain of the British staff in DGVI could not have been working there then. So I don't see how they could be involved. But we need to get some feel for the other staff – and this is the only way we can see of doing it."

"I understand. You will need to ensure that they treat your conversation as completely confidential....Who had you in mind?"

"We propose to speak to Derek Allenby. I understand he's an ambitious man, with loyalties only to himself. I believe it is made clear to him that if any word gets out about our conversation, the Secretary to the Commission will regard it extremely badly and would ensure it had an extremely adverse effect on any future career Allenby might be contemplating here in Brussels, he will understand the position."

"As indeed I would.....Was that all?"

"In order to preserve confidentiality, we thought it would be better if your office invited Allenby to a meeting....where he would meet Rosemary and me."

"On what pretext, might I ask?"

"Your office might hint that Allenby was regarded as a man with a promising career ahead of him in the Commission and that you were keen to get to know people like that?"

"He may be understandably disappointed, even annoyed, when he discovers he's meeting Detective-Sergeant Storey and yourself."

"I'm sure we can manage that...and without saying anything which would reflect badly on you."

"Very well. What time would you wish to meet him?"

"Ideally this morning, around midday?"

"My office will let you know."

I got a phone call from Vermeulen's secretary about half an hour later, confirming that Allenby was due to meet Vermeulen at 11.45. She would take him along to a room a few doors further along the same corridor, which we could use for our interview.

Rosemary and I made our way over to the Berlaymont shortly before 11.30. The room which had been selected for our meeting was, I guessed, a waiting room for those due to meet Vermeulen or other top brass in the Commission. Essentially it comprised a large coffee table with various Commission publications, notably the Official Journal, on it, four very low chairs and a bookcase – also crammed with Commission publications.

At 11.50 there was a knock on the door and a tall, smooth man in his early thirties was ushered in. He had longish, dark hair and gold-rimmed glasses, which gave a long, sharp face the look of an intellectual. He was dressed in a dark brown suit, with a dark orange shirt and florid orange, brown and purple tie. He looked at us with some irritation.

"I'm led to believe that my meeting – rather than being with Jérôme Vermeulen, as I was previously informed – is with Mr and Detective Sergeant Storey from an organisation called la Service Européenne contre la Fraude Fiscale. I take it that is you two?"

"That's so," I replied. "Perhaps when I explain, you'll understand the need for a certain amount of subterfuge."

"I was told it was a matter of utmost security and that you are working for Vermeulen. I assume that is the case and isn't also a certain amount of subterfuge?"

"That is correct. It concerns a fraud involving some £8 million of EEC funds, which M. Vermeulen has asked us to look into. He has asked us to treat it as a highly confidential matter. Indeed, so we completely understand each other, he asked me to make it clear that if anything concerning our conversation leaks out, he will not only hold you personally responsible, but will maintain a close and unfriendly watch on your future career in the Commission and elsewhere in Brussels, both directly and by way of his many top level connections."

"So you're the pair Robin Southern was muttering about! There've been rumours around the DG about someone sniffing about our activities. I assume it was you two?"

"That's correct. Mr Southern chose not to speak to M. Vermeulen, but preferred to talk to us instead."

"And plainly got nowhere as he's been going around like a man chewing a wasp for days."

"I guess if you were fairly sure the Secretary of the Commission had asked some people to investigate your DG without telling you, your nose might reasonably be out of joint."

"Well….I assume that the fraud you're investigating has taken place in DGVI? And presumably I'm in the clear?"

"I understand you arrived in the Commission after the UK joined the EEC?"

"A month later."

"That's what we understood. It puts you in the clear."

"So what exactly is this fraud all about?"

"I guess you could probably work it out. All I need to say is that it required knowledge of DGVI procedures for subsidies and grants, along with a fair amount of knowledge about certain companies in West Germany, France and Belgium which received large sums of money from the EEC. The fraud needed information about who had signed the various application documents in these firms, copies of their signatures, information about their bank accounts, for instance. We've been investigating fourteen firms, all of which were sent at least a quarter of a million pounds to a bogus bank account, which was then emptied and the money sent on to another bank. The only place where this information is held together is in DGVI. We've been told that security there is fairly lax, so pretty well anyone could get hold of almost any information and lay their hands on virtually any document."

"That's certainly true. But what do you want from me?"

"I'd like to show you our list of the frauds we've been looking at, including the names of those who handled the work in DGVI. Also whether, from your experience in DGVI, is there anyone who might be involved in a fraud of this nature. Of course, they may have left…."

"And that brings us on to the final question," added Rosemary. "Monique Lefebvre has disappeared. Anything you can tell us about her, including whether it's at all possible that she might've been involved in this fraud, would be appreciated."

"OK. I'll see what I can do."

For a man with the air of a "blue-blood", the warning about Vermeulen's continuing hostility seemed to have worked a treat. Moreover, to give him his due, he didn't stare at Rosemary's legs, despite the fact that the shape of the low chairs meant that she was revealing several inches more thigh than usual, a fact that was making her a little self-conscious, I realised.

I showed Allenby the list of fourteen companies and people involved *(as set out in the table at the beginning of chapter 3 above)*.

"You realise that both Cardle and Griffiths have moved on, don't you?" he observed.

"Oh? Are they still working here?" I asked.

"Yes. Both applied for the Commission in 1970 and ended up in DGVI. Cardle was ex-Board of Trade, like me, and took the first opportunity to work on trade policy when work was being divvied up anew after UK accession. Griffiths came from the Treasury – absolutely detested it in DGVI and is now happily managing part of the EEC budgets."

"When did they leave DGVI?"

"Cardle went at the end of '73. Griffiths just after the summer break in '74. If they were involved in any fraud, they're keeping their ill-gotten gains closely concealed. I've been to David Cardle's flat in Etterbeek every month or two ever since I've been here. If he's suddenly become vastly wealthy, it'd decidedly not evident. I don't know Griffiths socially. He's a keen cyclist and has a small flat in Wemmel, in the north-west of the city somewhere. Cardle's wife and mine play tennis together, so we keep in touch. Though I wouldn't say I know him well, I'd be astounded if he'd get involved in any sort of fraud…if for no other reason than he's a confirmed pessimist, who'd be bound to believe he'd be caught."

"Since you've been there, is there anyone or anything suspicious that you could recall? It'd be mostly last year. Both people who are still in DGVI and those who've left."

"I've tended to work with my direct colleagues - Philippe Wouters, my line manager, and the rest of my unit, Gianpaolo Ricci, Charles Vautroux, Heinz Groebler and Maire Grimes. Wouters has a sort of 'at home' in early July. Other than that I've never met any of them socially. The people I know best are Jürgen Schwenk, André Fontaine, Florence van Dooren and Katrin Eriksen. We play bridge together and Jürgen and I also play squash. We meet socially, with our wives and families. Other than that I know people only as colleagues…..Anyone or anything suspicious…..? I suppose Monique Lefebvre's disappearance is certainly suspicious. One of the quietest people I've ever met. Extremely punctilious. Probably the only person in DGVI who actually follows the strictest rules of security…."

"Would you say she gives off an aura of disapproval when things aren't done to her standards?"

"Not that I'd noticed….But I'm probably not the best at detecting other people's auras."

"Is there anything you can think of that might explain her disappearance? What have people being saying in the office about it?" asked Rosemary.

"You'll understand that there's been a certain amount of rumour about you two and it's inevitably been linked with Monique Lefebvre's disappearance. Suggestions that she was somehow involved in some sort of irregularity have generally been met with incredulity. But she might have family in Vietnam or Australia, I think, that might make her persuadable….and I imagine that passing on a few pieces of paper might not feel too heinous a crime. But if she was dealing with people who don't want to get discovered, she's the obvious link in the chain…so perhaps they might consider it safest if she was to disappear without trace….I'm just speculating, you understand…and it only came to me after you'd explained a bit of what you're up to…..Within the office, people have largely lost interest. She was a long way from being the life and soul of the office. Indeed, she's only marginally less noticeable now she's absent as when she was in the office. If you asked people, they'd probably think she'd killed herself...though as she was almost certainly a Catholic, that strikes me as unlikely."

"So people are either not interested or think it was suicide. Nothing else?"

"Hit by a car and got amnesia? Someone suggested that. The other favoured one was that her mother in Paris somewhere is desperately ill and she's gone back there to be with her...and that's taking up all of her time...and that she's probably sent some sort of explanation which unaccountably failed to arrive."

"I realise you don't want to point any fingers – but are there any members of DGVI, past and present, who we might take a greater interest in?" I asked. It seemed to me he'd ducked that issue so far.

"None of the names on your list...for a start. Not that they're necessarily 100% honest, but from what you've said, someone involved in a fraud like this wouldn't go putting their name in the frame...or that's how it seems to me. Similarly, there are about a third of the staff in DGVI who are basically there to get as much for their home countries and put the kybosh on as many bids from competing countries as they can without it being too obvious. That's Graham Peacock's job essentially. But in view of your timescale, you could rule out the Irish, Danes and Brits because they wouldn't've been around when this was being planned. Beyond that, it depends whether you believe this fraud was set up in DGVI or whether someone else picked one of my colleague's brains and got them to get copies of the relevant documents..."

"We have to consider both possibilities at this stage."

"The ones with the brains to set it up would be Robert van der Broeken, Gerhard Schäfer, Luc Beffroi and Frans te Haarden. They're all at my level and as they've been there longer, are beginning to face some awkward decisions: Do I stay where I am? Do I move on? What are my chances of progression? Please understand, I know none of them well. We don't meet socially.

But if I was looking a people clever enough to have planned this and ensured there were no traces of evidence pointing to them, they'd be the ones I was looking at."

"Any who might've left since you joined?"

"Paolo Castagnoli went off to Faccioli's cabinet about a year ago. He's certainly bright enough….and possibly Korthuizen….though I always thought he was a bit of a thug….He punched Creac'h on the nose, just for a bit of teasing….though that was the Lefebvre woman, if I remember what I was told….and Creac'h too….though he's not just left DGVI but the Commission altogether…a gamekeeper turned poacher. Korthuizen is a cyclist, of course. One of those who appears in the office all the Tour de France gear….I don't know why that made me distrust him…I suppose it's when someone puts on such an obvious show….."

"And Creac'h?"

"Clever chap. One of those who says outrageous or rude things and then claims it was all just a bit of a joke. I certainly never felt I knew where I was with him….There was another one who left for some group of lobbyists at about the same time…..Roger Dufour, a native of this fair city and a man of few words, but considerable cunning and insight. Went to work for EUROSITRO, the umbrella organisation for SITPRO and their ilk in other Member States. But the line between working for the public service, the private sector and lobbying groups like that is a vastly more blurred in these parts."

"The only person who's definitely involved in this has been described to us as a small man with very dark hair. It's possible that he might be Chinese or from south-east Asia. Is there anyone who might fit that description working in DGVI or who might've worked there previously?" asked Rosemary.

"No. Certainly not in my time. The only person who could possibly fit that description would be Monique Lefebvre. The rest of us are all European."

"Is there anyone else you can think of who we might look further at?"

"Not that I can think of. Of course, you might assume that someone clever and cunning enough to pull off a fraud that was likely to be traced back to someone in DGVI would want to appear as unassuming as possible….which brings you back to Monique Lefebvre…..though that really would astound me…"

"And you don't come across any of them socially or happen across them out of the office?"

"Not apart from those you've mentioned. Naturally one might bump into someone in a restaurant or a supermarket…But Sue and I live in Saint-Josse ten-Noode and we try to avoid the restaurants in the streets around the Grand Place for obvious reasons…..And now you mention it, we did come across Monique Lefebvre in a little Chinese restaurant over towards Uccle on the chaussée d'Alsemberg not far from the junction with the rue de Nieuwenhove. Someone had told us it was quite new and quite good…more like the sort of Chinese you get around Leicester Square in London. But it turned out to be dire. Run by Indo-Chinese with lots of their dishes…..I wouldn't've been surprised if we hadn't been served up cat or dog. But Monique Lefebvre was in a booth in a corner with a man. All I could see was the back of his head. My impression was that he was eating his native food, but I imagine he could've been Chinese or Indonesian….but we ended up being seated out of sight of them. They weren't there when we left, but I didn't see them go…For what it's worth, they weren't sitting there like lovers…or a married couple, either…."

"Could the man have been the one I mentioned just now?"

"I suppose so, in theory. I don't think I got a sufficient impression of him to tell whether he was small or not…and, of course, they were sitting down."

"But you haven't come across anyone else?"

"Not that I can recall. I probably have come across people in a shopping aisle in a supermarket or a queue for the cinema, but nothing that would've seemed out of the ordinary. I only recall Monique Lefebvre because she was one of those people who one tended to assume had no life outside the office…so the fact that she met someone….and, of course, it could've been her uncle or whoever….must've made it register in my brain cells somewhere…."

"Is there any reason you know of why Robin Southern and Jérôme Vermeulen should mistrust each other as much as they seem to?" I asked.

"I couldn't really say. I believe Southern was a member of the EEC Accession negotiating team at some stage. It's possible they got up each other's noses then. But it might just be personal chemistry….but from where I sit in DGVI, no-one seems to like or trust Vermeulen very much…so I trust you are supping with a very long spoon at his table…."

"We're not only using a long spoon, we're at arms' length and returning to the UK in the spring…"

"So you're national experts, as they're called……You're not tempted…..?

"Definitely not."

9. VIETNAMESE BANKERS

"He was less unpleasant than I expected," I remarked to Rosemary as we walked back to the SEFF office.

"I'm not sure how far I'd trust him….and we've only got his perspective…though it did put Korthuizen and Creac'h in a different light…"

"…and raised even more questions about why they were chosen as the people to give us information and guide us."

"But at least he'll keep quiet…that's my impression…"

"I agree. In fact, it probably made him relax a bit because he also knew that we could hardly disclose what he told us….though I'm not sure how much we really learnt, other than some names of people we might take a greater interest in….."

"The Chinese restaurant he mentioned where he saw Monique Lefebvre. That wasn't the one we went in was it?"

"No. It must've been at the other end of the rue de Nieuwenhove, I think…I suppose it might be worth paying it a visit…."

"With Emily and Sarah, perhaps? They quite like Chinese food."

"Assuming it isn't hot and sour like the only Thai food I've ever eaten."

"But apart from eating there…and the chances of picking anything up there will be practically zero…"

"…apart from food poisoning possibly…"

"Please be serious! What else can we do? We can hardly interview those people Allenby named. Even if one or more of them is involved, we've nothing to test what they say against, so they can lie happily and we'd have no way of spotting it."

"We could ask Vermeulen to get us their personnel files…including Korthuizen and Creac'h…I'd like to know what's going on there. Why were they the two offered to us? Was it just because they're no longer in DGVI? Or are they suspects and we're supposed to work that out? Before we get a lot further, it's worth asking Vermeulen some questions about them."

"He'll probably have a plausible answer, which may or may not be the truth, but we wouldn't be able to tell....But it's worth doing. If it ever turns out he has been lying to us or misleading us, we may be able to use it in some way."

"And the personnel files may give us some sort of check on what Allenby said to us....I don't think he was lying...I reckon he's too canny for that...But he'll have his own view of people and reading the reports will let us do a bit of triangulation."

"I know I'm going to regret this, but what is triangulation?"

"I was taught it during my National Service. Our instructor gave a very good example of a mountain in North Wales somewhere.......Aberglaslyn, I think........and it was called Cnicht...From one angle, near Portmadoc if I remember correctly, the mountain looked steep and sharp, almost like a shark's tooth. But from the side, it looked rather tame, basically just a long ridge. He showed us a couple of photos to make the point. ...But it also means that it's a way of fixing a point on a map. If I'm in Portmadoc I draw a line towards the summit of Cnicht on a map. Someone else looking at the peak from the east also draws a line towards it. Where those two lines coincide enables you to mark the exact spot on the map where it is. Otherwise you can only tell the direction, not the exact spot."

"I imagine you could have found the top of the mountain by looking at it."

"Very funny! If you can't see where you're supposed to be heading.....But as I never tried it out for real, who knows whether it works in practice. I never got nearer North Wales than a stint in Catterick and I can't say we ever felt the need to do anything like that when I was in Kenya."

"As you're so experienced, you can have the pleasure of reading the personnel files."

In order to get my hands on the personnel files, I realised I'd have to speak to Vermeulen again. As Rosemary had a meeting with some Interpol colleagues about what she'd been learning about the ways in which the Soviets had been hiding their money in Swiss bank accounts, I went to see him on my own.

"I thought I should let you know where we've got to," I began.

There was a faint air of discontent about him. But whether that was that because he was missing the chance to leer at Rosemary's legs I couldn't really ask.

"Very well. Please proceed."

"We've now met Derek Allenby, who gave us some useful information about people in DGVI, including those who he felt might have been involved in planning the fraud or supplying the relevant information and documents. But plainly, just his views aren't sufficient for us to interview anyone. We've no evidence against anyone and if any of them were involved, we'd have no idea whether they were lying or not….."

"So you've not got very far."

"We know how the fraud was carried out and we know where the proceeds were transferred from the banks which were used initially for the money. But it's inconceivable that the money wasn't transferred on from there…not least because every time they transferred it into a bank account and then out again, they had to reveal the bank and the accounts they were using. We also have a description of the man who appears to have carried out all these transactions, as well as doing a recce of all the companies, so he could get the information he needed from them. From what we've seen, someone had to have a good knowledge of the procedures used by DGVI – not least the fact that they relied on the annual check to pick up any discrepancies, rather than doing it as they went along. That doesn't necessarily mean that it was planned in DGVI, but that someone needed that information and copies of relevant documents….One thing we're not sure about….and it'll mean having a look at some of the larger firms which weren't targeted for this fraud…is why these firms were chosen, rather than others. That might help us get closer to who was involved in DGVI. But it's plain to us that this was very carefully planned….and as it must've been evident to whoever planned it that the path of the fraud would lead directly back to DGVI, whoever it was is plainly clever enough to ensure that his or her tracks were carefully covered."

"So even if we looked into people's finances, we might well discover nothing…..and, indeed, if someone in DGVI was involved, they'd be careful not to give any impression they'd come into possession of a vast amount of money? Or perhaps they'd just vanish without trace, as Mlle Lefebvre appears to have done?"

"That's what I'd expect. But we've no evidence that Mlle Lefebvre was involved….which could mean that she supplied the information or planned the whole thing, of course. Though if she did, she seems to have completely fooled her colleagues for many years."

"So what are you doing next?"

"I'd like to examine the personnel files of the people whose names were suggested to me by Allenby….and Allenby's too, if I may. That's mainly so I have a wider view of them. I should mention that two of the people he suggested were Gérard Creac'h and Piet Korthuizen. Assuming there's still a file for Creac'h, I'd like to see their files too. In view of what Allenby had to say about them – including the fact that Korthuizen appears to have hit Creac'h on the nose for teasing Mlle Lefebvre – I'm a bit bemused as to why they were offered to us as people who could help us understand DGVI…."

"I chose them because they no longer worked in DGVI and therefore were less likely to spread information or try to defend the reputation of their DG. I asked de Klerk to identify a couple of officials who had worked in DGVI, but no longer did so. My knowledge of them is nil. Did you think there was some ulterior motive, Mr Storey?"

"The thought had crossed my mind that they were at or close to the top of the list of suspects and that was the reason why they were pointed in our direction."

"You should certainly check with de Klerk. But that certainly had nothing to do with me."

"There was also another former member of DGVI, Roger Dufour, whose file I'd like to see too, assuming it has been retained."

"I fear the name means nothing to me…..What else? Or it examining these files your last hope?"

"If someone can let me have back the files of a dozen or so firms who are receiving perhaps between 20 and 50 million Belgian Francs in subsidies from DGVI, I propose to visit a few of them to see why they weren't chosen for this fraud….I take it that the Belgian police have found no trace of Mlle Lefebvre or why she has disappeared?"

"Not that I know."

"I'd be grateful if your office could let me know when and where the personnel files are available. Shall I arrange to get the DGVI files through Commander de Klerk?"

"Yes," he replied, still with a grumpy air, opening up a shiny and expensive-looking leather document case as I left.

I gave his secretary a list of the personnel files we needed. Then I called in on de Klerk's office so that his secretary was completely clear what files I wanted….Unfortunately the ones we'd been looking at previously had gone back a week or so previously, so I knew no-one would be best pleased. But she promised to get a dozen or so files over to us in the next couple of days.

In mid-afternoon (or, more accurately, after Vermeulen returned from lunch), I got a call from his office to say that the personnel files I'd asked for would be made available in the room I'd used before from 11 am the next day.

Meanwhile Rosemary and I took Emily and Sarah across town for a meal in the Chinese restaurant. Allenby had been unable to remember its name, but his description of where it was gave us sufficient information and after a couple of tram rides and a bit of walking, we arrived at the "Cochinchine". Even with my limited knowledge of the region, I was aware that this was a Vietnamese, Cambodian or Laotian restaurant and not Chinese. I hoped that the food in Cochin China was sufficiently tasty and not too hot so that my daughters would eat it without visible expressions of revulsion.

A small, dark-haired man greeted us and found us a table in the middle of the room. I was able to confirm that there were several booths and certainly from where I reckoned Allenby had sat, he wouldn't't've been able to see Monique Lefebvre or the man she was with. Fortunately, the menu was both in the local script (whether Vietnamese, Cambodian or Laotian I had no idea) and in French, with a description of the dishes and whether they were hot, sour, etc. It seemed a very large menu and I wondered how long we'd have to wait for our food – Emily and Sarah not being the most patient of children. We chose food that seemed least spicy or hot, with ingredients we knew and liked.....along with "xoi", a sticky rice, but which seemed to be as plain as it got.

As we waited, I looked around. The restaurant could probably seat about eighty people. But it was less than a quarter full. But it was a weekday evening and I guessed Allenby would've been there at the weekend. The pictures on the walls were of rivers and wooded hills, but also what I could tell were of Saigon. This suggested that the place was probably owned by Vietnamese, presumably refugees from the Viet Cong's steady advance into South Vietnam, which had led to the eventual victory of the forces formerly led by Ho Chi Minh, and a large diaspora of former residents of Saigon and the surrounding areas. As this was somewhere she could eat food from "home" – at least on her mother's side – I wondered whether Monique Lefebvre came here often?

Our first course came – "pho", a clear soup with noodles and strips of rare beef, and "banh cuon", a Vietnamese version of the more familiar spring rolls. Somewhat to my surprise, Emily and Sarah pronounced them delicious – something with which their parents could happily agree. It was followed by "bo luc lac" (described as "shaking beef" in the menu), marinated beef cubes sitting on watercress, which we ate with "xoi". This, too, went down well…and the children knew enough from Chinese restaurants to avoid the tea, which Rosemary and I drank, but Vietnamese émigrés plainly had no ideological objections to coca-cola, which they consumed contentedly enough.

The fact that we were visibly enjoying the food seemed to warm the waiters up a bit. From when we'd walked in, they'd treated us as what we looked like - a family exploring unfamiliar territory, which, of course, to them was home. I reckoned their clients were probably either Vietnamese and other south-east Asians living in Brussels or Westerners doing a bit of culinary tourism. And though Emily and Sarah were no more sensitive to cultural differences than the average child of their ages, they were - unlike their parents – relatively uninhibited about their likes and dislikes. So their enthusiasm drew one of the waiters over to speak to us. He was quite tall, scrawny, with a pallid complexion and friendly eyes.

"You like Vietnamese food?" he asked, in French naturally.

I wondered whether, if he'd lived in Saigon, whether he knew any English from the US soldiers stationed there….as it would've been obvious that we had been speaking English. If so, he wasn't letting on.

"Yes," I replied, as the most confident French speaker among us. "We have never tasted Vietnamese food before, but it is very good. None of us like food that tastes too strong, especially if it is very spicy or fiery."

"Some Vietnamese food can be quite hot. But it is traditional in Vietnamese cooking to balance tastes so that the food is most good for you."

"I believe that we probably have not done that, as the food we chose did not have tastes that were too strong."

"I am sure you will have done your health good with the food you have chosen......You are tourists perhaps? You seem to have come a long way from the centre of the city....."

"We work here and our daughters attend the international school. We shall return to London next spring. We live in Woluwe St Lambert."

"That is a long way to come for your evening meal....especially for food you have not eaten before."

"That is true. We heard about this restaurant from a colleague who works in the EEC Commission like us. Her mother was Vietnamese and she has eaten here and recommended it."

"A number of Vietnamese eat here, as you might expect....Has your colleague visited here recently, do you know?"

"She didn't say. She mentioned your restaurant in a conversation a few months ago. I don't know how often she came here. She is naturally a very quiet person. Indeed, we are a little worried about her as she appears to have gone missing and we have been unable to contact her for about three weeks....She lives in this neighbourhood, I believe. But we do not meet outside work."

"I believe I know of the woman you are talking about. Her mother comes from Saigon, but lives in Paris. She eats here once a month and always with a man from the Banque de l'Indochine, which he recently informed me has just become the Banque Indosuez. I do not know whether he is a friend or a relative perhaps. But I do not think they are lovers. He is of Vietnamese origins, I believe."

"Perhaps our colleague wishes to keep her knowledge of Vietnamese in practice?" I suggested. "Though she is not a person to talk about her private affairs, I do not believe she is able to visit her mother as often as she would like. But she plainly wishes not to lose the Vietnamese part of her heritage."

"That is certainly possible. They always seek out one of our booths, so that they can speak in private. I would think it would be easier to practice a language there than in the middle of the restaurant....You would not think it, but at weekends the restaurant is generally full....But whether they are speaking Vietnamese I do not know, of course. The young lady never speaks and the man always addresses me in French."

"I wonder whether this man from the Banque Indosuez might know where she has gone? As I said, we are getting quite worried about her. I expect you do not know his name?"

"Regrettably not. He pays with cash, rather than a cheque or credit card. Indeed, I know no more about him than I do of the young woman. The only reason I know about his profession is that he mentioned to my boss that he'd just changed his employment, without changing his job. A rare moment of being sympathique. Normally he is polite, but reticent, like the young woman."

"Well, we must hope that she is perhaps with her mother but unable to get in contact. That she has been missing so long is of great concern to her colleagues."

He went about his business. I didn't see how I could have asked more questions without appearing to pry. And there was no way I was going to get more out of him than he was prepared to tell me....and if she wished her colleagues (and the authorities) to believe she'd disappeared, but the staff at "l'Indochine" knew precisely where she was, I couldn't see them taking sides against her.

But though the attitude of our waiter and of the "maitre d'" as we paid - by cash – and left, didn't alter, I felt that we were being a little more closely observed than before my conversation with the waiter. Whether they suspected what I'd been up to, I couldn't tell, of course. But that'd been the reason for going to the restaurant and we had learnt a little more about Mlle Lefebvre....and had discovered an acquaintance who must surely know about banking procedures. And Rosemary didn't feel I'd pushed my luck – but then her French was less proficient than mine and, as she accepted, most of the time she was trying to keep up with the conversation rather than try to judge the waiter's reactions.

And I largely forgot about it as I ploughed my way through the different personnel folders of Robert van der Broeken, Gerhard Schäfer, Luc Beffroi, Frans te Haarden, Paolo Castagnoli and Piet Korthuizen, as well as the "closed" files on Gérard Creac'h and Roger Dufour. Fortunately, the Commission currently required personnel files to be completed in French, with a copy in the person's native language. So I didn't find myself faced with mostly unintelligible Dutch or Italian.

I started with the two men I'd already met. As in C&E, the reports weren't shown to the person being reported on, so some of the reports were quite forthright. But as I didn't know any of the reporting officers, plainly I couldn't tell what their day-to-day relationship with these individuals was like. Essentially Korthuizen came across as intelligent, but idle and an outstanding bullshitter (my translation of an idiomatic French word "con"). Plausible and likeable, he had occasionally shown a sharp temper when roused. He did not appear to be ambitious, but seemed content to live comfortably off his almost untaxed Commission salary.

On the other hand, Creac'h was regarded as quite intelligent, but ambitious and eager to increase his wealth. There were suggestions that he helped French firms bidding for DGVI money to fill out the applications in a way that guaranteed success, even to the extent of "dressing up a cow as a horse". He had sought several interviews to press his case for promotion, but the accession of the UK, Ireland and Denmark had put the kybosh on that. So he'd been casting around for another vehicle for his ambitions and had hit on CLIF. He was regarded as sarcastic, not a team player, intolerant, but could put on the charm when it suited him. There was evidently no love lost between him and his reporting officer – Heinz Groener.

Van der Broeken appeared bright, conscientious and quiet. He was relatively young – in his later twenties – but with a nonworking wife and four children. Though keen to get promotion, he was sensible enough to go about positioning himself discreetly. His trick was to become Mr Indispensable. Schäfer was an intellectual, a lawyer by profession. Erudite, verbose, but prone to errors of judgement and enthusiasm. "Resembles Tigger", remarked David Cardle in his report, a comment which must've meant little to any German or French reader of the report. Beffroi was sharp, prickly, but essentially a rather cold man. In his later forties, he had a chip on his shoulder about not receiving the promotions he felt had been his due within the French administration and had gone to the Commission in the – probably vain – hope of advancing his career there. So far he had met with no success and appeared to be at the stage where he either decided to move on again or "retire on the job" – in other words, did as little as he could to get by: something I'd encountered from time to time in C&E. Te Haarden was Belgian and had joined the Commission from university. He knew all there was to know about the work of DGVI, having been there for over ten years. He appeared content to remain there for the remaining twenty years or so of his career. His interest was largely concentrated outside his work, as a grower of miniature rhododendrons of international repute. However, despite what such a close interest in plants might imply, he was probably the most gregarious person in DGVI and the best-liked. Castagnoli was smooth and unpredictable. He was regarded as highly intelligent, but working more for the Italian government than for his employer, the Commission. As one of the few Italians in DGVI, he was felt to be somewhat aloof and not greatly interested in the work. On the other hand, Dufour was regarded as a bit of a star. He could both see the wood for the trees, but knew a lot about each individual tree too (David Cardle's idiosyncratic prose again). It was all rather a surprise when he moved to EUROSITRO on a semi-promotion. Cardle's successor, Jean-Pierre Jourdain, mentioned his watchful quietness and a steely sharpness. But there were no criticisms or cavilling in his reports. He was seen as the one most likely to succeed. And the file contained no reason for his departure. Even his formal letter of resignation merely mentioned where he was going, without giving any explanation.

After I'd read the files and made my way back to the SEFF offices, I thought about what I'd read, glancing at my notes from time to time. After a while, I realised that I could pick any of them as a possible suspect – or none of them. Some of them had a character that might be tempted to get involved in a fraud like this. Some had reached a point in their lives where resentment might encourage them to defraud their employer. It would've been useful to see something like the records kept in the UK relating to people's vetting. But the Commission didn't seem to do any of that – or perhaps I wasn't allowed to see such files. Plainly, it would've been useful to know if any of them had money troubles, were divorced or were womanisers – or perhaps liable to blackmail as homosexuals. But the personnel files contained virtually nothing about anyone's private life unless it spilt over into their work.

The files on a dozen or so of the firms which had received similar amounts of money from DGVI as those where the frauds had been perpetrated arrived as promised. Rosemary and I examined them together. What was immediately apparent was that there seemed no difference between them. From what we could judge, the firms seemed similar, engaged in the same sort of business. They used national banks, rather than local or regional ones. There was nothing in the documents that set them apart at all.

"This looks like a complete blind alley," remarked Rosemary after about an hour and a half of slogging our way through the documents. "It looks as though the fraudsters picked out the firms at random."

"That doesn't quite feel right to me," I replied. "This all feels a bit too carefully planned for some part of it to have been done like that. Plainly they've avoided the huge firms that you might expect to be too well-known and too well organised and they evidently don't seem to have wasted their time on the smaller fry. But it seems to me that having identified those firms that fitted in between, they'd surely go for as many as they could. After all, it's probably a once-in-a-lifetime chance to get away with tons of money. So why wouldn't you try to get as much as you possibly could?"

"Well, I can't see anything that distinguishes the sheep from the goats here."

"Nor can I. I think this may involve a few more visits…or at least perhaps starting with a few phone calls…There has to be some reason why they weren't chosen….."

"Well, we haven't got much else…..I take it we're not going back to the 'Cochinchine' soon? Emily and Sarah were saying that they'd be happy to go once more before we return to Beckenham, but not more often."

"I doubt we'd learn anything more from them anyway…..But it might be worth following up on Mlle Lefebvre's companion – the man from the Banque Indosuez, formerly the Banque de l'Indochine. He'd certainly be someone who' know how banks operate – and how to make large sums of illicit money vanish from sight and be as untraceable as possible….But just a name or two would be a start."

"Those are both for you, Nick. If we're having to speak French over the phone, you're a lot better at it than I am….and your average banker is going to take you on trust a lot more than me."

"Yes. It's been painfully apparent at times how many of these bankers pretty well ignore you, even though you undoubtedly know a lot more about their business than I do."

"I ought to be writing up some of what I've been doing chasing up that Russian money anyway."

So I phoned the Banque Indosuez to make an appointment, explaining who I worked for - as I thought it might sound more impressive than the reality – and that it was a confidential matter possibly involving Banque Indosuez staff. Then I looked through the files of the firms that hadn't been chosen for the fraud to find a suitable manager to speak to on the phone. I hoped that I might be able to get sufficient information on the phone, without having to make yet another series of visits.

My hope about SEFF's name turned out to be more effective than I'd ever expected. After a brief phone call with a secretary and then with a "M. Baudoin", I was asked to await a call back. Within twenty minutes, I got a call from a secretary offering me a meeting with "M. Albert" at 3pm. Naturally I accepted.

I decided to try a couple of West German firms first, as I would undoubtedly understand them better than those speaking French. I managed to get through to Vondern Kohlenbergbau AG based in Oberhausen. They were due to receive around £2 million to close down their coal mining operation, from what I could tell. Dieter Schnorr (Chief Executive), Johan Fischer (Financial Officer) and Hans-Georg Rausch (Legal Director) were the names on the application documents. Their bank account was with the Westdeutsche Landesbank. After a while I was put through to Rausch. We spoke in German.

I explained that I was working for the EEC Commission, carrying out an audit of certain transactions and checking whether our financial and documentary controls were adequate against possible fraud. On that basis, I'd picked a sample of organisations that received EEC funds and wished to carry out a reasonably detailed audit. But, as that would take up a considerable amount of their time, as well as mine, I was carrying out initial conversations over the phone, so that where possible, I could get the information which I needed in that way. Rausch replied that he'd do his best to answer any questions I had. If he couldn't, he'd get back to me that day or the next.

"I see that you've drawn just under a million Deutschmarks from the overall amount you've been granted by the EEC?"

"That is so. It was to cover closing down of one of our mining operations here and assisting in the redeployment into other work of those whose jobs were lost. The whole operation will close in a little over a year's time and we shall draw down the remainder of the money then."

"Could you possibly explain to me what the nature of your contacts with the EEC Commission have been, please?"

"After we produced the required documents and information for the Bundeswirtschaftministrie in Bonn, we received a phone call from a Philippe Wouters from Directorate-General VI of the EEC Commission. Mostly it was about details of our submissions. But he also suggested that he might visit our company to see for himself how we were managing our business, so that he could obtain a clearer view on exactly what the EEC funds would be supporting. I explained that this would be entirely acceptable to us, but that we would naturally inform Herr Paul Heidegger, the official who has been advising us in the Bundeswirtschaftministrie. M. Wouters said that he'd already been in contact with Herr Heidegger, who was aware of his proposed visit to Vondern Kohlenbergbau AG. I told him that while it was helpful to know this, I'd always considered it a matter of courtesy to keep Herr Heidegger informed myself. I said that I realised he might regard this as what we call 'belt and braces', but we had got into problems with officials – both federal and from our local Land – when communications appeared to have become mixed-up, garbled or lost. So we were now punctilious about ensuring that everything of relevance to the Bundeswirtschaftministrie was passed on to Herr Heidegger. M. Wouters then asked me several other questions about our business and explained he thought he probably had sufficient information that a visit to us wouldn't be required. If a visit was necessary, he'd be in touch again."

"So you received no visit from any official from the Commission?"

"No. Frankly, I didn't entirely understand why one should be necessary. Officials from the Bundeswirtschaftministrie have visited us regularly – Herr Heidegger most often. Though I could understand that occasionally officials from the EEC Commission might wish to see for themselves to what their funds are contributing, I felt that this was probably an official who wanted a couple of days out of the office. The alternative – that the EEC Commission do not trust officials of the Bundeswirtschaftministrie – is surely unthinkable!"

"Am I correct in thinking that this M. Wouters was one of the Commission officials who approved your application for EEC funds?"

"That is so. Of course, as he never visited us, he is just a signature on a page and a voice over the phone."

"And I expect there was nothing unusual about his voice?"

"We were speaking in English, which was evidently a second language for both of us. So I confess I was concentrating more on what he said rather than his manner of saying it. His accent when speaking English was, I guess, French. Just as mine would sound German...."

"And just as my German accent sounds English....I am most grateful for your time, Herr Rausch. When I have completed a number of similar phone calls, I shall decide which companies I may need to consider in greater depth....But I believe it is unlikely one of them will be Vondern Kohlenbergbau AG."

Though I couldn't expect it to be the same in all cases, evidently the threat of a witness from the Bundeswirtschaftministrie, who might possibly know the real Philippe Wouters (who would have to be the idiot that whoever planned this fraud was plainly not, to use his real name) was sufficient for Vondern Kohlenbergbau AG to be dropped from the companies selected for the fraud. I realised that these visits to the companies were an intrinsic part of the fraud. That was how a lot of the informal details - like de Mettet knowing Verstappen at the Namse Krediet Bank – were picked up and probably some of the documents needed to convince the local banks obtained one way or another. Though it might also be regarded as "belt and braces", it seemed to me that it was not just necessary but vital to avoid being caught. The whole essence of this fraud was to get away with the money months before anyone caught on. But whether that meant whoever had organised the fraud was also long gone – or merely had loads of time to cover his or her tracks - was impossible to say.

Ideally I needed to find some company where "Philippe Wouters" had made an actual visit. But, having told Rosemary what I'd picked up from Vondern Kohlenbergbau AG, I needed to prepare myself for my meeting at the Banque Indosuez. As she suggested, I swapped the colourful tie which I'd bought in one of the Brussels "galeries" for a more sober one. Otherwise, it was more about ensuring I had a believable reason for checking out one of their staff, without giving away information about the fraud.

The Banque Indosuez was in the Rue Pletinckx, not far from the Bourse. It was one of those typical, heavy, vaguely classical buildings that bankers seem to favour the world over. Inside was a large entrance lobby, displaying various shades of dark marble and ornate chandeliers, along with dark wooden seats, the entrance to the public counter, a couple of offices and the inevitable reception desk, with a prim, young receptionist with a thin face, fierce glasses and a tightly ornate hairstyle drawn into two buns on either side of her head.

"Do you have an appointment?" she demanded, in French of course.

"Yes. At 3pm with a M. Albert. My name is Nicholas Storey."

She looked at a large schedule in front of her.

"I must telephone the secretary. Please wait for a minute or two."

Within a couple of minutes, a large woman in her thirties appeared. She seemed cheery, with unkempt shoulder-length blonde hair and a red business suit.

"Please come with me," she announced in a suitably large voice.

We took the lift up one floor, along a corridor tiled in intricate patterns, through a heavy dark wood door into a small room which contained two comfortable chairs with a small dark wood table between them. I guessed this was normally used for select clients.

"M. Albert will be along in a minute or two," boomed the young woman and departed.

Within less than a minute, M. Albert appeared. He was of average height and build, but with a very bony face, which he'd attempted to disguise with a beard. His hair was light brown and thinning. His eyes were brown, his age fiftyish and his clothes what you'd expect of a banker.

"Alain Albert, at your service," he began.

"Nicholas Storey. Good day to you. I'm grateful for you agreeing to meet me so quickly."

"When we get a call out of the blue from a part of the Commission we've never heard of, but which seems to be concerned with fiscal fraud, we naturally wish to be as helpful as possible....You mentioned on the telephone that it was a confidential matter?"

"Yes. Thank you. I should explain that I am a National Expert on a two secondment from HM Customs & Excise in London. My wife, who is working with me on this matter, works for the Metropolitan Police, also in London. We had been asked to examine some financial irregularities in one area of the work of the EEC Commission. We had not reached any conclusions about the matter when a member of staff who worked in that area disappeared. She hasn't been seen for about three weeks. She left no messages and has not been in contact with her colleagues or her relatives. We are concerned for her welfare, not least that if she was in any way connected to these irregularities she may have wished to take her own life. So we are searching for any and every contact she was known to have. And we understand that she regularly dined with a friend who claimed to work in the Banque

Indosuez, having until the recent merger worked for the Banque de l'Indochine."

"I see. You are hoping that we may be able to identify this individual so that you can learn whether he has had any contact with the lady who has disappeared?"

"Exactly."

"May I take it that you do not have a name?"

"No. Unfortunately not. All I know is that he is of Vietnamese origin and otherwise appears to have no noticeable characteristics. I realise that is very little to go on...."

"We have but a few staff of Vietnamese origin working here in Brussels. As you might imagine, as Belgian engagement in that region was so small, we had little business there. Of course, our head office in Paris and no doubt several branches in French cities would undoubtedly undertake considerably more business. Indeed, the former Banque de l'Indochine had but a small branch here in Brussels. Most of us here come from the other side of the merger - Banque de Suez et de L'Union des Mines. Several of the staff from the Banque de l'Indochine transferred back to France after the merger, including a couple of Vietnamese staff. It is possible, of course, that the man you have mentioned was one of those."

"I suppose so. But I believe he has been seen with the young woman quite recently."

"You will understand that though we are not a large branch, there are several staff who I do not know....and I certainly do not know the names of all, especially those who joined us from the Banque de l'Indochine. I will ask Mlle te Hoorn to get me a list of staff here."

He picked up the phone and asked the woman at the other end (her voice audible from where I was sitting) for a staff directory. We waited, while he sipped a cup of some herbal tea. The large young woman appeared with a leather folder.

"The Banque de l'Indochine would have had a section dealing with Vietnam. Typically there would be a European manager with a Vietnamese under-manager and clerks….."

He leafed through the folder.

"Ah…here we are manager - Gilbert Verney; Under-manager – Bao Tran; various clerks, among whom are Duong Lac and Minh Pham…The other one is Belgian or possibly French….I believe I've met Bao Tran. If I recall him correctly, he's well into his fifties. A spare man with almost bright grey hair. The other two I have not met. You could see Bao Tran, if you wish? He may well be able to give you the assistance which I, regretfully, cannot."

This wasn't quite what I'd expected. But Bao Tran appeared not to fit the description of the man who had dined with Monique Lefebvre in the "Cochinchine" – nor that of the "little man" who'd visited various firms and banks as part of the fraud. So it seemed to me, if I was careful, I should be able to avoid arousing any suspicions.

"That would be helpful. Thank you."

"If you will, may I suggest you remain here and I will arrange for Bao Tran to join you."

He departed, with evident relief and I waited for a while. I was beginning to get a little surprised that no-one had come in and offered me a coffee or tea, but just as I was beginning to mutter to myself about their inhospitability, a short, silver-haired oriental man entered the room. He was more thickset than the Vietnamese we'd seen in the "Cochinchine", but then he was also quite a lot older.

"Good afternoon. My name is Bao Tran, under-manager. I understand you are seeking a female colleague who has become lost."

I quickly realised that his French was fairly idiosyncratic.

"That is so. My name is Nicholas Storey. I work for the EEC Commission. I am trying to find the whereabouts of a colleague who seems to have disappeared about three weeks ago. She left no note and we have been unable to contact her through friends or relatives. We know that she regularly met a Vietnamese man who said he worked in the Banque Indosuez, previously the Banque de l'Indochine. That is almost all we know about him, though we believe he is likely to be between thirty and forty years of age. When I met M. Albert, he suggested that you would know your colleagues better than him."

Bao Tran gave me a strange look – one of servility mixed with suspicion and a dash of hostility.

"If the woman has disappeared, perhaps it was by her own choice. If she does not wish to be discovered, perhaps that is a decision for her?"

"As she is paid by the EEC Commission, she is expected to carry out her work for them and comply with the rules set down for employees. I am sure you have something similar at the bank here. In any case, she was not the sort of person who would break the rules in this way. So that is why we are concerned about her. Even if one of your colleagues does meet her occasionally for dinner, I realise that does not lead to the conclusion that he must know where she is. Indeed, as she is of mixed parentage, Vietnamese and French, it is possible that she only meets with this man to practice her use of the Vietnamese language."

He was silent, continuing to regard me with what I can only describe as a mixture of servility and distaste.

"Might I ask whether there is some problem with my request?"

"What exactly is the nature of your request?"

"I merely wish to know whether either of your colleagues….Duong Lac or Minh Pham….have met a young woman called Monique Lefebvre, whose mother's name was Nguyen…and if they know anything about her whereabouts, they would be prepared to tell me."

"They may prefer to say nothing."

"That would be their right. This is solely a matter where Mlle Lefebvre's colleagues are concerned about her welfare. It is not a legal matter or one where the police are involved….though as I am sure you will understand, her disappearance has been reported to the police."

"I will talk to my colleagues and see whether they are prepared to say anything to you."

He too vanished. I wondered whether he'd return. I was also puzzled by his attitude. Did that mean he knew a lot more about Monique Lefebvre's disappearance than he'd ever let on? Or as I was someone plainly not French, did he think I was an American? But would a Viet-Cong sympathiser really have worked evidently for many years in a colonialist, capitalist bank? But he could be an undercover agent, I supposed. Or was it merely the common resentment held by members of a small community when someone from outside was trying to poke his nose in?

I waited for about twenty minutes. I was beginning to wonder whether someone would appear and tell me that I'd be meeting no-one else that afternoon, when Bao Tran returned, with two younger men, who he introduced as Duong Lac and Minh Pham. Of course, it could've been vice versa and I'd've been none the wiser. Both were short, spare, with short black hair, small heads and thin, quite bony faces. Duong Lac was in his later thirties, I guessed, while Minh Pham was perhaps five years younger. Duong Lac wore small wire-rimmed glasses. Both greeted me with servile, insincere smiles – the sort I recalled from the locals who I met when I was doing my National Service in Kenya.

"I have explained what you told me," said Bao Tran.

"I believe we have both met Mlle Lefebvre," continued Duong Lac. "You will understand that the Vietnamese community in this city is small. Someone like Mlle Lefebvre, who wished to maintain her command of our native language, would seek people to assist her within our community."

He spoke French well – better than I did.

"She would perhaps seek at the embassy, the Banque de l'Indochine or maybe a restaurant habituated by members of our community," added Minh Pham, in rather more accented French.

"From time to time, the embassy or the bank would arrange an event for the community – usually a meal or perhaps a film showing," Duong Lac went on. "We would've met Mlle Lefebvre at one of these events. It'd be some years ago, so I cannot recall which. I agreed to meet her for dinner from time to time to converse with her in our native language. Naturally, after the 'Cochinchine' opened, it was an appropriate place for us to meet."

"I met her for the same reason at a small restaurant called 'La vieille porte verte', not far from where she lived. It was on my way home....I live out by the Chaussée de Neerstalle....She said that her father had disapproved of his wife and daughter speaking Vietnamese once they returned to France and, of course, there was no possibility for her to be taught the language at her schools, so she felt she required quite a lot of practice," said Minh Pham.

"How long have you been having these conversations?" I asked.

"Four or five years, I suppose," replied Duong Lac. "But that doesn't mean either of us knew Mlle Lefebvre well. She was a very private individual. Never spoke about her life – other than to explain about her mother in Paris and her upbringing. We would talk about the news or perhaps the cultural life of Brussels when we met...in Vietnamese, of course...."

"Or about the food, or the difficulties of getting to work when the trams are delayed," added Minh Pham.

"But I fear we know no more than you do about her disappearance," continued Duong Lac.

"So how did you realise she was missing?" I asked.

"We always met on the second Saturday of the month," explained Duong Lac. "I went to the 'Cochinchine' as usual, only to discover she wasn't there. She has no telephone in her apartment and she told me she cannot accept telephone calls at work. So I called on the concierge, who told me that she was away, but hadn't left word where she was or when she was coming back…..Evidently, my next date for our dinner has not arrived yet."

"When I met her for dinner was less regular," said Minh Pham. "She would telephone me. I expect it must have been from a telephone box and we would make an arrangement to meet. As she had not telephoned me, I had not noticed her missing. But my colleague told me that she appeared to have gone away for a while, so it was possible I might not anticipate a telephone call for a while."

"Do you have any idea where she might have gone? Does it seem strange to you that she should just go off in this way?"

"As she spoke so little about her life, I have no thoughts as to where she might have gone," replied Duong Lac. "I suppose I'd assumed she'd gone to visit her mother, who was perhaps sick and required her daughter with her full time. I agree it'd be somewhat out of character for her to do such a thing without informing anyone, but I suppose a message might've gone astray, but she believes it will've been received by those for whom it was intended."

"From what we've learnt, she isn't staying with her mother. So we are at a loss……I realise that she was reticent about her private life, but do you think there might have been any reason why she might have decided to kill herself?" I asked.

"I should certainly say that'd seem unlikely," replied Duong Lac hurriedly, giving me an irritated look. "Mlle Lefebvre was a good Catholic and would assuredly never do such a thing."

"I'm relieved to hear that. It was something that has been worrying her colleagues. I suppose you don't know where she worshipped, do you?"

"No. I would imagine in the church of her quarter."

I decided I'd asked enough and was beginning to risk them becoming considerably more suspicious of me than they were already. So I thanked them and, having located Mlle te Hoorn, made my way out of the bank, with many thanks and apologies for having taken up their time.

Though I could reasonably have gone straight home, I returned to the SEFF offices and remained there apparently looking at papers, but actually thinking in a disorganised way. If nothing else, I hoped this would discourage the person who I felt had been following me on the tram from the Bourse stop to the rue de la Loi from shadowing me all the way home.

10. A PUSHME-PULLYOU RELATIONSHIP

However, when I mentioned it to Rosemary later that evening, I had to confess that it was no more than a feeling, possibly brought on by the somewhat creepy nature of the three Vietnamese bankers I'd just met. Certainly I had no certainty they were telling me the truth, however plausible their accounts. There was an equivocal undertone to what they said and a shiftiness behind the servile courtesy. How much of that I was reading into the normal reserve of a small and probably embattled community towards outsiders, I found it hard to tell. Similarly, I couldn't definitely say that a small man had followed me on to the tram, keeping me in his sight without me being able to see him properly, staying on the tram after I got off. But it would've been apparent that I'd got off at my place of work, not my home. But I hadn't had the same feeling on my tram journey back to Woluwe St Lambert. So it was more than likely I'd just imagined it.

In any case, was there really any reason to suppose there was a Vietnamese connection to this fraud? The only link was Mlle Lefebvre and a slight possibility that the "little man" who'd visited the firms and banks caught up in the fraud was "oriental". If the fraud was planned in DGVI, which seemed most likely considering the knowledge required to carry it out, the only person who could've done it would've been Monique Lefebvre, who seemed a distinctly unlikely candidate for that role. It was more likely that the Vietnamese didn't really believe my story and wanted to check whether I wasn't from the police or security services checking up on potential Viet Cong sympathisers or undercover agents. It was conceivable that one or more of them was, of course. But that was other people's concern, not mine....and if I had been followed and had been seen to get off at the rue de la Loi tram stop, perhaps that'd been sufficient for them to believe what I'd told them.

But whatever we felt about Monique Lefebvre's possible involvement in the fraud, it did seem worth following up where she might - as a "good Catholic" – go to church in her neighbourhood. In the event, this turned out to be simpler than we expected. There seemed to be only one church in the neighbourhood – the Église St Pierre, within easy walking distance from her apartment. As it seemed almost too obvious, I wondered whether there might not be a church elsewhere in Brussels where Vietnamese Catholics might worship together. But I had no way of finding that out. Rosemary suggested that she went over to Uccle the following morning to speak to whoever she could at the church. I encouraged her to wear trousers or a rather longer skirt than usual if she wished any priest to take her seriously. In her usual mini-skirt, she might look like an unwelcome temptation!

The following morning, I continued to phone firms that hadn't been used for the fraud. Having done a German one, I decided to try a French one next. Cie ACT, based in Roubaix, were due to receive around £3 million of funds from DGVI. After the usual faffing about, I was put through to the company secretary, Hervé Colombe. I explained the circumstances of my call in the same terms as I had to Hans-Georg Rausch the previous day – though rather less confidently and in less grammatically-correct French.

"Naturally, we normally deal with Patrick Ploucanet in the Ministère de l'Industrie in Paris," he explained. "They supported our application strongly – no doubt because Guy Jacq, the mayor of Roubaix, is also the Ministre de L'Emploi. We received a couple of letters from a Philippe Wouters in the EEC Commission, which we referred to Ploucanet, who responded on our behalf. These were requests for information which we had already shared as part of our application, so the request seemed superfluous to us. Perhaps it was some form of checking. But that was the sole contact between us and the EEC Commission."

That didn't surprise me. If Cie ACT were in the habit of referring Commission requests to an official in Paris, those involved in the fraud would assume that if they suggested a visit, there was a fair chance that Ploucanet or a colleague would also be there. I could only assume that French, German and Belgian officials must've met several of the people working in DGVI at some stage, so they might reasonably be expected to recognise the real Philippe Wouters and know when someone else was impersonating him. So I thanked M. Colombe and rang off. I wondered how Wouters had responded to letters from Ploucanet referring to letters he hadn't sent? It seemed to me that the time was approaching when he'd be worth interviewing.

I tried Acier DeBruine et Cie of Sambreville, speaking to M. Guillaume Laspeyre, who was the commercial relations director, which apparently also included dealing with the Belgian Ministère de Commerce et Manufactures. As with the other companies I'd spoken to, he dealt normally with his national authorities – in his case a man called Piet Haan, whose name I recognised from several documents I'd seen. He had also spoken on the phone to Louis Chastelin from the Commission.

"We discussed our application in a manner which surprised me a little," explained Laspeyre, "as it seemed to replicate what we'd already submitted. When I mentioned this, he said that his managers were keen that a certain proportion of applications should be double-checked. I told him that I'd been at school with Philippe Wouters in his office and if it was him being so pernickety, he'd certainly changed a lot over the years. The conversation didn't last for more than a few minutes after that."

A pattern of sorts was emerging. But it was entirely due to the potential risk of someone visiting the company impersonating Wouters or Chastelin and being found out, rather than the nature of the business or the transactions. At this point it also struck me that we'd never asked the first companies we visited whether

169

they'd had any official from the Commission visiting them or contacting them before a visit. We'd got that from the later ones, but we'd never asked Cie CCR, CW & Cie or Charbonniers de Courcelles. So I phoned them up a confirmed that all three had received visits from a M. Louis Chastelin, following a preliminary phone call, whose description was one I was already familiar with and whose punctilious behaviour, bordering on nosiness, surprised me not at all.

A couple more phone calls to other companies not used for the fraud revealed similar risks to those I'd identified at Vondern Kohlenbergbau AG, Cie ACT and Acier DeBruine et Cie earlier. Whoever had planned this fraud was meticulous and cautious. I felt more than ever that he or she would not leave a trail that could possibly lead to him or her. While suspicions would be directed at DGVI because of the nature of the fraud, as it was gradually revealed, they could go no further than that. Which also suggested to me that the disappearance of Mlle Lefebvre was almost certainly entirely unconnected or just possibly a false trail intended to waste the authorities' time, but lead nowhere. Which led to the unpleasant possibility that Mlle Lefebvre might well have been murdered and her body disposed of in a way that would ensure it was never found. Assuming she wasn't involved in the fraud and knew nothing about it, it seemed an extremely cold-hearted way of treating a colleague. But someone as meticulous and cautious as this might well also be ruthless....But perhaps I shouldn't rule Mlle Lefebvre out as the mastermind, despite all the indications to the contrary?

Rosemary's morning was less productive. She found the church, apparently an old one but rebuilt in the eighteenth century

"It's quite a fine church," she observed, "but nothing terribly special....at least as far as I'm concerned.....But I'm not sure about your advice about wearing trousers....There were a couple of clergymen there, both of whom gave me very old-fashioned looks.....I don't know what they thought I was...and I'm not going to guess…But they looked uncomfortable talking to me and weren't particularly friendly either….."

"I suppose you'd expect me to say that the ideals of Christianity are often not lived up to by its representatives….."

"The opium of the people, of course……But if I'd been offering them opium, I could scarcely have been worse received……I did my explanation about a missing colleague who we believed attended their church. They pointed out that they regularly had several hundred worshippers and tended not to know each one well. I explained that the missing woman was half-Vietnamese, so she might be a little more distinctive than their average parishioner…and as a good catholic, presumably she'd also make her confession fairly regularly. They hummed and hawed and generally muttered about the secrets of the confessional. I reminded them that I wasn't interested in what she said to them in her confessions. I was just trying to find out the whereabouts of a missing colleague, if I could. As she'd been missing for more than three weeks and nothing had been heard of her, her colleagues were becoming worried….

'The police have presumably been told?' remarked the older, thinner priest, a man with small, pale blue eyes.

'Yes,' I replied. 'But they seem to have found out nothing.'

'I believe I know the woman you mention,' said the younger priest. He was plump and rather owl-like, with old-fashioned round rimless spectacles. 'She is a regular almost every Sunday for early morning Mass – unless she is visiting her mother in Paris or is away. She makes confession every month. You would not expect me to say more. I realise with confusion and regret that I hadn't remarked on her absence. I tell myself that I imagined she must be on holiday or perhaps her mother in Paris was unwell. But I fear I know nothing more about her. I do not even know her name or where she lives – other than it seems likely that she lives in this quarter.'

'Does she always attend church on her own?'

'Invariably. To my mind, she was a person who was on her own.'

"At that, the older priest gave a very visible frown, almost tut-tutting. The younger priest looked embarrassed. I realised I'd get no more out of them – even if there was anything, which I doubted. So I thanked them and left."

"I suppose they'd get to know a little about her from her confessions – like her mother in Paris, for instance," I suggested. "You didn't get the impression that they were holding anything important back?"

"No. I reckon Uccle is quite a large parish and unless their parishioners force themselves on their attention, they're all the same sheep that go past them every Sunday. Even though Monique Lefebvre looked a bit different, unless she did something or demanded attention – which seems completely out of character – she was just an unnamed member of their flock."

"Oh well, it was worth a try, I suppose…."

"….and pushed my French to the limit!"

I explained what I'd got from my phone calls and my further thoughts.

"If this was a fraud organised by these Vietnamese and, as you say, carried out so meticulously and cautiously, why did they use someone who might be recognised as Vietnamese…or certainly oriental…as the man who was the only public face of the fraudsters?" remarked Rosemary. "You'd think if they wanted the trail to lead away from them, they'd use someone less distinctively like them."

"Unless this was a purely Vietnamese operation – and they don't trust anyone else. I agree, a Westerner would stand out less, but they'd have to trust him and either pay him oodles of money or promise him tons of cash and then make him disappear. I don't think they'd want to do that."

"So on that basis, Monique Lefebvre provides the information and documents as necessary to her fellow-countrymen. Is she the mastermind? Perhaps she is – and is very good at concealing a

172

devious criminal mind? Or perhaps one of her fellow-countrymen is the mastermind and when she describes in passing how open the DGVI arrangements are to being defrauded, he devises this plan. She can easily lay her hands on the right documents and names, she knows the processes…"

"So why does she disappear? Doesn't that risk the finger being pointed in her direction?"

"Yes. But either she's been disposed of somewhere no-one is going to find her for ages. Or she's hopped it with the loot and is now somewhere safe…perhaps even Vietnam. Indeed, perhaps she was recruited by North Vietnam years ago and the money isn't going to line her nest, but to provide funds for whoever replaced the late Ho Chi Minh?"

"Presumably that'd suggest that the man these firms and bankers met has also scarpered, disappearing without trace…."

"You seem disappointed….."

"Well, if that's what's happened, we'll be able to tell Vermeulen exactly how the fraud was committed and our suspicions about Monique Lefebvre and her accomplice, but basically we'll've drawn a blank."

"But they were a long way ahead of us…and we've only had a few weeks. I reckon this was several years in the planning."

"And I was going to invite a couple of the people we've met to have a meal in the 'Cochinchine' to see whether they could identify any of the waiters there as the man who visited them. I'd even though of positioning them outside the Banque Indosuez to see whether Duong Lac or Minh Pham fitted the bill…I certainly wish I could find out a bit more about them…There was something about Duong Lac in particular….."

"Why don't you contact your friends in the Security Service here? They owe you the odd favour, after all."

"I bet it doesn't work like that. But it's worth a try…..and even if we are in the office, I'm going to give you a big kiss…"

"But we should also remember that if the person who thought this fraud up is as clever as you think he or she is, getting

Monique Lefebvre to disappear and using someone who looked like a Vietnamese for the only part of this operation which involves anyone being seen could be a clever ploy to send anyone investigating the fraud in completely the wrong direction….and that gun left in her apartment looks very odd to me, if that wasn't the intention."

The Security Service man in Brussels – working in NATO rather than the EEC – had been called "David Watson", the last time I'd been in touch with them over Soviet heroin smuggling. I also remembered a colleague – "Callum MacIntosh" – who made me think of a monk dwelling in a monastery on the Scottish borders. I tried to contact them as I had before, but was told that "Watson" had moved on and that "MacIntosh" was out of town. A secretary with a very posh accent took my phone number and said someone would ring back. About an hour later I got a call from someone calling himself "Simon Stone", who suggested that we met for coffee in a little café just off the rue de la Loi.

"Simon Stone" was in his mid-twenties, blond-haired, with a long face and unsettling pale blue eyes. He spoke with a strong public school accent, with something of the army officer in it. I wondered whether he'd done a short service commission and gone into the Security Service from there. He ordered a cappuccino. I decided to have tea – even though it'd probably be something poncey like Earl Grey.

"You wanted to see someone from our office?" he began.

"I've dealt previously with a couple of your colleagues about some Soviet heroin smuggling. Were you aware of that?"

"Yes. I assume your wish to meet has nothing to do with that?"

"Quite so. My wife and I have been asked by the Secretary of the Commission, Jérôme Vermeulen, to investigate a fraud amount to around £8 million in one area of the Commission. I can fill you in on the details if you wish, but…."

"I'd be grateful if you would."

So I did.

174

"So you have a missing woman who's half-Vietnamese and a little man who may or may not be oriental fronting up the fraud. Is there any particular interest here for us?"

"There may not be. But as I've mentioned, Mlle Lefebvre had a couple of Vietnamese connections, which may or may not be innocent. Her disappearance may be unconnected with the fraud or with any Vietnamese she met. But hanging in her cupboard was a Chinese manufactured pistol with about fifty rounds. It was utterly and completely out of place, but either she didn't expect anyone to find it – which suggests she didn't disappear of her own free will – or someone placed it there after she left, presumably for a reason….though at the moment I can't fathom what that reason might be. But it does suggest a link between Mlle Lefebvre and a more violent world. We've also been asking ourselves whether among Vietnamese employees of a bank like Banque Indosuez, especially in its former incarnation as the Banque de l'Indochine, there wouldn't be some agents of the North Vietnamese? How would a pistol made in Communist China end up in the cupboard of a half-Vietnamese Commission official, who supposedly makes quite long visits to relatives in Australia, about which we have no evidence? I'm not saying that there's anything more to it than a series of coincidences; and the information we have could support several more innocent circumstances, I realise. But I wondered whether you or your people knew anything about these Vietnamese we've met and, if so, whether you'd be prepared to share any information with us? Or whether it'd be worth a little bit of your time doing some checking?"

"As I imagine you'd expect, I can't give a response today. I've got down the names of the men in the bank and you've give me the names of the two restaurants where there may also be Vietnamese employed. All I can say to you today is that what you ask will certainly be considered and we know how to get back to you."

"Thank you."

I hadn't expected any more. Indeed, I suspected that "Simon Stone" and his predecessor "David Watson" were essentially legmen for the people like "Callum MacIntosh", who were the ones who took the decisions. I had to hope that I still had sufficient credit with them for them to be prepared to share some gen or perhaps do a bit of checking. If these Vietnamese in the Banque Indosuez hadn't come to their notice already, perhaps they were worth a look anyway?

Moreover, I didn't anticipate that "Simon Stone" would get back to me particularly quickly. But I felt I'd give him a few days, including the weekend, before trying to chase him up. I had made him aware that we were on a short timetable, so I'd rather be told they'd do nothing or knew nothing quickly, rather than get something useful in six weeks' time.

But we'd also got to the point where there were no obvious directions to follow. I wondered whether further phone calls or visits would serve any purpose, but decided that they wouldn't. Instead I wrote to the remaining companies and banks which had been used for the fraud to ask them to tell me about the man who'd visited them from the EEC Commission. I also wrote to the similar firms we'd identified who hadn't been involved, asking for a brief description of any contacts they'd had with the EEC Commission during their applications for EEC funds. The reasons for these enquiries were plausible and told no lies, even if they concealed the whole truth. It was, I told myself, a vain hope that somewhere the person who'd devised this fraud had slipped up. But from what we'd seen so far, that seemed highly unlikely.

But in any case, I felt I was getting too close to being unable to see the wood for the trees. I needed some time thinking about different things. With luck, that might allow my mind to sort out the mass of information about this case and come up with something that made sense – or at least suggested new paths we might follow.

However, my wish to leave these issues alone for a day or two was confounded by a summons from Robin Southern the following morning.

"I wonder what he's going to moan about this time?" I remarked, as Rosemary and I made our way over to the Berlaymont building.

"Perhaps it's plus ça change plus c'est la même chose," replied Rosemary, with a smirk. (I tended to tease her about her French from time to time and she took suitable opportunities to respond).

At any rate, we didn't have long to wait. We were shown into Southern's office almost as soon as we'd arrived. He looked more relaxed than the previous time we'd met him….and to give him his due, he never once cast a glance at Rosemary's legs.

"I believe I now know what you two are up to," he began. "And I'm not asking you to confirm or deny anything. I've been getting a bit of background on you two and I now appreciate that if you've been given a piece of work to do by someone, you'll do what you're asked to do, perhaps in unorthodox ways, but in ways that appear to achieve results. As I don't propose to go cap in hand to Jérôme Vermeulen, I realise there are several questions which you won't be prepared to answer. I take it that remains the case?"

I nodded.

"Then so be it……I'm led to believe that there has been a fraud involving not far short of £10 million carried out through businesses in receipt of funds from my DG. You don't need to confirm or deny this….and I can assure you that I have kept this knowledge confidential….though you should be aware that staff in my DG are under no illusion that the DG isn't being investigated in some way or another. I also understand that it seems likely that the fraud was either planned in my DG or a member of staff provided information about how the fraud could be carried out, along with copies of the various documents required. I'm making an educated guess here – but if the fraud was discovered when Vermeulen's people did their annual audit, we're looking at the frauds being executed in 1974 with the planning and other preparatory work taking place the previous year. I trust you realise that this cuts out several members of staff of my DG, including me, from any involvement?"

"Certainly," I replied.

"But I guess you are still left with over forty possible suspects, along with as many as a dozen who've left in the last couple of years….and presumably even more who departed before that….."

"As someone would've needed to get hold of the relevant documents during the latter part of 1973 and during 1974," Rosemary explained, "We believe you could safely cut out anyone who left before September 1973. The only exception to that would be if the person who planned this left DGVI before the fraud got under way and had an accomplice who remained – and possibly still remains – in DGVI."

"In any case, which you may well not have known about, the audit system changed in 1973. Prior to that year, there had been a quarterly reconciliation, which should've identified such frauds faster and certainly reduced the amount that could be stolen in that way. But in order to save money, the Commission Secretariat altered the system to an annual reconciliation. Though it might seem risky, I'm reliably informed that no fraud had ever been detected under the previous arrangements…."

"Possibly because they made frauds of this nature more difficult to perpetrate. It's a bit like saying we didn't let any goals in during the first half, so we don't need a goalkeeper in the second half."

(I wondered whether my infrequent references to football and Charlton Athletic had rubbed off on Rosemary…or perhaps she was just thinking of her hockey-playing past).

"Did this change of procedure apply only to DGVI or did it cover every DG that spends EEC money?" I asked.

"As far as I'm aware, it applied to all," replied Southern.

"Presumably DGVI isn't the largest spender of EEC money?"

"Not at all. We're dwarfed by the CAP spending….and almost certainly the CFP too."

"Yet, as far as we know, the fraud has only occurred with DGVI money."

"I believe we can safely say that someone who has either worked in my DG or who can get information from someone in my DG has executed this fraud…..I hope you understand that I'm as keen as you are to identify who that is. This is bound to get out sooner or later. If no-one gets caught, the finger of suspicion will continue to be pointed at the whole of my DG. Anyone who could've been involved will be suspected and will realise that they are under suspicion. In most cases they'll have no way of proving their innocence. So we shall have a dysfunctional organisation, with colleagues suspecting and blaming each other. I shan't know whether one of my senior managers might not have been involved. It isn't conducive to good management or an effective organisation. Indeed, if no-one is identified, I'll recommend to Commissioner Chevrou de Polignac that the whole DG should be disbanded, with the staff moving to other parts of the Commission and new staff brought in from elsewhere. It won't solve the problem, but it'll make DGVI a more harmonious and effective organisation for the future."

"From what we've seen, the fraud was extremely carefully planned and whoever was involved has covered their tracks effectively," Rosemary explained. "The only thing that looks odd is the disappearance of Monique Lefebvre, though it's always possible it isn't connected at all."

"As you may imagine, I've been thinking about that. I barely know Mlle Lefebvre, who is evidently a quiet and retiring sort of person. Her line managers are Heinz Groener and her Director, Joop van Nieukerk. Neither can offer any reason why she might've disappeared. Indeed, I doubt whether van Nieukerk encounters her more than once or twice a year. Groener appears to regard her as hard-working, competent, but otherwise of no interest whatsoever. Apparently she joined the Commission direct, so she has no advocates from the French administration – as, for instance, press constantly for the advancement of another of my Directors, Pierre-Henri Dumoulin, whose competence, in my view, equates roughly to that of a bog-standard fast-stream Principal. I had no reason to come into contact with her. Indeed, I'm not certain if you put her in a line-up of similar looking women I could even pick her out. My impression is that she was barely noticed by any of her colleagues…"

"We've been told that she'd been teased about being an undercover agent for the Viet Cong and one former member of DGVI, Piet Korthuizen hit the man doing the teasing, Gérard Creac'h, another former DGVI employee….."

"I'd heard that too. I believe it occurred not long after I arrived here. For what it's worth, my impression was that Korthuizen was regarded as something of a bully and may have taken the opportunity of some fairly gentle teasing to impose himself on one of his weaker rivals in the office. If I'd known about it, I'd've had him disciplined. I don't condone violence in the office….or anywhere else for that matter. If people have problems with each other, there are plenty of procedures…Indeed, the Commission is awash with procedures for making complaints, appealing issues, etc, etc…And as far as I'm aware, it was an isolated incident."

"Do you think it might be why Creac'h decided to leave?"

"I doubt it. From what I know of him, he's greedy, ambitious and crafty….Oddly enough, he was once referred to me as Vermeulen's nark in DGVI. It struck me as unlikely. Why would a Belgian Commission apparatchik like Vermeulen use a Breton Frenchman as his stool pigeon? We've got plenty of Belgian Commission lifers who'd be more suitable…….I should explain why Vermeulen and I don't get on. He was in the Commission team during the UK Accession negotiations in the early days in 1971. I was in the DTI team. It was clear to me that Vermeulen wasn't acting on behalf of the Commission, but the Kingdom of

Belgium. Basically they didn't want the UK to start creaming off funds going to decrepit Belgian industries. At some point I, undiplomatically and probably unwisely, made a point about that. There was a bit of a furore which ended with both of us being removed from our respective teams. Ironically, he got promoted to his present position almost immediately afterwards and I ended up as a DG here a couple of years later….by no means the UK's first choice portfolio, of course….So when I learnt from Emil de Kock that you'd been sniffing round certain companies and banks in Charleroi about an alleged fraud and that it was thought you were working under Vermeulen's orders, I'm afraid I put two and two together and made five…..But I bumped into Martin Finlay at some do or other and muttered about what was going on. I doubt whether Martin has much time for me, but he did mention a few things that suggested that even if Vermeulen had set you off on this affair, you'd follow it where you felt it needed to go and certainly weren't being used to set me up in some way."

This was probably the closest we were going to get for an apology for what'd happened the previous time we met. It seemed best to let it pass in silence.

"Mlle Lefebvre's disappearance is a puzzle," he continued. "From what I've learnt and from what I imagine you've found out, the only link between her and these frauds is that she worked in DGVI and has now vanished. But if there was no evidence linking her to the frauds, why did she need to disappear, as it must surely result in drawing attention to the likelihood that she was involved? Unless she has an extremely secure bolt-hole, she must reckon that the authorities will be on the look-out for her. Whereas if she just remained in post, no-one would be the wiser. If, for example, one of her colleagues had seen her taking away or photocopying papers she wasn't supposed to have, that'd be a different matter. But when line managers asked her colleagues for any information that might be relevant to her disappearance, nothing of that sort emerged. So I conclude that either her disappearance is unconnected, possibly a deliberate blind alley, or most likely in my view is that she was doing this on behalf of the North Vietnamese government and that she is probably safely in Hanoi by now."

"But leaving one or two people potentially exposed here," observed Rosemary. "Whoever organised this fraud had at least one accomplice, who might easily need to remain here. From what we've seen, the Vietnamese community here is very small and if any of them were involved as the accomplice, they might well be identified. It's possible that the accomplice was none of them, of course. But as far as we know, none of the ones we've come across has skipped town…."

"Though it's possible they finished their part in this six months ago or more and could've been in North Vietnam ever since then," I commented.

"Which would be very convenient for Vermeulen, of course," remarked Southern. "The whole affair could be put down to incompetence in DGVI. Without anyone to bring to justice for the actual crime, there'd still have to be a scapegoat – and you're looking at him."

"Surely you could remind those concerned that it was the changes made by the Commission Secretariat in moving to an annual reconciliation exercise that made this fraud possible….and certainly made as big as it is?" Rosemary said.

"In theory….But Vermeulen is the one with the inside track here…."

"But there might be a possibility of seeing whether the North Vietnamese theory is correct," I suggested. "Rosemary has been doing a lot of work chasing Soviet money through various Swiss and other banks. They've been fairly cooperative because it's drugs money and because it's been carried out by Soviet agents. I wonder whether we couldn't put similar pressure on the Banque Luxembourgeois about money they've been handling which appears to be headed for North Vietnam. Plainly, they weren't the final link in the chain, but if we could get a bit further down the line, I wonder whether it'd be possible to find out whether where we got to had links with the North Vietnamese or other Communist regimes?"

"I guess it'd be worth a try. I might be able to get something through Interpol about which banks the North Vietnamese are known to use…and I can probably disguise this among the Russian stuff I'm doing anyway," replied Rosemary.

"Is there anything I should be doing?" asked Southern.

"All I can suggest is keep your ear to the ground," I replied. "It's possible something unusual might happen or some rumours get around, for instance about Mlle Lefebvre's disappearance."

We left on considerably better terms than we'd expected.

"It was good of Martin to put Southern straight about us when he had the opportunity," remarked Rosemary as we headed back to the SEFF offices. "He seemed to be genuinely keen to help."

"To be cynical, it's his head on the chopping block when all this gets out and I suppose he needs as many friends as he can get….and needs to know as much as possible about what's going on. But as I can't for the life of me see how he could've been involved, I felt we could trust him a certain amount….and you don't get to his level in the Civil Service without being pretty bright….Are you happy to chase up the Banque Luxembourgeois stuff? I'm sorry I rather dropped you in it, but it just came to me as we were talking."

"It's not a problem. It's possible I won't get very far, so I hope no-one is going to build up too many hopes on it."

"No….and you might not get too far without something from my Security Service contacts – and whether they'd be prepared to give us anything in relation to this matter I don't know."

"They certainly owe you….us…for getting that unpleasant man, Yeremeyev."

"My impression with blokes like that is that their gratitude doesn't last long….But there is something that we might be able to do a bit more about…."

"Why the reconciliations were changed from every quarter to annually? That struck me as a bit odd."

"I wonder why it was necessary? I've never come across any pressures from anyone in the Commission to reduce costs, so that reason doesn't look awfully credible to me. It's possible there was some short-lived economy drive, perhaps before all the British, Irish and Danes started to demand places working there. But if it came out of the blue, I'd begin to wonder whether someone hadn't spotted an opportunity for a large fraud with a change that must've seemed quite innocent."

"But not something to ask Vermeulen."

"Definitely not. I don't know whether he would've had a hand in it. But it's his patch and with all this antagonism between him and Southern, I'd quite like to keep clear of him."

Unfortunately my wish wasn't to be granted. The following morning we were both summoned to Vermeulen's office. Evidently his "nark" in DGVI had spotted us meeting Southern and had reported back. Unsurprisingly, we weren't kept waiting in his outer office for more than a couple of minutes.

"I'm led to believe that you've met Southern again," he began, his eyes fixed on Rosemary's legs as usual.

"He asked to see us," I replied. "There seemed no reason not to do so, especially as it was always possible he might have some information, for instance in relation to Mlle Lefebvre's disappearance."

"And did he….have any useful information?"

"Not much. My impression was that he wished to apologise in a rather roundabout way for the way he treated us the last time we met….As far as he's concerned, the planning of this fraud took place before he was placed in charge of DGVI, so it's possible he might not even know who was doing it. We speculated a bit about Mlle Lefebvre, but not very profitably."

"In what manner?"

"That she might be linked in some way to the North Vietnamese. But if so, both she and any accomplices are likely to be safely beyond our reach by now…and presumably it was planned that way…..."

"So that's your conclusion?"

"No. At present there's no evidence to support it. It's an interesting theory – and might even be true – but that's all it is. We still have no evidence that Mlle Lefebvre was involved in the fraud….and by the same token, we've no evidence that she wasn't."

"So where exactly have you got to?"

"We know how the fraud was carried out. We know why certain companies were selected rather than others. We have a description of the man who visited the companies and banks involved. It's also plain that whoever planned the fraud either worked in DGVI or had an accomplice there giving him or her information and getting hold of documents which would be needed to carry out the fraud. Beyond that, we have no evidence linking any individual working in DGVI at the appropriate times more than any other individual in the same position," Rosemary explained.

"So what are your prospects for going further?"

"I'd say our chances of identifying who did it are less than 10%," I replied. "This fraud was carefully planned and carried out sufficiently well in advance of its discovery for those involved to have covered their tracks. The person who planned it strikes us as meticulous and cautious. For instance, plainly firms receiving a particular level of DGVI payment were chosen. But each one seems to have been contacted in advance and where there any risk that one might cause any problems, it was dropped. So I'd expect that when documents in DGVI were needed – photocopied, of course – it would've been carefully organised so no-one knew."

"Well, I suppose all you can do is what you can do in the rest of the time available."

With that, we were dismissed.

"It'd be nice if we could avoid being in the middle of this pushme-pullyou relationship between Vermeulen and Southern," remarked Rosemary.

"But it has given us a few possible areas to look at more closely," I replied.

11. "THE GOLDEN FLEECE"

"And what do you mean by that?" demanded Rosemary.

"As I was speaking it struck me, we've never tried to work out how these documents were copied. Assuming it was done in a way that no-one else in the office noticed, that might suggest times of day when other people weren't around. Then if we know roughly when these documents might've been copied, we might be able to be a bit of checking on who was in very early and who stayed late…especially if it wasn't what they normally did."

"I'm not sure how we'd be able to do that. Not least because the two people foisted on us as our contacts both seem to have lied to us….or at least been a lot less helpful than they could've been….and could just as easily been involved in the fraud as anyone else."

"I need to think about that…..But Knud has been around long enough to tell us about the change in the reconciliation procedures…or at least whether there was an economy drive going then and who was around in the Commission Secretariat, assuming the change was really promulgated from there."

"Well, you have a word with him….I'd better start chasing up the Banque Luxembourgeois."

Knud Henriksen wasn't available until the afternoon. I explained why I wanted to speak to him.

"It sounds a bit as though you may be going round and round in circles. But I guess you know your business better than I do," he commented. "As you know, I was one of the officials from the Accession countries who were brought into the Commission in the middle of '72 to give us experience of what working in the Commission was like. I assume they didn't want hordes of Danes, British and Irish all arriving in '73 wanting to run the Commission in the way they did at home. Because we weren't allowed anywhere near any area subject to Accession negotiations, I was seconded to work on trade agreements with the Maghreb, a subject I was passionately uninterested in. But I did learn how things were done round here….and formed a strong desire to change them….which is probably why I ended up in SEFF, rather than anywhere else….and no doubt why they are happy to see me disappearing back to København….But to answer your question – I certainly recall no economy drive in '72 or '73. Indeed, if there had been one, I'd've fallen over in complete surprise! I can't say I noticed any edict to alter these annual reconciliation procedures, but we didn't dole out any EEC money in DGXI, so we wouldn't't've had any interest either."

"That was rather what I felt."

"So you believe it's possible that someone in the Commission Secretariat deliberately changed the reconciliation procedures in order to allow this fraud to happen? It seems a bit far-fetched to me."

"From what we've been able to find out, this fraud could well've been carried out by possibly as few as two people. If you see an opportunity to get away with ten million quid because of what you know about Commission procedures for controlling payments and you have the opportunity to make it easier to commit the fraud and get away with it without leaving any traces, wouldn't you take that opportunity."

"But why go for the relatively small amounts being paid out by DGVI, rather than the much larger payments by the various CAP DGs?"

"The way this fraud was carried out suggests to us that it was run by someone who is cautious and meticulous about the details. He or she would rather lose a bit of money than take the risk of being caught. My guess is that the links between people in receipt of large CAP payments and their national administrations might well be regarded as too close for comfort….I also reckon that though a lot more is spent on the CAP, most of it is paid out in relatively small payments. I reckon that this fraud was never going to involve more than twenty firms, in order to minimise the risks…..After all, there's no point in devising an extremely clever fraud if you get caught…or, so I believe, if you can be identified afterwards."

"So you really need to know who was behind the change in reconciliation procedures in '72."

"I need to know who was around in the Commission Secretariat at that time. I keep getting the feeling that whoever set this thing up does his or her best to work through other people, so they remain as anonymous as possible."

"I guess you know at least one person who was working in the Commission Secretariat then?"

"Jérôme Vermeulen. And I wouldn't mind betting it was his name on the bottom of the internal memo setting out the new reconciliation procedures."

"And a good reason why he needs to find out who did this, otherwise he's likely to come in for some strong criticism for making a change which allowed this fraud to occur."

"Exactly. I'd been wondering why he was so keen for us to identify who carried out the fraud. It's only as we've worked our way through all the stuff that I've begun to realise that."

"One thing the Commission is good at is publishing staff directories every six months or so. You might be able to get hold of ones from '72 in the library in the Berlaymont."

"Would I be able to dig out the memo which changed the reconciliation procedures there somewhere?"

"Probably. They should keep copies of all the internal memos."

I hurried back to the Berlaymont, conscious that I'd got no more than an hour before the library closed. I hoped that the documents I wanted hadn't been transferred over to the archives, as that would mean another journey and greater delay.

Fortunately, the Commission library appeared to keep documents going back about three calendar years, so I was able to get my hands on both a staff directory and the offending memo.

Not to my surprise, the memo had been signed by Jérôme Vermeulen. From glancing through the box file of internal Commission memos one of the librarians had given me, it seemed that anything emanating from the Commission Secretariat was signed by the Secretary to the Commission. However, it confirmed my view as to why he was keen to get some greater clarity about the frauds.

Naturally, Vermeulen's name also appeared in the staff directories in 1972 and 1973. Two other names stood out - Joop van Nieukerk and Heinz Groener, both currently working in DGVI, but members of the Commission Secretariat during 1972, transferring around the time of the British, Danish and Irish Accession in early 1973. They suddenly became considerably more interesting.

Of course, I told Rosemary where I got to when I got home that evening. She hadn't got very far with the Banque Luxembourgeois, but experience had taught her that it took a while to get to the right person.

"Didn't Groener sign some of the documents used in the frauds?" asked Rosemary.

"Yes. And some of the ones that weren't selected…..In a way I'd think that was an argument against him being involved, because I'm sure whoever ran this fraud was determined to leave no trace…But perhaps that wasn't possible…and actually leaving no trace in places where you'd expect to see someone's name might be more risky. So it might seem odder if he didn't sign any of these documents than if he did."

"Besides, assuming he didn't work in DGVI before he worked in the Commission Secretariat, he only knew about the procedures after he went there in 1973. So would he have known enough to have planned the change in the reconciliation procedures before he got there? You reckon this whole fraud was planned well in advance. Doesn't that suggest that whoever was behind the change in procedures must've worked in DGVI or knew someone who worked there pretty well?"

"You're absolutely right! It's a pity the Commission doesn't have anything like the old C&E stud book which gave you some idea of where people had worked previously. And I doubt whether Vermeulen is going to let us crawl all over the personnel files of everyone who was working in the Commission Secretariat in '72 and '73."

"Couldn't you work your way back through the staff directory for a few years. Assuming that the person who planned this fraud worked in DGVI at some stage, would you really expect them to have worked there much before 1970? Assuming you're not intending to work there again, there's a risk that you may have an out-of-date idea of the procedures."

"But don't forget he or she must've had an accomplice working in DGVI during 1973, so perhaps that wouldn't be so much of a risk....But I'm sure it'll be worth me having a look to see if any interesting names crop up....I just hope I don't have to go back too far before 1970."

Of course, even if some names emerged from this work, it didn't prove that any of them would've been involved in planning or carrying out the fraud. It certainly wouldn't constitute evidence....and was insufficient to encourage any but the most querulous to admit to anything. And I was confident that the mastermind was far from querulous.

The following morning I headed for the Commission library again to look over any staff directories they had going back before 1972. As I walked over there, the Chinese pistol hanging in Mlle Lefebvre's cupboard suddenly popped into my mind. At that moment it felt as though the whole theory of North Vietnamese involvement went out of the window. If Mlle Lefebvre was either a North Vietnamese undercover agent or constrained by them in some way, there was no way anyone would leave something as suspicious as a Chinese military pistol so barely concealed that anyone examining her apartment would

191

discover it. And much as I recognised North Vietnamese tenacity, intelligence and cunning, I found it hard to believe that it was some kind of deliberate double bluff. After all, if Mlle Lefebvre and a North Vietnamese agent had carried out the fraud, it seemed to me all the rest of what they'd done was intended to leave no trace. So why on earth would you leave something that would inevitably point towards you? It didn't make sense.

On the other hand, it did fit my idea of the person who planned the fraud being meticulous, careful and extremely cautious. Exactly what'd happened to Mlle Lefebvre remained a mystery. Perhaps she was the person in DGVI who supplied the information and the documents and was now safely beyond the reach of the authorities? Or perhaps – a less pleasant thought – an expendable partner, who'd been "expended" once her value had ceased? And then a false trail pointing at North Vietnamese involvement was a convenient way of answering possible questions. But perhaps her disappearance wouldn't be enough. And though her meeting with the Vietnamese from the Banque Indosuez would eventually emerge, perhaps the mastermind considered that would be insufficient to lay the false trail – and for that, the pistol was required.

It struck me as a rare occasion when the mastermind had, in the immortal phrase of the C&E "blue-bloods", "over-egged the pudding". It was the one thing that didn't fit properly. Moreover, the gun had to be procured from somewhere. I wondered whether the Belgian police had eventually spotted it and done something about it? But how could I find out, without having to explain all the stuff about the fraud which needed to remain confidential? Was this, perhaps not the only occasion, when the mastermind had been too clever by half?

I knew where the Commission archives were – in the rue van Maerlant – from our work on the wine fraud, so I set off there and toiled for several hours through old Commission staff directories. What emerged certainly added to my knowledge and list of potential suspects, but otherwise just seemed to confuse the issue. Pierre-Henri Dumoulin, the Director in DG, whose cause was being promoted by the French to Southern's evident irritation, had been apparently seconded to the Commission Secretariat between 1971 and '72, possibly as part of the Accession negotiations. Korthuizen also worked there in 1970, but seemed to have gone to DGVI the following year. Robert van der Broeken, one of the people singled out by Allenby, was in the Commission Secretariat in 1972-3, but had previously worked in DGVI and went on to work there afterwards. He immediately went to the top of my list, but began to drop down it a bit when I remembered his equivalent grade in the UK Civil Service would be Principal or possible Senior Principal: and I doubted whether someone at that level would have had the clout in the Commission to bring about the change in the reconciliation procedures. The same applied to Roger Dufour, who seemed to have been seconded to the Secretariat for a year in 1972-3 from DGVI. On the other hand, Louis Chastelin, who'd done pretty well the same thing, was one rung higher up the greasy pole. I thought I'd better check with Knud Henriksen my assumption that this was all part of the Accession negotiations. But at least I'd found a few people who seemed to have been in the right places both to have identified how the fraud could be carried out and to engineer the change in the timing of the reconciliation procedures. Finally, I discovered almost by chance that Jérôme Vermeulen had worked in DGVI as one of the Directors before moving across to the Commission Secretariat at the beginning of 1972. I probably should've realised that from what Southern had told Rosemary and me. Perhaps he should be going to the top of my list? But it seemed to me that if he'd been involved, his previous experience in DGVI and signing the memo changing the timing of the reconciliation procedures were traces which I'd always felt the mastermind sought meticulously to avoid.

What I'd really like to find out was how the changes in the reconciliation timings came about, but I couldn't see how I could do that without potentially alerting the man who'd run this fraud......And though I didn't trust Vermeulen, I couldn't quite see why he would've brought Rosemary and me in to investigate a fraud he'd carried out, because the only things he could've heard about us was the successful uncovering of the Soviet heroin smuggling ring and the unmasking of a Soviet mole and a blackmail victim in SEFF. If you wanted to go through the motions, it'd surely be easier and completely explicable to use Commander de Klerck's people.

In any case, something else was puzzling me. We'd discovered that the fraudster had only chosen to use those firms where there was no risk of the person pretending to be "Philippe Wouters", etc being unmasked as a phoney. The same would presumably also be true with the banks. So why did he go ahead with the fraud involving Cie CCR and the Namse Krediet Bank when it became apparent that de Mettet and Verstappen knew each other? I guessed he might only have discovered that when he carried out his preliminary visit to Cie CCR, but it would still have been possible to abort that fraud.

I was about to set off for home and mention this, along with what I'd got from the staff directories in the Commission archives, when I got a phone call from "Simon Stone" to meet "Peter West" in the "Golden Fleece" by the Porte Namur at 6pm. This meant hanging around for another hour or so...and unfortunately Knud Henriksen was out of the office, so I couldn't check my assumptions about people involved in the Accession negotiations with him. So I continued to worry away at the various loose ends and even the ends that looked neatly tied up without getting anywhere fast, before ringing Rosemary to tell her I'd be a bit late and setting off for the Porte Namur.

It was about a half an hour's walk, but I preferred to give myself the exercise and the time to clear my thoughts a bit. "Peter West" – a man born to be a secret agent because there was absolutely nothing memorable about him – was waiting for me, with a copy of the "la Gazzetta dello Sport" , which seemed incongruous, but was conveniently pink. We sat down in one of the booths which guaranteed a fair amount of privacy if you didn't speak too loudly. We both ordered beers, mine a Jupiler, his a Duvel. Naturally, they arrived in their own special glasses. We waited until they arrived - in silence. To any observer, it must've looked exceedingly strange.

"Mr Storey?" he asked, in a BBC accent.

"Yes," I replied. I would've liked to have made some sarcastic point about code names, but I needed his cooperation.

"Callum MacIntosh sends his regards. He also said that you and your wife seemed to have a nose for matters that might interest us. We've had a look at those Vietnamese you mentioned. By and large, Vietnamese aren't of much interest to us, as we haven't been fighting any of them. But our friends take a strong interest in them. They reckon that virtually all Vietnamese in the West who arrived more than a couple of years ago when the tide was plainly turning against us, are stooges of the North Vietnamese in one form or another. Bao Tran is thought to run a post office, if I may put it like that. Various people come into the bank and they may or may not pass on or receive money or just messages. He is a useful link. Duong Lac is reckoned to be more active, examining bank accounts for those who might be blackmailed. But he isn't a courier and may well be the ideological spy who makes sure Bao Tran and any other Vietnamese agents in Brussels – probably Belgium as a whole – don't get lazy, go native or, worse still, get turned. Minh Pham appears to be a sort of general dogsbody, substituting for either of the other two as necessary."

"So would they be trying to get Monique Lefebvre as an agent?"

"I'll come on to that. Perhaps the most interesting person isn't any of those you pointed out, but someone who's been and gone. Our friends tell us that shortly before the time your Mlle Lefebvre disappeared, one Ho Quyen Diep arrived in Antwerp by ship from Bremerhaven. He is an active agent of the North Vietnamese security service, mostly involved as a courier, notably transporting money, drugs and diamonds. And though there's no proof positive, he's been around when several murders of prominent anti-communist Vietnamese have occurred. So it's suspected he may also someone who makes problems go away, as our friends like to put it."

"Including possibly Monique Lefebvre?"

"That seems a distinct possibility. Of course, if he didn't want her body to be discovered, the authorities won't be able to find it, except by chance. But I doubt he was in this fair city long enough to 'case the joint', as they say. So probably Duong Lac was tasked with finding a suitable spot where someone could disappear without trace and little likelihood of being discovered. But with nothing concrete to put to him, he'd be under no pressure to tell us anything…and probably wouldn't even if we'd got his fingerprints on the body of the deceased. Our friends could always sweat him, as they term it, but that wouldn't guarantee any results. Besides, they'd rather keep the whole team in the Banque Indosuez under surveillance to see who turns up there….NATO, rather than the EEC, being their interest, of course."

"As you may know, there's a theory going around that these frauds we're investigating might've been carried out by the North Vietnamese…."

"It seems implausible to us…and to our friends. Essentially it's too sophisticated and using one of their number to visit all these companies and banks just looks too risky. These guys are in it for the long haul…and even though the war is over, they're not letting up their guard one inch."

"And Mlle Lefebvre? What do you…or your friends…think her part in all this may have been?"

"Difficult to say. There's pretty well a consensus that they wouldn't've invested so much time in her if she wasn't going to be of some use. But whether she was keen to join the club, a gradual convert or still outside the tent, you can make your own guess."

"Apart from helping them get access to this EEC money, she wasn't going to be of much use to the North Vietnamese where she was......And she'd shown no signs of wanting to move somewhere more helpful..."

"Perhaps she, too, was playing a long game. She wasn't thirty yet, was she? I guess she might be more trusted in NATO, for instance, if she'd had a good solid ten years in the EEC?"

"She joined the EEC direct...which was unusual, I believe.....Do you happen to know what the vetting arrangements are like for the EEC, compared to those of the French?"

"EEC vetting arrangements are so minimal to be vestigial. There are areas where we and NATO won't deal with them unless they get their people massive additional checks. I don't know the French procedures off-hand, but I doubt they're less than the UK's."

"Naturally, she wasn't the sort of person to say why she'd applied direct to the EEC. But it makes you wonder....."

"...whether she might already have had some ropey connections she wished to keep secret. I see what you mean."

"This is all pretty speculative, of course. There's no hard evidence underlying any of this...."

"That's about par for the course in my line of business....."

"But what do you reckon about the pistol? If some North Vietnamese hitman bumped Mlle Lefebvre off surreptitiously and made sure her body couldn't be discovered, why on earth would he leave such large indication of her possible involvement with his fellow-countrymen in her cupboard? This seems all far too meticulous for someone to miss that, if the gun was already there. And why would you place a gun there afterwards?"

"A good question, to which I fear I have no satisfactory answer. Other than we understand it's a type 54 pistol widely available in China and North Vietnam."

As I stood waiting for a tram in the Chaussée de Wavre and while I sat on the two trams I needed to get home, a little light began to dawn in my head. The man – and I was now convinced it was a man – who'd devised this fraud was cautious, neat and had been able to plan the fraud so that there'd be no links back to him. But in his cleverness, he could be too clever – like leaving the pistol in Mlle Lefebvre's flat to set off a false trail - and I reckoned disposing of her both removed a potential witness and someone who might have to share some of his ill-gotten gains. It was a pity we didn't know who "the little man with the dark hair and thick spectacles" was, because I'd've put a fair amount of money on him having disappeared without trace too…….Always assuming he wasn't the mastermind himself?

When I got home and had completed the normal bedtime routines with Emily and Sarah, I explained why I'd been delayed. That sort of meeting certainly wasn't the sort of thing to be mentioned on an open phone line.

"I finally got something out of the Banque Luxembourgeois," said Rosemary. "There were two accounts – essentially the same name in French and German. They were set up – would you believe it – by a small man with dark hair and very thick glasses. I suspect the bank is essentially a route for rich people to hide money from the tax authorities. In any case, as Luxembourg is part of the EEC, rich people who live in the EEC tend to be a little nervous of their money sitting in a bank located in an EEC country. Why, I don't know. From what I've seen, Luxembourg pretty well operates Swiss-style rules about banking secrecy, contrary to what I've always understood to be the principles of the EEC. But anyhow, most of this sort of money doesn't seem to stay there very long. It heads for Switzerland or Liechtenstein, where chasing up money like this becomes more difficult. Fortunately, the fraudsters seem to have started with one of the banks I've been dealing with about the Russian drugs money. It was too late to have a go at them today, but I'll see what I can dig out of them tomorrow."

I explained what I'd got from "Peter West".

"So all they can really say is that the three Vietnamese in the Banque Indosuez are North Vietnamese agents and that another man came over at about the time Monique Lefebvre disappeared. The rest is assumptions. As they don't know whether she was an agent for the North Vietnamese or not, they can't tell whether she was killed, made to disappear or has fled back to Vietnam. I'm sure they'd've had a suitable passport for her if it was needed. They've actually no idea whether these frauds were carried out by the North Vietnamese or not."

"There's a couple of things that I think make it unlikely. The first is that evidently none of the men in the Banque Indosuez was the 'little man with the dark hair and the thick spectacles'. If they'd been travelling around as much as that, the Americans would've noticed and would've told 'Peter West'. There'd be no reason not to. But no-one has mentioned any other Vietnamese about the place…"

"Always assuming this 'Peter West' actually asked. If he didn't ask, I doubt they'd volunteer anything."

"On reflection, you may be right. I should've pressed him. But if you come up with the name of a bank we want them to check, I'll ask the specific question….But there's also the pistol. If the North Vietnamese had run this fraud, why on earth would they leave a clue in Mlle Lefebvre's flat that so plainly pointed to their involvement? If nothing else, it made us look at her acquaintances and we've come up with three North Vietnamese agents. Why would they want to do that?"

"I agree…It does look rather odd….But it's pretty odd anyway…."

"Hmmm…I'm not so sure…I think that despite his meticulous and cautious planning, the man who organised this can occasionally be too clever by half. I believe the pistol was placed in Monique Lefebvre's flat after she disappeared – to put us, or whoever was investigating the fraud, on a false trail…the one supposedly leading to North Vietnam. The other thing is that I believe that Monique Lefebvre almost certainly was a North

Vietnamese agent. I'm guessing that being bullied or ignored at school when she was a child made her resent the French, the West and all they stood for. She deliberately didn't enter the French civil service because their vetting procedures would probably have uncovered inconvenient associates. On the other hand, the EEC's vetting procedures are apparently a joke and if she kept her nose clean here long enough, I guess she could've got a transfer to a job in NATO in a few years."

"So why wasn't this done by the North Vietnamese?"

"Because I believe someone discovered what she was and used it to blackmail her into providing the information needed to carry out the fraud…Then, if you want my guess, once it became apparent we were sniffing around, it'd be easy to get some sort of message to the North Vietnamese that Mlle Lefebvre was in fact a double agent, involved in a dirty little capitalist conspiracy. Then the North Vietnamese would send in their hitman to dispose of her neatly, tidily and permanently."

"That sounds neat and tidy too. But it's only a theory based on not much evidence…and it doesn't tell you who blackmailed her either…..or how whoever it was found out about her."

"But it enables me to search in a particular direction…which may turn out to be a blind alley, of course."

"It'll keep you out of mischief while I'm chasing up these banks, I suppose."

First I needed to check out a couple of things with Knut Henriksen.

"It's possible that the change in reconciliation procedures was made deliberately to facilitate this fraud," I explained. "Plainly, Vermeulen's name is on the internal memo – but it is on every memo emanating from the Secretariat. But presumably there's no reason to suppose that he was the author of change in policy, is there?"

"It could've been him, of course. But the Secretariat covers a wide range of functions and I know Vermeulen regards himself as the ruler of this particular Belgian empire, even though he's only equivalent to any other DG, most of whom are doing vastly more important things. But within his empire there are personnel specialists, accountants, maintenance staff…you name it, they'll be there. But plainly, no-one is going to take seriously a change suggested by anyone too junior. So you could assume if not Vermeulen, it'd be one of his directors or assistant directors. No-one below that level, unless they were highly regarded….a future star or heavily supported by their home government."

"I know who was there at the time, so I'll have to dig around them – discreetly of course."

"Occasionally I wonder how Rosemary and you are going to adapt to returning to London. I can't imagine Customs & Excise has the sort of free-wheeling jobs you've had here….and I'm sure the Metropolitan Police don't. Indeed, I'm contemplating my move with a modest amount of trepidation – not least because I've begun to realise just how circumscribed my time is going to be…..But though I know you enjoy this sort of thing, I'd encourage you to spend a bit of time between now and the spring thinking about how you're going to fit in again."

"That's a good point and I thank you for it. I think by and large, Rosemary and I just slot into the jobs we're given…..But she's going to have a bit of a problem anyhow as she wants to continue to be part time for a while. So we're keeping our fingers crossed that a former boss she's worked for will keep his promise to find her a suitable job when she gets back….and we were intending to look in on our offices when we're back in London over Christmas….and also check out about Emily and Sarah's schools. I reckon they could face as many difficulties as Rosemary and me."

"Evidently the Belgian empire holds no lasting attraction for you?"

"No. It's too much of a bubble. While it's been great working in SEFF, I doubt there's anywhere else in Brussels remotely like it…..which I accept is a lot down to Gerry and you….and what I see of places like DGVI makes me feel that even the Valuation Branch in C&E would probably be more satisfying."

"Don't remind me! I shall be taking over one of those in København and doubtless from time to time will have to visit and show enthusiasm for their work!"

From the names I'd written down in the Commission Secretariat, there were relatively few who'd either worked in DGVI before they moved there or worked there subsequently - Pierre-Henri Dumoulin, Robert van der Broeken, Roger Dufour, Louis Chastelin and, of course, "the ruler of the Belgian empire" himself, Jérôme Vermeulen. Any of them could have proposed changing the timings of the reconciliation procedures. Van den Broeken and Dufour were relatively junior – but Dufour had been regarded as a star before his surprise move to EUROSITRO. And was that to distance himself from any subsequent goings-on in DGVI? Van den Broeken was regarded as quiet, but effective. From what Allenby and his line managers had said about him, he struck as the sort of bloke who'd have no difficulty in insinuating a suggestion to his line manager, with all the advantages neatly provided, while keeping out of the limelight himself. Indeed, that struck me as exactly the modus operandi of what I felt I'd picked up about the mastermind of this fraud.

But this was still almost entirely based on speculation. I could hardly interview these men on the basis of the exiguous evidence I had at my disposal and the tenuous ideas in my head. I needed something more concrete. I needed to look back at what we'd already learnt and see what that told me.

12. "IS MORE INFORMATION GETTING US ANYWHERE?"

I spent the afternoon looking back over my notes and over the various tables and other scribblings Rosemary and I had created to record what we'd seen, read and heard and to try to make sense of it. Eventually, a couple of things emerged which I hadn't really spotted before. Partly because we'd been doing our visits sequentially, we'd picked up certain patterns – notably that the process of setting up and carrying out the fraud was pretty well the same everywhere. The one that stood out was Cie CCR. When "Philippe Wouters" realised that de Mettet and Verstappen were squash-playing mates, why didn't he just pick another bank in the Charleroi area, rather than continue with the Namse Krediet Bank?

The second thing was even more significant, so it struck me. The visits by "Philippe Wouters" to the various companies in Belgium, France and West Germany had taken place in the same week. So all the Belgian ones were carried out in one week, the French in the following week and the West Germans a week later. This pattern was also followed up with the setting up of the bogus bank accounts and the withdrawal of money from them into the Banque Luxembourgeois. Though it would've involved some risks - not least of being spotted by someone he'd already met in circumstances that looked incongruous - presumably it cut down travelling and his absence from wherever "the small man with dark hair and thick spectacles" normally worked. Presumably, he would've taken annual leave or sick leave from his normal employment…. Though if he was a career criminal, I realised he might not have that sort of regular employment.

If it was someone from the Commission, would it be possible to check? Unfortunately, a phone call to the personnel people in the Commission Secretariat informed me that though records were kept of sickness absences – because people could claim days off sick as exempt, even from the minuscule levels of tax they actually paid – records of annual leave were a matter for the individual official to maintain and agree with his or her line manager. I doubted whether anyone would want to declare around nine weeks of sickness absence without a very compliant doctor and an extremely gullible line manager. The pattern didn't work. You might have three weeks off with a bad case of 'flu or shingles, for instance. But it'd surely be too risky to have three weeks off in early '73, early '74 and then later '74 with plausible-sounding illnesses? So possibly one lot were taken as sick leave, but the rest would've been annual leave. The only thing about that, I reminded myself, would be that someone might remember a large chunk of annual leave being taken outside the traditional Brussels summer leave period of the month of August. I also reckoned Commission officials had probably learnt the art perfected by certain C&E staff of finding plausible work reasons for being out of the office for days at a time.

However, one thing I could check was how many of the names I'd identified of men who'd worked both in DGVI and the Commission Secretariat at the right time could conceivably have been "the small man with dark hair and thick spectacles". Of course, I already knew of one - Jérôme Vermeulen. Unfortunately, a phone call to Allenby only ruled Philippe Dumoulin out, as being over six feet tall. The rest were small - around 5' 6" or less. Though some had blond or brown hair, plainly that wasn't an insuperable obstacle. Vermeulen was the smallest by several inches, according to Allenby. It struck me that if the "small man with dark hair and thick spectacles" had been him, more stress would have been put on his unusual shortness. Besides, I wasn't at all sure how someone in his elevated position could disappear for three weeks at a time without it being far more noticeable than the person who carried out this fraud would want to risk.

"Well, I've got as far as the Banque Commercial de Vaud," said Rosemary, coming into my room. Hans-Georg Meyer was attending yet another of the interminable committee meetings which seemed to fill the days of so many eurocrats. "But without something extremely sensitive or explosive, I'm not going to get any further. I doubt very much whether they're crooks or even that they knowingly channel crooked money through their coffers, but they're being unremittingly Swiss in standing on their dignity and the ultimate principle, as they put it, of Swiss banking secrecy. If I could show they were holding drugs money, I might've had a sliver of a chance, but this is EEC money and they've pretty well worked out we wouldn't make a public song and dance about it. I've threatened them with a bit of heightened Interpol interest, but it was pretty well water off a duck's back. Some of these men are so self-righteous! They find it impossible to believe that their virtuous bank could possibly be used to transfer ill-gotten gains….And, of course, we've no powers to compel them to do anything…..They wouldn't even tell me something I knew already, that the contents of the account of 'DG6 Comptes' from the Banque Latour in Geneva had been transferred to the account of 'AXQ44617B' in their bank."

"Though an account called DG6 does give the game away a bit."

"It's also pretty cheeky! The alphanumeric account will probably link to a similar account in another bank from where our mastermind will obtain his cash at some stage."

"Would he have had to set up these accounts in person?"

"Yes. But if he looked the part and had the right documents, no-one would question him. If you're talking to Swiss bankers about millions of pounds, you'll be assumed to be honest and reliable unless you do something extremely odd or alarming to put them off…..I know that sounds a bit cynical, but there's loads of hot money, especially from drugs, that has to somewhere to be laundered and Switzerland is favourite because of their banking secrecy laws. I'm sure there are some people there who know perfectly well what must be going on, but they'd rather make money than do the decent thing."

"You would've agreed with my father on at least one thing….though he would've put it in more ideological terms, of course…..And presumably Swiss banking secrecy includes not telling us what the person who set up the bank account looked like."

"Oh, certainly! But I wouldn't mind guessing it was a small man with dark hair and glasses - possibly not thick ones as he wouldn't've needed to disguise himself once he got within the hallowed portals of a Swiss bank."

Yet another thing we couldn't do anything about. And as it seemed likely that the Banque Commercial de Vaud wasn't the final resting place for this money, there'd be no point mounting a surveillance there, even if we could've persuaded anyone to do it for us.

"How did you get the info out of the Banque Latour?" I asked.

"I guess the money had already passed through their account and they didn't expect to receive any more so they didn't get their knickers in a twist about it – especially as they could score a brownie point or two with Interpol, while knowing that no information about the actual owner of the money would ever be disclosed."

"So what we've basically got is either it really was a North Vietnamese fraud and Mlle Lefebvre is either safely in Hanoi or at the bottom of a deep lake somewhere, or it was run by someone from the Commission…..with a few possibilities that we've identified….but mostly on the basis of hunches rather than any evidence."

"But the timings of when the little man visited the companies, the banks and then transferred the money are genuinely firm evidence. I realise it's more than likely that the little man didn't come from the Commission, but surely we could at least see whether any of the names you've identified were away from the office at those times. Taking nine weeks leave outside August seems improbable to me. So at least one lot would've been taken as sickness absence, I reckon....and didn't you say the Commission keeps records of sickness absence?"

"It's worth a shot. It'd certainly give us our first opportunity to ask someone some awkward questions and we might be able to get one or two of the more observant people from the firms or the banks to see whether they could identify them....Unfortunately, the records will be kept in the Commission Secretariat and I doubt we'd be allowed to look at them without Vermeulen's permission....and though I can't see how he could be involved, he fits the pattern to some extent and if by any tiny chance it was him, I wouldn't want to tip him off."

"And you have a natural tendency to believe that it's the bosses who are most likely to be at it....admit it!"

"I suppose so....and my experience so far bears it out to some extent....But I agree...and if Vermeulen has taken three weeks of sick leave at one of those times, I'd be amazed! He really is too short to take the risk of doing all those visits....and the man who planned this fraud strikes me as being very careful to avoid any risk.....apart from Cie CCR and the Namse Krediet Bank. When he learnt about the friendship between de Mettet and Verstappen, why didn't he just call the whole thing off? Or use a different bank? As it was, he must've had to take some risks to find out when Verstappen wasn't in the bank, just so he could turn up then......I wonder we shouldn't go back to Cie CCR and the Namse Krediet Bank and try and work out how he managed to do that....and why."

"We could try a phone call first, perhaps? I can't say I really fancy yet another railway trip to Charleroi."

"I think this is something which needs to be done face to face. There was something a bit fishy about de Mettet and Verstappen when we met them.....and I really don't know why de Mettet needed to phone Verstappen immediately after we'd left to fill him in. It seemed more like that they needed to get their stories to fit...."

"As Storeys like to....." observed Rosemary with a smirk.

"...and I think it's worth checking up on anything they said. Of course, de Mettet didn't need to have an excuse, but plainly Verstappen needed to be out of the way on two occasions...The first time was in January 1973...."

"26 January to be precise," said Rosemary, looking at her notes.

"I see we're back taking this seriously.....and he said he'd gone skiing, didn't he?"

"Yes. A place called Sölden ...He said he thought de Mettet was with him..."

"That's a bit fishy, don't you think? Surely he'd know! I reckon de Mettet and he hadn't agreed a line on that, so it was safer to be indefinite."

"It's a long shot, but would be able to find out what the snow conditions were then? If they were fine, it wouldn't be much use. But supposing it was unseasonably warm or there were blizzards all week, you'd expect Verstappen to remember....and if you can catch him out in one lie, it's easier to push him on everything else."

"You said 'you', rather than 'we'. I take it there's a reason for that?"

"Yes. I agree you meet them face to face. But only you. I can't see they've actually profited from the fraud in any way, so we're not going to be letting anyone off the hook. But I think they'll find it easier to confess to another man, rather than with his wife sitting next to him."

"Oh! I see what you mean! You think this was some sort of alibi-providing friendship which allowed them to slope off and have it away with ladies who weren't their wives!"

"That's my guess...Hence the shiftiness........If I'm right, they'll find it much easier to confess if I'm not there...and if I'm wrong, we both know you do that sort of interview at least as well as I do."

"But how on earth could you find out what the conditions were like in a single ski resort nearly three years ago?"

"Ruggieri claims to be something of an expert…and he certainly disappeared for a fortnight in January last winter. I'm sure I've seen forecasts of conditions of the 'piste' when I was reading 'Le Monde' to improve my French…"

"While avoiding the political bias of 'Libération'…."

"No…Well, not really. It's just 'Libération' is much heavier going than 'Le Monde". Your French and your patience may be up to full pages of dense prose – mine isn't!"

At any rate, after a conversation with her colleague from the Guardia de Finanza, she appeared to get some useful information and I didn't see her again until I got home that evening. It was unusual, because normally we'd have lunch and unless one or other of us was unavoidably absent, we'd usually part with a kiss.

"I'm sorry I didn't see you at lunchtime, Nick," she explained when I arrived home. "I was in the press archive in the basement of the Berlaymont looking through old newspapers and I didn't realise the time. As it was I was quarter of an hour late for picking up Emily and Sarah…and they didn't let me forget it…I've had three hours of Inspector Clouseau ever since. Could you get them ready for bed?"

"OK. I'll tell them that if they insist on being Inspector Clouseau, I might start pretending to be Cato."

After we'd eaten, Rosemary told me what she'd found out.

"You're actually quite lucky. There was heavy snow for four days that week….always assuming they travelled at the weekend….and they might've got one day's skiing at most….You'd think that might've stuck in Verstappen's memory."

"I'll ring the pair of them tomorrow and get a meeting on Friday with them both…."

"Both…..? Together?"

"Yes. If this is what we think it is, if they're apart, they'll stick to their story for fear of betraying the other. But if I worry them a bit about possible involvement in a multi-million pound fraud and then come up with the evidence about the snow when they were supposed to be skiing, I think they'll find it easier to agree to cooperate….and they can still maintain their dirty little secret…."

I decided I needed to meet them somewhere where they weren't on familiar ground. Naturally, once they got my phone call they would confer and probably agree how to deal with any questions I might have for them. But I wasn't going to tell them much – just enough to make them realise that it was serious and connected with a large fraud. And as it was going to involve two train journeys for me, I felt I should avoid having to traipse half way across Charleroi, but that we would meet in the station or nearby. I recalled that the station was quite large and grand, in the style generally favoured by continental railway architects. We'd crossed a large square to get to it and I couldn't recall any cafes around the square.

"If there isn't somewhere to get coffee, croissants and croques messieurs, I'll be amazed," observed Rosemary. "You'll just have to hope that if you tell them to meet you in the station café, there isn't more than one."

I reckoned I could probably sort that out on the phone. Indeed, it'd be a lot simpler than the rest of the call.

I rang de Mettet the moment I got in, conscious that Cie CCR probably started work at the crack of dawn.

"Mr Storey. I'm surprised to hear from you again. I thought we'd dealt with all the matters which you were interested in," he began, in good English, after I was put through by the secretary.

"You'll recall our conversation related to a large fraud. We've recently come across some evidence that indicates that what you told us and what M. Verstappen told us seems not to be entirely accurate. In view of the high value of this fraud, we need to confirm to our own satisfaction that none of the businesses or banks involved had any guilty knowledge of what was being perpetrated, which would be a serious criminal offence, of course. However, I felt that before I brought the Belgian police in, I should allow M. Verstappen and you the opportunity to explain the incongruities in your statements to my wife and I."

Silence at the other end.

"I…I…I…. can assure you I've never been party to any fraud…and if you were to say so in public, you would be hearing from lawyers immediately afterwards."

"In that case, you should expect a visit from the Belgian police within the next week or so. I had hoped it might prove possible to resolve this without unpleasantness, but if that's your attitude…."

Further silence. I could almost hear his brain ticking away over the phone line.

"Very well. I suppose a meeting would prejudice nothing…."

"I propose that we meet tomorrow at 11 o'clock in the station café in Charleroi Sud station. The meeting shouldn't take more than half an hour, but I have to back in Brussels by lunchtime for a meeting with our lawyers about this case. That's why our meeting is both urgent and needs to take place where I've proposed…"

"But…."

"I also propose that M. Verstappen should join us. As you plainly know each other's phone numbers like the back of your hands, I'd be grateful to you if you could make sure he comes along too. And I must emphasise, if either of you come with any lawyers or anyone else, the meeting will not take place and the unpleasantness which I've referred to will commence rapidly."

I rang off – to make sure he had no time to come up with any excuses to postpone the meeting – not least because they might be entirely genuine and reasonable. Indeed, I half-expected a call back or perhaps something by way of Robin Southern or someone in DGVI. But the lines from Charleroi into my office remained silent for the rest of the day.

I got up early the following morning, to make sure I got to Charleroi at about ten o'clock. I didn't anticipate any violence from this pair - apart possibly of the tongue – but it seemed wise to be careful. I also needed time to check out the station café and how best I could position myself so that they'd feel comfortable admitting to what they been up to, without feeling too defensive.

It was a pleasant, sunny Autumn day and the leaves on the trees looked at their best. I realised we'd probably ignored large parts of the Belgian countryside while we'd been in Brussels and that there were probably walks, even small adventures, which Emily and Sarah would've enjoyed…and without any attendant dangers.

I got into Charleroi Sud just before 10 am. As a big, grand station, it had a large café whose original grandeur had succumbed somewhat to age. However, it plainly served a range of food, from the ubiquitous coffee and croissants to soup, salads and even various forms of sausage and stoemp. Naturally, it also sold a wide range of beers from the mass market Jupiler and Stella to the exotics like 'Mort Subite', "Brugse Tripel" and "Edelschott", the last an unholy alliance between barley wine and scotch, as far as I could make out the only time I tasted it. I chose tea, reckoning that with the best part of an hour to wait, I didn't want to be helping myself get edgy or desperate for a pee by having the usual coffee. I found a table in one corner, which couldn't be seen from the outside, but gave me a good view of the door. I picked up a copy of the "Nouvelle Gazette" and half-read it, half kept an eye on who was in the café and who was going in and out.

As Iain Cogbill had reminded me on several occasions, surveillance is boring. Arguably, sitting around waiting is worse. However, I reckoned the staff in the café were used to people hanging around for hours, as no-one encouraged me to buy another cup of tea. The room was never more than about a third full. Half-past ten came and went, the minutes hand on the large clock above the bar ticking by like an old-fashioned funeral procession. But at least no-one who looked like my idea of someone who might have been brought along to "encourage" me to go away appeared.

Indeed, at 10.45, de Mettet and Verstappen arrived together. They saw me instantly and came over to where I was sitting. De Mettet was calm. Verstappen was plainly boiling.

"Thank you for agreeing to meet me at such short notice and at this inconvenient spot," I began in English. It seemed to me I had to stop Verstappen expostulating all over the place, trying to put me on the defensive. "As you both know a substantial fraud was undertaken using Cie CCR and the Namse Krediet Bank. As we've seen more instances of how this fraud was carried out, one thing stuck out like a sore thumb – the fact that the two of you were friends. Thus the fraudster would be unable to make his two visits to the bank, posing as M. de Mettet, when M. Verstappen was there, because he'd be found out. Yet miraculously, he managed to pick two occasions when M. Verstappen was out of the bank. How on earth could he do that, we asked ourselves? M. Verstappen explained that he was at head office on one occasion and the other time – the week of 26 January 1973 – he was skiing in Sölden, Austria. However, my evidence is that he was never there. Indeed, your mutual squash matches are, in fact, a way of giving each other an alibi for meeting ladies who aren't your wives. I believe that the fraudster picked it up when he was visiting Cie CCR, M. de Mettet. I guess he probably asked you about the bank which you used and what other banks one might use in Charleroi. I suspect you recommended the bank run by your friend, but some of your staff know what your 'squash matches' really are most of the time. I also reckon you told him you were going off to play M. Verstappen at squash that day. Of course, he didn't need you any more…and you'd actually seen him. So he drove into the centre of town and waited until M. Verstappen left the bank to enjoy his 'cinq a sept'. It was a bit of a long shot, but it paid off. Of course, you didn't hear anything until early January 1973. He was about to come to Charleroi for the week to set up the various fraudulent bank accounts. But I guess that at that stage, he didn't know which day he'd be coming to the Namse Krediet Bank. So he mentioned a time and an address and your home telephone number – and possibly even indicated there were photographs. But if you made sure you had a credible reason for being away from the office during the week of 26 January, your wife need not be troubled. The second time, he knew which day he was coming, so he phoned you and told you to make yourself scarce that morning. Which, of course, you did – indicating also who was the least experienced member of staff he should deal with – and, of course, facilitating a fraud of tens of millions of Belgian francs….Now then, how am I doing?"

There was a stunned silence on the other side of the table. Confusion, guilt, incredulity, even the occasional glimpse of anger crossed their faces. I felt a bit as I had when I unmasked those merchant bankers in Whittingtons in the Houndsditch – I'd been doing rather an ostentatious bit of skating over extremely thin ice. But I always felt I could trust Rosemary's intuition – and the looks on their faces proved she was right.

"How in God's name do you know all this?" demanded Verstappen.

"I take it you both confirm that what I've just said is substantially correct?"

Both nodded, looking down at the table, like a pair of guilty schoolboys.

"Then there are just a couple of things I need to check. I take it, M. Verstappen, you were contacted by phone?"

"Yes. On one occasion I would've said it was from a payphone on a large station, but I couldn't tell you which," replied Verstappen.

"And when you made your visit which enabled the fraudster to blackmail you, did you notice anything different or untoward, like a car that you hadn't seen before perhaps?"

"No. You understand I usually pull my coat collar up round my ears, duck down and head inside as fast as I can. That probably appears suspicious enough without me looking about myself right, left and centre."

"Thank you. One final question. M. de Mettet when you were visited by the man from the Commission, I assume he drove? Do you recall what make of car it was?"

"It was a Renault 5, dull crimson, three doors I think. We probably have the number somewhere, as visitors have to give a registration number otherwise we won't let them in. You'd like me to let you know?"

"Yes please."

Though I realised that if the car number was going to be recorded and the "little man with the dark hair and the thick glasses" was bound to know it, there'd be no way that the car would be traceable back to whoever he really was. But tying de Mettet in to being helpful seemed too good not to accept.

As I sat on the train on my way back to Brussels, I recognised that my meeting hadn't taken the overall investigation much further forward, if barely at all. But a car number might be useful. Presumably the "little man with the dark hair and thick glasses" must've stayed in hotels or pensions while he was on his travels. He must've - presumably – hired the car somewhere. More occasions where he might've left traces which could lead us to his identity. He was surely not so amazingly careful that he hadn't slipped up somewhere?

Hans-Georg Meyer had a message for me when I walked into the office. The number of the crimson Renault 5 – KLV402. Evidently I'd either scared de Mettet sufficiently for him to have jumped to do my bidding or, more likely, he wanted me out of his hair so he could forget me for the rest of his – to my mind – somewhat sordid little life.

I went along to see Rosemary, but she was busy on the phone, so I didn't get a chance to speak until lunchtime. I explained how I'd got on and that I'd now got the number of the car used by "the little man".

"That was a bit silly of us," she remarked. "We should've realised he'd probably be using a car to get around. I'd assumed that the little man would use public transport because it's anonymous…and I suppose we've tended to use it….and taxis, if necessary….What made you realise he'd been using a car?"

"I'm not sure I ever realised. It was when I was doing my skating on thin ice thing with de Mettet and Verstappen. It seemed to me that the only way the little man could've known about them was overhearing something when he was at Cie CCR, but he'd need something a bit more concrete than that to blackmail Verstappen successfully. So I guessed he learnt de Mettet was meeting Verstappen for a game of squash that day and the only way he could possibly get from Cie CCR to the Namse Krediet Bank would be by car."

"I guess it must've been hired. But I can find that out from Interpol."

"Not that it'll take us much further forward. He will've undoubtedly used a false name when he hired the car."

"And false papers…including insurance and….."

"…a driver's licence? In Belgium?"

"We can find out from a car rental place….At least there's a chance he made have given us a bit more to go on than usual."

"But he's had plenty of time to plan all this. So no doubt he's got several false identities with papers that look kosher as well as whatever insurance he might need….though I thought the car hire company usually include insurance in the price of the rental?"

It didn't take Rosemary long to confirm that the Renault 5 KLV402 was owned by AVIS. Naturally, all their rental cars were registered in the same place – Brussels.

"So where would the small man be most likely to pick up his car?" Rosemary asked, putting her head round my door for a kiss before she went off to collect Emily and Sarah. "You can think about that this afternoon."

In fact, I'd already started thinking about it. It seemed likely that the small man would travel to the car rental place by public transport and he'd also choose a large place where he was unlikely to be remembered. The two together suggested a main railway station…and if you were proposing to head out of Brussels in the direction he'd've been going, you'd pick Brussels Midi as the most convenient. I looked through the local phone directory in the secretaries' room and found an AVIS at Brussels Midi. I rang them and confirmed that KLV402 was normally stationed there, though it was currently undergoing its final service before being sold off. I also found out that they kept records of customers going back up to five years, so I decided to get a tram there and see what else I could discover.

AVIS car rental was on the western side of the station, a glorified garage with large signs. It looked as though they could park around sixty cars there. At present at least half the parking spaces were empty. I went to the reception and had to wait until a couple of customers were dealt with. Then I explained my business to the smart, brisk French-looking young woman behind the counter. She made a phone call and a similarly smart and brisk young man, with short, brylcreemed hair and a permanently cheery face emerged from a back room and escorted me through to a small office of nondescript metal furniture and pictures of a dozen or so different models of AVIS cars on the walls.

I explained who I was, who I worked for and in very general terms why I was interested in knowing the name of the man who hired KLV402 in January 1973. The man – whose name badge pronounced him to be Jean-Pierre Michelet – made a phone call and a few minutes later a young man appeared with a large lever-arch file.

"This is the history of KLV402," explained Michelet.

I leafed quickly through the pages back to January 1973. I was unsurprised to find that the car had been hired by a 'Philippe Wouters', who had collected it on a Monday and returned it on a Friday evening nearly three weeks later. He had paid cash, but the boxes for identification papers were ticked. I should've realised that the little man was too fly to use a different identity when he already required plausible false papers to show the firms and the bankers."

"I assume you don't keep any records of your customers, do you?" I asked.

"Not those who hire for a day or two. But if you're hiring for a week or more, we like to take down further particulars and keep the car you used previously available if you let us know in advance that you'll be needing to hire one. The company has found that people who spent a fair amount of time in a car either want to use it or a very similar model again in future…or complain and want something very different. It's worth knowing that too, of course."

"Of course….So you might have some information about Philippe Wouters?"

Another quick phone call. The young man reappeared with a smaller lever-arch file….S – Z. I found Wouters had used different cars – but both Renault 5s on his other two three week periods of visits to the banks. The cars were KMC114 and KLN955."

"M. Wouters has used us on three occasions," observed Michelet, looking over my shoulder. "I can't say that I recall him."

"I took him through the paperwork the last time he used us," said the young man, in a disconcertingly deep voice which didn't fit with his generally rather weedy appearance – despite the inevitably smart uniform. "I recall him being quite insistent that he didn't have a crimson or a grey car…but it had to be a Renault 5. He hadn't phoned in advance, so it meant I had to talk someone else into taking the crimson model so he could have a green one….He didn't get nasty, you understand. He was just insistent and would undoubtedly have taken his business elsewhere….and there was something else about him. He was quite short, but when I went to hand back the paperwork, he was already sitting on the front seat of the car, taking his shoes off and putting on some sort of moccasins. He said that he didn't like driving with soles that were too thick as he couldn't feel the pedals as well as wished."

"Did you see what his normal shoes were like?" I asked.

"I'm sorry – no. He'd already slung them behind the front seat."

"Can you remember what he looked like?"

"Short, dark-haired….oh yes, he was wearing sunglasses."

"Sunglasses?"

"Yes. I asked him why as it wasn't a sunny day…Indeed, if I remember it was raining a bit…He said his eyes were weak and badly affected by the light, so he had to wear dark glasses to drive. I asked him how he managed when at night. He told me he didn't drive in the dark."

"What sort of person did he seem like?"

"Someone who knew what he wanted…and wanted to get on his way….Not someone I'd want to get on the wrong side of…Not that I think he'd be nasty – it'd be the phone call to my manager or head office putting the knife in…..At any rate, that was my impression….and perhaps he could read my mind, as he hasn't been back since….."

"I believe I can reassure you in that score. From what I know, he hasn't needed to hire a car since then……But from what you've said, it'd seem he used a crimson car the first time he hired one from you and then a grey one?"

"Yes. We've got six Renault 5s…all different colours and I know which number goes with which."

Nothing else occurred to me at that point so I thanked them for their time and left, promising that if I ever needed to hire a car I'd use AVIS. And though I found the uniforms and resolutely friendly approach a little overwhelming, I couldn't fault them for their helpfulness or the quality of their record-keeping.

I told Rosemary what I'd learnt later that evening, but as she rightly said, "Is more information getting us anywhere?"

It was a fair point. Perhaps it was time to take a bit of risk?

13. VIOLENCE BEYOND THE VIETNAM WAR

"You intend to go and meet those North Vietnamese bankers and tell them their man killed Monique Lefebvre by mistake!" exclaimed Rosemary after I'd explained what I proposed. "Don't you think you've been doing enough skating on thin ice for a year or two? And this ice is so thin, it's practically water!"

"I don't think it's that bad. I wasn't planning to ask them to admit to what they really are. I thought I'd just go along and tell them a tale about what's been happening and how the little man has played them for fools and got them to kill one of their own. It's just possible they might tell me about how they were informed about Mlle Lefebvre and when. Or it might just encourage them to do some digging around of their own."

"And if they work out who it was and make them disappear?"

"I guess that we'll know who the fraudster was – and be confident he wasn't able to enjoy the fruits of his crime."

"Perhaps they already know and they've already made him disappear?"

"I don't believe so. I'm as sure as I can be that whoever organised this fraud works in the Commission – and Mlle Lefebvre is the only person we know of who's disappeared without trace. If someone else had, don't you think Vermeulen would've told us?"

"Hmmm…I'm not sure I'd trust him to tell us anything he didn't want us to know."

"But I reckon Knud or Gerry would've picked something up. They're over there even more often than we've been recently."

"I can see you've made up your mind. In which case, I'm coming with you. I know you won't like it. But if there's to be any nastiness, two of us are better than one and I may be able to keep a closer eye on them while you're doing your skating over thin ice act."

"Then I suggest we turn up first thing tomorrow morning, without giving them warning."

I knew from the look in her eyes that there was no point in trying to dissuade Rosemary. Besides, as she'd rightly said, dealing with two inconvenient people when there were only three at most on their side was going to be a lot more difficult than one. I realised that my Security Service contacts might not be best pleased at what I was doing – but if Bao Tran, Duong Lac and Minh Pham didn't believe they were under surveillance by the CIA, at least, they were a lot more foolish than I took them for. The anticipation of the following morning ensured we enjoyed more lovemaking than usual on a weekday evening – and I was glad we were planning to meet these spies first thing, as I suspected I'd be feeling quite jaded by mid-afternoon.

We arrived at the bank at 9.30. The bank staff would be in the building by then, but the public counter wouldn't open until ten. We went to the reception desk, where a smart young woman of Mediterranean origin dealt with us.

"We need to have a short but very urgent meeting with Mr Bao Tran," I explained. "The matter we need to discuss is in this envelope which I'd be grateful could be passed to him immediately, please?"

She gave me a look of mild irritation, but spoke briefly on the phone. A messenger in a sort of semi-uniform appeared and took the envelope away. Within ten minutes, Bao Tran appeared, looking as impassive as ever.

"You may wish to come with me…..This lady, she is with you?"

"Yes," I replied. "She works for the same organisation as me."

We made our way to a different meeting room, slightly larger and less elegantly furnished.

"I do not understand the meaning of this note," Bao Tran began.

"Let's come on to that in a moment. I would be grateful if your two colleagues could join us, please?"

He glided out and returned with Duong Lac and Minh Pham within a couple of minutes. Both stared at us with barely-concealed hostility and unconcealed suspicion.

"Now – what do you mean by this?" demanded Ba Tran. "We know who killed Mlle Lefebvre. So do you. If we cannot talk about it, we shall have to inform the police'. We know nothing about this matter, as we told you when you were last here."

"Allow me to explain, please. My intention here isn't to cause you any more trouble than you are already in. We know who you really are and what your real jobs are here. I'm sure you'd expect the authorities here to be aware of that. That's not our job or our interest. As the person who followed me back to my office after we last met knows, I genuinely work for SEFF. Neither of us are involved in security matters. Our interest is in dealing with fraud – at the moment a particular fraud….and one which you know about. I'm not asking you to admit anything – though after I've said what I've had to say, I hope you might be prepared to give me a piece of information….."

"Say what you have to say," grunted Bao Tran.

"Let me tell you a tale and you can see whether you recognise any of it. Working in the EEC Commission is a very greedy and calculating man who sees a way of making an enormous of money for himself through a clever fraud which won't be detected for months after it's happened. He needs an accomplice in a particular part of the Commission. Naturally, he would prefer not to have to share his ill-gotten gains with the accomplice. So he seeks someone he can blackmail. As it happens, within the right part of the Commission is a young woman of mixed French and Vietnamese parentage. Unlike almost everyone else, she joined the Commission directly, rather than having first worked in the French administration. This is sufficiently unusual for him to check out some of her life. For instance, she meets certain North Vietnamese regularly and she takes regular flights off into that part of the world, supposedly heading for Australia. But he's heard that her knowledge of Australia is only skin-deep. So my guess is he takes a few days off and noses around the places where she was brought up. What he finds is a girl who's teased, bullied and ostracised at school because of her Vietnamese blood. Though she's good at hiding her true feelings, he picks up that she made contact with Vietnamese while she was still living in the Paris region and that at that stage she gave her allegiance to North Vietnam. She was encouraged to apply directly for the EEC Commission in the hope that if she gave nothing away about her true allegiance and did well, she might be able to get a posting to NATO. And, of course, her North Vietnamese connections might well have been detected by the vetting procedures of the French authorities. Naturally, once he'd got enough to go on, the man blackmailed her with it. In any case, he didn't require much of her – just some names and some documents, normally photocopies. Rather than have her cover blown, she did what she was told...."

"If this woman was what you say, if she had any sense, she should've told her Vietnamese contacts who might've found a way of dealing with the blackmailer," remarked Bao Tran.

"That assumes that the man let her know who he was and that they met. He is an extremely careful, calculating man and I'm sure he would've contacted her by phone and would've arranged for the documents to have been got to him without her ever knowing who he was. You should understand that this could've been planned as long as ten years ago, so the processes which this man has used have been extremely carefully thought about with the sole intention of ensuring he can't be traced."

"If you say so...Please continue."

"With the help of the woman who we'll call Monique, he carries out the frauds. Inevitably, they are discovered some months later and the Secretary of the Commission asks us to investigate. The most obvious thing that immediately strikes us is that someone in the part of the Commission where Monique works has to have been heavily involved. At this stage, the man telephones one of you. He tells you that Monique has been playing you along, while really she's been involved in a very large fraud involving Commission money which she is planning to disappear with. This is probably accompanied by some incriminating documents. This adds to the previous suspicion that there was something not quite right about Monique and after a tribunal at which she is not represented, she is sentenced to the penalty appropriate for all traitors. The executioner arrives, carries out the execution and departs. Of course, Monique wasn't a traitor. Why she didn't appear quite right was because of the torment inside her about being blackmailed; because she guessed what the information she was giving to her blackmailer was being used for and because she feared what'd happen when she was no longer useful to the blackmailer. I certainly wouldn't want to argue that perhaps Monique was feeble and lacking in initiative, but in your terms, she wasn't a traitor."

"And interesting story. You are evidently well-named. But you cannot explain why did this blackmailer not arrange to have this Monique removed as soon as the fraud was complete?"

"That would've been incredibly stupid! If she disappeared, people would be out looking for her. The police would be involved. People might start to look at her work. There'd be a risk that the frauds could be discovered months before he intended. The time for her to disappear was once the frauds were discovered through the normal procedures. And then he could point the blame towards the North Vietnamese by leaving a Chinese type 54 pistol with some fifty rounds of Chinese ammunition hanging up in her cupboard. Of course, he placed it there a day or two after the executioner had been and gone....I should say that our investigation will cease in a few weeks' time and I've no idea who will take over. It's quite possible that everyone will decide that the most convenient solution will to blame Monique Lefebvre and a North Vietnamese connection……..But anyway, that's my tale. I don't expect you to confirm it. But I do ask you to consider whether there's any information you could give us that might help us identify the man who did this."

"As I said earlier – an interesting story…..Do you mind waiting here for a short while?"

"Not at all."

They trooped out. It would've been interesting to heave heard what they were going to say to each other, but as it'd undoubtedly be in Vietnamese, it wasn't going to happen. I reckoned it'd be a battle between their natural hostility to a representative of capitalist, colonialist imperialists; a desire for revenge; a common reluctance to admit that they might've been fooled and sent an innocent young woman to her death, probably without giving her the chance to explain; and a wish to put that right in some way. But, as Rosemary had said, they might well prefer not to share such information that they had and use it to mete out justice in their own way.

After about twenty minutes they reappeared. Their expressions remained the same mask of impassive suspicion and underlying hostility.

"There are questions which we must ask you," began Bao Tran. "I expect you won't tell us where you got your information from?"

"No," I replied.

"You do not know the identity of the man who you say committed these frauds?"

"No. If we did, we wouldn't be here. Though many people might regard what happened to Monique Lefebvre as cold-blooded murder, that's a matter for the Belgian police, not us."

"You believe that Mlle Lefebvre could not have devised and controlled the fraud herself?"

"No. The fraud was only made possible by a change in the way checks were carried out. This took place in 1973 and it appears to us that it was done deliberately with the aim of allowing this fraud to be carried out. Mlle Lefebvre was never in a position to have made this happen. In any case, we never met her. You knew her a lot better than us. Do you believe she was capable of devising and carrying out a fraud of this nature? And who was the man who actually did all the work in checking out the firms and banks involved and then collecting the false payments? He was small, dark-haired and wore spectacles with very thick lenses. We think he was intending to give an impression that he might be oriental, possibly Vietnamese."

"But he was not?"

"We think it's unlikely. As I guess she probably told her executioner, Monique Lefebvre was a pawn in a game played by a much smarter player. Once he told her that he knew she was really working for you lot, she did what she always did, from what we can judge – hid the problem even deeper into herself and hoped that if she remained very small and very quiet, it might blow over. Unfortunately for her, the person who was blackmailing here is greedy, but also ruthless in ensuring he cannot be traced."

"I do not understand why she did not say something to her comrades," interrupted Minh Pham, earning himself looks of impatience from his colleagues.

"Because she had no evidence to show you. I guess she feared she'd no longer be regarded as being any use to you, with her identity compromised. I imagine a desire to hit back at the West – the French, in particular – was a ruling passion in her life. If she couldn't carry out work to achieve her revenge on them, she didn't have much else of a life. I don't know whether you've ever seen her room and I assume when we saw it was after her executioner had been, but it was as it'd normally look. It looked like the room of a soldier or perhaps a nun. All the important part of her life went into her work for what she regarded as her homeland. I suspect she felt...or perhaps hoped.... that once she'd passed on these few photocopied documents, the anonymous blackmailer would leave her alone."

"If he was anonymous, why did he need to get her killed?" asked Bao Tran.

"I guess because he has a mania for avoiding any loose ends, any possibility of traces that lead back to him. He may also have reckoned that once the frauds came to light, she might admit her part in them – and point the finger at someone within the EEC Commission. Whereas if she disappeared, the false trail leading to North Vietnam could be neatly established....and as the chances of the money being recovered are zero, in my view, the authorities might end up as finding that the most convenient explanation."

Silence resumed. Bao Tran was thinking. His colleagues were trying to work out what he was going to do next.

"You should understand that we find your story interesting," Bao Tran resumed. "But you will realise we regard as just a story. In the course of the story you suggested that information was supplied to certain people with whom the lady called Monique had contact that suggested she was involved in illegal activities. Such information was provided by way of documents containing EEC Commission forms and various company and bank details which demonstrated the creation of false bank accounts which were subsequently cleared. When put to the lady called Monique it is understood that she didn't deny her involvement. Indeed, her manner and behaviour gave herself away without a word being spoken. Regrettably this means the man who devised this piece of evil provided no clues as to his identity."

"That was what I feared. I hoped....but didn't expect....But I'm grateful to you for being prepared to listen to my tale...and perhaps in the light of it you might consider rehabilitating Monique Lefebvre to some extent. I don't believe she ever betrayed your cause…but the man who blackmailed her is extremely skilful in working out the vulnerabilities of other people…and she was more vulnerable than most…..We'd been led to believe there was a Vietnamese mother living near Paris….Perhaps…..?"

"Though she preferred to marry a colonialist exploiter, her daughter died as the result of a capitalist conspiracy, so…..."

That was the most we were going to get out of them, or that we'd get for poor Monique Lefebvre. I hoped she hadn't had to undergo a long interrogation at the hands of Ho Quyen Diep, but I suspected her body would never be found unless by accident. I also reckoned that if the North Vietnamese ever worked out the identity of the "little man", he could expect his last few hours to be unbearable. But I wasn't convinced they'd put much effort into it. These blokes were essentially couriers and a post box. They'd had to call in a specialist, presumably from Hanoi, to carry out an interrogation and execution which were probably unnecessary. My guess was that they'd keep what I'd told them between themselves and keep their heads down.

We departed. Their faces were as impassive as ever – and, naturally, we didn't shake hands in the normal Continental manner. I felt that they were perhaps a little less hostile – but that could just have been my relief at completing the meeting.

"That ice wasn't as thin as I expected," remarked Rosemary as we waited for a tram at the Bourse stop. "It was a pity they had so little information."

"You didn't think they were concealing something?"

"Not that, I don't think. If they'd got something I think they'd've tried to do some sort of deal – as we've probably got more scraps of info about the man who blackmailed Monique Lefebvre than they have…..But I reckon we'll have to expect we get tailed from time to time. If I was them I'd want to find out who fooled them into getting her killed."

"I'm not so sure. I think they'd rather that particular sleeping dog lie undisturbed. I doubt whether they're the executioner types, so they'd have to send for someone and then they might have some difficulty explaining how they got a comrade wrongly executed. If I was them, I'd keep my head down."

"But I don't see why we can't deal with someone who's also been keeping their head down….the concierge, Mme Vliets. She must've known what was going on when Monique Lefebvre was abducted. Either she sat in her cubby-hole with her eyes closed or she was encouraged to go out for an hour or two. But someone came back to tidy up – and probably check for any evidence…and then someone also came and planted the pistol and ammunition. Don't you think we've got enough to call her bluff?"

"Why not! And there's no time like the present."

So we changed tram stops and headed out to Uccle. As we opened the door of the building where Mlle Lefebvre had her apartment, the concierge emerged on cue.

"You two again," she grumbled. "What do you want?"

"You should understand that you are facing a lengthy gaol sentence as an accessory to murder," I began, having agreed with Rosemary that we'd better stick with my more confident French.

"I don't understand what you mean!" Mme Vliets gave me an angry stare.

"Yes, you do. On the last evening Mlle Lefebvre was in her apartment here, a man telephoned you. It's possible he called, but it's more likely he phoned. He told you that if you valued your life, you'd get yourself out of the building for a specified period. My guess it was several hours, possibly even as long as a day. While you were away from the building, Mlle Lefebvre was interrogated and killed. We don't know whether it was here or elsewhere. But someone undoubtedly searched her apartment and tidied it up neatly afterwards. It wouldn't take a good concierge like you to know that it was Mlle Lefebvre who had gone missing and you also guessed that she wouldn't be coming back. But you've never told anyone about being warned off or that someone - indeed, several people – had been in her apartment….including the police. As you'll no doubt be aware, that makes you an accessory to murder."

She promptly burst into tears. I doubted whether they were genuine, but a tactic which she'd evidently used successfully on many occasions.

"It's true…..I got a phone call…..I was to stay away from the building between six in the evening on the Saturday until midday the following day. I didn't see anyone….I was scared they'd do something to me if I told the police…." she mumbled, between great sobs.

"But as there was only a phone call, you couldn't identify anyone. So why would anyone care what you said to the police later? You didn't hang around and look did you?"

"Not on my life! I went to visit my cousin in Etterbeek. I didn't come back 'til the evening on the Sunday…But I'm not Belgian. The Belgian police wouldn't believe me. They'd believe I knew more than I do….."

More sobs.

"But you do know a bit more, don't you. After all, during the following week, you had at least one visitor who looked at Mlle Lefebvre's room, didn't you?"

"On the Thursday morning, a small man with dark hair and round, thick glasses with a large moustache like M. Thomson in the 'Tintin' books. He told me he knew what'd happened during the weekend and that I'd better keep my mouth shut. He said he needed to check Mlle Lefebvre's room to make sure his associates hadn't left anything. He went up on his own with the key and came back about five minutes later."

"Was he carrying a bag or a package?"

"A bag."

"Has anyone else been in the flat, apart from us and the Belgian police?"

"On the following Tuesday. Another man. Tall – taller than you, but quite broad. Narrow face with spectacles. Short fair hair. Spoke French like a Flamand."

"What did he want to do?"

"He said she was a colleague and wanted to know whether Mlle Lefebvre was unwell. I told him she'd gone away a week previously. I showed him into her flat, but he just glanced around the rooms briefly and came out….I didn't think he was a colleague. He looked like some sort of flic to me….and I began to wonder what sort of things Mlle Lefebvre had been up to…..It made me even keener to keep my mouth shut."

"I shouldn't put too many hopes on that. You may be called to identify one or both of these men at some stage."

I wondered whether my final remark might just cause her to flee. But I reckoned she was made of sterner stuff than she'd been showing us and would resume her habitual hostile grumpiness the moment we were out of the building.

We decided to take an early lunch nearby – in "la vieille porte verte", naturally.

"It hadn't occurred to me that Korthuizen or one of the others might've been working for Dutch intelligence," remarked Rosemary. "I guess he's only part-time. I suppose everyone suspected Monique Lefebvre, and he was there to keep an eye on her."

"And probably the reason why he hit Creac'h when he was teasing her about being an undercover agent for the Viet Cong wasn't because of the teasing, but because it was bringing into the open something they didn't want. After all, if you suspect someone, you can keep a discreet eye on all her contacts….which might lead you to someone a lot more interesting than her…so you probably wouldn't want a person as harmless as her chucked out of the Commission because of suspect loyalties. You'd actually want her to progress to NATO where her contacts might be a lot more important."

"What a strange world these people live in……But let's hope they don't feel we stepped heavily on their corns this morning."

"I can't imagine we told the Vietnamese anything more than they didn't know already….And if they'd kept proper tabs on this Ho Quyen Diep, Monique Lefebvre might not have been killed and the little man might be more worried than I suspect he is today."

"Do you think we should do anything about Korthuizen?"

"No. If one of these security service people cuts up rough, we can use him to divert them a bit."

Rosemary was silent for a couple of minutes, sipping at a bowl of soup.

"No. We do need to speak to Korthuizen. It's quite possible it was him who told the little man about Monique Lefebvre in the first place. Probably not intending to, probably a slip of the tongue. He may not remember…."

"But then he might."

However, it was Friday. I phoned Korthuizen when I got back to the office, Rosemary having decided to take a shorter day and take Emily and Sarah out by tram for an afternoon walk in the Auderghem forest, as it was a sunnier, warmer autumn day that recently and we weren't likely to see too many more of them….and the weekend promised heavy rain. Unsurprisingly, Korthuizen had already left - perhaps taking the opportunity to do some cycling in the leafy lanes round Tervuren….Though, on reflection, I'd been told he was a serious cyclist who wore all the "Tour de France" gear, which I'd always considered faintly indecent. So he was probably pedalling all the way to Maastricht or somewhere like that. Rather him than me. Though I'd owned bikes from time to time, not least when I started as an OCX in Harwich, I'd always felt that when the cycling was flat it was uninteresting and when it was interesting, it was too much like hard work.

I was pleased that Emily and Sarah had enjoyed their walk in the woods on Friday, because the rain didn't let up all weekend. We braved it for a Saturday afternoon excursion to the Royal Art and History museum and Rosemary escaped to the local supermarket later for the basics of our week's shopping, returning with dripping trolley and pretty well soaked to the skin, as the wind had got up and ripped her umbrella to shreds. While she soaked in a hot bath, the rest of us played "Contraband" and, when she rejoined us, "Cluedo" and "Scoop", which I'd found in a second-hand shop not far from the Palais de Justice. Of course, the children wanted to play "Pit", but the neighbours were in and we'd banned it whenever there was anyone else in the building.

On Monday morning, I rang Korthuizen's number, but a man on the other end told me that he hadn't come in yet. For an idle moment, I wondered whether the rain had been so heavy he'd been unable to get back over the River Maas. At any rate, I left a message for him to ring back and settled down to a bit of my day job, while wondering from time to time whether I'd be receiving an admonitory call from some security service or counter-intelligence agency or other.

It was only at lunchtime I heard the news. Rosemary and I were eating with several of our SEFF colleagues in the Commission restaurant when Gerry Fitzpatrick, of all people, came over to our table and indicated that Rosemary and I should follow him to a vacant table in a different corner.

"I'm right in thinking that you had some dealings with a fellow called Korthuizen, Piet Korthuizen?" he asked.

We both nodded.

"Then you'll wish to know that on Saturday morning, he was killed just outside a place called Bertem on the Louvain road, He was on his bike on his own, apparently. They're saying he was hit by a car and the driver didn't stop. I guess it was pouring with rain at the time.....As a very keen cyclist, he was braving the weather and heading for Louvain from his apartment in Tervuren. What I've been told is that the car heading in the opposite direction appeared to lose control in the wet, swerve towards him, smash into him and then drove away as fast he or she could."

"That sounds more as though it was deliberate," remarked Rosemary. "If you'd really lost control of your car and hit a cyclist, the decent thing would be to see how he was and do something to help him."

"That may be the case. But from what I was told, he was killed instantly...If you need to know more, you'll have to see if you can speak to the Belgian police...though which particular version I've no idea."

"Thank you for telling us."

We sat in silence, stunned. Though neither of us had particularly liked Piet Korthuizen, his murder – for that's what we were sure it was – showed yet again that the "little man" would stop at nothing to ensure that he wasn't discovered. Indeed, he was prepared to kill even if the chances of anyone discovering a link between him and his victim were remote. Of course, we had surmised that Korthuizen was possibly...probably...the person who deliberately or inadvertently put him on to Monique Lefebvre in the first place, but the knowledge took us no nearer to who had carried out this fraud than we were already. But there was something odd about this murder....several things, actually....

"Why now?" asked Rosemary. "If we're right and Korthuizen put the mastermind on to Monique Lefebvre originally, why did he kill Korthuizen now? We'd worked out why Monique was killed when she was, but what happened to require Korthuizen's death?"

"And something that may well not have been long planned. After all, someone could've got the car number. There'll be a damaged car somewhere. It will've come from somewhere. All add to the risks. And presumably the mastermind did it himself?"

"Assuming Korthuizen was deliberately killed and we're not adding up two and two and making five, you'd have to know what he looks like....and the MO of this man is certainly to involve as few other people as possible in what he gets up to."

"So why now? Could it've been our visit to the Banque Indosuez on Friday? It's possible that the bank is watched by some security service people pretty well permanently, just to see what likely suspects go in and out. Because we went in, it may be that someone from there told Korthuizen. And did he perhaps mention it to the mastermind?"

"And the mastermind suddenly realises that Korthuizen might speak to us about our visit to the bank. We'll work out what his part-time job is and make the link to Monique Lefebvre. We're then only one question away from finding out who else Korthuizen has been talking to about this. So Korthuizen has to go…and quickly."

"With all the possibility that doing it in a hurry may have left us some traces……Though if I read the mastermind right, he's probably had some sort of plan to deal with Korthuizen for some time….as he was perhaps his most vulnerable spot."

"Well…You'd better see if you can get anything out of the Belgian police…."

"With you, I think. I may speak French better, but you're another flic, or whatever the feminine of 'flic' is."

But before we could go anywhere, we were found by an emissary from Jérôme Vermeulen who wanted an immediate word. Plainly it was important, as I couldn't imagine him normally breaking into his lunch hours without good reason. He met us, as usual in his stocking feet and gave Rosemary's legs his usual long appraisal.

"You have heard about Korthuizen?" he began.

"Yes. It sounds dreadful."

"I understand the police aren't suggesting it was a deliberate act aimed at killing Korthuizen. But was there anything in the course of your investigations that might suggest that he was linked to these frauds? Or any other reason why someone might wish to kill him? I barely knew the man, but our paths had crossed a few times….and naturally, I'd hope that the good name of the EEC Commission isn't dragged unnecessarily into what may well be a completely different affair."

"Though we weren't convinced that Korthuizen was always entirely truthful with us," I replied. "There was no reason at all to suppose he was involved in the fraud."

"Any possible link between his death and the continuing disappearance of Mlle Lefebvre?"

"Not that we know. But all we know about Korthuizen's death is what Knut Henriksen has just told us at lunchtime. Apart from working together in DGVI, the only link we've come across is that it seems likely that it was Korthuizen who supposedly thumped Creac'h on the nose for teasing Mlle Lefebvre about being a Viet Cong sympathiser. As that seems to have been some years ago, I can't imagine it had any bearing on what happened on Saturday."

"And your investigation? How is it proceeding? You have but a few weeks to go, if I remember correctly?"

"It's more than likely we'll never know who carried out the fraud….and the money is long gone and will be untraceable by now. We know how it was carried out. We know what the man looked like who made the necessary visits to the firms and banks involved and we think it's likely – but without much evidence – that Mlle Lefebvre may have been involved in some way, or made to look as though she was involved, to create the impression the fraud was carried out by North Vietnamese. It's even possible that's who it was."

"So what are you doing at the moment?"

"We know the cars which the man hired to make the visits to the firms and banks. We're planning to try to see where he stayed. We hope that might produce some more evidence about him – but so far he's shown himself to be extremely adept at avoiding leaving any traces of who he really is."

"But you still believe the fraud was planned in the Commission?"

"We believe that whoever carried out the fraud needed to know about the procedures in DGVI and needed access to relevant documents and names. So, someone who works or worked recently in DGVI had to be involved, but they could've been working for someone outside the Commission."

"And presumably, among those who it could've been was Korthuizen, as well as Mlle Lefebvre?"

"I think Korthuizen had left DGVI before some of the documents were copied, certainly according to what he told us. Someone might've mentioned it if he'd reappeared later on. So I doubt whether he would've taken the risk."

"Very well. Keep me posted."

We departed, Rosemary shooting off to collect Emily and Sarah. I decided to try and find out who in the Belgian police was dealing with the death of Piet Korthuizen. Fortunately, Rosemary's colleague, Marc Dierich, was knowledgeable about the Belgian police services, if not about the Korthuizen case. However, he had contacts who informed him after about half an hour that it was being dealt with by the local gendarmerie for the municipality of Bertem. He said that this indicated that they were almost certainly treating Korthuizen's death as a traffic accident, rather than as anything more serious....Though he'd been told that the Brussels and Louvain police had been contacted to see whether they could trace the car that had hit Korthuizen and then driven away.

"It's a pity it's one of these local police forces," observed Rosemary when I explained later. "They don't like other forces taking over. Which is no doubt why they're treating it as a hit-and-run, rather than murder. Fortunately, we don't really need to deal with them. What we really need to know is about the car that killed Korthuizen....And I think it must've come from Brussels..."

"Why? Why not Louvain? It was travelling from there."

"Because it must've been nicked. Where would you try to steal a car with the least risk, here or Louvain? Besides, if someone was deliberately trying to kill Korthuizen, they'd hardly park on the Louvain road until they saw a cyclist coming in the opposite direction, rev up and swerve over and kill him. In the rain, there's no way you could be certain who you were killing…and I'll bet there are enough crazy cyclists around these parts that you couldn't just assume the only cyclist would be him. So I reckon whoever killed him must have been keeping an eye on his flat. When he left, he'd know what he looked like. Then all he'd have to do would be keep behind him until he was definitely heading for Louvain, overtake him, turn round and smack into him on his way back…He's also heading for Brussels, where it'd be much easier to hide the car."

"But there's always a risk if you use a lock-up…."

"I wouldn't use a lock up. I'd park in a supermarket car park or station car park right next to some convenient public transport and head away from the vehicle as fast as I could. Who notices people parking cars in supermarket car parks? Especially when it's pouring with rain. And hitting a cyclist might well not cause much noticeable damage….and the rain would've conveniently washed off any blood, so it'd look like loads of cars here that've had a small bump or two…"

"And presumably it'd be stolen in the first place?"

"Probably that morning," Rosemary suggested. "But possibly Friday night. I guess you'd nick it from a car park and stick it in another one – an undercover one, probably a multi-storey – until you needed it. But if you were really slick, you'd nick it and drive straight over to wherever Korthuizen lived in Tervuren. Indeed, you could even stick it back in the same car park if you were confident you wouldn't be seen and could get away on the next tram or bus without anyone noticing."

"And you'd wear gloves – so no fingerprints."

"I wonder how the man stole the car? If we're still assuming it's someone who works in the Commission, he's acquired some interesting criminal skills along the way."

"I suppose if we're right and it was Korthuizen who told the mastermind about Monique Lefebvre originally, he may've had to have a plan for getting rid of him ever since then. And while he could get someone else to bump her off, the North Vietnamese wouldn't do his dirty work for him in Korthuizen's case. So he may have had a couple of years to polish his skills."

"Unfortunately, if the police are looking for a hit-and-run, they won't do much if they find the car involved was stolen. They'll dust for fingerprints, but they'll be pretty sure the thief wore gloves and the only prints they'll find will belong to the owners. It might not even be worth getting in touch with them – not least we'd have to explain our interest."

"I suppose it might be useful knowing where the car was stolen and where it was dumped, but assuming it was the mastermind who drove it, he won't have made a simple journey to get there – or to get back home again."

"We may not need to do it ourselves anyway. You'd expect the local police to keep Commander de Klerk in the picture…..It'd be nice to think he kept a diary with incriminating names in it, but I suppose if he'd had some security service training, there wouldn't be anything we could lay our fingers on…."

"But would that be enough for the mastermind? When you think how meticulous he's been about ensuring there are no links back to him, how confident would he be that there might not be something in Korthuizen's flat or his room at work that might identify him in some way?"

"Of course, checking them out might be at least as risky as doing nothing. After all, even if Korthuizen had a name in a diary that said he'd spoken to Mr X about Mlle Lefebvre, who's going to know the significance of it, other than us?"

"Hmmm…That doesn't quite feel like the mastermind we've got to know…But, of course, it's possible he could check out Korthuizen's room at work without being noticed…But it'd be even easier to get the stuff removed from his room and, unless there's some relative to send the personal stuff, bung it in the waste."

"Which would probably happen in the normal course of events."

"Which leaves his flat.....But apart from not knowing where it is, we've also no idea whether he lived with anyone…"

"I can't say he gave that impression – but if he was a homosexual, of course, he'd've been doing his best to give the impression of being single."

"I guess the mastermind knows.....I must say I'd like to see whether he has visited the flat…We can already guess what he looks like, but there's always the chance he might've given something away."

"We've been saying that for a while now without him slipping up so far....."

"Apart from the Chinese pistol. I still think that was a bit too clever by half. With any luck, that arrogance might've caused him to slip up somewhere else.

14. A TRIAL OF ASSUMPTIONS

It would've been convenient to have been able to look at a couple of the bits of Korthuizen's personal file which I hadn't seen. But that'd mean going through de Klerk or Vermeulen. And while I'd long dismissed de Klerk being the mastermind of these frauds, Vermeulen – however unlikely - fitted enough of the profile for me not to wish to trust him with anything I didn't have to. In any case, it was something Rosemary was better at: and she managed to get an address out of the personnel people by explaining we were colleagues and acquaintances and wish to send some flowers to his home.

The following morning, we went straight to Vermeulen's flat in Tervuren. It was the ground floor of quite an elegant brick house in a pleasant street of similar houses, smaller and less grand than a few of the rather magnificent houses we'd seen on our way there. It was opposite the church, slightly smaller than its neighbours. But this was one of, if not the, poshest suburbs of Brussels. Apart from several stunning large private houses and a smart barracks, there was the Royal Museum for Central Africa, which we'd visited a couple of times with Emily and Sarah - with me continuing to bite my tongue about how the Congolese people had been exploited to provide, not just the exhibits, but the wealth to build the magnificent museum, the splendid avenue leading back to Brussels and probably many of the beautiful houses in the vicinity. I reckoned the rent for this flat must take a pretty huge chunk out of Korthuizen's pay. We knocked on the door, but there was no answer. I'd already concluded Korthuizen had almost certainly lived on his own, so this wasn't a surprise. Unfortunately, there was no front garden or step on which we could leave our bunch of flowers.

We stood outside, wondering what to do, hoping our presence might attract some neighbours. After a few minutes a young Filipino woman came out of the house next door.

"He not there. He dead. Police came Saturday. Killed by car," she said in primitive French.

"We are colleagues of his. We had heard about his death. We wished to leave some flowers for him, as is the custom in our country," I replied in straightforward English, reckoning she might well be more fluent in my native tongue.

"You speak English? I can take flowers if you wish and give to someone who comes for them. But he lived on his own and I do not know whether he had relatives. He was from Netherlands, I think."

"Yes."

"The police told Mrs Helder....my mistress....that he was hit by a car and it was possibly not an accident. Have you heard that?"

"We had heard that the driver didn't stop after he'd hit Mr Korthuizen, but the police weren't sure whether the driver lost control of his car or whether he swerved deliberately. But we know no reason why anyone would wish to harm him."

"Perhaps he had something someone wanted? I thought I heard someone in his apartment the night after he was killed....Saturday night. My room is in the basement and I could hear movement in his flat. I asked Mrs Helder whether I should inform the police, but she said I'd probably dreamt the whole thing and she wasn't calling the police to tell them about something as insubstantial as a maid's imaginings."

"You didn't hear a car?"

"No. Just movement in the apartment. I didn't even hear the man come in or go out."

"A man?" asked Rosemary.

"It could've been a woman. I can see nothing of the street from my basement."

"Could you tell what sort of noises were being made in the apartment?"

"The person was moving around quite a bit and opening cupboards and drawers….the noise is quite distinct…I assumed he was looking for something."

"Do you know when he left?"

"No. It went quiet and I must have fallen asleep again….Why are you so interested in this?"

"If someone was looking for something in Mr Korthuizen's flat, it might've been documents which relate to his work. His work involved paying out money to certain sorts of farmers," I explained. "Someone might have wanted to get their hands on them for personal gain."

"You will inform the police?" She suddenly looked extremely worried. "Mrs Helder will…."

"I believe not. First we should check whether any documents are missing from his work. Then I think it'd be best if a colleague came to his apartment and checked, rather than involving the police at this stage."

She breathed an audible sigh of relief.

"Mrs Helder is not in the house at present?"

"She works in the city during the day. I collect the children from school and she returns for the evening meal – with Major Helder at the same time."

"If we needed to contact you again – is there a telephone number we could use?"

She gave me a number, with the proviso that I should only call during the day. Without seeing her, I couldn't say I warmed to Mme Helder.

We handed over the flowers and thanked her and spent ten minutes wandering round Tervuren, just to see where the driver who had killed Korthuizen might have parked his car. In the event it was pretty straightforward. The way out of Tervuren on to the Louvain road came past a couple of places where someone could park a car easily and without attracting any notice.

Korthuizen could've come sailing past on his bike and then the driver just had to drive past him and smack into him on the way back.

"Why didn't he just run into the back of him on the way to Louvain? Why did he need to go past him and turn back? Surely you'd be risking hitting another vehicle?" asked Rosemary.

"In theory. But it was a wet morning and I bet not many cars were about.....But if you hit him from behind I reckon your chances of killing him would be a lot less. You're travelling in the same direction, so the impact would much less and you might just knock him off the road. But when you hit him head on, the impact combines both your speeds – and you're hitting his head first, rather than his bum….and I guess you also want to get back to a big anonymous city like Brussels as soon as you can after you've committed the murder….?"

"That's sufficiently convincing, Sherlock….But do you reckon the Filipino maid was dreaming, or whether she really heard something?"

"It's an odd sort of dream, if it was one. It seems more likely that the mastermind wanted to make sure that there was nothing hidden in Korthuizen's flat that might give him away."

"It could've been the Dutch security service?"

"Why would they go creeping around at night? They'd just make a few phone calls and one of their blokes would accompany the Belgian police when they had a look at the flat."

"And if he found what he was looking for, he's now home and dry."

"But, of course, if he didn't find anything – perhaps because there's nothing there to find – he's never going to be quite sure there is something there, but he missed it."

"And it might be possible to make use of that…."

We travelled back to work, mostly in silence, thinking our own thoughts. As we kissed before going into our separate offices, Rosemary said,

"I think it's time we looked through all our notes and then thought about what we've got. When we were talking out in Tervuren, you realise we were always making the assumption that it was the little man who killed Korthuizen. But we've practically no evidence for that. We don't really know whether the man we call the mastermind is the same as the small man. And Korthuizen could easily have any number of enemies….or conceivably just been unlucky…and I was involved in several hit-and-run cases in Leicester where the driver just panicked…they certainly hadn't intended to kill the victim."

"OK."

I spent the rest of the day doing as Rosemary had suggested. It was only as I did so that I realised how many assumptions I'd been making, drawing inferences from evidence mostly based on these assumptions. All we really knew was how the fraud had been carried out and the fact that "a small man with dark hair and spectacles with very thick lenses" had plainly been directly involved. Virtually everything else involved speculation, assumptions and sometimes, just guesswork…though I might dress it up as something else. I lay awake during the night for a long time, Rosemary's head resting on my shoulder as usual. I had a slight, but pervasive headache and a growing feeling that we'd been wasting our time for the last few weeks. My initial fears – that this whole matter had been offered to us to enable us to fall flat on our faces – returned to the surface.

Though the following day was one of those sunny, warm days in which Brussels looked its best, we resisted the temptation to consider what we knew, what we thought we knew and what we didn't know in one of the parks near the Commission building, but borrowed an empty room in the SEFF offices.

"What we actually know is remarkably little," Rosemary began. "We know how the fraud was carried out and we know that 'the little man with the dark hair and thick spectacles' was the contact both with the companies and the banks involved. He's actually the only person we can reliably tie into it. We also know that the fraud depended on knowing DGVI procedures, not least the fact that there'd be no checking until after the year-end. So we can make the reasonable assumption that whoever carried out the fraud either worked there, had worked there or had an accomplice working there. Is there anything else we can say which depends on evidence, rather than assumptions?"

"I think there's a bit of evidence. From the car rental company, we know what cars the little man used and we could probably trace where he stayed – though I don't believe it'd be worth doing that. There's also something which you may say is an assumption, but I feel is carried a bit more weight than that. When I told Bao Tran and his colleagues my story about Monique Lefebvre, they never challenged me about it. You could say that they preferred not to say anything to a running dog of Western imperialism, but the story didn't put them in a particularly good light and they made no comment about my suggestion that Ho Quyen Diep executed Monique Lefebvre…"

"I'm not so sure about that….I think they were determined to say as little as possible…."

"So you don't think Monique Lefebvre was connected to these frauds?"

"What I'm saying is that I don't think we've got any firm evidence for that."

"So her disappearance at the time the frauds were discovered was pure coincidence?"

"Maybe. Maybe not. I just don't think we've established a link that rests on evidence rather than our assumptions….I'm not trying to be difficult – but I think if one of us doesn't play devil's advocate, we could easily go haring off down particular tracks…and we've only got a few weeks left to sort this out if we can."

"OK. But equally, we shouldn't treat everything that's happened as coincidental. For instance, the conjunction of the frauds being discovered, Ho Quyen Diep making his short visit and Monique Lefebvre's disappearance. We've found no other reason why she should disappear. The security service blokes didn't know any reason why he'd been and gone. And Bao Tran and his colleagues looked distinctly uncomfortable when I suggested how they'd been played by the man who carried out the fraud. It may not be firm evidence – but if we don't use some of what we've learnt that isn't firm evidence, it seems to me we might as well stop now."

"I'm not disagreeing with you. But as we examine what we think we know, I believe we really need to keep testing every assumption. For instance, Korthuizen's visit to Monique Lefebvre's flat after she died. We made the assumption he was working for a Dutch security or counter-intelligence service. But that was purely an assumption. And then when he got run over, we made another large assumption that it was the man behind the fraud because it was Korthuizen who'd put him on to Mlle Lefebvre's supposed involvement with North Vietnamese intelligence and enabled him to blackmail her. But we've no evidence wasn't a run-of-the-mill hit-and-run."

"The movement in the flat heard by the Filipino maid next door?"

"A burglar. Word gets about that someone has been killed. A local burglar realises his opportunity. It happened at least once in Leicester in my time."

"OK. Then let's go from what we can make reasonable assumptions about. Would you agree that the little man who carried out the frauds must've had an accomplice in DGVI - either someone who worked there or has worked there? And that it wasn't him?"

"I guess so."

"And what we can tell from where the little man hired his cars, he probably lives in Brussels?"

"OK.....But why do you assume that the little man didn't work in DGVI or hadn't worked there?"

"Because when the fraud was discovered, as it was bound to be, people with knowledge of DGVI procedures and the ability to get hold of the documents needed to carry out the fraud would inevitably lead the authorities to suspect someone working there or who'd worked there…..And I don't think I'm making too big an assumption when I say that the evidence supports a view that the man who carried out this fraud is extremely cautious. My evidence for that is the firms where he decided not to run the fraud….and as far as we know, no-one in DGVI fits his description either."

"I can certainly go that far. But there's no real evidence that the little man is the mastermind or that either of them work in the Commission. They could just be a gang of local crooks who managed to get their hooks into someone in DGVI with gambling debts, for instance."

"Well, let me try another assumption. It's not as strong as the last one, but I think it's worth thinking about. The only time this fraud could be committed was after the rules for reconciling DGVI balances were changed from quarterly to annual. There appears to have been no pressure for this to be done. There was no cost-cutting drive in the Commission, no O&M report, no staff inspection report….."

"Mostly because the Commission doesn't go in for such things…."

"Exactly. So it seems to me we can reasonably ask why it was changed? And since this fraud took place very soon afterwards, is it too great an assumption to suggest that someone changed the reconciliation timings in order to commit the fraud?"

"There might be other reasons. You're always saying…or you were when you were back in Customs…about all these fast-streamers coming up with lots of bright ideas, most of which were completely impracticable. Perhaps this was just someone's bright idea that someone important liked, and the crooks just took advantage of it."

"So someone in DGVI has a gambling habit and racks up a big debt to some crook. In order to pay off the debt, he suggests how the crook can make millions through a fraud on DGVI, with his help. He provides the names and documents and the crook does the rest. But surely, when the fraud is discovered and the authorities start poking around, they're likely to find out about this bloke's gambling habit? Doesn't that risk blowing the whole thing open?"

"I suppose it could be pictures he wouldn't want his family and colleagues to see in the papers?"

"I suppose it depends on whether the crook trusts him to say nothing when the authorities start poking around. And you have to admit that the way this fraud was carried out has shown that whoever has been running it to be extremely cautious and, we've kept saying, meticulous in not leaving any traces to come back to him.....or her, of course. Would someone like that leave his or her informant in DGVI in place when there was even the slightest prospect that they may end up shopping them?"

"So?"

"Wouldn't the crook do something to ensure he couldn't be traced? By getting rid of his informant one way or another?"

"So?"

"If it has to be someone who worked or had worked in DGVI - that leaves only Monique Lefebvre and Piet Korthuizen as people who've disappeared from the Commission one way or another. And then you have to ask yourself from what we've learnt about Monique Lefebvre, was she likely to have a gambling or drug habit? Or put herself in a position where she could be blackmailed? I agree – it's unlikely, but not impossible. And as a good Catholic.....and I'm aware I'm making an assumption there.....the thought that indecent photographs of her might get out might well've been more than enough to get her to give the crook the information he needed."

"But I think there's a problem with that. It assumes that the crook already knew there was big money to be had from frauds on the Commission and that Monique Lefebvre could provide all the information he needed. She was hardly the sort of person you'd line up to blackmail, surely? Indeed, knowing that she was supposedly a good Catholic, wouldn't there be a risk that she'd blurt it out in the confessional…and who knows where it might go from there?"

"Korthuizen?"

"Why kill him now, rather than when the fraud was discovered? Has anything happened to make a crook feel he was suddenly less reliable now than he was a few months ago?" asked Rosemary.

"Perhaps he used our investigations to demand a larger share of the loot?"

"Hmmm…Would he really be in a position to demand anything, assuming the blackmail threat had been sufficiently persuasive in the first place? In any case, I'm not sure whether he was still working in DGVI to be able to get his paws on all the documents used in the frauds."

"If I remember, he was a bit unclear about that…..perhaps deliberately?"

"But suppose he was – would you say his death was an accident or deliberate?"

"I don't know. It was raining hard on Saturday morning, so someone could've skidded and swerved into him, even though it seems a pretty straight road. If it was deliberate, I can't see any reason why it should be linked to him being the man who gave crooks or someone else details from DGVI. I agree with you. The timing doesn't really seem right."

"I agree we haven't really looked in any depth at the names Allenby suggested. The trouble is, it means getting into the Commission personnel files without any justification. And if we're trying to avoid acting on assumptions, there's no strong reason why Allenby's names should be any more likely than any others."

"I agree……So what do we make of the Chinese pistol left in Monique Lefebvre's flat? It's certainly evidence. But of what? We heard nothing about her that suggested she'd be the sort of person who felt she needed to own a weapon like that. And why would Mme Vliets mention the little man with the dark hair and thick spectacles and someone else who certainly resembled Korthuizen if they hadn't been there? We never suggested either of them to her. Did you feel she was lying?"

"No. I wouldn't say I was completely certain about that. But I agree, we never mentioned either of them, so what she told us goes beyond a pure assumption."

"Do you think it's reasonable to assume that the little man Mme Vliets saw was the same one involved with the firms and the banks?" I suggested.

"It's possible that there's more than one of them, of course. But it'd be fair to say it was probably the same man."

"So what assumptions do we make about him going there at the time he did?"

"We know he was involved in the frauds. Monique Lefebvre worked in DGVI and subsequently disappeared at the time the frauds were discovered and began to be investigated. But there's no evidential link."

"Which it seems to me, there won't be – because the man who carried out this fraud, whether it was the little man or someone else, has made sure that there won't be…..But assuming he was the little man involved in the frauds, what reasons could there be for him to go to her flat unless she was involved with him in some way?"

"Assuming it was the same man, I guess you could reasonably say they were linked in some way."

"OK. Then what about the Chinese pistol? It was there when we went to the flat a couple of weeks later. But I think we can apply something that goes beyond assumptions to how it got there. First – we don't know whether it belonged to Monique Lefebvre or not. Do we agree on that?"

"That's impossible to argue with."

"So when the person who rang Mme Vliets and told her push off if she valued her health turned up on the Saturday, the gun was either there or not. And we don't know whether it was there when the man who went to the flat - let's call him Ho Quyen Diep – or not. And I realise I'm assuming the person who warned Mme Vliets off might not have been him, but let me follow this path a little longer. If there was a Chinese pistol in the flat already, why would he wish to leave it there? The only thing it could possibly do is to point to probable North Vietnamese involvement, in view of Monique's Lefebvre's family background. Would he really want to advertise that? Otherwise, we have to assume he brought it with him. But how many people like that would take off their pistol, its holster and fifty-off rounds of ammo and leave them all neatly hanging in a cupboard? It makes no sense? Surely if it'd been there when Ho Quyen Diep came to the flat, he'd've taken it away with him and presumably disposed of it with Monique Lefebvre's body.....or if he was really cautious, somewhere quite different. Does that seem logical to you?"

"Yes. Though you've got to remember your assumption about the man being Ho Quyen Diep, which we haven't really established."

"Well, someone plainly scared Mlle Vliets off. Or did you think she was lying?"

"No. That rang true enough."

"Well, if it wasn't him, who was it? The little man and Korthuizen both came along later, after Monique Lefebvre had disappeared, when she'd reverted to being the normal crocodile-concierge."

"What?"

"She looks fierce and intimidating, but when put under pressure releases large volume of crocodile tears.....She must've guessed that something nasty was going to happen to someone in those flats, but she preferred just to shove off....Not even an anonymous phone call to the police!"

"I guess she felt someone would find out and then they'd have it in for her."

"Sorry…We're diverting….But that leaves us with the likelihood that Monique Lefebvre has been removed, but also there's no Chinese pistol there. So how does it get there? I assume you're prepared to discount Mme Vliets?"

"I can't see any reason why she'd be involved."

"So that leaves the two visitors – the little man and Korthuizen. I realise I may be taking a risk that there was someone else who visited Monique Lefebvre's flat, but Mme Vliets didn't - or didn't want to - tell us about him or her, but let's assume she was telling the truth. Assuming she was, that means that either the little man or Korthuizen left the Chinese pistol."

"And begs the question why?"

"Let's stick with the assumption that Korthuizen was working part-time for Dutch intelligence….We might even be able to use my contacts to check that…What could his interest in Monique Lefebvre possibly have been? My security service people believed that the North Vietnamese working in the Banque Indosuez wouldn't have spent too much time with her unless she was likely to be of use. Is it unreasonable to think that if our people knew that, someone on a security service payroll working within the Commission would be detailed to keep an eye on her? And as with the men at the Banque Indosuez, all they wanted to do was to keep a look-out, in case she or they did something that might lead them to some bigger fish. So isn't it reasonable to conclude that he was making sure there was nothing that the security services needed to know about lying around somewhere in her flat?"

"Why didn't they do the usual security service thing and get someone along with the local police?

"I could theorise, but perhaps the simplest answer is that they've got Korthuizen, who's a colleague. Why not get him to look around, ostensibly for some papers missing from the office? You don't have to tell the local police anything and they've no reason to think you owe them one."

"Just make sure you keep Ockham's Razor out of this! I felt you were getting closer by the second then!" She smirked.

"OK. But I may need to come back to it at some point......But all that suggests that if Korthuizen was doing what we think he was doing, there's no reason for him to bring a Chinese pistol with him and leave it there. All it does is advertise her possible links to North Vietnam. And why would any of the security services wish to do that?"

"So you conclude that it had to be the little man who took it there and left it...to divert suspicion on to the North Vietnamese? So why didn't Korthuizen take it away?"

"I don't know. I'd guess that when he was doing his security service stuff, he did what he was told. He wasn't told to remove the pistol, so he didn't. No doubt he reported it back, but they probably then started their games of treble- and quadruple-think about who'd left it there and why, and what sort of a trap it might be. So they decided to leave it where it was.....After all, no-one really knows whether the building wasn't under surveillance at least some of the time.....and if you work in the security service, I guess you're more paranoid about that sort of thing than most of us."

"And I suppose everyone just left it there.....including the Belgian police.....So, do you think it's that thing that appears in all those Hitchcock films....."

".....The 'McGuffin'?"

"That's it! Do you think the Chinese pistol is one of those?"

"No. McGuffins only fire .22 calibre bullets!"

"Very funny! Shall we get back to where we were? I think we've probably convinced ourselves that Monique Lefebvre was involved in the fraud. But the only other person we can be sure was involved was the little man."

"I agree."

"So that leads us on to the next question – was the little man Mr Big?" Her smirk was the largest since we'd been in Brussels.

"You've been waiting to use that for weeks!"

"Serves you right for the McGuffin!"

"Very well…. Concentrate, woman!"

"But it's actually the question we can't answer. Or do you believe we can?"

"It depends on whether you believe Korthuizen's death was a pure accident or deliberate murder. This is where I admit to quite a bit of skating on thin ice. If it was Korthuizen – deliberately or, in my view, inadvertently tipped off Mr Big about Monique Lefebvre, he was always at risk. I reckon that one of these security services have got a deal with Mme Vliets. She tells them about anyone who calls about Monique Lefebvre – including our latest visit. This gets back to Korthuizen, not least because someone needs to warn him that we might be asking him some awkward questions. Where I'm really guessing is that Mr Big also gets to hear about it. Perhaps Korthuizen has been asked by de Klerck or someone else to let them know if anything happens in relation to Monique Lefebvre. But Mr Big realises that when we start asking Korthuizen questions he probably doesn't ask himself, we may come up with a conversation Korthuizen has had with someone who wishes to remain utterly and completely anonymous….Now to my mind, that doesn't suggest some sort of crook, but much more someone within the Commission who doesn't want to have to spend the last thirty or forty years of his life in Paraguay or North Vietnam, but in some nice places where he can live in luxurious obscurity, rubbing his hands at the way he outsmarted everyone."

"There are one or two quite large leaps there, you know."

"I realise that. But to some extent I'm basing them of what we seem to have learnt about this man's character in how he's operated…."

"Always assuming the little man is the same as Mr Big? The smirk hovered round her lips again.

"And I don't quite see how we can resolve that. Common sense suggests that if you worked full time in the Commission, you wouldn't go off for three weeks at a time, when you'd be bound to leave some sort of trace – especially when it was on three separate occasions. Also you're the one out doing stuff and running at least some risk of being caught. After all, suppose you got in a traffic accident, how would you explain where you were and what you were up to? On the other hand, you've got to share the loot – even though there's a lot of it – and you've got a partner who presumably must know who you are, who you've either got to trust with that knowledge for the rest of your life or get him bumped off."

"And after what happened to Monique Lefebvre, you might think you could be next......and the little man hasn't been seen since shortly after her death, of course....."

There's no reason why he should've been...and quite a few why he shouldn't."

"Maybe so...But after all this digging around and sifting what we know and what we think we know, are we really any closer to finding Mr Big – whether he's the little man or someone else?"

"I'm not sure we'll ever lay our hands on any evidence that conclusively proves who Mr Big is, but I'm beginning to wonder whether there isn't a way of flushing him out. It's possible it might not work. But there are two things I need to do before that....and one of them may allow us to kill two birds with one stone...."

"And how do you propose to do that, may I ask?"

"Personally, I don't think you really have much chance of finding something hidden in someone's flat if you're examining it at night, when you can't make too much noise. So I reckon when whoever it was visited Korthuizen's flat, he probably didn't find what he was looking for.....especially if there wasn't anything to find, which is more than likely. But if he were to believe that the Dutch security services had decided he might've been killed because of the work he was doing for them and were going to take his flat apart in the next couple of days, what do you think Mr Big might do?"

"You either go round and carry out another search or you set light to the place…..I wouldn't want to have several charred bodies on my conscience."

"Hmmm…I think you'd want to have a butchers first….After all, unless you've also picked up some clever skills in fire-starting, you risk being seen and associated with a fire….if nothing else."

"But how are you going to get Mr Big to believe Korthuizen still has some incriminating documents there, when you don't know who he is."

"I believe I know a way of doing it….and I think I've just had a spark of light which is based almost entirely on unprovable assumptions…"

"And you're not going to tell me, are you?"

"Not until I've tested a couple of theories out first."

15. A BURGLAR IS ARRESTED IN TERVUREN

I needed to manage the next couple of days carefully. My first step was a short phone call to the man at AVIS, which confirmed what I expected to be told. After the first feelings of pleasure and relief, I also reminded myself that I shouldn't completely ignore the possibility of coincidence, which might lead me into making a complete fool of myself. However, what I was proposing was more likely to prove a damp squib than a custard pie in the face.

A phone call to "Simon Stone" reinforced my belief that I was heading in the right direction. A further call to one of the names on one of our lists encouraged me still further.

For the next stage, I needed information that took me too close to my main suspect, with people who knew me a lot less than they knew him. One element was straightforward to do, but I couldn't guarantee whether it'd be successful. The other required a certain amount of subterfuge, but which told me what I needed to know. As I was expecting a further visit by my main suspect to Korthuizen's house, I rang the Filipino maid to phone our number if she heard any untoward noises next door overnight. I thought it'd be unlikely. My suspect wasn't the sort of man to reinforce failure. If he couldn't search the place adequately at night, he'd do it during the day. I also suspected he'd choose a time when his absence wouldn't be noticed.

"I suggest we head to Tervuren in mid-morning," I told Rosemary. "The Filipino maid has my number here until then and we'll need to find a café with a phone, so I can give her that."

"So you aren't planning a stake-out outside Korthuizen's house, then?"

"I believe that'd frighten Mr Big away."

"So what's the name of this operation then?"

"I don't think C&E really go in for things like that...Perhaps the IB do, I don't know....But if you like, this is operation Brussels Sprout."

"I wonder why they were called that? I don't think I've ever come across any all the time we've been here. We've certainly never been offered them to eat in a restaurant."

"Perhaps the Belgians...or whatever they were called then...gave them to their pigs and a passing Norman saw they were cheap and reckoned they'd allow him to cut the cost of feeding his serfs.....Or the only way the growers could get anyone to eat things that taste so awful was to give the impression they were some sort of foreign delicacy?"

"Or possibly, because no-one in our household likes them, I haven't looked for them here....How are you planning to get to Tervuren?"

"By public transport. If there's any sign of movement in Korthuizen's flat, I intend to phone the local police and tell them there's a burglar in there. I hope we can find somewhere to wait that's completely out of sight and only a couple of minutes' walk away....I got a map of the area on the way in."

Rosemary started to study the map carefully.

"You were right about the man who killed Korthuizen. He'd've had to follow him quite a way before he could be sure where he was heading. But once you're through these villages like Vossem, you could tell....and then you'd have several places where you overtake him and hit him on the way back....He could've had a problem if Korthuizen had decided to go on to Louvain by the main road."

"It's the main road east. Even on a Saturday it'd probably be pretty busy and there might well be loads of trucks...If you were a cyclist, which road would you use?"

At mid-morning, we set off for Tervuren. It was one of those heavy, grey days with the occasionally flurries of rain, which threatened more. I felt we shouldn't be seen outside Korthuizen's house, so we walked into the "markt", which was just round the corner and found a bar-and-café, which appeared to offer Leffe as the standard late-morning drink and had a patron with an addiction to "American Pie" by Don Maclean. While it was a song I'd enjoyed when it first came out a couple of years previously, hearing it all the time could make me detest it. The only thing that could be said for it was that it wasn't the prevalent Continental pop, generally anaemic covers or copies of British or US hits, or the originals – for that matter. I was evidently too old to be enthused by Glam Rock or the middle-of-the-road stuff which I suppose was inevitable after the excitement and innovation of the sixties and early seventies….and the music almost certainly wasn't aimed at people of my age anyway.

We ordered a burger and chips each, along with bottled water, while I phoned the Filipino maid with the phone number of the "Oude Zaak". She confirmed that there appeared to be no-one in the flat next door at present. Rosemary and I discussed how high the chances were that the burger would be horsemeat, consoling ourselves that, at least, the chips (and mayonnaise) would be reliably good.

It was at this stage when the usual negative thoughts started to pour through my mind. We'd sit here for the best part of three hours, probably hearing "American Pie" at least fifty times, without any phone call from the Filipino maid. Either the information which I'd tried to get to my intended target by the route I felt was most likely to work hadn't, or "Mr Big" had smelled a rat and decided not to come…or he'd come at a different time when our chances of catching him were less….Perhaps I'd been too predictable? Perhaps I'd been completely wrong in who I thought Mr Big was and I'd been sending a message to someone who would've found it incomprehensible? I still felt I'd identified the right person, but my confidence was slipping as the minutes ticked by….not least that perhaps my attempt to catch him had been spotted as the amateurish long-shot that it undoubtedly was.

However, shortly after quarter past two the barman called out "Mr Storey" and I went to the bar. The Filipino maid was on the phone.

"It's Maria here. Someone has just gone into the apartment next door. I can hear them moving around."

"I shall call the police immediately."

Naturally, I already had the number of the local municipal police. I dialled the number and spoke to the operator – in French, of course. Although this was plainly a Flemish area, they were sufficiently close to Brussels not to refuse to acknowledge anything spoken in French. I explained that a burglar had gone into the house in Kerkstraat where the man had recently been killed, and that it looked like a burglar. The lady thanked me and said they would send a car round.

I couldn't really tell them their business, but I hoped this would be done pronto, while at the same time, they'd decide to spare the use of their sirens…especially as presumably they were coming from just round the corner. Unfortunately, from where we were sitting, we couldn't see along Kerkstraat, though we could see the very occasional car coming past.

"We could go outside," observed Rosemary. "I don't think we could be seen from Korthuizen's house."

"Let's leave it five minutes and then we might just wander past as if we're going to the church. It'd be particularly annoying if the local police thought we were lookouts for the burglar."

The five minutes felt like as many hours. But as we got into Kerkstraat, we could already see a police car parked outside Korthuizen's house. As we arrived outside the front door, two young uniformed policemen were bringing out their suspect in handcuffs, complaining volubly, if not loudly all the while. They were also carrying a large brown briefcase.

"Him!" exclaimed Rosemary. "I never dreamt it was him for a moment!"

Jérôme Vermeulen spotted us, just as the policemen were about to put him in the car.

"You two!" he shouted. "What do you think you're up to!"

"I think the right question is what do you think you're up to?" I replied.

"Do you know this man?" asked one of the policemen, a thickset young Fleming with a blond moustache.

"Yes, you've just arrested not just a common burglar, but the man who ran over and killed the man who previously lived in the flat, who arranged for the murder of an EEC Commission employee and carried out a fraud on the EEC Commission in the amount of around five hundred million Belgian francs."

"You will come with us to the municipal police offices please?"

"Certainly. Is it far?"

"A few streets away. My colleague will wait with you while we send another car."

"He's lying…I was in this flat to collect possessions which I'd lent Korthuizen and wished to get back!" exclaimed Vermeulen.

I realised he would probably have a plausible cover story for if he got caught. But unless he'd actually brought with him something other people knew he owned or he'd got positive proof of ownership, it wasn't going to be easy to prove. I knew that some of my allegations were going to be equally hard to prove – but his greed and the temptation sometimes to be too clever by half meant that I several aces up my sleeve…and he already must know they were there. But I thought I'd give him a taste of what was in store.

"I see you're wearing your about-town shoes," I observed.

He gave me a dirty look, but said nothing. No doubt his fertile brain was whirling away. I suspected he'd try to get out of the clutches of the Tervuren police somehow – probably by pulling strings – and then either brazen things out – or more likely, flee.

Indeed, as we stood for five minutes with the officer who'd spoken to me, I began to get more and more worried that Vermeulen would be able to talk his way out – or, at least get to make a phone call to someone who'd tell the officers to release him. But a police car came (possibly the same one – I wondered just how many the Tervuren police actually had); we got in; and arriving at the police station, found Vermeulen still there, shut in onihis own on an office.

An officer with insignia I didn't recognise, but who looked as though he was in charge, came up to us.

"This man claims he's a very senior official in the EEC Commission. He claims you are working for him…So just exactly who are you? And what's been going on?"

We went into a neighbouring office. Rosemary and I explained who we were and showed our SEFF passes, Rosemary's Met identification card and my C&E Commission.

"You will now explain, please," said the officer in English. "My name is Inspector van der Leyde and the officer is te Bos. He will take a note of what you say."

"The man you've arrested is called Jérôme Vermeulen," I explained. "He's the Secretary of the EEC Commission. We are both National Experts from London, on a two-year secondment which will end next spring. Vermeulen asked us to investigate a fraud of five hundred million Belgian francs which was carried out in the Commission last year. We discovered where it had been carried out and how. I can give you as much detail as you wish. The only person who could be definitely identified as being involved was described to us as a small man with dark hair and spectacles with very thick lenses. This was, in fact, Jérôme Vermeulen and I propose to ask a dozen or so witnesses to identify him. He was also absent from his office during the times when the small man was carrying out his work involved in the fraud."

"You made various allegations about murder and arranging a murder back in Kerkstraat, so I'm told."

"Yes, I did. I fear I may well not be able to prove either. But the fact that he went to Korthuizen's house today suggests that he did. But we may well not have sufficient evidence to get him into court. To explain – to carry out the fraud, certain details and documents were required from a particular Directorate-General in the EEC Commission. Vermeulen learnt – probably by accident – from Korthuizen that a young woman working in DGVI was a sympathiser for the North Vietnamese. She was half-Vietnamese by birth and evidently wanted to work for them. Vermeulen blackmailed her, so that she would provide the documents and information he needed. The fraud worked essentially because no checking of payments was undertaken until after the year in which they were made. This change took place a couple of years ago and was arranged by Vermeulen. Previously, checks had taken place every three months, so the fraud would've been impossible. But, of course, when they came to light, they had to be investigated…..”

"And for some reason Vermeulen chose you two?”

"I reckon he probably felt that involving the Commission security people would look too feeble – especially as he didn't intend anyone to discover who'd really carried out the fraud. And since we've been here, we've identified and caught a Soviet heroin smuggling operation and identified two Soviet moles within the Commission. So I suppose we had sufficient credibility…”

"And the Belgian police might well have had access to information which could be awkward for him,” added Rosemary. "But we were told that the Commission weren't required by law to involve the Belgian police in a matter regarding its own money.”

"That may be true,” said van der Leyde. "We have nothing to do with any of that.”

"Almost at the moment we began our investigation,” I continued, "a young woman disappeared…the half-Vietnamese woman who we believe got the information and documents Vermeulen needed. We'll never get positive proof about this, but it seems pretty certain that Vermeulen tipped off the North Vietnamese agents who were the woman's contacts in Brussels that she'd betrayed them and had been involved in a large fraud against the Commission. We know that about the time she disappeared, a North Vietnamese agent was in Brussels and he's apparently the sort of man who gets sent to resolve local problems, usually in a conclusive manner."

"And presumably leaving little trace of what he's done….so little evidence that links him to M. Vermeulen."

"Indeed. As I said, the only thing I'm confident I can link him to is the actual fraud. But you wanted to know why he was in Korthuizen's house. As I said, we believe it was Korthuizen who - deliberately or inadvertently - tipped Vermeulen off about the half-Vietnamese woman. I confirmed this morning that he worked part-time for the Dutch counter-intelligence service. Because of her contacts, he'd naturally keep an eye on her – but as she wasn't doing anything, we can assume everyone was waiting for her either to change jobs where she'd have access to material of interest to North Vietnam or make more interesting contacts. Several days after she disappeared, Korthuizen visited her apartment in Uccle. We discovered this only recently. Indeed, that was why we started to ask ourselves about his possible counter-intelligence connections. I have to assume that someone was keeping watch on the apartment or the person we spoke to - the concierge – informed Korthuizen or someone else in Dutch counter-intelligence that we'd been there - and knew he'd been there. There was an oddity left at the apartment – a Chinese pistol with about 50 rounds of ammunition. It was evidently intended to point the authorities towards the lady's involvement with the North Vietnamese and, we believe, suggest that the fraud had been undertaken by them. But the North Vietnamese agent was a professional. Why would he leave something so obviously pointing to him? And if we could ask that, I guess Korthuizen might too. He might also start thinking, how come the half-Vietnamese woman was involved in the fraud, since he believed it was completely against her nature. So he'd start to think of blackmail, just as we did. And he'd know what might make her vulnerable to blackmail…and he'd start to wonder whether he'd let on to anyone, deliberately or not? I believe Vermeulen feared that Korthuizen might remember that he'd shared a certain amount of classified information, either with him or someone who he could guarantee would pass the information on to him. Vermeulen doesn't take risks like that. The only risks he takes are those he controls himself. And when he knew that we now knew that Korthuizen had been to the half-Vietnamese woman's house shortly after she disappeared, he reckoned the questions we might ask him could well jog his memory inconveniently. So Korthuizen had to be killed and, as a cyclist so keen as to go off for long rides even in the pouring rain, he wasn't difficult to run down on the Louvain road, near Bertem.....and in the conditions, it'd be virtually impossible to prove it was deliberate, even if you could find the driver."

"So this may be true or it may be supposition – but you can't prove it either way."

"No. But you might ask yourself why he was in Korthuizen's flat today. I told Commander de Klerck, head of the Commission security staff, that I'd been told that Dutch counter-intelligence believed Korthuizen had been deliberately killed and that they believed he had important material stashed away in some secret place in his flat...and that they were going to take the place apart either tomorrow or the day after. We believe that Vermeulen had already been here at night, to make sure Korthuizen hadn't left any documents – a diary, for instance – which might lead to him. But you can't really do a thorough search at night and I felt he couldn't risk Dutch counter-intelligence stumbling across something that pointed to him. So he'd have to take the risk and have a thorough search in broad daylight."

"He claims Korthuizen had certain documents that belonged to him. He says they're confidential and he can't disclose to us what they are."

"Well, if you wish, we're certainly cleared to the same level as Vermeulen, so you could suggest he could tell us."

"He also told us he barely knew Korthuizen," added Rosemary.

"As it is, he's made an unlawful entry to Korthuizen's apartment, but he was apprehended before he appears to have removed anything. A lawyer might well persuade the local judge that his client is evidently a very senior official in the EEC Commission, with a distinguished record and no criminal connections or antecedents. He's already suggested the names of several important people in the Brussels police and judiciary he wishes to telephone. We cannot deprive him of his rights indefinitely."

"Of course not. If you'll agree, I'll make a couple of phone calls to summon witnesses here. They will provide sufficient evidence for him to be held on charges of fraud against the EEC Commission. All those I'm contacting have access to cars, so they can be here quickly."

"I believe that'll be satisfactory. M. Vermeulen may be angry – but he was apprehended on someone else's property….and none of the names he mentioned have any authority over the Tervuren municipal police anyway."

I phoned Commander de Klerck and the AVIS car rental, asking them to come to the Tervuren police offices as soon as possible. Fortunately we'd got beyond the end of the Brussels lunch hour and they were able to come. Within half an hour, the young man from the AVIS car rental and Commander de Klerck, along with Vermeulen's personal assistant, arrived.

I decided to take the easiest one first. Inspector van der Leyde and I led the man from AVIS into the room where Vermeulen was waiting, apparently calm.

"May I look in the briefcase which you brought away with M. Vermeulen?" I asked van der Leyde.

"Certainly."

Inside were what I'd expected…and, to be honest, fervently hoped for – a pair of spectacles with very thick lenses….and also a pair of sunglasses…along with a pair of leather moccasins.

"Would you put the sunglasses on, please, M Vermeulen?" I asked.

"Why should I?"

"For the purposes of identification."

With evident reluctance, he put on the sunglasses.

"That's him!" exclaimed the young weedy man, with the deep voice. "That's Philippe Wouters…or the man who called himself Philippe Wouters, certainly."

Vermeulen said nothing, merely removed the sunglasses, which van der Leyde took from him.

"M Vermeulen, would you be so kind to remove one of your shoes please?" I asked.

He gave another show of impatience, but complied. It took a couple of minutes. These were special shoes. They were constructed so that when he wore them he looked at least three inches taller than he really was.

A foot in a sock was visible – a grey and black striped sock.

"And those are the socks I saw on M Wouters when he was in the car," added the young man.

"Thank you," I said.

All but Vermeulen left the room. Te Bos locked the door. Van der Leyde indicated that he should take the young man's statement.

"What that proves is that Vermeulen has been identified as a man calling himself Philippe Wouters who used three different cars in committing fraud against the EEC Commission," I explained. "I can also produce a dozen or more witnesses who will also identify him as such….But this bloke was the nearest by far."

"Very well. What about the other two? Are they going to identify this man?"

"No. Both know him well. I suggest we interview them separately."

We started with Vermeulen's personal assistant, Mlle Louise Legros.

"You know who I am?" I asked, continuing in English.

"Yes. And your wife." She was nervous, suspicious, defensive.

"You'll recall I asked you yesterday about occasions when M. Vermeulen was away from the office for more than a couple of weeks?"

"Yes. I wasn't sure why you needed the information….and certainly why I shouldn't tell M. Vermeulen…"

"But you didn't?"

"As you said it was an important security matter, no, I didn't."

"Will you confirm that M. Vermeulen was away from the office during these periods of time?"

"I don't see why it's necessary….But I can confirm that on the first occasion he was away looking at how EEC money was being used in Germany. The second three weeks he took as private family business. The third was to examine how EEC agricultural funds were being used in central France."

"But he claimed no expenses on any of these?"

"I would not expect it if he was away on family business. As for the rest, he informed me that he was staying as a guest of several acquaintances and that he could not be bothered about relatively insignificant travel expenses."

"We are extremely grateful to you."

"Is that all? I've been dragged over here just for that!" she exclaimed, reverting to her native French.

"We are grateful to you for doing what the law required of you," replied van der Leyde in perfect French.

"If you will have a look at these photocopies," I explained, "you'll see that the times when a man described as "a little man with dark hair and spectacles with very thick lenses"…..in fact, those on the table there….was engaged in carrying out the fraud with these firms coincides directly with M. Vermeulen's absences from work."

Van der Leyde looked through them carefully.

"I should certainly say that if anyone from these companies or banks identified Vermeulen as the man generally calling himself 'Philippe Wouters', you've made strong case against him."

"I take it you don't want us to get in touch with some of them?"

"No. You've got enough for me to hold him and pass him on to colleagues in Brussels who'll be dealing with this…..Now what did you want this other man for?"

Commander de Klerck was brought in. He looked irritated, but confused.

"Might you explain why I'm here?" he said in his strained English.

"When we spoke yesterday, I indicated that I knew that Piet Korthuizen worked in a sort of part-time way for Dutch counter-intelligence, didn't I?"

"Yes."

"You knew that already, of course."

"Of course. It's important that I know such matters so that I and my men don't inadvertently hinder the work of people like Korthuizen."

"So you knew Korthuizen suspected Monique Lefebvre of being an agent for North Vietnam?"

"Certainly."

"And you knew he'd visited her apartment after she disappeared?"

"Yes. He told me."

"Did he tell you about his suspicions about Monique Lefebvre?"

"Yes. Mainly to make sure that no-one gave the impression that we knew about her."

"Did he tell you quite recently that my wife and I had visited Monique Lefebvre's apartment for a second time and now knew that he'd been there shortly after she disappeared?"

"I don't know how you could know that – but yes. Apparently the concierge is under instructions to pass on anything about anyone who goes there and anything they say."

"And presumably you briefed M. Vermeulen about this, as about every security matter which could have an implication for the good name of the EEC Commission."

"Yes, certainly. M. Vermeulen has the interests of the Community at his very heart."

"So when I told you yesterday that I'd learnt that Dutch counter-intelligence were going to search Korthuizen's apartment tomorrow or over the weekend, you believed it appropriate to inform him?"

"Of course. There might have been items there which could prove embarrassing for the Commission. I did not find M. Korthuizen an entirely trustworthy man."

"Thank you, Commander de Klerck."

"Is that it? Why was I required to rush to a provincial police statement to tell you things you already know – or I could've told you at any time within the confines of the Berlaymont?"

"Because the fraud which Rosemary and I have been investigating was carried out by Jérôme Vermeulen, with Korthuizen and you as his unwitting agents, and Monique Lefebvre as his blackmail victim. In view of what has happened to Mlle Lefebvre and M. Korthuizen, it's probably a good thing for you that Vermeulen believed that you trusted him completely and implicitly…"

"Oh my God!"

I confess that I'd expected de Klerck to defend Vermeulen to the hilt and probably beyond – but I guess a series of small unanswered doubts and question suddenly plonked into place in that rather thick skull. Unfortunately, I doubted whether what he'd be able to tell a court would be enough to get Vermeulen convicted of any of his more heinous crimes.

But I also realised that Vermeulen was almost certainly the sort of person who had sufficiently influential friends – certainly to help evade justice, possibly to get him off the hook altogether. Since he'd evidently had plans worked out in advance for the removal of Monique Lefebvre and Piet Korthuizen, had he also worked out some way of getting rid of us?

It suddenly seemed urgent to get back to the Brussels and ensure that there was a wider knowledge of what Vermeulen had been up to. It'd still be possible to contain it to Tervuren, Rosemary and me. But I also needed to be sure that Inspector van der Leyde wasn't pushed around by some high-up from Brussels, summoned by Vermeulen, the instant he had access to a phone.

Rosemary was already there.

"You realise that they can't deny Vermeulen his phone call much longer?" she said, as we sipped a well-earned cup of coffee in the Inspector's room. Commander de Klerck and Mlle Legros had departed, having signed short factual statements. "He's almost certainly got some bigwigs who can get him out of here in next to no time. The Inspector is a good man – but we police don't tend to be good at standing up to very senior ranks or judges….You can bet Vermeulen has got a couple of them in his pocket….And I don't know whether you've got all your evidence here, but I wouldn't rely on it getting back to Brussels in those circumstances…."

"I'm with you. One of us has to stay here and be as difficult as we need to be…not least about getting receipts for all the evidence…and whoever goes back to Brussels takes our stuff with them…Though actually I have at least one more copy of it all stashed away.."

"And what are you expecting one of us to do back in Brussels?"

"We need to get Gerry - and Robin Southern as well, if we can – to get to see the most senior people we can in the Commission – the President, if possible. So they know what's been going on, what the nature of the evidence is about Vermeulen and what could be alleged against him on top of the fraud. The real risk is that they prefer not to sully the good name of the EEC and sweep the whole thing under the carpet…which is why we need people like Gerry and Southern along…."

"And Knud…"

"And Knud….Otherwise, you could see them pensioning Vermeulen off quietly and, in practice; allowing him to live in luxury beyond anything we could dream of on the proceeds of a fraud and two murders. But it's only people like that who can counter what Vermeulen will now be trying to do….and we need to be in there urgently to stiffen their backs…or at least remind them what the consequences will be if they duck this."

"That has to be you, Nick. These middle-aged men aren't going to listen to me. Half the time they won't be listening to what I say anyway…They'll be staring at my legs, as usual. I can deal with senior police as well as you can…and I'm not someone who gets overawed by rank….certainly not Belgian rank."

"OK."

We kissed and I prepared to leave, leaving Rosemary to stop Vermeulen from evading the justice he so richly merited.

16. A SMALL MAN GETS WHAT HE DESERVES

I should've given Inspector van der Leyde credit for greater intelligence and probably the natural suspicion provincial police forces have for central ones.

"You are going to try to prevent Vermeulen from getting help from powerful friends in Brussels?" he asked.

"Yes. I hope if I can get in quickly enough, they'll see there's too much evidence for this to be quietly swept under the carpet."

"Swept under the carpet….? Oh, I understand what you mean. So you need to get back to Brussels rapidly?"

"It's already later than I'd like."

"One of our cars will take you….To the EEC building?"

"That will do."

I was a little afraid we might travel with sirens sounding, but fortunately we were back into the city before the rush hour began, so I was able to get off at the Berlaymont and make it hot-foot for the SEFF offices. To my immense relief, Gerry and Knud were in. They were evidently having a meeting together. I knocked and went in.

"We were actually…." began Gerry. But looking at me, he stopped.

"OK. What's up?" asked Knud.

"We've just got Jérôme Vermeulen arrested for the DGVI fraud out at Tervuren and we need to stop him using his influence to get out of it," I replied, attempting to put it in a nutshell.

Knud started laughing. Gerry looked appalled.

"Jérôme Vermeulen? What on earth! You'd better explain some, Nick."

I did so, as tersely as possible, setting out the main evidence I had against Vermeulen, ending with what I acknowledged were unprovable assertions about his involvement in two murders.

"I'm not sure why you find this so comic, Knud," remarked Gerry, stiffly.

"It's just so like Vermeulen. Such an arrogant idiot! He thought he could play you two for fools. Half of these middle-aged crooks don't think beyond Rosemary's legs and that you work for Customs. I'm sure Vermeulen was confident you'd find out how the fraud was done and even identify what those involved looked like – but he'd never give you credit for outsmarting him!"

"But he's certainly got the contacts to get him out of it. We need to get in to see a Commissioner….and not ours, soonest….one of the British or Irish…or ideally more than one….You were going to say, Nick…..?"

"I wondered about picking up Robin Southern on the way."

"I suppose he'll add weight, if not substance."

"With any luck he might've met one of the British Commissioners. I've never met either of them."

"There is that, I suppose."

After a quick phone call, we hurried over to the Berlaymont and up to the top floor, where virtually all the Commissioners had their offices. Robin Southern was waiting for us in the lift lobby, looking vaguely irritated and his customary pompous self.

"Jérôme Vermeulen has just been arrested by the Tervuren police for carrying out the fraud in DGVI," I explained hastily. "We're trying to make sure he can't use his influence to worm his way out of it. So we're trying to line up a couple of Commissioners. Do you know either of the British ones?"

"Bloody hell! Vermeulen was behind it!" Several curses followed.

"British Commissioners?" demanded Henriksen curtly.

"I've met Peter Horspool about twice. I was the main secretary to a couple of Cabinet Committees Harold Marks chaired. He should certainly remember who I am, at least."

"OK. Gerry seems keen to speak to Padraig O'Hare first....and even Nick can't split himself into two, so we'll try Harold Marks if we don't get anywhere with O'Hare."

"That's likely to cause a delay. Vermeulen is as slippery as an eel. Storey – can you give me a two minute summary?"

I did. He shot off in search of Commissioner Marks, former financial wizard for the Labour Party, but a bit too pro-EEC in the aftermath of the referendum. So he'd been sent to Brussels as one way of healing the wounds in the party, probably to balance the removal of Tony Benn from his beloved Ministry for Industry.

We got in to see Commissioner O'Hare almost immediately. From what I'd heard of him, he was a longstanding Fianna Fail politician – essentially the town boss of the city of Cork – who'd been rewarded for loyalty and a lack of longer term ambition to supplant the current Taoiseach.

"An essentially stupid man who's survived through low cunning and an ability to drink his opponents under the table," was Gerry's opinion of him. However, he was all subservience and affability now.

"Ah, Mr Fitzpatrick. To what do I owe this pleasure?" he asked, in the soft, friendly accent of south-west Ireland. His room was vast, with modern furnishings, with various pictures and other artefacts advertising his native Ireland. I hadn't the faintest idea what portfolio he held.

Gerry introduced Knud and me and then explained that a senior Commission official had been caught with his hand in the till to the tune of around five hundred million Belgian francs. It struck me that when you wanted someone to take something like this seriously, it was handy having a currency like the Belgian franc or the Italian lira which always made it sound so much larger.

"The name of this senior official, if you please, Gerry?"

"Jérôme Vermeulen, Secretary to the Commission."

"The dwarf?"

"Yes."

"And you think he'll use his connections to get out of it?"

"I think he'll decide whether he just wants to get out of police custody and make his escape or whether he can brazen the whole thing out. But both will need important connections which we'd like to stop."

"Some details, please Gerry. If I'm going to throw my weight around – especially with top policemen – I'm going to need chapter and verse."

"It'd be best if Nick Storey explains. He's been carrying out the investigation into the fraud and he and his wife are the ones who managed to identify Vermeulen as the culprit."

"Explain please, Mr Storey."

I gave him a reasonably potted version, largely covering over the involvement of Monique Lefebvre and her and Piet Korthuizen's murders. Though they were more heinous, to my mind, they were also going to be unprovable....and time was passing all the while."

"And you have reliable witnesses who will identify Vermeulen?" asked O'Hare, eyeing as I suspect any Irish Catholic in the Fianna Fail tradition would look at a Londoner, and an employee of HM Customs & Excise to boot.

"One has already. The rest are in places like Charleroi, Lens and Gelsenkirchen. Provided we can get Vermeulen securely under lock and key, they can be produced within a day or two. But he's also got in his possession a couple of items mentioned by eye-witnesses to his fraud. We need to make sure they don't disappear somehow."

"So what do you want from me?"

"Nick?" Gerry looked at me.

"I suggest that if you could phone the Tervuren police, explaining who you are and telling them that if anyone of whatever rank appears there to get Vermeulen out of their custody, he should refuse to do so unless they have cleared what they propose to do, in person, with you. As a Commissioner, it seems to me you're his legal employer and the crime was committed by him against his employer. So it strikes me you have the absolute right to determine what happens to him in the first instance."

"And if it's a senior judge or the Chief of Police for Brussels….or whatever he's called…?"

"It depends what they're proposing to do with him," I replied. "If there's any suggestion they plan to release him in any way - even if it's on mammoth amounts of bail – you should refuse, using the argument that I've just proposed. If they're proposing to bring him into safe custody in Brussels, I think you need to demand that his transfer is fully documented and all items of evidence are recorded, photographed and copies kept by the Tervuren police and brought direct to you here."

"And if he lines up another Commissioner? A fellow Belgian, for instance?"

"I believe you could point out that the international press might find it somewhat strange if senior official suspected of embezzling five hundred million Belgian francs from the Commission was allowed to escape justice through the intervention of a Commissioner from the same country as that official," remarked Gerry, showing the cunning and steel which his academic manner concealed.

"And it cannot be said that the EEC Commission is universally popular…..I believe that probably covers it…But I'd be grateful if you could be on call if required Gerry….and you too, Mr Storey?"

"We'll give our contact phone numbers to your PA," replied Gerry.

"Will he do the right thing?" asked Knud, as we left the Commissioner's outer office.

"Oh yes," replied Gerry. "He may hate my guts, but he knows when someone's got hold of his short and curlies....Now what about Harold Marks?"

We made our way along the central corridor, past statues and portraits of "great European leaders" – plainly excluding Napoleon and Hitler, while paying homage to Charlemagne, who was probably viewed in a similar light by many contemporaries. Gerry explained the purpose of our visit to the tall, thin, ascetic young man in his outer office and he ushered us in.

"Robin has been telling me about your errant, Mr Vermeulen," observed Harold Marks. He was short, balding, unobtrusive, with a friendly, unmistakeably Jewish face. He was one of a number of former Manchester Grammar School scholars in the Labour Government, widely regarded as brilliant, amiable, but too rich and too close to the City for left wingers like Tony Benn. I had no idea what Commission portfolio he had either. "I understand you're the expert, Mr Storey?"

"My wife and I have been leading the investigation into the fraud against DGVI, at Mr Vermeulen's request, I should add."

"Didn't you find that rather unusual?"

"A bit. I expect Mr Southern may have explained how my wife and I fit in here. We're National Experts on secondment from London for two years. Rosemary, my wife, works in the Met. I work in Customs & Excise. In our first year we uncovered a Soviet heroin smuggling ring and a couple of Soviet agents here in the Commission. We're also investigating what we believe is a large scale wine fraud...."

"I should explain that being in SEFF gives Mr and Mrs Storey a fairly broad rein to examine criminal acts relating to the EEC," added Gerry.

"Yes. Robin did explain SEFF to me....a curious beast....But do go on, Mr Storey."

"Vermeulen explained that as the fraud was carried out on EEC funds, it wasn't strictly speaking a matter for the local police and he didn't think that the Commission security people were up to it – but he'd heard about what we did with the Soviet stuff. Gerry and Knud agreed we'd only have about ten weeks before the wine fraud investigation resumes – so we'd do what we could.....And it quite quickly became plain how the fraud had been carried out. We also worked out quickly that you needed to know the procedures used in DGVI and also have a certain amount of information and some documents from there. It meant that some form of internal involvement was necessary. Also the fraud could only have taken place after the banking reconciliation procedures had been changed from quarterly to annual. Whether someone made that change deliberately or just took advantage of it, we couldn't tell at that stage. Anyway, we followed up with the firms who appeared to have made false claims and the banks into which the money was paid and taken out and we quickly identified the same man described as 'a little man with dark hair and spectacles with very thick lenses'. Of course, he disguised part of his appearance by using a beard or moustache sometimes, but it was plain that it was the same man. The traces linking him directly to the Commission were purely the documents and information, which he could've got from someone inside DGVI, for instance.....He always used the names of people working in DGVI – often that of 'Philippe Wouters'. However, M. Wouters bears no resemblance to the description of the man who carried out the fraud."

"So it was evidently well planned...and made.....?"

"Around five hundred million Belgian francs...."

"That's a fair amount – even in real money!" He grinned, a cynical, but pleasant grin. "But you managed to track him down."

"He needed to get information to blackmail the woman in DGVI who supplied him with the detailed material he required. Though she couldn't identify him....indeed, she was subsequently killed....he thought the person who gave him the original information might work out what'd been going on....so we believe he killed him too....But I felt I'd worked out how he was getting his information, so I used that route to entice him to the flat in Tervuren where the man he killed lived. Fortunately, he took the bait….and brought along a pair of the spectacles with thick lenses, which I reckon he used to disguise himself….”

"But I've met Vermeulen. I practically tower over him – even me!”

"When he's in the office he wears no shoes or things like slippers….but when was carrying out the fraud, he wore specially built-up shoes, which I reckon raised his height about three inches….sufficient for the people he met to regard him as small, but not like a dwarf. He's actually wearing those shoes at the moment, I noticed…and we need to make sure that they are photographed and aren't allowed to disappear….”

"So what exactly do you want from me?”

Before anyone could answer, a secretary came into the room – a typically slim, attractive brunette of a type that flourished greatly in the Berlaymont.

"There's a message for Mr Storey,” she announced, in accented English.

"That's me.”

"It's the Cinquantenaire international school. They were aware that neither you nor your wife would collect your daughters at the usual time, but they're about to close and they've been unable to contact your wife.”

"Hell's teeth!” I exclaimed. "I'd completely forgotten the time! I'll have to get over there pronto….I'll head over to Tervuren from there…”

"We can explain to the Commissioner what we're asking him to do,” added Knud.

"Take my car!” called out Commissioner Marks.

After a phone call of few words, the secretary took me down to the basement of the Berlaymont in what seemed to me to be a special lift. Waiting for us when we got out was plainly the Commissioner's driver. The secretary explained where he was to go – in Italian – and went back into the lift. We got into the car (in my case, in unaccustomed luxury), and the driver sped off – at breakneck speed, apparently the done thing by drivers in Brussels underground car parks. Naturally, we hit the rush hour and I suspected I could've got to the international school faster if I'd jogged across the park, but I was grateful for the kindness shown by the Commissioner, also reminding myself of a few unkind (and palpably unfair) words my father used to say about him.

There was only one teacher keeping Emily and Sarah company. She looked irritable, they looked anxious and relieved.

"About time too," said the teacher firmly and did an about-turn before I could provide any excuses.

"Is Mummy all right?" asked Emily, with tears in her eyes. "Miss Heathcote she hadn't been able to contact her…or you until just now…..We were worried…."

Sarah had her arm clasped firmly round my waist. She didn't need to tell me what she was thinking….and it showed how upset she was because normally she would've done.

"Mummy is all right. It's just our work meant that she had to be stuck out at Tervuren making sure a criminal and some evidence didn't escape. I had to come back and sort a few things out with some high-ups in Brussels and I'm afraid I didn't realise what time it'd got to."

At least from there the journey to Tervuren was straightforward….indeed, pretty well dead straight.

"Were you and Mummy involved in catching the criminal?" asked Emily, as we sat towards the front of the tram.

"No. Actually we phoned the local police and they arrested him. He wasn't carrying a weapon anyway."

"But if you're worried he might escape – does that mean some people with guns might come and try to free him from the police?"

"No. We're worried that he has important and influential friends who might tell the Tervuren police that they must let him go. I've been trying to make sure that doesn't happen. But Mummy had to stay there to prevent it happening there."

Whether that reassured them, I wasn't entirely sure – not least because I suspected Sarah listened more to her fears, inevitably influenced by what she'd seen in Riga, than to my words. At any rate, we all sat in silence until the tram stopped in Tervuren and we got off, heading towards the police station. Of course, by now it was dark. Fortunately it wasn't raining, but it felt quite bitter under the orange streetlights.

However, as we approached, the scene was utterly unexpected. There were several police cars and an ambulance drawn up. Three or four policemen were directing people and traffic away from the road in front of the police station. The special rope police use to cordon off areas – usually crime scenes - was being tied round the whole area. In the middle there was a lump on the ground, with a couple of men and a woman in what looked like medical uniforms bent over it.

My heart leapt into my mouth. Remembering what I'd seen that night in our flat in Beckenham, the horrendous thought shot into my head that the person lying on the ground was Rosemary. I grabbed Emily and Sarah by the hands and rushed almost blindly forward.

"Where is my wife?" I demanded, in French. "Who is that?" I pointed.

Rosemary emerged from among the group of police standing at the front of the police station. We ran into each other's arms and embraced, kissing each other fiercely.

"Thank God!" I whispered. "For a moment I thought that was you."

We held our daughters in our arms. Sarah was sobbing, tears of immense relief. Emily was always less emotional and more perceptive.

"Was that the criminal you were trying to stop escaping?" she asked Rosemary.

"Yes. He got what was coming to him, I suppose." Rosemary was white-faced, shocked.

"Were you there when it happened?" I asked.

She nodded. She was close to tears, making a tremendous effort not to break down.

"You've got some blood on your hair," remarked Sarah. "Have you been shot Mummy?"

"No. But I was quite close to the man over there when he was shot."

She closed her eyes and looked as though she was about to faint.

"Let's go indoors and sit down," I said. "You need a glass of water."

With my arm round her shoulders and Sarah holding my hand, Emily holding Rosemary's, we made our way into the police station. Inspector van der Leyde was already sitting in the entrance room, blood spattered over his shirt, sipping at a cup of coffee.

"That definitely is Vermeulen, I take it?" I asked Rosemary, as I handed her a plastic beaker of water.

She nodded.

"Don't feel you need to say anything….In fact, is there any reason why we can't go home?"

I went over to the Inspector. He, too, looked shattered. I guessed Rosemary and he must've been right next to Vermeulen when he was shot.

"Is there any reason why I can't take Rosemary home?" I asked him. "We can come back first thing tomorrow and make any statements we need to."

"I shall be going home myself shortly," he replied. "Such things don't happen here! Tervuren isn't a place like that!"

I doubted whether that really constituted permission to go. But it was good enough for me. In any case, as I took Rosemary and my daughters out of the police station, a middle-aged Fleming with a bushy moustache and short, bristling, fair hair came up to me. He wore the fawn, doule-breasted raincoat beloved by Continental detectives……..according to the cinema, at least

"Mr Storey?" he asked, in English, with the familiar Flemish accent.

"Yes."

"We are aware who this man is and who killed him. There are many details which will need to be accounted for, but that is for tomorrow. This man isn't going anywhere. I would be grateful if you and your wife could attend here at say 10 tomorrow morning?"

"That'll be fine."

"Wait a second....After what she's just been through, your wife doesn't need to endure public transport....You live in Sint Lambrechts Woluwe?"

"Yes."

"A car will take you there."

We only had to wait for a couple of minutes, but Rosemary was already shivering. Just as the car arrived, I could see they were picking up the corpse to put in the ambulance. I noticed that, as they picked him up, a small moccasin fell back on to the road. I got Emily to sit in the front of the police car, while Rosemary sat next to me, with my arm firmly round her shoulders. We travelled in silence.

We were home in next to no time. We went into the flat, took off our coats and sat down.

"How are you feeling?" I asked.

"I just want to sit with my family.....and have a cup of tea?"

I kissed her and went into the kitchen to make tea, while Emily and Sarah sat next to her on the couch. I brought mugs of tea for both of us, hot chocolate for Emily and Sarah and packet of gingernut biscuits, recently acquired from the Commission store. Rosemary seemed more composed. She gave me a watery smile.

"Do you think you could make us some dinner, Nick, please? After I've had this I'd like to change....and I should probably have a quick bath."

"OK."

So I boiled up an instant soup and grilled cheese on toast....I would've spoilt anything more complicated....while Emily and Sarah looked at their books. That told me how worried they were about their mother. Being quiet and reading were not normally things they did voluntarily – even less after they'd been stuck at school all afternoon doing exactly that. As I served up the food, Rosemary came out in her dressing gown.

"How do you feel, Mummy?" asked Sarah, with tears forming in her eyes.

"A lot better......I was standing right next to the man when he was shot and some of his blood spattered on to me. I knew no-one was trying to shoot me, so I wasn't scared. But I've never been right next to someone when they were shot like that before and I found it rather upsetting....But I'm all right now....and I'd really prefer to talk about something else.....And I'm sorry I forgot about getting you out of school. Unfortunately I was completely occupied from almost the moment Nick went back to Brussels until just before you arrived...which was not long after the man was shot."

"You can tell us all about it tomorrow," I said. "You need to relax and rest and try to think about something else."

After we'd eaten we played some card games before getting Emily and Sarah off to bed, where we both read them their bedtime stories and sat with them until they were asleep.

Afterwards, Rosemary lay on the couch with her head on my shoulder, silent.

"Do you mind if I don't tell you what happened until tomorrow?" she whispered. "I really just want to go to bed now and sleep."

"Of course. You get into bed and I'll be along in a moment with a mug of tea."

But by the time I got there, she was already asleep.

About an hour later, she turned over and muttered "sorry", as I put my arms round her. I kissed her short dark hair. Sometimes she seemed too slight and vulnerable for all that courage.

17. AND BACK TO THE WINE FRAUDS

Everyone seemed in better spirits by the morning. We took Emily and Sarah to the school without complaint and without demands to know what had so upset their mother the previous evening. What was more surprising was the attitude of the teachers. I anticipated being given a telling-off for forgetting about our children and putting the staff to such inconvenience. Instead, we were met with a civil, if not friendly approach, and a few words which showed they understood why we'd been "unavoidably detained". I guessed someone in authority must've spoken to some there...or possibly was married to one of the teachers, as virtually all of them seemed to be the spouses of high-ups in the Commission or NATO. At any rate, a piece of unpleasantness had been averted – though I doubted whether I'd ever find out who we had to thank for that.

It was far too soon to go over to Tervuren and neither of us felt like going into the office to face the inevitable questions...at least, not until we'd had time to talk it over between ourselves. So we walked in the Park de Cinquantenaire, close to the school. It was another grey day, but at least it was a little warmer and not raining.

"Thank you for last night," Rosemary began, kissing me on the cheek. "I really wasn't up to talking about anything then. It was so unexpected! And so horrible!"

"How do you feel now? Can you tell me what happened? Or is it still too soon?"

"I'm going to have to tell the detectives from Brussels shortly anyway.....But I'm OK now.....I'll start from when you left…..For a while nothingreally happened. Inspector van der Leyde told me that, if possible, he preferred to wait until you got back before he formally interviewed Vermeulen and he'd still got nearly six hours before he was required to detain him formally or let him go. I'd already explained that you'd plainly worked out something about Vermeulen's involvement in the fraud which I hadn't. But he was also nervous about what'd happen when Vermeulen made his phone call, which couldn't be delayed much longer. Indeed, about twenty minutes after you left, van der Leyde reluctantly gave him his phone call…..and, of course, we weren't permitted to know who he was phoning. One thing I did notice when he stood up to make the call was that he seemed to have shrunk…."

"I hope you spotted his shoes?"

"Yes. I'm not a policewoman for nothing! When we went back in to remove the phone, I noticed he'd moved his shoes under the table. I pulled them out, from the other side and told van der Leyde that I suspected they were quite important evidence….Indeed, it was at that point I realised the significance of the evidence of the man from the AVIS rental place…..Vermeulen couldn't drive in shoes as built-up as those. But when he was carrying out the fraud, he needed to look two or three inches taller, so people just thought he was short, not a midget. So when the man from AVIS saw him sitting in the car in just his socks, he'd just taken off his special shoes and was about to put on a pair of driving shoes…like the sort he was wearing when he was shot."

"It was something that didn't quite add up. How many people do you know who change their shoes to drive? And the man from the AVIS rental place was also able to confirm that the small man was wearing black and grey striped socks. I've never seen Vermeulen in any other style of socks. It wasn't conclusive, of course. Lots of people may favour socks like that, but it was fitting into the pattern….But go on…Sorry!"

"Don't be silly! I'd only be asking you questions like that later on......After Vermeulen made his call, there was a brief respite, while van der Leyde asked about you and me and I found out why someone as plainly clever as him should end up being in charge of a quiet leafy suburb like Tervuren....After nearly fifteen years in Antwerp and Brussels, he was fed up with the violence and steaminess of what he encountered on a daily basis and felt he was becoming the sort of man who couldn't bring up his children properly, or be a proper husband to his wife. So when Tervuren came up, he took it. Though he welcomed the occasional bit of excitement, like arresting someone like Vermeulen, he said he could happily put up with the routine of occasional burglaries, speeding or inconsiderate neighbours complaining about each other...He said he'd even got used to doffing his cap to the many extremely rich people who live in the huge houses in Tervuren....Then we got the phone call...from a very senior judge called Rosselaere, or something like that...That's what van der Leyde wrote down. Basically, he said we'd no grounds to hold Vermeulen, no reason to charge him and his continuing detention would be illegal. He'd have perfect grounds for levelling civil charges against us for illegal arrest and criminal charges of conspiracy against you and me for blackmail and attempting to pervert the course of justice. That was probably about half of the charges which he claimed could be filed against us. Finally he demanded that Vermeulen should be released immediately with all his possessions returned to him and a car provided to take him back to his home."

"What bloody cheek!"

"In any case, it rested on a fundamental weakness, which van der Leyde and I'd already talked about and he now deployed it. He pointed out that Vermeulen had been found on the property belonging to another person. He had entered it illicitly and had no credible explanation as to why he was there. Moreover, he had in his possession items which were evidence of his involvement in a serious crime and van der Leyde had in his possession sworn written statements supporting that. He therefore had more than sufficient grounds for the continuing detention of Vermeulen and added that unless he or Vermeulen could produce any evidence of the various allegations he'd made about you me and himself, he'd be wise not to say them in public, because he, at least, would undoubtedly sue him for slander......That pretty well stopped this Rosselaere in his tracks. He blathered on for about five minutes, but I could tell from the expression on van der Leyde's face, he wasn't getting anywhere. Then he evidently slammed the phone down."

"You'd think that people as clever as Vermeulen and presumably knowledgeable about the law like a senior judge would've worked out they weren't likely to get far using those arguments," I commented.

"I reckoned they were hoping it might work, that van der Leyde might just be overawed by a very senior judge. I guess they reckoned the police in Tervuren would be typical woodentops, just as the Met do about Leicestershire....But he and I agreed, it was unlikely that it'd stop at that....I was a bit disappointed that he didn't point out to the judge that his friendship for Vermeulen appeared to override any thought that justice should be served properly.....But then perhaps you and I push these things further than we ought to...."

"Probably....But it's also completely true...and quite worrying. If you can ignore any sort of rules of justice and demand that a friend who's been arrested should be released, purely on his say-so, you're a disgrace as a judge."

"Perhaps I won't join you on that particular soapbox..." Rosemary gave a happy smirk, which warmed my heart. I hugged her and gave her a long kiss. We didn't need to say why.

"Sorry....I take it you had further phone calls?"

"Naturally. The next one was from the police....which was what we expected - from a Deputy Chief of Police in Brussels, called Dombrois. He tried to order van der Leyde to release Vermeulen, but when he was reminded he had no authority over the Tervuren police and that if he wanted Vermeulen released, he could come to Tervuren and sign the release papers himself, he evidently slammed the phone down. This was another attempt to pull rank, I thought. It'd be a fairly brave policeman, even one so senior, to get his signature on something that might turn out to be ill-founded....It's one of the advantages of the Belgian system that the equivalent of the Met can't bully much smaller police forces...My impression when I was in Leicester was that, though they'd resent it, the locals would defer to the Met, especially if they were waving the Home Secretary at them...and they'd know to keep their mouths shut too."

"I can't imagine Vermeulen's friends gave up at that point?"

"No. But I think they'd realised that phone calls weren't going to get them anywhere. About twenty minutes later a couple of police cars drew up outside, and we were visited by four detectives from Brussels, led by a Commander Dulac, one of those rather slimy, political detectives you find in the Met from time to time. He announced that he'd come to 'take charge' of M. Vermeulen, in tones that he thought brooked no disagreement. In that he was wrong. Though he evidently thought his considerably senior rank would overawe van der Leyde, he was mistaken. I guess van der Leyde had seen plenty like him when he was in Antwerp and Brussels...but he also knew that Dulac had no authority in Tervuren, unless someone had called a national emergency...and we felt that even Vermeulen couldn't pull the strings to make that happen.....So van der Leyde demanded to know what his authority was and what he was planning to do with Vermeulen. Dulac said that allegations had been made about Vermeulen committing a fraud in relation to EEC Commissions money. He'd been assigned to deal with these allegations. I stepped in at this point, to Dulac's evident irritation....

'May I ask who assigned you to examine these allegations and under who's authority?' I asked. 'I work for the EEC Commission and as far as I'm aware the Belgian police have no jurisdiction over offences carried out against EEC funds. You could only be brought in with the express authorisation by a member of the Commission.'

"I wasn't absolutely certain about that last bit, but I doubted whether he knew - and his face betrayed his ignorance anyway.

'And who exactly are you?' he demanded.

"I explained. I then repeated my question. He was plainly not a happy bunny....I guessed he'd got some sort of authorisation, but didn't feel comfortable about it. I thought I'd keep him off his guard...

'Knowing the EEC Commission, there'd have to be an authorisation form....probably in triplicate....for anything like this. I expect you have a copy?'

"He glared at me and muttered something about having to make a phone call and disappeared into another room. I should say that, apart from the man keeping an eye on Vermeulen, he was treated like a complete pariah throughout. Indeed, I began to wonder whether van der Leyde wasn't breaking some regulation or other by not keeping him going on something to eat and drink....But evidently, the phone call put some fire into Commander Dulac, as he came out and told us he was going to take Vermeulen into his custody and that if we attempted to resist him, he'd arrest us and lock us up....and he was plainly going to ignore van der Leyde's protestations that this was not just illegal, but would have extremely unwelcome consequences for him. When I was about to speak, Dulac announced that he was proposing to arrest me as well, on charges of conspiracy. I made very much the same point as van der Leyde, but he ordered his men to get the keys to the room where Vermeulen was being held, when the phone rang. Dulac ordered van der Leyde to answer it, but within a minute or so, he handed the phone over to Dulac who listened for about five or six minutes. When he put the phone down, he'd gone as white as a sheet.

'I can only apologise,' he muttered. 'My previous orders have been countermanded. You also appear to have influence.'

"I guessed you must've managed to get through to someone important in the Commission and they'd managed to prevent whatever Vermeulen had arranged."

"Yes," I replied. "As I mentioned last night, Gerry managed to line up the Irish Commissioner and Southern appeared to know Commissioner Harold Marks. I don't know whether it was one of them or both – but both seemed to be prepared to do something…and I had to shoot off to collect Emily and Sarah."

"It's a good thing we know some people with influence, otherwise who knows what might've happened. At any rate, Dulac now said that his orders were to take Vermeulen into custody in Brussels, but that we should itemise all the stuff in his possession, and any other evidence. Van der Leyde and I would each keep copies of all the documentary stuff – and of the receipts. Of course, we'd already done this in case the worst came to the worst, but we got Dulac to put his signature on every copy…and on the receipt for Vermeulen's possessions…."

"…including the glasses and his special shoes?"

"Particularly those. We all told Vermeulen what was happening. He plainly worked out his attempts to get himself out hadn't worked….yet, at any rate. But apart from informing Commander Dulac he was a spineless poltroon and giving van der Leyde and me the most poisonous stares he could muster, he said nothing. I reckoned he was working out who his next phone calls would be to and his next plan of escape. Naturally, he didn't like being handcuffed, but I guessed Dulac had worked out which side his bread was buttered and wasn't going to allow any slip-ups. A couple of the Brussels uniformed police took Vermeulen outside and we followed. They were just about to put him into a police car when suddenly a man came out of the shadows from the other side of the street and I heard several shots. I was just diving to the ground as I felt blood and flesh hitting the side of my head and my shoulder. It all felt as though it was in slow-motion. I could even see a young Vietnamese man firing an automatic pistol at Vermeulen, before turning and running off in the direction of the church. As everyone recovered, several police ran after him, but I thought I heard a car draw away at speed....It was evidently well-planned....."

"And Vermeulen was very dead."

"Yes, he must've been hit by at least six bullets. By the time I'd got up, it was plain he was already dead.....I assume the North Vietnamese must've been following us?"

"I guess so. I must admit I'd rather forgotten about them. I felt that even though they now knew they'd been conned by the man who carried out the fraud into getting Monique Lefebvre killed, they weren't allowed to take any revenge themselves and they wouldn't want to admit how they'd cocked up by asking for someone like Ho Quyen Diep to come back and make amends. Besides, it wasn't until a day or so ago I was reasonably sure I'd got the right man."

"Yes...I'd quite like you to explain how you got there, rather than just setting a trap and seeing who blundered into it...But perhaps I should continue telling you what happened yesterday evening."

"Certainly."

"Initially it was complete chaos. I was definitely suffering from some sort of shock – as was van der Leyde. He kept muttering that things like that didn't happen in a place like Tervuren. If I was thinking anything rational, it was I was glad that the Vietnamese knew how to shoot straight, but I suspect the rest of me just felt I'd had a narrow escape and was extremely lucky. But basically I think I was still terrified, re-living the moment when I saw the young man step out and start firing that gun in my direction."

She shivered and I put my arm round her.

"And I'm not sure I noticed a lot more. Various policemen moved van der Leyde and me away from the crime scene....and I think I noticed Commander Dulac's car leaving. The man you spoke to was his number two....and I've no idea what he was called...."

"We may find out a bit later......And though you don't need me to say it, I'm not surprised you were in shock. At the time, you must've felt the man was as likely to shoot you as anyone else. You were incredibly brave!"

"I didn't feel like that......not at all...Actually I kept feeling I was about to burst into tears – especially when I saw you and Emily and Sarah chasing up, looking as though you though it was me that'd been shot...."

She was silent again and I held her against me, kissing her head.

"It's a good job you got me away so quickly...I couldn't've held out when you're so kind to me," she said, tears streaming down her face.

"A good cry is probably just what you need," I said.

After a couple of minutes and a borrowed handkerchief, she was herself again.

"It's a good thing I don't wear much make-up," she observed, "or I'd need to find somewhere to make some running repairs.......Now you tell me how you worked out it was Vermeulen.....? As I didn't have a clue – even after you gave me one with the name you gave yesterday's operation."

"I suppose it really came from thinking about two aspects. The first was what I felt I'd learnt about the character of Mr Big. He was extremely careful, even ruthless, in preventing any traces of anything that could lead back to him...or at least his real identity. But on things he felt he could control, he seemed to be a bit too clever by half. The Chinese pistol was one thing. The other was the way he manipulated de Mettet and Verstappen. Wouldn't it've been easier to drop them? But because he knew he could blackmail the two of them, he couldn't resist the temptation. That made me wonder about a couple of other things....But I'll leave them for the moment. The second came from thinking about how he knew about Korthuizen – both originally when Korthuizen let slip about Monique Lefebvre, but also that we'd been to Monique Lefebvre's flat again and had learnt that Korthuizen had been there not long after she disappeared. I decided to check that Korthuizen was a part-time agent for the Dutch security service and our people said he got a few hundred Guilders a year for any general intelligence he might pick up – and for keeping an eye on Monique Lefebvre…and making sure no-one blabbed about her identity."

"So you were able to turn that assumption into a fact."

"Yes. But I was still puzzling about how Vermeulen got his information from Korthuizen. I couldn't quite see Korthuizen jabbering away in front of Vermeulen. Not least because if he had, I think he'd've cottoned on to him – but I don't think he ever did. Eventually I began to wonder whether Korthuizen didn't make some use of Commander de Klerck. After all, he was 'Mr Commission Security' and is probably pretty highly-cleared. He'd be a good person to keep an eye out for anything that Korthuizen might find interesting and he might also pick up any rumours about Monique Lefebvre. Korthuizen could be confident a fellow-security person would know about keeping his trap shut. But I couldn't see de Klerck as Mr Big somehow. On the other hand, it wasn't much of a leap to think that Vermeulen seemed to have de Klerck pretty well in his pocket. I reckoned that on the basis of 'the good name of the Commission', de Klerck would keep Vermeulen informed about anything and everything of possible interest. So he'd pass on what Korthuizen told him about Monique Lefebvre…and the subsequent stuff about our second visit to the flat and our learning that Korthuizen had been there. I think when de Klerck passed this on, Vermeulen realised we'd have a chat with Korthuizen and he'd eventually put two and two together. Hence his early demise. Of course, de Klerck trusts Vermeulen implicitly…and I doubt he does a lot of thinking anyway. I went to see him and explained that I'd been in touch with the UK security people about the fraud we were investigating an they'd told me that they'd been told Korthuizen knew about Monique Lefebvre's secret allegiance to North Vietnam. He confirmed that Korthuizen had told him that. I was very tempted to ask him whether he'd told Vermeulen, but that'd be testing his loyalty too far. But he did confirm that Vermeulen was out for the day. So I went in to see Vermeulen's personal assistant. I'm afraid I both bullied her and told her less than the truth. But I needed to see her records of Vermeulen's whereabouts when 'the little man' was doing his bits with the firms and the banks. Sure enough, he was out of the office on all three occasions….with perfectly plausible reasons….and there were three or four similar instances over the last couple of years, so these didn't stick out like too much of a sore thumb…"

"Weren't you worried that she'd blab to Vermeulen?"

"That was my main worry. But I told her I was working for British Intelligence and if the slightest word of my visit to his office, let alone what I'd asked to see, reached his ears, not only would I know about it instantly, but she could expect to find herself in prison for the next ten years, somewhere not very nice. My experience as a UO at passenger ports stood me in good stead…..Even so, I was relieved when he turned up at Korthuizen's flat yesterday……Oh, and I also managed to contact Roger Dufour, ostensibly to seek a meeting about why he'd proposed to change the banking reconciliation dates for the Commission from quarterly to annual. He told me that he'd mentioned it in passing in a conversation with Vermeulen, who'd suggested he made it a formal suggestion. As he'd always felt himself a bit of a protégé for Vermeulen, he didn't think anything of it. It was only when he decided to test the water to see whether he couldn't achieve an accelerated promotion, that he found that his protégé status appeared to have been replaced by a profound indifference, which was why he was currently stuck in EUROSITRO."

"How did you know it was him?"

"I didn't. I was lucky that he was the top name on my list."

"You did well…..Though it still strikes me you were riding your luck until you got some confirmation…..and you were a bit lucky that neither de Klerck nor Vermeulen's assistant didn't blab to him."

"That's true...But I kept getting this feeling about Mr Big being too clever by half.....and Vermeulen deciding to use us for the investigation. Though his reasons were perfectly plausible, they were also a bit odd, if you think about it for a while. So I began to ask myself why he'd gone for us, rather than the Belgian police....who I'm sure are more competent than us and have vastly more resources. And that brought me back to de Klerck. I couldn't imagine it'd take de Klerck long to tell senior Brussels detectives that he passed on pretty well everything of interest in the Commission to Vermeulen...."

"So why didn't he bump off de Klerck?"

"I suspect he felt he couldn't eradicate the links between de Klerck and him sufficiently for him not to be tracked down. After all, we agreed that his name was in the frame – though for various perfectly sensible reasons, we tended to discount him. But I wonder what we'd've thought if de Klerck had met a sticky end, probably not long after Monique Lefebvre?"

"I guess you're right......Heavens! Shouldn't we be telling the office where we are?"

"It's OK. I phoned Knud last night when you were in bed and told him Vermeulen had been shot and that we'd be going over to Tervuren this morning. They're not expecting us....Indeed, I think I even recall speculating it was one of the North Vietnamese who shot him."

"Ockham's Razor, I suppose. As you haven't mentioned it yet, this has to be the moment!"

"I wasn't thinking specifically about Ockham's Razor, but I suppose that was how I got there. It seemed to me that there were really only two reasons why someone would shoot Vermeulen when they did – revenge or to keep him quiet. The people who'd be keen on revenge would be the North Vietnamese and possibly the Dutch counter-intelligence people. The Dutch could get access to him at any time – always assuming they go in for that sort of thing. But the Vietnamese would reckon that once he was safely locked away, they'd have no chance of revenging themselves on him....and it was quite a public execution too."

"And those who might wish to keep him quiet?"

"I was moving into areas where I couldn't even guess. It's possible he knew secrets about people with influence who knew he'd use that information either to get them to let him escape or, if the chips were down, to take them down with him. But revenge by the Vietnamese seemed to be the most likely answer....and if Duong Lac or Minh Pham are found to have left the Banque Indosuez in a great hurry, I'd feel that'd pretty well confirm my opinion."

"But you think it was them."

"And I suppose a bit of me hopes it was them. Vermeulen must've made Monique Lefebvre's life a complete misery....and it didn't strike me had much of a life up to that point anyway...."

"And whoever it was has saved the Belgian taxpayer the cost of a trial...and the Commission will probably make sure details of his fraud don't get out....."

"Yes – assassination by ruthless North Vietnamese agents of a dedicated servant of the Commission sounds the sort of thing.....I hope Gerry and Knud can do something to prevent it from becoming too disgustingly unctuous."

"There are enough scandal sheets printed in this part of the world for them to make sure Vermeulen's death is treated factually and his obituaries too."

We had an expensive cup of coffee in a café at the edge of the park and made our way to Tervuren. The formalities were straightforward and, though they would just end up in some archives somewhere, we handed over copies of our notes, including Rosemary's remarkable record of our long discussion about assumptions. We also formally noted the evidential value of various items belonging to Vermeulen which remained temporarily in the Tervuren police station. Then after a round of handshakes – especially with Inspector van der Leyde, who still seemed a bit shaken – we headed back to the SEFF offices.

Naturally enough, we had to give a pretty full explanation to Gerry and Knud and a subsequent one to Southern – but not Commissioner Chevrou de Polignac of DGVI, who evidently appeared to believe that the whole affair was passé and beneath his dignity. We also tried to pass back through them our thanks to the two Commissioners for the timely intervention at Tervuren the previous evening and various other small acts of kindness, without knowing whether these would reach their rightful recipients.

Vermeulen's death passed almost without notice in the press. For all his status within the Commission, he meant little to the Belgian public and perhaps "Secretary to the EEC Commission" wasn't a title to inspire much interest. We learnt a few weeks later, just before we were setting off for Verona, that the gunman appeared to have been Duong Lac, as it was he who'd disappeared from the Banque Indosuez. And no doubt lovers of financial detail would discover the fraud on DGVI eventually. But, there being no-one to face charges, no fraud case could be brought. And Vermeulen seemed to have taken to his grave the secrets of where he'd stashed his ill-gotten gains.

I kept finding "American Pie" going round and round in my head, along with the words which generally meant as much as those of Bob Dylan. I was never quite sure whether there was some deep meaning to them or they were words and phrases haphazardly flung together for effect. But in the end, as Rosemary pointed out to me, if you just let the music flow over you, it didn't really matter. We spent a lot of our time picking through the small bones of things, but what really mattered was the two of us and Emily and Sarah – and that music could play all day and all of the night!

And, in any case, Rosemary and I were just about to set off for the romantic city of Verona, to try and solve a large wine fraud......

Glossary

AT	Administration Trainee (UK Civil Service fast stream entrant)
CAP	Common Agricultural Policy
CFP	Common Fisheries Policy
CLIF*	Comité de Liaison des Industries Françaises
Coreper	EEC Committee of Permanent Representatives (= ambassadors to the EEC)
DG	Directorate-General or Director-General
DGVI	Directorate–General VI of the EEC Commission
DOI	Department for Industry
DTI	Department of Trade & Industry
EUA	European Unit of Account, a basket of currencies used by the EEC
EEC	European Economic Community (later European Union – EU)
EUROSITRO*	Umbrella organisation for trade simplification in the EEC
MAFF	Ministry of Agriculture, Food and Fisheries
Met	Metropolitan Police
OCX	Officer of Customs & Excise (obsolete)
SEFF*	Service Européenne contre la Fraude Fiscale
SITPRO	UK lobby group for trade simplification
UO	Unattached Officer (obsolete C&E grade)

*Imaginary organisations

Lightning Source UK Ltd.
Milton Keynes UK
UKHW020748300322
400827UK00008B/302

9 781326 761882